THE WINGS THAT BIND

ALSO BY BRIAR BOLEYN

BLOODWING ACADEMY

On Wings of Blood
The Bond That Burns
The Wings That Bind

BLOOD OF A FAE SERIES

Queen of Roses
Court of Claws
Empress of Fae
Knight of the Goddess

WRITTEN AS FENNA EDGEWOOD

The Gardner Girls Series

Masks of Desire (The Gardner Girls' Parents' Story)
Mistakes Not to Make When Avoiding a Rake (Claire's Story)
To All the Earls I've Loved Before (Gwen's Story)
The Seafaring Lady's Guide to Love (Rosalind's Story)
Once Upon a Midwinter's Kiss (Gracie's Story)
The Gardner Girls' Extended Christmas Epilogue (Caroline & John's Story—Available to Newsletter Subscribers)

Must Love Scandal Series

How to Get Away with Marriage (Hugh's Story)
The Duke Report (Cherry's Story)
A Duke for All Seasons (Lance's Story)
The Bluestocking Beds Her Bride (Fleur & Julia's Story)

Blakeley Manor Series

The Countess's Christmas Groom
Lady Briar Weds the Scot
Kiss Me, My Duke
My So-Called Scoundrel

BRIAR BOLEYN

THE WINGS THAT BIND

HQ

ONE PLACE. MANY STORIES

HQ
An imprint of HarperCollins*Publishers* Ltd
1 London Bridge Street
London SE1 9GF

www.harpercollins.co.uk

HarperCollins*Publishers*
Macken House, 39/40 Mayor Street Upper,
Dublin 1, D01 C9W8, Ireland

This edition 2026
1
First published in Great Britain by HQ,
an imprint of HarperCollins*Publishers* Ltd 2026

Copyright © Briar Boleyn 2026

Briar Boleyn asserts the moral right to be identified as the author of this work.
A catalogue record for this book is available from the British Library.

Interior image: Whitney Law at New Ink Book Services

HB ISBN: 9780008792336
TPB ISBN: 9780008792343
SPECIAL EDITION ISBN: 9780008819910
SPECIAL EDITION (EXPORT) ISBN: 9780008804589

This novel is entirely a work of fiction. The names, characters and incidents portrayed in it are the work of the author's imagination. Any resemblance to actual persons, living or dead, events or localities is entirely coincidental.

All rights reserved. No part of this publication may be reproduced, stored in a retrieval system, or transmitted, in any form or by any means, electronic, mechanical, photocopying, recording or otherwise, without the prior permission of the publishers.

Without limiting the exclusive rights of any author, contributor or the publisher of this publication, any unauthorised use of this publication to train generative artificial intelligence (AI) technologies is expressly prohibited. HarperCollins also exercise their rights under Article 4(3) of the Digital Single Market Directive 2019/790 and expressly reserve this publication from the text and data mining exception.

Printed and bound in the UK using 100% Renewable
Electricity by CPI Group (UK) Ltd

For all of my readers who have made this incredible
journey possible, this is for you. Thank you
for sharing my love for magic, books, wings,
fangs . . . and, most important, fluffins!

PS: Please don't throw your Kindles too hard.

A NOTE ABOUT TRIGGER WARNINGS

Bloodwing Academy is a dark fantasy romance series with bully vibes. The series deals with topics which some readers may understandably find triggering.

A trigger and content warnings list may be found on the next page.

Please keep in mind that reading the trigger warnings list will spoil certain plot elements.

Avoid reading the trigger warnings list if you do not have any triggers and do not wish to know specific details about the plot in advance.

TRIGGER WARNINGS

Abduction and Kidnapping
Blood and Gore
Blood Play
Child Abuse
Death and Loss
Dubious Consent
Emotional Manipulation
Graphic Violence
Mental Health Issues
Mistreatment of Animals
Murder
Nonconsensual Mind Control
Physical Abuse
Power Imbalances
Psychological Abuse/Bullying
Sexual Assault
Strong Sexual Tension
Substance Abuse
Suicidal Ideation
Torture
Trauma

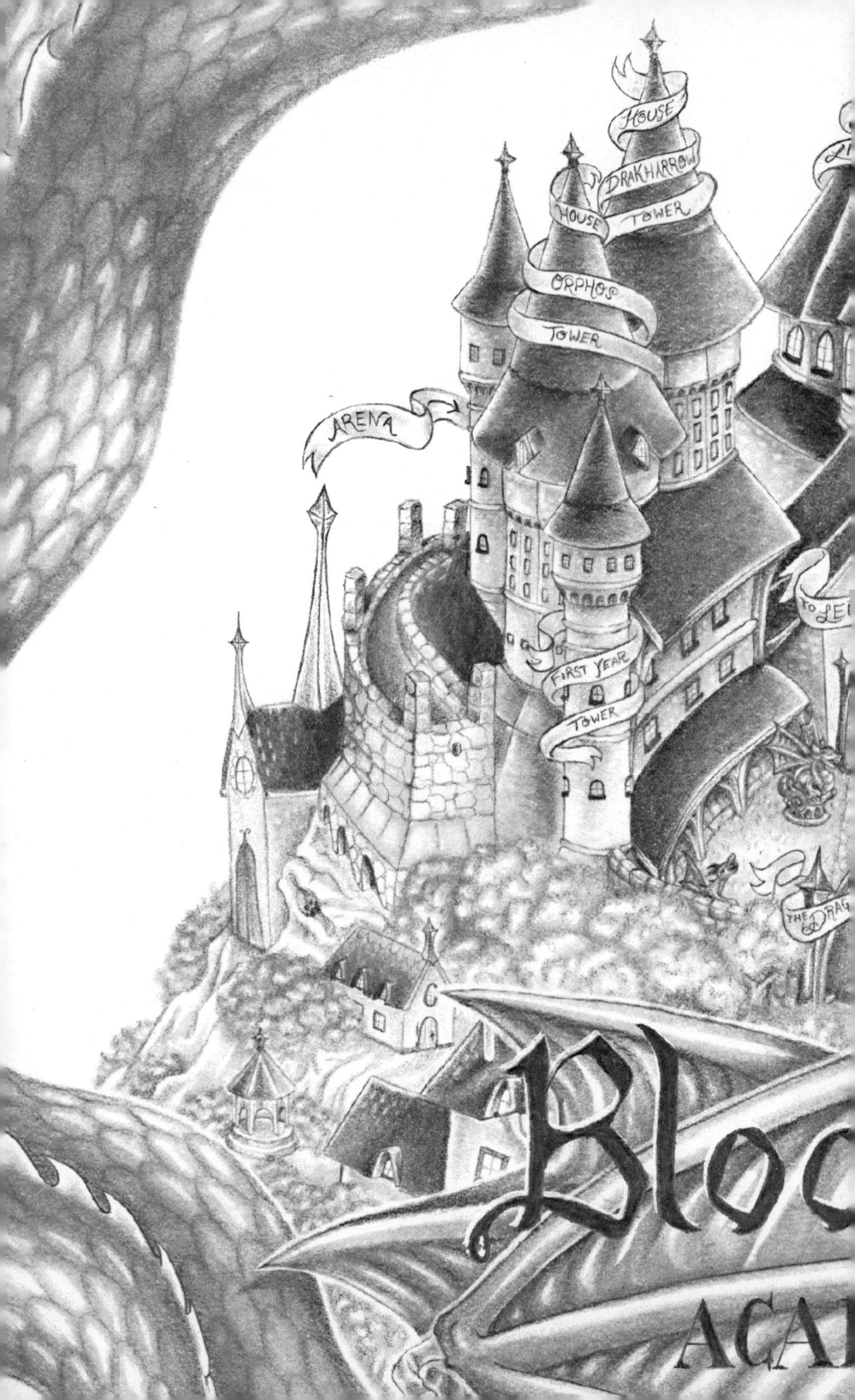

PROLOGUE

NEVILLE

A heavy snow was falling, whirling outside the windows and lashing the panes, blocking out light and making it seem closer to midnight than a mere four o'clock in the afternoon. Along the stone corridor, a small creature padded along, their little frame replete with self-assurance. The air carried the scent of sausages and cinnamon, both flavors they were rather fond of.

The smells of cooking were good ones. They helped to cover over the scent of fear. Fear had been thick in the halls of Bloodwing these past few days. Not merely the sharp, panicked fear of students who had forgotten to study for exams, but a deeper kind. Closer to terror. The kind that tasted like blood and heartbreak.

Neville had known that kind of fear before. He didn't like it.

Continuing on towards the kitchen, he passed unnoticed—as he always did unless he decided it should be otherwise. Professors glanced past him. Students stepped around him, almost without realizing it.

Leaping onto a polished wooden banister, he scampered down its slope—half sliding, half running—before jumping onto the ancient flagstone floor at the bottom. From there it was a short jaunt into the kitchens. They were busy at this time of night. Preparations were well underway for supper, which would be carried up to the students in the refectory hall. Professors had their own table in the refectory, but many preferred to dine in their chambers. Trays would be carried up to them. Dozens and dozens of servants all working in harmony three times a day to bring food to the denizens of the academy.

Ignoring a pair of undercooks arguing at one of the hearths about whether or not the beef was properly cooked, the fluffin approached the spot where a tall thin woman was stirring a pot with a grim expression. Her eyes were narrowed as she watched the undercooks quarrel. In another moment, Neville knew she would lose her temper and snap at them. He made a low chirping noise, with just the hint of a purr, and the woman turned around instantly, looking down at him, the expression of annoyance falling off her face to be replaced by one of pleasure.

"Ah, the little lord has arrived for his supper." She was already reaching for a plate behind her. "Well, here you go, milord. I hope it doesn't disappoint."

Neville gave another chirp of appreciation before turning his full attention to the plate. Slices of sausage. A butter biscuit. Some greens—which he disliked. Still, he ate them with dignity, knowing they held necessary nutrition.

He held very still as he sensed the woman look around carefully, then drop to her knees as he finished licking the plate. Reaching out a hand, she gently ran it over his head.

She really was a soft-hearted human, despite her tendency to snap at her underlings.

Neville licked her wrist in thanks, looking up at her and meeting her gaze, letting his eyes shine wide with his appreciation. The cook's lips parted slowly, and a small smile appeared. Thus the exchange was concluded. The cook would have a more peaceful evening. She would be less bothered by the silly mistakes made by those around her. A little more inclined towards grace.

As for all those around her? Neville slipped out of the kitchen. For the rest of them, it was as if he had never been there at all.

While he was in the lower recesses of the castle, he decided to explore. There were deeper areas, below the kitchens. Areas which frightened him and over which he had no purview. Then there were areas riskier to visit, farther afield from the hub of academy life, but which he nevertheless knew fell within the boundaries of his domain. And as with all domains, inspections must be conducted.

Back through the kitchen door. Down another corridor. A turn, then another. The walk became monotonous. The passages were unlit. Few came this way. Another turn and he was in an area of the castle few knew even existed. A shortcut. There was a prickle behind his ears. He didn't wish to go this way, to visit this part of his kingdom. Bad things lay this way. But it was his responsibility. Sometimes not even the darkest shadows could be turned away from. The light must go everywhere.

Another prickle. His fur twitched. A slight pressure. A nudge.

Nyxaris. The dragon's presence poked—like a cool nose touching his. An almost teasing gesture. The dragon was bored. Lonely. Morose. Not for the first time, nor probably the last.

The little fluffin gave his fur a shake. There was a dilemma there, a puzzle to be solved. But first, the shadows called, and he would answer.

A mouse scrambled by, and the fluffin gave a playful pounce. The mouse ran on, shaking, but intact as it reached a crack in the wall and skittered inside. Neville snuffled, twitching his nose. On a different occasion, the mouse might have been a tasty snack, but he had been well-fed too recently. He felt a kindness towards the humble little creature and let it go on its way.

The air chilled. A shift. There were places on the border of his realm where the stones felt colder than the rest. Where there was a wrongness. The Black Keep was one of these.

He walked for a while, then entered a space behind a cracked column and vanished into a narrow, dark place no map remembered and no blightborn or highblood had walked. Eventually, there was light, a shard of warmth peeking out from behind a tapestry. Neville nudged his nose against the hanging, moving forward for a better look.

There, sitting on the edge of the bed. The girl was there again. The one with the broken heart. Her hair gleamed dully in the firelight, unwashed and uncombed. Her eyes were listless, but she did not weep.

Neville hesitated. The urge to enter and go to her was very strong. There was something there. Something that had been, something that would be. He felt it very powerfully. Then a voice, coming from just outside the room. Harsh, guttural, yet still smooth as poisoned honey. Everything about it was *wrong*.

Neville growled, a faint sound low in his throat. He knew it was only a small indulgence. He would not engage the wrongness. He could not. He knew the extent of his own abilities too well for that. He had done enough to ease his own mind, simply by confirming it was still indeed *there*. Existing where it had no right to. But there were many things wrong that still endured. This was a time when fluffins were needed in abundance. Yet as far as he knew, he was the only one.

The nudge came again. Nyxaris. The dragon had no idea where Neville was, yet he sensed . . . something. Enough to send a warning. Neville backed up, the tapestry swinging back into place, the girl disappearing.

His fur bristled. He turned. Not from fear, no. He really feared very little. He had been afraid once, very afraid. Then the red girl had come. She had found him on the beach. She had brought him home.

Still, some ancient instinct—a kind of animal wisdom—told him this was neither the place nor the time for fluffins. Neville vanished into the dark, paws silent on the stone, the taste of sausage still sweet on his sandpaper pink tongue, and the feeling of the girl's sorrow still lingering behind him.

REGAN

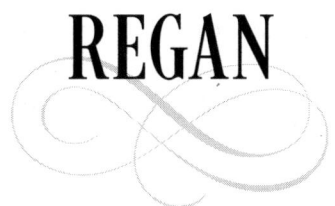

There was no point in wailing, gnashing teeth, or whining. Though one or all of those things might have been the recourse of other girls. I was not like them. I never had been. I was special. Perfect. Hadn't my father always said so? Besides, if I shone here, now, he'd let Persis come home. He'd promised my father that. So I sat stiff and rigid, my back straight, waiting. The trick was to remember to breathe. To breathe slowly. In and out, in and out. Chin up. Shoulders square.

My bloodline was pure. I was practically a goddess. Not far off from the Bloodmaiden herself, bless her blood. I was a *legend* in the halls of Bloodwing. Everyone looked up to me. I could do anything, get away with anything. So I could do this.

Still, legend or not, I'd trade every whispered compliment for one letter from my father telling me that my little brother was safe and home again.

The room was quiet, save for the ticking of a rectangular metal clock on the mantle. It was ugly and repulsive, the front glass over the face cracked as if someone had dropped it yet decided throwing it away would be too merciful. It wasn't to my taste, but no one cared about my taste. Not today. Certainly not in this room.

I forced myself to look towards the door when it opened, a small smile I hoped would look coy already forming on my face. I already knew who it was. A chill seemed to always enter with him, like death chasing at his heels. Was it waiting for him? Or for me?

He began speaking as if resuming a conversation we'd been having all along. "The reopening schedule has been finalized. Students have been arriving all day. Staff have been informed of what to say." He looked at me as if I didn't know all of this already, and I nodded dutifully. He resumed. "The Dragon Court is a mess. As of today, it's officially off-limits to students. Notices are being posted. No one needs to know the details of why."

"But it's an access point," I noted. "And many windows overlook it . . ."

He waved his hand. "They'll take the long way around or walk outside. What do we care? You may cross it if you wish. Though, you're liable to break your neck if you try. Stones are strewn everywhere. It will take weeks to clean up."

I nodded again. It didn't really matter. I knew why he wanted to keep people away.

He moved closer. The scarlet velvet robe he wore dragged along the floor. He wore it long. I think he believed it made him look taller. Bigger. More imposing. Men were such fools.

Besides, Viktor didn't need a robe to look imposing. He was fucking terrifying with or without it.

"They'll fall in line," he said.

I lifted my chin. "Of course they will. We'll see to that."

We. We were a pair now. No more triads. No more sharing. So why wasn't I filled with joy?

"So efficient," he murmured appreciatively, eyeing the scanty gown I wore. "We'll use the outer courtyard tomorrow for the assembly. You'll make a wonderful first impression."

I looked down at my lap, smiling slightly, trying to appear modest. "I'll try. There must be unity. Especially now."

"I value our unity greatly," he said. I didn't have to raise my head to know he was making an effort to smile. I held back a shudder. "You must be eager to step into your new role," he added.

"You've honored me. Elevated me. I won't fail you," I responded.

"Of course you won't. You wouldn't dare." The words were light. But my stomach churned.

"House Mortis has been beheaded. What could Catherine have been thinking to disappear like that? Pure political suicide." He chuckled. Many things about the events of the last few days had made him furious, but not this—this was a delight. A rare opportunity.

"Catherine's absence leaves Mortis vulnerable," I agreed. I knew he would not wish to discuss where Catherine had gone. Or who had gone with her.

"She trained her house well. You'll find them an advantage waiting to be taken."

I'd already determined that for myself. Catherine had always cultivated sly cruelty amongst her most favored. With her gone, they'd be a lost flock of mean little sheep—looking for someone to follow, someone to lead.

Someone like me.

He moved again. Closer to the bed. I could see him now in my periphery, just the edge of his silhouette. "I permitted Blake to complete the Rite of Dissolution," he said. "I might have opposed it."

My breath hitched. I tried not to let it show. In and out. In and out.

Blake. He'd chosen that blightborn girl over the betrothal our parents had spent years arranging.

"I was ecstatic," Viktor murmured. "Could you tell?"

I licked my lips slowly. "No, Lord Drakharrow."

"Please. Dispense with the formalities."

I forced my head up, made myself look at him—really look. "I had no idea, Viktor. Or I would have been much happier in that moment," I lied.

He stretched what was left of his lips into a smile. I held my gaze very still. "I gave Blake an opportunity. He was a fool to discard you. Yet now I can claim what I admit I've always seen as mine." He moved closer. Much closer. A hand reached out. He gripped my chin.

I lifted it eagerly with a sigh, as if the touch was everything I'd always wanted—and more.

"You're exquisite. Perfect," he murmured. "I've watched you since birth. Always on the sidelines. Always admiring. Waiting, watching. It was a mistake to give away something as perfect as you are. I should have claimed you myself, right from the start."

It took everything I had not to shudder. "It was. How grateful I am to be free of him now." Inside of me, another girl was weeping with rage and fear. Still trying hard to convince herself that this all could be undone, that Blake's rejection might not be forever, that Father wouldn't sign a contract selling his daughter in the hopes of regaining his son.

She was a stupid, silly girl. I told her to shut the fuck up.

Viktor's fingers were trailing lower. Down my throat, skirting the tip of my collarbone. Then his hands were gone.

I breathed. In and out. In and out.

His hands were on his belt. Loosening his robe. My smile froze.

"I'm going to take my time with you, Regan. When one gets to be as old as I am, pleasures tend to fade." He laughed softly, and for a moment I let myself wonder just how old he truly was. "But having to wait for you all these years? I expect the pleasure will be . . . Well, perhaps nearly as exquisite as you are."

As he slid the robe off his shoulders I made myself look—but not directly. I let my gaze land just to the right, past him to the door behind.

He was inches away now. I could smell him: blood and the medicine he'd been prescribed. And something else. I stole a glance. A thick, shiny ointment was smeared across his skin, coating every part that I could see.

My stomach turned. Soon it would be all over me, too.

"Take off your gown."

My fingers obeyed before my mind could react.

He watched me, saying nothing. I sensed the time for compliments was over. When the fastenings were undone, I stood up, even though it meant coming closer to him, and let the dress fall to the floor. Blessedly, he didn't touch me then.

"Good girl. Now lie back on the bed."

I did as I was told. The mattress was too soft beneath me. I closed my eyes and tried not to breathe through my nose as he joined me. I could do this. I had to. If I bolted now, Viktor would have Persis shipped home in pieces. As it was, my little brother was far from here. Sent as a ward—such a noble word for *prisoner*—to live with the family of one of Viktor's most loyal followers until our family's honor was restored. I didn't even know where Persis was. Which family held him. No one had told me anything. But if I ran, if I failed, if I said the wrong thing? He'd pay the price. My father would pay the price. My entire house would pay.

Pay. I thought about the word. I was being paid—for all of this. Wasn't I? In power. In prestige. All would fear me. And fear was close to envy, was it not?

So I let him touch me. Because every caress bought Persis another sunrise.

And while he did what he wanted, I went somewhere else.

I was standing on the balcony—the one just above the entrance to Bloodwing—looking down upon the students as they gathered for the first day of school. Watching them gape, watching them stare, as the realization dawned that I had ascended far above them all.

I would look down at all their faces, my own expression cool and remote. A queen in her tower.

And then I would finally see Blake.

I'd smile. And I'd watch as the disdain I'd grown so used to seeing there finally melted away, changing into something else. *Fear.*

If he couldn't bring himself to love me, then he would fear me. Oh yes, I'd make him fear for himself and everyone he held dear.

The time passed. When it was over, I reclothed myself—fingers numb but steady.

Viktor rose, grunting like a pig as he reached for his robe and pulled it around him.

I glanced over despite myself. The luxurious velvet fell unevenly across his ruined frame, like a curtain trying to mask a nightmare. I looked away. I'd already looked enough for a lifetime. But then, this was my life now. I had to get used to it. There was no room for the weak in the Black Keep.

He moved to the door and wrenched it open. "Davies," he barked to the guard standing in the hall. The one who'd probably been listening to us this entire time. "It's time. Fetch my nephew. Drag him here if you must. Tell him Headmaster Kim wishes to see him and sends his regards."

There was a murmuring answer, then the sound of retreating footsteps. Viktor turned back to me. His eyes lingered over my hands as they worked to fasten the dress. For a horrible moment, I wondered if he was going to tell me to lie back down.

Then he smiled almost wistfully—or as wistfully as a vampire who'd lived longer than any highblood had any right to could. "All good things must come to an end," he said, his voice like graveyard dust. "Even my time with you, my precious gem." He turned to the door. "It's time to give my dear nephew a delightful surprise."

Then he was gone, not even bothering to close the door behind him. Another guard had taken up position outside. The man peeked in for a moment before my glare warned him away.

I stalked over and slammed the door, then smoothed down the

front of my dress. My hands were trembling. I forced them to stillness. I'd bathe and wash the scent of my new husband away down the drain, along with every memory of his touch.

Then I'd do it again and again.

I could do this. I could play their tyrant queen. Let them all watch and see.

Book 1
Wintermark

CHAPTER 1

MEDRA

I was flying.

Well, not quite. I was bouncing. Held in some sort of a sling contraption, I swayed with every heavy step my caregiver took. I flailed my arms—pudgy, uncoordinated, utterly enthusiastic, while my legs kicked just as eagerly at the open air. I heard squealing. Loud. Joyful.

It took me a moment to realize the sound was coming from me.

"Easy now, little cub." The voice was a warm rumble, familiar and comforting. "You don't have to get quite so excited each time you see me."

"I don't think she's gotten quite as used to talking bears as Morgan and I have." The voice was rich and deep and came from somewhere behind me. A man's voice. The man holding me. A strong hand came up, checking the straps of the contraption. Some sort of a baby carrier. I grasped for the hand, squeaking and squirming. Everything shook as the man holding me laughed. He let me raise his fingers to my face. They smelled warm and earthy. Like pine and sandalwood. Safe.

I couldn't turn to see him. But warmth radiated from him like sunlight. I knew who held me. I could feel him, sense him. He was *love*. My uncle. My protector. Draven.

"Wrigglier than a fox in a henhouse," the great booming voice intoned again.

I looked up in delight as a huge brown bear peered down at me, then leaned in to nuzzle their cool, wet nose against mine as I gurgled and gasped in delight. A warm summer wind crossed the glade, and I closed my eyes. When I opened them, something silver caught my eye. Hair like shimmering moonlight flowed down her back. My aunt, Morgan.

She was dressed like royalty, in a rich scarlet gown trimmed with gold. She stood tall, head bent in conversation with a young knight. The half-fae woman could have been no more than twenty-five, and yet her expression was thoughtful, her smile warm and wise.

There was something sharp about the young knight, something edged like a blade. Unlike my aunt, she was mortal. She wore her steel armor as if it were a second skin. Her blond hair was cropped short, with just a slight curl over her ears. She was intimidating. Fierce. Violence obviously became her. But when she looked across the glade at me, there was nothing hard in her expression. I saw only warmth and fondness.

The two women slowly approached me, their faces soft in different ways—both ways I loved. Then Morgan bent forward. I closed my eyes as she kissed my forehead with lips so soft.

"Our little Medra," she murmured. "Oh, how precious . . ."

And then it was all gone.

My heart lurched. I woke up, coated in sweat, my heart hammering. The dream was scattered like ash in the wind. My sheets were damp. My breath fogged the air. I sat up, the ache in my heart still sharp and all too real. The room was quiet. I turned towards the other bed, Florence's name on the tip of my tongue, everything in me calling for comfort and consolation.

The bed was empty. Another pain stabbed through my chest. I'd forgotten.

Florence was gone, too.

The morning dawned cold and gray. It was still snowing. I hadn't slept well, not after that dream. I was used to intrusive thoughts—hell, Orcades had been nothing but. Still, the dream had been something different entirely. A reminder of my past life. Of who I really was. Of the family I'd lost. The last time they'd seen me, I'd been that baby. Giggling and gurgly. Would they even recognize me now? And what would they think of me if they did? What would they think of who I'd become, of what I'd done?

My aunt, Morgan le Fay. My uncle, Draven Venator. Hawl, the Bearkin warrior with a heart of gold. And Lancelet, my aunt's dearest friend and faithful knight of Camelot.

They were legends in my mind, not real people. A world where fae and mortals and other fantastical creatures coexisted? From where I stood, with both feet fixed solidly on Sangratha's blood-soaked soil, it all sounded like nothing more than fiction. I'd idealized them since I'd arrived in this place. It had been easy to do, considering how long it had been since I'd seen any of them in the flesh. What would they think of *me*? Maybe that was the wrong question. What would they think of the people I was surrounded by?

The highbloods. The vampires. Blake.

I tried to ignore the throb of questions in my head as I quickly got dressed.

Today was the first real day of classes after Frostfire. The midwinter break had been unexpectedly extended. We'd all been restricted to our respective house towers since the events of a few nights ago. Since I was in House Avari, that meant I hadn't really had a chance to see, well, anyone but Kage. And we weren't exactly on speaking terms at the moment.

I'd mostly stayed in my room, alone. But sometimes, when I came down to snatch a tray of food, I'd hear rumors swirling in the common room. Scattered bits and pieces of what had happened that night, most of them wildly off base.

I'd caught more than a few looks from Avari students. I knew everyone wanted to ask me what had really gone down that night . . .

but no one dared. Maybe Kage had warned them off. Or maybe it was just the look on my face that told them it was better not to risk it.

Of course, I wasn't the only one who had been through a lot.

Trying to tally up the losses from that night was still enough to leave me reeling.

Visha had lost her girlfriend Lace Ironstride, a sweet yet tough dwarven girl I'd just begun to get to know, but who I'd truly liked. She'd been one of Professor Stonefist's star pupils, too. I wondered if Stonefist had been told Lace was dead.

Blake had lost Aenia, but not until after she'd brutally murdered Lace. The death of a child should have been horrible. We all should have been in mourning. And yet, what I mourned was the loss of Aenia the child. Because the Aenia who'd died had been a monster.

Back in the Dragon Court that night, Theo had briefly told me what had happened. How he'd been forced to stab his youngest cousin, while shielding Florence from Aenia's blood lust.

Poor Theo. In some ways, he'd always been the most innocent of us all. Now he'd lost some of that, lost a piece of his own blooddamned heart. I wondered if he'd even been able to see his boyfriend, Vaughn, yet and talk to him about everything that had gone down.

Meanwhile, Lysander had lost his younger sister, Lunaya. Not to death—but to something even more malevolent. Did the House Orphos leader even know the full story yet? Had anyone bothered to tell him exactly what had happened? Had Blake or Kage?

Lunaya had been blood-bound to Marcus Drakharrow. From what I'd seen, she was basically in servitude to him and Catherine Mortis. She'd gotten onboard that terrifying, corrupt dragon and ridden off into the sunset—taking my mother's soul along with her.

Right. As if things weren't fucked-up enough already. Orcades had gone from being dead, to being in my head, to being in a fucking enchanted knife, to now being inside of a godsdamned dragon. Molindra, that was the dragon's name.

I wasn't crossing my fingers that my mother had survived the transition. Even if she'd managed to survive, our connection seemed to have been broken when Molindra flew away. I might never see her again. I wondered if there was any way to tell if Orcades was still alive. A spell, a ritual, a bit of light blood magic. Anything. Of course, there was one person who might have had an answer to that. But there was no chance in hell I was setting foot in his bloody office ever again.

Thinking of Professor Rodriguez raised the pace of my heartbeat immediately. I slammed the door of my wardrobe shut with a little more force than I'd meant to, tugged on the hip-length black sweater I'd pulled out, and headed for the door.

Today was going to be such a shit show.

Theo leaned over the breakfast table, making sure to keep his voice low. I'd lost track of how many times I'd glanced towards the refectory entrance. Breakfast was more than half-over. We'd be heading to class in a few minutes. Obviously, Visha wasn't coming. And, apparently, neither was Blake.

I glanced back at Theo. Who was now standing up and making his way around the table to my side. He slid onto the bench beside me. I raised my eyebrows. "Changing seats?"

He shrugged. "I decided this was too important to risk sharing." He leaned his head as close to mine as he could without us kissing, and I tried not to snicker. He'd been reserved so far this morning. But at least he was *there*. He was eating. He was talking. He wasn't rocking back and forth sobbing or hiding in his room. Or, worse, furious with me. That was more than I'd hoped for, honestly. It was more than we'd gotten from Visha so far.

"What?" Theo questioned, seeing my smile.

I shook my head. "Nothing. It's just . . . really good to see you, Theo."

"Oh." He looked taken aback. "It's good to see you, too, Medra." He glanced around one more time, then lowered his voice to less than a whisper. "So I'm not hallucinating again, right? Tanaka can turn into a fucking wolf?"

"Again?"

He ran his hands through his hair, looking sheepish. "I mean, yeah, it's been known to happen. After imbibing . . . certain substances."

I rolled my eyes. "Right. Of course it has. Well, you're not hallucinating this time, Theo. It happened."

"Did you know that? Before, I mean. That he could . . . you know, *do* that?"

I met his eyes. "I'd actually expected you to tell me it was no surprise."

Theo's eyes widened. "What? Me?"

"You're a highblood," I pointed out. "Aren't you all supposed to have special tricks like this up your sleeves? Sanguimancy? Necromancy? A little extra fur?"

Theo snorted. "I mean, magic, yes. But usually just being, you know, a fucking vampire is good enough. We don't need to turn into wolves, too." His eyes suddenly lit up, and he rose from the bench.

"What's going—" I started to say. Then I saw the reason for Theo's excitement. Vaughn Sabino was striding between the tables. Clearly he'd already spotted Theo. A huge grin covered the tall dark-skinned young man's face.

In an instant, the two had collided. I watched in delight as Vaughn folded Theo into his arms, one hand firm at his waist while the other cupped the back of his neck, then drew his lips into a slow, breath-stealing kiss.

There were a few whistles and groans, but to my surprise, no one threw food or shouted anything nasty. I saw a few dark looks from some highbloods at the House Mortis table and a few from Theo's house, Drakharrow. But none from Vaughn's, House Orphos.

But then, in a world of cutthroat vampires, Orphos was kind of the exception. I still wasn't sure what to make of Lysander's house. There were those who said Orphos was weak. And yet once, they'd been allies of House Drakharrow. Unfortunately, the loss of Lunaya—basically the princess of House Orphos—wasn't going to put those claims of weakness to rest.

I glanced around again, wondering if anyone knew about Lunaya, then shifted my focus back to where Vaughn and Theo were still embracing. The looks they were getting weren't necessarily because Theo and Vaughn were both male either, I reminded myself. Theo was a highblood, and Vaughn was blightborn. In Sangratha, a pairing like that was still fairly taboo. My skin prickled. Just like Blake and me.

Except, I told myself, rising as I looked at the clock on the nearby wall, there *was* no Blake and me, was there?

Theo, Vaughn, and I left the refectory with just a few minutes to spare to get to the entrance to Bloodwing Academy. A sort of back-to-school assembly had been called. Usually events like these were held in the Dragon Court. But this one was being held outdoors in a vast courtyard at the entrance of the school. I could still remember coming through those huge front doors the day Blake had escorted me from the Black Keep. He'd told me he'd never mingle his blood with mine. Rather ironic now.

I walked ahead with Theo and Vaughn trailing behind me through the corridors, hand in hand. We were nearly at the entrance when we heard it: voices, sharp and jeering, tinged with the kind of tone that screamed *asshole* and that seemed to come easily to those with power undeserved.

"J-j-just leave me alone," a girl's voice stuttered, and I cringed, knowing the sound of her weakness would only excite whoever was bothering her.

I glanced behind me. Theo was already scowling, his fists clenched by his sides. Vaughn's entire body had stiffened, his warm and open expression shuttering. I took a deep breath and rounded the next corner at a jog. A handful of students stood clustered beneath an archway. Six of them. All highbloods.

I spotted Quinn Riley first. She leaned lazily against a stone column, her arms crossed over her narrow chest, pretty lips curved in a satisfied smirk. Two other girls were there. Larissa, a Drakharrow girl with mellow golden skin and silver hair that fell in thick waves. And Gretchen, a tall curvy girl with straight chin-length hair and a pretty-enough face, if you liked the weaselly ones. I'd once stuck a knife in that face, so I guess that counted me out.

The other three were males. One boy lounged against the wall close to Quinn. I wondered if this was her betrothed, the infamous Edward Ashveil, who I'd once heard her and Regan discussing. Apparently, Quinn had worked pretty hard to land him. Elegantly dressed in the colors of House Mortis, the highblood young man stood picking at his nails with a dagger, a faint look of boredom on his handsome brown face. I was a little surprised to see the House Mortis colors. I'd assumed Quinn would be matched to someone from Drakharrow.

The last two were the biggest surprises, however: Lucian Aleron and Evander Sylvain. Both were Visha's consorts. Evander stood slightly apart from the group, looking stiff and uncomfortable. He'd helped me once, but that had been mostly Visha's doing. I was a little surprised to see him there, but I told myself I shouldn't have been. Most highbloods were capable of such casual cruelty.

I spotted the girl they'd cornered as I drew nearer. She was right in the center. Dwarven, curvy, with mousy-brown hair and threadbare gloves. The blue coat she wore was hanging off her shoulders, far too big for her small frame. Maybe it had been a hand-me-down from an older brother or sister. She was in First Year colors, probably training to be a healer or a scout—if she ever made it that far. I thought of Naveen.

Her eyes were wide with fear. I watched carefully to see who she was looking at. Who was she most afraid of? To my surprise it wasn't Quinn but Lucian. He was smiling as he tossed something from one hand to another—a shiny crimson apple. I frowned. Not exactly threatening. Not like the knife Edward was still busily cleaning his cuticles with.

"I'm just trying to help," I heard Lucian say. "You look pale. We thought maybe you could use a little snack. It's a gift. Go on, take a bite."

The girl shook her head, smart enough to know something was wrong, even if she couldn't quite pin down what. "No, thank you. I . . ."

Quinn peeled away from her pillar. "Refusing a gift from a highblood? Do you know how deeply offensive that is, girl?"

"I—I—I'm sorry, my lady," the girl stammered. "I didn't . . ."

"Oh, hell no," I muttered. No one was calling Quinn *my lady* without an intervention. I started forward without even glancing back at Theo and Vaughn.

"Hey, *Lady* Quinn," I called, letting my voice drip with sarcasm. "Why don't you back the fuck up and let the First Year breathe?"

The entire group turned to face me. I took in their expressions. Quinn was eager. She was obviously delighted to see me. She knew I'd be much more fun to play with than a random blightborn First Year. Lucian was wary. Edward had paused his knife play. He looked curious but not put off. The only one of the six who looked at all intimidated by my arrival so far was Evander. He seemed like he'd scurry off like a rat from a sinking ship, given half a chance. I wondered what Visha would say when she knew what her consorts had been up to this morning.

"You there, First Year. What's your name?" I called, moving closer and reaching the edge of the group.

"D-dani," the blightborn girl managed.

"Why don't I walk you to the assembly now, Dani?" I offered. The girl gave a tremulous nod, but Gretchen and Larissa were suddenly blocking my way. Gretchen looked back over her shoulder and snickered. That was all I'd needed. With a sigh, I grabbed their shoulders and shoved them apart none too gently, then moved into the gap and stepped up to the blightborn girl.

"That's better," I began to say—just as Lucian stopped tossing the apple.

They must have had it all planned, for the next instant he'd turned towards Quinn and given her a sly, conspiratorial wink. "Catch." The apple flew through the air.

Quinn caught it easily, cradling her prize close to her lips as she smiled and showed her fangs. For a second, I thought she meant to bite into it herself.

Then, with no warning, she spun her arm forward and hurled the thing straight at the First Year's head. It hit with a wet, unnatural splat.

Dani screamed as thick, congealed blood exploded from the apple, matting her hair and running down her cheeks.

I gagged as the rancid scent hit me—sweetly rot-tinged, like pig's blood gone sour. A few of the drops had sprayed me. I hastily wiped at my face with the back of my hand as the girl's scream cracked into sobs. "Dani!" I tried to reach for her, but she was too upset to even look at me.

The highbloods surrounding her backed up as she moved, laughing and shrieking, trying not to let any of the blood drip onto them. The gap between Quinn and Lucian widened. Her eyes still squeezed mostly shut, Dani stumbled towards it and bolted. This time no one tried to stop her.

"By the Three," I snarled, reverting to an expression I'd grown up with. "What the fuck is wrong with you all? When are you going to grow the fuck up?"

"Calm down, Pendragon," Gretchen drawled. "What's the big deal? It was just a little joke."

"Just a little blood," Larissa agreed with a titter that made me want to smack her in the face. "This is Sangratha, after all."

"At least it wasn't dragon blood," Edward offered, beginning to polish his stupid dagger with a small cloth. "At least, I don't think it was dragon blood."

"It couldn't have been dragon blood, Edward," Quinn said sweetly. "Pendragon's stupid dragon hasn't been seen in days. It flew off and abandoned her. This time for good, I think."

Gretchen gave a fake gasp of sympathy. "Oh, poor little Pendragon. You're all alone."

"She sure is," Quinn continued, her voice venomous. "She probably thought Blake would come running to defend her. But oh, no, it seems like he's disappeared, too."

Her words shouldn't have mattered to me. Still, they hit me like a punch to the gut. I tried hard not to show it, but I must have flinched a little, because Quinn's eyes lit up as if she'd scored a point.

"That's right." She lowered her voice to a whisper and stepped forward. "Without him, what do you have left? You're dragonless. Mateless. Just pitiful blightborn trash."

"Seems to me we should have saved the apple," Lucian drawled nastily, eyeing me up and down. "You're less than trash, Pendragon, you're—"

"You're boring," Theo interrupted loudly as he stepped into the center beside me. He slowly turned, looking at each of the highbloods with an expression of aristocratic disgust and shaking his head. "And wow, that really is impressive. Six vampires should be badass. Intimidating. But what do you have? One blood apple and a First Year." He gave a slow theatrical clap. "Bravo. That'll really show your enemies what you can do."

Quinn growled and leaned forward, opening her mouth, but Theo was already turning away. He looked at Evander, then Lucian.

"Does Visha know where you two are? Because if she did, I have a feeling we'd be mopping your blood off the floor right now."

"I didn't—" Evander said quickly, his face flushing.

"Oh, you didn't?" Theo echoed. "You didn't just stand here and watch them bully that poor First Year? I'll be sure to tell Visha that later. I'm sure you'll like how it plays out." He looked down his nose at the other highblood. "You're a waste of space, Evander. Absolutely pathetic."

I doubted Theo had even seen Visha since that night in the Dragon Court. But since he was doing a damn fine job of schooling her two consorts, I wasn't about to stop him.

"Come on," Evander muttered, grabbing at Lucian's arm. "Let's go."

Lucian glared at me. I had no idea what I'd done to bring out this side of him. Before this, I'd had a casual relationship with Visha's future consorts. We'd said hello in the hallway, waved once in a while. We'd never been close, but at least we'd been polite.

But now . . . there was something in Lucian's eyes that made me wonder what else was going on.

"You're right," Lucian snapped, not taking his eyes off me but beginning to walk backwards. "She's not worth it."

"But the year is young," Edward said lightly, finally sheathing that fucking dagger. He reached out and grasped Quinn gently by the wrist. "Plenty of time for this later. The assembly, remember?"

Quinn lingered for a moment, her eyes on me. "You have absolutely no idea," she said, finally smiling cruelly. "Things are about to change, Pendragon. And I promise you, you're not going to like the new rules."

Gretchen and Larissa were already walking ahead down the corridor. Taking Edward's hand, Quinn started to follow them. Gretchen glanced back and took one last shot. "Start practicing your curtsying, Pendragon. You're going to be spending a lot of time on your knees from now on."

Edward waggled his fingers and grinned. *"Sanguis et Flamma Floreant."* Then they turned a corner and were gone.

I didn't move. Not right away. My blood was still burning. Theo was still staring after them down the hall. Vaughn stepped up beside him with a worried expression. I opened my mouth to thank Theo—and felt a hand touch my shoulder from behind.

My body reacted before I could even think.

Fist already forming, I spun and punched. There was a grunt of pain as my fist connected.

"Bloodmaiden," someone groaned. "What in the ever-loving fuck was that for?"

Shit. It was Blake.

CHAPTER 2

BLAKE

I took a step back. Not because the punch had been that hard—though, it was—but because I knew I'd screwed up. I shouldn't have touched her. Shouldn't have dared to get that close. I deserved worse.

Theo gave a low whistle. "Well, that's one way to say hello."

My cousin, the ever-helpful bystander. I shot him a glare, then exhaled, slowly. Tried to let the sting of pain blooming in my jaw ground me. "Guess I deserved that." I finally looked down at her. She hadn't moved since she'd struck me, her fist still half-raised. I wondered if that meant she was thinking about doing it again.

I stood my ground. I wouldn't dodge if Pendragon came at me. I'd meant what I said: I deserved it. Then I took in her expression. Somewhere between furious and broken. Something wrenched inside. *Oh, Pendragon.*

But that was the hell of it—I couldn't touch her. Couldn't even say her name out loud.

She had dark specks of blood spattered across one cheek. She smelled . . . a little strange. But beneath it all I caught the familiar scent of *her.* Her entire posture screamed *Get the fuck away from me!* from the power in her stance to the fury in her eyes, the way her whole body radiated a pure kind of grief that demanded the world get its shit together and do a hell of a lot better.

She was the most alive thing I'd ever seen. The most beautiful thing I would ever see. I wanted to step closer. Wrap her in my arms. Soothe her, say all the comforting words I could think of—which weren't many, under the circumstances, but damn if I wouldn't give it a try.

But I couldn't. Didn't dare. Didn't have the right.

I looked around the hall, saw the blood spattered on the floor. Clearly, I'd walked into something. But just what, I wasn't sure. Pendragon was breathing hard—not just from hitting me but like she'd been running. For all I knew, she'd been running since the moment I'd betrayed her in the Dragon Court and hadn't stopped until now, when her fist had finally found my face. Wasn't I the target she wanted? I'd fucked her over completely. Gone behind her back. Lied to her. Made her lie to her dragon. I'd tried to turn Nyxaris back to stone. I'd done a lot of shitty things in my life. But that one kept me up at night. When I wasn't thinking about Aenia, which was a lot of the time, I sometimes let the guilt gnaw at me. Just for fun. It wasn't as if I was actually sleeping anyhow.

Pendragon was still looking at me. I wondered what she saw. I dropped my hand from my jaw. My fingers itched to raise it again, to touch my left eye—or what was left of it. My body was healing. Benefits of vampirism. But the damage would never be entirely undone. The skin around the eye socket was still tender, taut. The eye was still, well, *gone*. The healers weren't sure if it would ever grow back. Highbloods had sometimes been known to grow back limbs, but it wasn't guaranteed. In the meantime, I didn't need a mirror to know I looked like something a dragon had chewed up and spit out.

Blake the highblood golden boy? Not anymore. Not with a red-scaled monster hiding under my skin.

Pendragon's expression had changed into something less angry but no less guarded. I longed to ask her what she saw when she looked at me. But just having her look at me at all would have to be enough. One of her red curls suddenly plunged over her face. I stared, transfixed, as she brushed it back, tucking it behind an ear.

Hell, it was the loveliest thing I'd seen all week. I'd never stop being in awe of that hair. Of her hand. Of every little thing she did.

I closed my eyes briefly, trying to get a fucking grip. I'd tried to redeem myself that night. I'd stood between Nyxaris and Florence. Offered myself as a dragon snack to try to save a friend who mattered to her. But the fact that if all had gone according to plan, I'd have betrayed her that night and rendered my attempt to atone hollow. It didn't matter what I'd done afterwards. I was a bastard. A villain.

Still, those words she'd said to Nyxaris? I'd never forget them. But that didn't mean she'd really meant them. Not in the way I hoped she did. She'd saved my skin. I hadn't deserved it then—I didn't now. I wasn't foolish enough to think she'd ever truly forgive me. But she was here. She hadn't walked away yet. So for a second, I let myself breathe it in. The shape of her. The memory of how good it felt to just be near her. I didn't have a shot in hell. But Bloodmaiden help me if I wasn't still hoping.

"Have you seen Visha?" Theo demanded, interrupting my thoughts—which was probably for the best. Pendragon and I couldn't just keep staring at each other forever, even if I would have been fine with that.

"Visha?" I shrugged. "Once or twice around the common room."

Theo frowned disapprovingly. I guess he was thinking I didn't seem concerned enough about Visha. She'd lost someone. I was her House Leader. I should be stepping up. He was right.

"You weren't at dinner last night. I didn't see you in the common room. Where'd you go?"

I stared at my cousin for a second. In some other timeline, I should have been furious with him. He'd killed Aenia. Taken my little sister away from me for good. I wasn't over her loss—in some ways I'd hardly even started to face it. I woke up every morning from dreams that seemed so real, dreams of Aenia and me running on that beach. Happier times. Every morning, I had to remember the truth. She was gone. No second chances. Some highbloods might have already ripped Theo's throat out for what he'd done, accident or not. But I knew—*knew*—in the very blood that ran in my veins that Theo hadn't wanted to hurt Aenia. It went against everything I knew about my cousin. He would never have caused her harm unless there'd been truly no other way.

Everyone had seen Aenia as a lost cause. But she was one I'd planned to never give up on. Still, I knew who was really to blame for it all. And I didn't have to look far to find him. The real culprit. The source of almost all my woes.

"Blake? Where'd you go last night?" Theo repeated.

I closed my eyes. "Viktor. I went to see Viktor."

CHAPTER 3

MEDRA

"*Viktor?*" I repeated. My eyes narrowed. "Why do you look like that?"

Blake shrugged. "Like what?"

I frowned. Something had shifted in his expression. I wasn't imagining it. He hadn't flinched, not exactly. But something close. His lips had become a hard line. His posture was wary, defensive. He hadn't looked like that a moment ago. Not when he'd been looking at me. He'd looked . . . softer. Now his hand twitched. Almost, almost reaching toward the left side of his face.

His face. I bit my lip, trying not to show how much seeing it bothered me. Behind me, Theo and Vaughn had gone conveniently silent.

"Why do you look like that when you say his name?"

Blake stared down at me, his eyes stubborn. But he didn't deny it.

My heart sped up. "Because you thought he was dead. Didn't you?"

Blake's lips tightened.

I was right. I knew I was right. "Why? Why would you think that?"

He held very still.

"Oh gods," I whispered. I'd been a fool. I'd had days to put this together. Why had it taken me so long? "Viktor did that to you."

Behind me, Theo made a strangled noise. But I couldn't take my eyes off Blake. I didn't want to think about what that meant exactly. He'd been hurt. That was all. Of course, I cared when someone was hurt. Even the highblood bully who'd tormented me, betrayed me time and again, and tried to turn Nyxaris to stone?

I cleared my throat. "Tell me, Blake. What happened?"

Blake forced a smile that didn't reach his good eye. "Look, we're going to be late for the assembly. I think we'd better—"

"No. Don't do that. Don't you dare. Don't deflect. Answer me, dammit."

We stared at each other. His eye. His poor ruined eye. His beautiful, wrecked face. The scars were already forming. It will all heal, I reminded myself. He was a fucking vampire. Of course it would. I tried not to question why my own hands were suddenly shaking. Why it was becoming so hard to keep them pressed to my sides. To resist reaching one hand out so I could run it over Blake's scars. Why? Why would I long to do something like that? What the hell was wrong with me?

Empathy. Absolutely ordinary empathy, I tried to tell myself. Completely normal.

Blake was hesitating.

"Blake." I softened my voice. "Tell us."

He looked at me, then his lips twisted in a bitter smile. "Fine. You're right. More or less."

White-hot rage flared through me. An anger that was as pure as it was terrifying. For a moment, I forgot everything. Where I was. Who I was with. My past with Blake. His betrayal. My grief. All of it went out the nearest window. All I could think about was *him*. Viktor. The smug, sick, arrogant highblood who'd haunted the edges of my nightmares since I'd arrived in this place. The man who'd manipulated me, manipulated Blake, used us both. And now, what he'd done to Blake . . . The pain he'd caused . . .

I was moving forward when hands shot out, gripping me by the shoulders. "Let me go." I struggled against them.

"No, Pendragon. Not until you tell me where you're going."

I looked up then, my eyes meeting his one good one. "I'm going to fucking kill him."

If I thought I'd see happiness, I was wrong. Blake looked stricken. "No. You can't."

"Why not?" I countered.

"Because you can't threaten Viktor and expect to walk away from that battle."

"So what? You think I'm afraid? I'm not afraid of your godsdamned uncle, Blake. This has been coming for a long time." I could hear myself. I sounded like a cocky, arrogant fool—and deep down, I knew it, too. Who was I, anyhow? It wasn't as if I still had a dragon. But I didn't *want* to know how wrong I was. I wanted to keep this anger burning, feed it fuel. It felt good. And it would feel even better when I hurt the man who had dared to do this to—

"No," Blake interrupted my thoughts. "I know you're not afraid. Though, by the Bloodmaiden, I wish you were." He let go of my shoulders, took a deep breath, but kept his body positioned in front of me, blocking me.

I thought of darting around but knew from experience just how fast he could be when he wanted to.

"You're not afraid, all right? I'm not saying that." He sighed. "*I'm* the one afraid."

"You?" I stared at him. "Why?"

"I'm afraid for you. Afraid for everyone I care about. Viktor . . ." His voice roughened. "Viktor has hurt every person he's ever known I . . ." He stopped, and my heart slammed against my ribs. Blake's jaw tightened. "He'll use you against me. You won't win. And deep down, you know I'm right."

The world was tilting. Vaughn had started pulling Theo down the hall. Now they were calling to us. I could hardly hear them.

Blake gave a low laugh full of bitterness. "You want to know why I'm really afraid of Viktor? Because I know exactly how far he'll go. I used to think I could handle it. I thought I could take whatever he threw at me and it wouldn't matter. But . . ." He trailed off.

I didn't say anything, already pretty sure I knew what he'd been going to say.

Blake cleared his throat. "I tried. I really did. I really fucking tried. But look at me, Pendragon. Take a good fucking look."

"Blake . . ." I blinked. Determined not to let the water in the corner of my eyes show.

"He'd love to break you. Just to watch me fall apart. And I can't—" He broke off, running his hands through his hair. "I can't let that happen. I know you don't owe me anything. But please, just . . ."

There was total silence for a moment.

"Fine," I said finally. "Let's go to the assembly."

He gave a hoarse laugh. "Right. The assembly. Nothing like an outdoor assembly in the middle of winter."

We started walking fast enough so that we could see Theo and Vaughn in the distance. Not quite fast enough to completely catch up. The space between Blake and me pulsed and throbbed like a beating heart.

"I'll bring him down, don't worry," Blake said quietly as we walked. "There's nothing I want more." I felt him sneak a glance at me. "So you feel better now? After punching me in the face?" He tried to put some levity in the words.

"Can't deny it was satisfying. Would have been better if you'd bled."

He smirked. "My nose has been broken more than once, as you can probably tell. Guess you just didn't hit hard enough."

Scowling, I made a move like I was going to hit him again, and he laughed and dodged.

"Anyhow, we Drakharrows are made of hardy stuff. For better or for worse." He was quiet for a moment. Then, "But I'm glad. Glad it felt good. I meant what I said. I deserved it."

Ahead of us, Theo and Vaughn had reached the huge double doors leading to the courtyard outside the school. Light streamed in. I could see a huge crowd of students already gathered. Blake and I stood on the threshold. Something between us had shifted. Some thread, broken and frayed, had been picked up again. I didn't know if we were starting over. But I did know he didn't want to be my enemy.

And gods knew, I couldn't afford to keep pushing people away. Not when I'd lost Nyxaris. Not when I'd already lost Florence.

We walked out into the courtyard, side by side, separate but together. There was still so much unsaid between us. So much that had been damaged. But when I glanced up at Blake—at the scars, the ruined eye, the jagged flesh, at everything that might have repulsed someone else—I didn't feel repelled. Not even a little. His face was somehow more beautiful, more haunted. Certainly more dangerous. And a lot more . . . well, real. It made me want to touch him. To remind myself I could. That if I wanted him to be, he was . . . Well. I wouldn't say the word. I'd said it to Nyxaris. Gods, I'd practically shouted it in the Dragon Court that night, in front of an audience. But I wouldn't, couldn't, say it to myself.

As we stepped out into the pale winter daylight, the first thing I saw was Headmaster Kim's head on a spike.

I stopped short, my breath catching in my throat. Blake's hand was on my arm instantly, pulling me forward in a way that was so subtly done most people probably didn't realize I was being pulled at all. I followed, half a second behind his stride, eyes still fixated on the decaying head.

It was mounted on a tall, black iron stake, right in the center of the snow-covered courtyard. Kim's skin had turned a grayish blue. His mouth was slack. One eyelid had frozen shut. He looked as if he had been . . . surprised.

Students gathered all over the courtyard, forming hushed, uneasy clusters. A few were gawking at the head. Most were ignoring it. A couple of students were crying. Kim hadn't exactly been a warm, beloved figure, but he'd represented something at Bloodwing: continuity. He was a steady, reliable presence. He stood between us students and the rest of the highblood elites, between blightborn and the rest of Sangratha. We'd never been exactly *safe* within the academy's walls. Naveen's death was proof of that. But we'd been lulled into a feeling of semisecurity, of being somewhat valued, thanks in part to Headmaster Kim. Now, in an instant, that had been shattered.

"How very kind of you to join us, Miss Pendragon. Mr. Drakharrow."

The voice came from above. Cool, composed. Laced with a familiar sweet malice. *Regan.*

I lifted my head slowly, turning around. Regan stood on the stone balcony that jutted out from the third floor, just above the entrance to the school. Climbing vines and writhing dragons with fierce, angry expressions were carved into the terrace. On the stone wall behind her was the Bloodwing school insignia, four intertwined dragons. I stared at it, remembering Edward Ashveil's earlier words. *Sanguis et Flamma Floreant.* Let blood and flame flourish. On either side of it, etched into the stone, were the four house names and their respective mottos. A good reminder of who the place really belonged to.

House Drakharrow's motto was *Sanguine Vincti.* Bound by blood. I pursed my lips. That one hit a little too close to home. House Mortis's *Mortem Excito* meant "I Summon Death." Well, Catherine had done just that, hadn't she? I hoped that was the one and only time I'd see such a powerful use of necromancy. But I wasn't about to bet on it. Avari's motto was *Luna Sanguinea Surgit.* Blood moon rises. I assumed that had something to do with Kage's ability to turn into a wolf. But I had no idea what exactly. Could everyone in his house do what he could? And then there was House Orphos's motto, Lunaya's house. *Sanguis Somniatorum.* Blood of dreamers. It seemed fairly self-explanatory after what we'd seen in the Dragon Court. But still, I wondered.

Up on the balcony, Regan wasn't alone. She was surrounded by highbloods—and only highbloods as far as I could see. I recognized some of the members of the board as well as some of our teachers: Professor Sankara, Professor Allenvale. And, of course, Professor Hassan was there, looking absolutely filled with pride. That couldn't be a good sign. Regan herself looked stunning as always, perhaps even more so today. Her long golden hair had been coiled in a sleek bun atop her head. Decked out in a formfitting dress with a bold flower motif of red, white, and silver, with a heavy black fur cape around her shoulders, she seemed to be paying homage to all of the noble houses except Orphos.

But my eyes didn't stay on Regan, beautiful though she was. No, they were already moving to the man at her side. I smothered a gasp as I saw Blake's uncle. Viktor Drakharrow's hand sat on Regan's waist possessively, gnarled fingers curled like claws into the silk of her gown. The touch was possessive—almost cruel. It must have hurt, but if it did, Regan sure wasn't showing it.

Still, I pitied her. I really did. If she thought that going from Blake to Viktor was some sort of an upgrade . . . Well, there was no accounting for taste, I supposed.

But it wasn't Viktor's hand on Regan's waist that had made me nearly gasp, it was everything else about him. Viktor looked worse than I'd ever seen him; I was surprised the entire courtyard around me wasn't filled with students chattering about it. But then, considering what had happened to Kim, I supposed it was no surprise they were keeping silent.

Since the last time I'd seen Viktor, Blake had tried to kill him. From the look of it, he'd nearly succeeded.

Viktor's white hair had been raked from his scalp and hung in stringy clumps. One side of his face was practically melted, as if someone had taken a candlestick and held it against the flesh. The skin had sagged and puddled. He wore a long red cloak that hid most of his frame and black leather gloves over his hands, so I couldn't tell just how bad the damage really was. But if his face was any indication, the battle had been brutal. I wondered what exactly Blake had done to make Viktor Drakharrow look like a walking corpse.

Still, I warned myself, he was a walking corpse that could smile like a man who still held the world by its throat.

I looked back at Regan, and my stomach turned. Her face was a perfect expression of serene defiance. With her chin high, it was as if she wanted that decaying monster's hand on her waist. As if being possessed by a disgusting predator like Viktor was something to be proud of.

Beside me, a soft growl came from Blake's throat, so low I was pretty sure I was the only one who'd heard. I knew—*knew*—that if he could, he'd drag me out of that courtyard right then and there.

But neither of us moved. Because something about that moment was telling him the same thing it was telling me: This was just the beginning.

Viktor lifted a gloved hand, and the low hum in the courtyard died down. "Students of Bloodwing Academy." His voice was raspy, as if he'd breathed in too much smoke.

I glanced at Blake, my mind filled with a million questions. *What exactly had happened between the two men?* I tried to turn my attention back to what Viktor was saying.

"The events of a few nights ago—" what a very subtle way of describing the night all hell broke loose, Viktor's nephew woke the deranged House Orphos dragon, and stole one of Bloodwing's noble highblood daughters "—have reminded us of a painful truth. Within Sangratha, there is an order. Every little child knows the words." He paused, and a blightborn woman came forward. She was dressed like a servant in a plain black dress with a crimson apron. She was neither old nor young, perhaps fifty, with curly brown hair tinged with gray. I vaguely recognized her, thought I'd seen her in the Avari tower. Yes, she was one of the housekeepers who cleaned the school after classes ended for the day.

Stepping to the edge of the balcony, she recited, "We serve the blood, we serve the line. The highbloods lead, by right divine. In blood we trust, in grace we stand. The highbloods guide us, hand in hand."

I thought back to the night I'd followed Blake into the city of Veilmar and listened to a different blightborn woman repeat those very same words as I watched small children beg.

"The Creeds of Faith," Viktor announced. "We all know them. Yet how often do we think upon the truth of the words? Their sanctity? Highbloods lead. Blightborn follow. Why? To ensure the safety and happiness of all." His face stretched in what I assumed was supposed to be a smile. He gestured to the stake in the center of the courtyard. "Our last headmaster sadly failed to uphold that cherished order. But we will not linger in the past."

A foreboding feeling filled me. I looked at Regan's face just as Viktor lifted his hand and gestured to his consort.

"Today, a new era begins for Sangratha—and for you, our Thralldom's most precious young people. Today, I am proud to present to you all the new headmistress of Bloodwing Academy."

Regan stepped up and laid her hands along the balustrade. "Thank you, Lord Drakharrow," she began. "As the new headmistress of Bloodwing, I shall implement urgently needed changes. This academy has been a highblood sanctuary for centuries. The most pure of the highblood houses send their children to reside within these walls. They must be kept safe. This is a place of power. A place of legacy." She paused, and the entire courtyard held its breath. "In recent years, that legacy has been besmirched by deviance, disrespect, and disobedience." Her lips curved slightly as she gazed down at me. "That ends now. Here. Today."

I held very still, refusing to flinch.

Our new headmistress continued. "As we resume the Wintermark term, improved security measures will be enacted to ensure the safety of our highblood students. A new task force will regularly patrol the halls. Lockdowns will be enforced whenever they are deemed required. No one who harms highbloods will walk the halls of our beloved academy unchallenged again."

My hands curled into fists, nails digging into my palms. Around me a few of the blightborn students were exchanging nervous, skeptical looks. Some highbloods were smirking.

The idea of highbloods needing protection from blightborn students was absolutely ludicrous: I'd seen all the proof I needed on the way to this absurd assembly. I glanced around, searching the crowd for Dani. When I didn't spot her, I wondered if she'd skipped the assembly altogether. I wouldn't have blamed her.

"Before classes resume today," Regan went on smoothly, "you'll all be treated to a demonstration. A lesson in accountability, which we would all do well to learn from." Turning, she gestured to the woman beside Viktor. The one dressed as a servant. "This blightborn woman," Regan pronounced, "was found stealing from the private quarters of a highblood professor." She glanced at Professor Hassan whose smile had deepened as if she was happy to be in the limelight. "What a heinous act. What a betrayal."

"Please, milady," the blightborn woman interrupted, sinking to her knees, tears streaming down her face as she looked down at us all from between the rungs of the railing, like a prisoner staring out of a cell window. "My son. He's sick. I needed the coin to send to the healer back in our vill—"

"Silence!" Regan slammed her hands down on the balustrade so hard it must have hurt. Her face was pale. If I didn't know better, I'd have said she was nervous. She certainly didn't seem to be enjoying herself as much as Hassan was. "Rise and be silent."

Trembling, the woman gripped the edge of the balcony rail and pulled herself back up.

"As I was saying," Regan went on, beginning to play with the fastenings on her black cloak, "this woman betrayed the trust we place in the lowblood servants who dwell amongst us."

Lowblood? That was a new one. But it made sense. If we were supposed to be the opposite of *pure*, the opposite of *high*, then of course we were *low*. Low and blighted.

"Crimes against highbloods will no longer be tolerated."

Silence.

I looked around in confusion, then back up at the balcony, waiting for something to happen. Too late, I realized it already had. I started to open my mouth in horror just as the thrallguard Regan was using made the woman's eyes go blank. A gurgling sound came from her throat. Then in one swift, unnatural movement, she reached both hands up to her own neck and *tore*.

Her scream lasted less than half a second, yet somehow it rang out and echoed through the courtyard as blood sprayed and her body slumped over the edge of the balustrade, hovering there for a moment before toppling down into the courtyard. Students below the balcony screamed and stepped back. There was a wet sound as the woman's body landed in a shallow grave of snow, reminding me of the splat the blood apple had made when it had hit Dani. I felt sick.

"Thank you all for coming. This assembly is dismissed," Regan announced brightly. "Please find your way to class. Blessed Blood to you all!"

From around the courtyard, hundreds of highblood voices echoed back "Blessed Blood."

The nausea in the pit of my stomach grew. I didn't say a word. Couldn't seem to find any. Blake hadn't repeated the highblood benediction. He stood near me, silent but stolid. I wondered if his stomach was roiling as violently as mine.

I stared at the servant woman's body lying there in the snow. Some students were walking respectfully around it. Others showed less care and stepped over. A few—highbloods, of course—laughed and jumped over the corpse like it was all some sick children's game. Meanwhile, above it all stood Viktor, watching us with an expression of triumph. How much triumph could the ancient highblood really feel—looking as ravaged as he did?

I turned to Blake. His single eye held mine. So much unspoken there. So much pain. So much wrath. But more than anything, I saw a plea. Not just for forgiveness—though, for that, too. But for hope.

CHAPTER 4

MEDRA

Kage had been in the courtyard. I'd looked away as soon as I'd spotted him in the crowd.

Seeing him pricked my conscience. I was furious with him. But if I were being honest, I felt angrier at him than I did at Blake. Both were equally culpable, but Blake had made an effort. He'd helped me convince Nyxaris. He'd been willing to die if it meant giving Florence a chance to live. What had Kage done besides turning into a fucking wolf and fighting an undead dragon?

All right, maybe he wasn't an entirely hopeless case. He wasn't as evil as, say, Regan or Viktor. But he'd *betrayed* me. The irony that I was now trapped in his house with him as my House Leader was not lost on me. I only had myself to blame for that move.

With a sigh, I heaved my book bag higher on my shoulder. The assembly and Regan's crowning as headmistress had eaten up the entire slot for Defensive Arts. My next class was Historical Strategy. The huge lecture hall felt colder than usual as Theo rejoined me and we walked in. Flames flickered in the wrought-iron lanterns that lined the walls. A cloudy winter light came from the row of narrow windows high up on the walls behind the lectern platform.

I slid into a seat midway up the tiers and dumped my textbook and parchment out on the table in front of me. Theo plopped down beside me, stretching out like we were about to see a theater production and not just attend another lecture in the school of hell. Vaughn had disappeared off to one of his House Orphos classes.

I snuck a peek at Blake's cousin. His expression was nonchalant, but I knew him well enough to know his heart was probably still pounding hard like mine was from the assembly. He wasn't immune to the sight of blightborn murder; Theo still had a heart. He possessed compassion and kindness: His uncle hadn't been able to destroy that part of him yet.

Students trickled into the hall slowly. I caught many whispering about what we'd just witnessed in the courtyard. Theo and I looked at one another, but we didn't say a word. Blake had vanished like a ghost as we'd reentered the school. He was supposed to be in this section. I wondered if he'd show up for class.

Then, just before the bell chimed, Visha marched in. Her head was bowed, her shoulders hunched under a black leather coat. She wasn't a tall girl, but still, I'd never seen her look so small. She moved stiffly, grief and anger clinging to her like a mist. When she slid onto the bench beside Theo and gave us a terse nod, I felt relieved. Something tight in my chest loosened. I wanted to say something, convey my sympathies for her loss, but the words stuck in my throat. So I just nodded back. There would be time to talk. To sort things out. To grieve.

Our teacher didn't show up until two minutes after the bell had rung. When the door banged open and Rodriguez walked in, a hush fell across the room. He looked . . . bad.

His usually clean-shaven jaw was coated in days' worth of black stubble. He was never the best-dressed faculty member, but now he looked even scruffier. His coat was wrinkled, the white button-up shirt he wore was stained dark with sweat stains.

I leaned forward, my body tensing as I noticed his right arm. It was bound in a sling across his chest. He'd caught a crossbow bolt in the shoulder, shot by Marcus Drakharrow. It must have hurt like hell. But funnily enough, I was having trouble feeling much sympathy.

Rodriguez threw his satchel on the desk with his good hand and walked to the lectern like everything was fine. "Turn to page one sixty-three in your textbooks. We'll discuss dragon warfare."

That wasn't exactly new. Dragons featured in a lot of Rodriguez's lectures. Still, my back went up. Theo raised an eyebrow at me. I gave the smallest shrug.

Rodriguez started his lecture. Instead of presenting things in an organized, chronological fashion as he would usually do—writing dates up on the board and going through events from start to finish—his lecture veered between battles, skipping from one to another and leaving out dates altogether. Some of the events we'd discussed in class before, others were new to me. Maybe Florence could have followed such a haphazard speech, but I started to get lost. Still, a theme of sorts began to prevail. Rodriguez's voice might have been a dispassionate monotone, but he'd clearly planned his speech with some focus in mind. He spoke of casualty numbers. Whole villages destroyed by dragon fire. Thousands dead. Civilians. Always *civilians*. And when he said that word, I knew exactly what he really meant: *blightborn*.

I gripped my quill.

"The Fall of Lutharion was, as you may recall, a turning point," Rodriguez droned. "Not for the highbloods—at least, not directly—but for the thousands of civilians caught in the blast zone of House Avari's dragons." Rodriguez paused his pacing and looked up at us. His eyes found mine. "The lesson here is clear to anyone who studies the historical record. Dragons destabilize order. While in the past, highbloods have valued them as a useful tool, they are a dangerous one. Capable of challenging the hierarchy. They incite chaos and bring vast loss of life. Not to mention . . ."

Not to mention it was bullshit. Such utter bullshit.

I stood up, shoving my textbook roughly into my bag, not caring about how much noise I was making. I knew what this was. It wasn't a lecture, not really. Or if it was, it was intended solely for me. This was a justification.

Rodriguez wasn't going to apologize. He was trying to rationalize what he'd done. What he'd encouraged Kage and Blake to do with him. He'd orchestrated the betrayal of Nyxaris, and he clearly regretted not succeeding.

"Miss Pendragon," he barked. "Sit down. This class is not finished."

I slung my bag over my shoulder. Ignoring him, I moved into the aisle and started down the steps to the bottom of the lecture hall. A ripple of whispers rolled through the room. Rodriguez moved towards the door, walking so quickly he reached it before I did. I paused in front of him. His eyes were bloodshot and hazy. He stank—and not just of days' old sweat. The predominant theme in the bouquet of repugnant fragrances was alcohol. The man was half-drunk. I couldn't help it. A bitter laugh escaped my lips.

"Is something funny, Miss Pendragon?"

I straightened my back. "Not really, sir."

"Then, sit back down."

I stared back at him boldly. "Are you drunk, sir?"

I heard gasps from behind me. I was being insubordinate. Rude. Maybe even cruel. But I couldn't find it in me to care. Nyxaris would be a lump of lifeless stone right now if Rodriguez had gotten his way.

He flinched, his face flushing. "Let's step into the hall for a moment, Miss Pendragon," he said through gritted teeth.

"Yes," I agreed. "Let's." I shoved past him, throwing open the door and stepping out without waiting to see if he'd follow.

"Your behavior is completely unacceptable," Rodriguez spat before he'd fully closed the door behind him.

"And you sound just like a highblood pawn, sir," I snapped. "Toeing the line, are we? You say you care about blightborn lives, and yet dragons are the best defense against highbloods. You and I both know it."

Rodriguez glared at me with something beyond fury in his eyes. "I should . . ."

"What?" I demanded. "Send me to see Headmaster Kim? Oh, that's right. He's dead. Speaking of the destabilization of order."

"You listen so well to my lectures, and yet you still haven't learned a thing, Miss Pendragon." Rodriguez's voice was cold.

"Learned what, that highbloods are evil? That blightborn are vulnerable? Oh, I think I've learned that pretty well. But unlike you, I don't resort to tricks and treachery. I don't attack my allies."

"Allies?" Rodriguez snorted.

"Yes," I retorted. "Because that's what Nyxaris is . . . Was." I stopped, confused.

Rodriguez smiled thinly, and I wanted to punch him. "That's right. *Was.* He's not your dragon anymore. Can you still hear him?"

I didn't answer.

"You're not his rider." Rodriguez's eyes softened slightly. "It must be quite a shock. Coming to terms with that."

My eyes flared. "I don't need your fucking sympathy. Don't pretend to feel compassion for my situation when you'd have gladly turned the only dragon on our side back to stone."

"On our side?" Rodriguez shook his head. "Nyxaris had never made a true position known."

"Yet here you are working in a highblood school," I pointed out. "Do you think your own position is so clear? Meanwhile, Marcus, Catherine, and Molindra are out there somewhere. Don't you understand what that means?"

"Perhaps better than you do," he responded coolly.

I wondered if that meant he knew where they were headed, what they'd do next—or just thought he did. Rodriguez had a lot of theories. Unfortunately, he'd just blown his credibility with me.

"Ah, yes, your precious knowledge of history," I said bitterly. "It's served you so well. Take a good look in the mirror. What you did allowed the greatest threat to blightborn lives to fly free. It's your fault Molindra is out there. You're a traitor to the very people you claim to want to protect." I'd never spoken to anyone so cruelly before, but the words just rolled off my tongue. "You failed. No, you didn't just fail. You made things worse." The knowledge of our true situation suddenly hit me like a ton of bricks. "If it weren't for Florence, you'd be dead right now for what you tried to do to Nyxaris, Rodriguez. Do you even realize that? *Dead*." I was coming undone. My body shook. I took a deep breath and tried to get myself back under control.

Rodriguez was silent. For a moment, I wondered if things were going to get ugly. Would he hit me? Would I hit him back? He was my teacher, yes, but he'd completely fucked things up.

The silence stretched on. For a moment I let myself wonder if he might actually be about to offer an apology, be the decent human being I'd always thought he was. But abruptly, he turned back to the classroom door.

"You're excused from today's class. But the next time you decide to throw a tantrum in one of my lectures, Miss Pendragon, think again. There will be consequences."

The door slammed behind him before I could even respond. I stood alone in the hallway for a long moment. The scent of stale alcohol lingered even after the door had closed.

Finally, I started walking. I'd head towards the library, I decided. Make another attempt. The halls were nearly empty. I passed a few students who were clearly skipping class. Unlike me, though, they were all highbloods.

I rounded the next corner and froze. "Dani!" Her name slipped from my lips.

The blightborn girl was surrounded by three young men I didn't recognize. Tall, broad-shouldered, good-looking. All highbloods. All arrogant, entitled pricks, in other words. To my surprise, Dani leaned against one of them—a muscular, hulking boy with long blond hair that fell around his shoulders. His arms were wrapped around her waist.

My mouth fell open in shock. He was drinking from her, right there in the open. Dani's head sort of lolled to one side. Her eyes were glazed.

"Dani," I said a little louder. "What the hell are you doing?"

She blinked, eyes hazy with bliss.

I thought I might vomit right then and there. I'd left her alone for less than two hours—nearly forgotten about her. Now she was enthralled. Someone had it in for this girl. I knew the lives enthralled blightborn led weren't all terrible. In fact, in some ways they were downright cushy, their room and board generally provided for as long as they served a specific highblood or highblood family. But overall, they were cattle. They were at the beck and call of whoever had enthralled them. And they balanced a strange position in Sangrathan society. They were supposed to be serving a vital role. They were treated better than sellbloods, and yet they were also subtly stigmatized. Most crucially, they weren't truly free to leave their . . . jobs.

"Get the fuck off her," I said loudly.

The highblood feeding from Dani ignored me, but one of his friends stepped forward. This one had mellow golden skin, brown eyes, and a square jaw. He was dressed in House Mortis colors, his jacket a dark crimson with white accents.

"Why?" His voice was falsely polite. "Is she your sister? I don't think I've had the honor." His eyes raked up and down my body in a lewd way I hated. "Miss . . . ?"

One of his friends punched Square Jaw in the arm. "You're such a dumbass, Silvio. Can't you tell who she is just by looking at her?"

"Dani," I said, ignoring Silvio Square Jaw and his delightful friend. "Get away from him. Come on. I'll take you back to your dorm."

The highblood feeding from her lifted his head. Blood dripped down his chin. "She's fine. See for yourself. Aren't you, sweetheart?"

"Of course, Brocklin," Dani murmured. She looked over at me dreamily. "Never better." She reached out a hand languidly. "Come join us. It feels so nice. Mm." Her eyes closed.

I'd never been less interested in a prospect.

"Excellent idea," said Silvio, still staring at me with far too much interest. "Who did you say she was again, Cade?"

The boy he'd called Cade laughed and elbowed him in the ribs. "The fucking rider, you idiot. Just look at her hair."

Silvio's handsome face flushed slightly. "Oh. Right." He stretched his hand towards me, like I was a dog he was entitled to touch. "Come here, pretty girl."

I moved before his hand reached me. Fast. So fast his eyes widened.

He whistled. "Shit. She's quick for a blightborn bitch."

My whole body hummed. Ready to move again. Ready to fight. I looked past him to Dani. Could I get to her? Would she cooperate with me? My heart sank as she let out a throaty moan and the highblood holding her latched on again.

"She's Blake's, you know," Cade observed. "Better watch out. You know how he gets."

Undeterred, Silvio looked at me with even more interest. "Marcus's little brother? I'd forgotten about that."

Cade nodded and grinned. "But I don't see Blake anywhere around. I think you should try again, Silvio. She obviously wants to play. If you catch her, maybe she'll give you a little taste."

Silvio stepped towards me, his brown eyes glowing at the thought of a challenge. "Come here, baby. I'm not going to hurt—"

He didn't finish. Because suddenly someone else was in front of me, blocking me completely from their view. I froze. For a split second, I thought it was Blake.

Broad shoulders tapering down to a narrow, lean waist. Lithe, muscular legs clad in perfectly fitted, silver-gray trousers. His dark eyes narrowed as he looked at the other highbloods.

Kage.

"Well, well," drawled Cade. "Hear you made House Leader."

Kage's lips pulled back in a snarl. "Old news. What the hell are you doing in my school?"

Silvio laughed. "Your school? Seems like it's still just as much ours as yours."

Still? Who were these assholes? I'd never seen them at Bloodwing before. They were older than even the oldest students, maybe twenty-five or twenty-six.

Then, the one feeding from Dani lifted his head again. "Relax, Avari. We're just doing what we were told. Regan called us in. Meet your new Bloodguard." Cade wore silver and gray like Kage, House Avari colors. Nice to know Regan was being so undiscriminating in her selections for her goon squad.

Silvio laughed. "That's right. Keeping the halls clean. Cracking skulls and sucking blood. This pretty little thing—" he gestured at Dani "—was out wandering the halls when she should have been in class. Naughty, naughty."

"Keeping the halls clean?" I spat. "Is that what you call harassing students?"

Silvio winked at me. "We don't have to stay in the halls. Come back to our rooms with us. I promise, you'll have fun."

"Fun like Dani's having?" I shook my head. "No, thanks. Let her go, and I'll take her back to her room."

I moved forward, but Cade jumped in front of me, his face suddenly less than pleasant. "Does this girl not know the rules, Avari? Do we need to put her in her place right here and now?"

"You'll keep your fucking hands off her if you know what's good for you, you prick." Kage's voice was so calm you'd never have known how pissed he was. But I was close enough to him that when he folded his arms over his chest, I could see his muscles trembling as if in eager anticipation of a fight.

"Come on, baby," Brocklin, the highblood feeding from Dani, said. He started to pull her away by the hand. "You're mine now, right?"

Dani nodded eagerly without even looking at Kage and me.

Brocklin glanced over at me. "There. That good enough for you?"

I shook my head slowly. "Not even fucking close."

He laughed. "Well, too bad. This is how it works. Sounds like you need some more schooling." He looked at Dani. "Let's finish this somewhere more private." He looked over at the other highbloods. "You two coming?"

"Wouldn't miss it for the world," Cade said darkly, glaring at Kage and me.

"Hope she tastes better than she looks. I'd have preferred . . . something with a little more red," Silvio said, looking at me wistfully. "You sure you don't want to come along, curls?"

"Fuck off," I said flatly.

"We'll see you around," Cade said to me, his eyes cold. "Sounds like Blake hasn't done a very good job instructing you in proper respect for the Pure of Blood. But the Bloodguard will correct that soon, don't you worry."

I refused to show him just how disturbed I was by that statement. Kage, on the other hand, let out a low growl that said he wasn't going to play around like this much longer. I wondered if we could take them, Kage and I together. Would he turn into his wolf form? Then, we might actually stand a chance. But the boys were already moving back down the hallway, Dani eagerly skipping behind.

"Are you really just going to let them take her away?" I demanded of Kage, my voice low.

He looked at me, his face suddenly tired. "You saw how it was. She's enthralled."

"So un-fucking-enthrall her," I suggested.

He shook his head. "Doesn't work like that." He gave me a curious look. "Sometimes I forget how little you really know about our world."

I leaned towards him. "I know a little. I know vampires aren't all what they seem. Isn't that right, Wolf Boy?"

He raised his eyebrows. "Wolf Boy?"

I glared. "I'll come up with something better, but the description is fairly accurate."

He shrugged. "You all right? Did they touch you?"

"I can take care of myself. I had things under control."

He stared down at me. "Sure you did."

My face heated. "They tried to touch me, and they failed. I'm fast, you know. I'm not completely helpless." I suddenly thought back to that moment in the Dragon Court. To that feeling of being trapped. Trapped because Kage's hands were pinning me, confining me.

"You have a lot of nerve," I said, my voice low. "Trying to play the hero after what you did to me. But maybe that's how you really see yourself. Kage Tanaka, champion of the weak, protector of the blightborn. Is that it? Do you really think you're any better than they are? That you're somehow superior?"

His black eyes searched mine, and I looked right back into the eyes of the man who'd betrayed me mere days before. I'd started to trust Kage. Hell, I'd started to like him a little. He was my House Leader; I'd purposely asked to be in Avari. I thought Kage could offer me more choices than I'd find in Drakharrow. What a fool I'd been.

He'd felt entitled to lay hands upon me. To hold me back as I struggled to protect Nyxaris.

I closed my eyes. Remembering that terrible moment. If it weren't for him, Florence might have . . .

"No."

My eyes popped back open. "No?"

"I'm not better than them, all right? I know that. The other night . . . I was wrong, Medra. I acted badly. I shouldn't have gone along with Rodriguez's plan. I should have been up-front with you. I hurt you. I betrayed your trust. I'm sorry."

I studied him, but it was useless. Kage was an enigma. Inscrutable as always. Hell, maybe he'd even meant what he said. Who could say for certain?

"Fine. I'm impressed that you actually apologized. It's more than Rodriguez bothered to do. But I'm not about to forgive and forget so easily."

He nodded. "I understand. Unfortunately, I have a favor I need to ask of you."

"Let me guess. You want me to keep my mouth shut about you turning into a wolf."

"Good guess."

"I'm a clever girl. Not clever enough to stay out of House Avari, though. And not stupid enough to just say yes to your request."

Kage smiled slightly. "I didn't expect it to be easy. So, what do you want?"

"How about some answers, to start?" I challenged him. "*Blood moon rises.* That's your house motto, right? You even gave me a half-moon pendant once." The necklace was back in my room, tucked in a little wooden box in my drawer. I hadn't worn it since that night we'd attended the Frostfire ball together. "Clearly the words are significant. So what do they mean?"

There was a trace of a mysterious little half smile on his face. Seeing it pissed me off.

"Can all of you do it? Can all of the Avari highbloods shift?" I demanded, starting to lose patience.

Kage glanced around. "Keep your voice down. But the answer to that is *no*."

"Does the moon trigger it? How is it connected?" I pushed.

He frowned. "I'm sorry, Medra. I'm not about to spill my house's most ancient secrets right here in the hallway."

"Not even after all you've done? You don't think you owe me a few little secrets to make up for what you've done to *me*?"

"I owe you your life," Kage replied. "And believe it or not, I mean for you to keep it. I want to protect you. That's why . . . that's part of why Rodriguez found me fairly easy to convince. Blake, too, I think. When it comes to you, we—"

"Oh, for fuck's sake," I exploded. "Don't you dare say you only want what's best for me."

He shrugged. "Trite, maybe, but true."

"You're not my godsdamned family. You're not my archon. You're more like my captor. You're a *highblood*." I said the word with such vigor, such hate, that my teeth nearly rattled.

"We're a despicable lot in many ways, aren't we?" Kage agreed. "But I stood up for you just now. It wasn't the first time. It won't be the last. You don't owe me forgiveness. You don't owe me kindness. But I'm your House Leader, so when I demand your Blood Vow, you will give me that."

I glared. I wasn't exactly clear on what a Blood Vow with my house leader meant, but I knew I wouldn't like it. "Oh, I will, will I?"

"You will," he said quietly. "Or I'll be forced to use some other means to get it from you. I don't want to have to do that."

"You're disgusting. Are you seriously threatening me with thrallweave right now, after you just apologized?" Let him try. I wasn't the vulnerable little rose I used to be. He wouldn't find it easy to get past my guards.

"I am sorry for what happened. But I used my powers to try to protect you, to protect all of you that night. Did you ever stop and think of that? I revealed something I was not supposed to reveal. Things could have been much worse, Medra. I put my life on the line to try to stop the damage. Now I'm asking you for your help." He held up one hand and pointed to his palm. "It's quick. Almost painless."

I gave a mirthless laugh. "Isn't that what you all say?"

"We mix blood. You're sworn to silence. If you break the vow in an attempt to harm me—"

"Oh, please," I interrupted. "Let me guess. I die?"

He smirked in a way that was practically Blake-ish. "Basically."

I rolled my eyes. "Here's how this is going to go. You've apologized. You did throw yourself into the fray that night, all of which is more than Rodriguez did."

"But Rodriguez—" he started to say.

I held up my hand. "No. Nope. Don't even try to defend him, Kage. We're not going down that road. He was the one behind it all. None of it would have happened if it weren't for Rodriguez."

A nagging part of me said that in that case, Marcus and Catherine might have found the Dragon Court empty—which would have made their plan much easier to carry out. But so what? It wasn't as if we'd actually stopped them just by being there. No, we'd lost more than we'd gained that night.

"I'll make the vow," I said.

Was it my imagination, or did the cool, calm, and collected Avari look slightly relieved? I wondered what his grandmother would say if she knew he'd used his powers in front of all of us. "But . . ."

Kage stepped towards me. He bared his teeth. "But?"

I refused to flinch. But the gesture did remind me of just what kind of a creature I was dealing with. I made myself smile as if I didn't care. "*But* you'll make one to me, too, House Leader. You owe me. Not just my life. The way I see it, I have a favor to call in. And when I call, you'd best come running."

He gave a tight nod. "Fine."

A knife appeared in Kage's hand. He slid it across his palm, and I watched the blood well up. Fucking entitled highbloods: Kage would probably heal within minutes. As a half-fae, I'd heal quickly too—but my palm would be stinging all night as I tried to hold a quill.

I stretched my hand out before he could reach for it and let him lower the knife. Then our palms met. I could feel the blood mingling, Avari blood mixed with Pendragon.

"Is this supposed to be magical or something?" I asked, looking skeptically down at our hands.

Kage pulled away. "Of course. It's a Blood Vow. It has a weight of power behind it."

I shrugged. "If you say so."

"It's binding, I assure you," he said shortly. "Just because you don't feel it, doesn't mean it's not there."

"*It?*"

He grinned wolfishly. "We're connected, Medra."

"You're *protected*, you mean," I snapped. "Just don't forget the vow works both ways. You owe me. No matter what I ask of you, you have to give it." Before Kage could reply, I slipped down the hall—using some of that rider speed I so rarely displayed openly. I let out a breath. *Had* I been bluffing? Honestly, even I wasn't sure I knew the answer to that. But having Kage owe me a favor couldn't be a bad thing, could it?

Unless it makes him want to eliminate you altogether, you stupid girl. I could almost hear my mother's voice in my head.

I sighed. Regan. Rodriguez. Kage. The Bloodguard assholes in the hallway. This had already been an exhausting day. And it wasn't over yet.

By the time I got to my destination, classes were over. The last person I expected to see waiting outside Jia Shen's suite of rooms was Rodriguez.

"Not you again," I growled, narrowing my eyes.

Rodriguez had cleaned himself up a bit since earlier in the day. He'd shaved and no longer smelled like a cheap bottle of liquor. He was even wearing a clean shirt. For a moment we just stood glaring at each other.

"What the hell are you doing here?" I finally said.

"In case you've forgotten, Miss Pendragon," he replied coldly, "I'm a faculty member at this school. I can come and go where I please. And if I choose to visit one of my students because she's missed a class, just how is that any of your business?"

"Haven't you done enough?" I said bitterly.

"I saved your friend's life. Some might say that was a reason for gratitude."

"Tell me, has she thanked you yet?"

"Librarian Shen has been extremely grateful, in fact, yes."

"Not her, you idiot. Florence. Has Florence thanked you?"

He pressed his lips together and didn't answer.

"I didn't think so." But I didn't feel victorious.

Rodriguez moved to step past me, then paused at my shoulder.

"I suppose I might ask you the same thing, Miss Pendragon," he said softly.

I glared at the shape of his back as he moved away. *Fucking Rodriguez.* Taking a deep breath, I turned to the door. For a moment, I stared at it. But I wasn't going to get any answers that way. I knocked.

Jia Shen answered the door with a book in her hand, of course. "Oh, Medra! How lovely to see you." The librarian pushed her spectacles up the bridge of her nose and gave me a warm smile that didn't quite reach her eyes. "I hope you had a good first day back."

I forced a smile. "It was . . . interesting." Jia had to know that Regan was our new headmistress. I wondered what the librarians all thought about that. "I was wondering if Florence was here."

Jia's face fell. She bit her lip. Once again I was struck by how much she looked like a slightly older version of Florence. They might have been mistaken for sisters, not mother and daughter. Jia was just a tad shorter than Florence, a little thinner. But they both had the same long black hair, the same intelligent dark eyes, wore the same dark-rimmed glasses, favored the same bookish yet softly feminine clothes—like the dove-gray dress Jia now had on, with small pearl buttons down the front. I glanced at Jia's sleeves. Sure enough, one was smudged with ink. She'd obviously spent her day in the library, working hard. Harder than her highblood colleagues probably did.

Jia played with a strand of hair that had come out of the knot she'd pulled her long hair into. "I'm afraid not, Medra. I haven't seen her all day."

"She wasn't in any of her classes," I said quietly.

"Oh?" But Jia wasn't all that great at lying. Her face told me she already knew.

"Well," I said, already starting to turn away, my heart sick with disappointment. "If you do see her, tell her I miss her. Our room . . . it's not the same without her there."

There was a scuffling, snuffling noise at my feet, and I looked down to see Neville trotting past. He went straight between Jia's feet and into the apartment behind her.

"Well," I said hollowly, "good night, Jia."

"Good night, Medra dear," Jia murmured.

I'd taken a few steps down the hall when I heard the door of Jia's suite close behind me. "Medra," a voice hissed. "Wait."

I turned around. Jia stood there, one hand on the handle, her face anxious.

My lips twisted in a smile. "At least she's letting Neville in to see her. I suppose I should be glad of that."

"Neville puts her at ease when even I can't," Jia agreed, not bothering to deny that Florence was inside the apartment behind her. She studied me, compassion in her eyes. "Medra, you brought her back to me. You saved her life. I'll never forget that—never. She might have been lost forever."

A lump formed in my throat. I knew there was no point in reminding Jia that I'd actually lured Florence into danger. Danger she'd never have been in if she and I hadn't become friends. But Jia had made up her mind about me, and there was no changing it. Part of me didn't even want to. I was grateful to have her in my life. Grateful for her calm, kind heart, for her loyalty—even if I didn't deserve it.

"She's not lost," I said carefully. "But I feel like I've lost her."

Jia nodded understanding. "I know. Give her time. She's going through something . . . Something even I don't understand."

I wondered just how much Florence had told her mother about how we'd saved her life, what we'd done that night. I'd only given Jia the briefest of explanations. No wonder she felt gratitude towards Professor Rodriguez, too. She didn't know the full story.

Jia took a small step closer, her voice still low. "She's afraid of what's happening to her, Medra. She wants to . . . deny it. Have everything just stay the same."

"I'm not sure that'll work." I thought of Nyxaris, of trying to deny him—and he and I hadn't even been bonded to one another. I had no idea what the depth of his connection to Florence was like, but surely it was even stronger.

Jia shook her head. "I don't think so either. But she needs time to process all of this."

"I understand. Well, good night."

Jia stepped towards me, slipping her slender arms around me and pulling me into a gentle embrace. "I'll tell her you were here. I'll tell her I couldn't fool you. You're still her dearest friend."

I tried to smile. "Thank you. I appreciate that." But as I walked away, I knew the truth. I wasn't Florence's dearest friend. Not anymore. She blamed me for what happened to her—how could she not? I'd nearly stolen her life. And then, to give it back to her I'd had to sell her, body and soul, to a creature I knew she was fascinated by, yes, but also utterly terrified of.

A dragon.

CHAPTER 5

REGAN

I stumbled out into the freezing air, gasping and choking for breath. My high heels slipped on the icy flagstones. I quickly threw out my hands before I could topple over.

Steadying myself, I clutched at my throat, unbuttoning the high-collared dress. All day I'd felt as if I could barely breathe.

I looked around. The area where I stood was deserted, thank the Bloodmaiden. I'd come out of a side door, one few even knew existed. Above me loomed Bloodwing, the castle's towers rising into the night like sharp-edged teeth. I glanced upwards at the high-paned windows glowing faintly with candlelight, blurred slightly by the falling snow. The wind howled past my ears, and I shivered. I'd left my cloak behind in my new office. But I didn't mind the cold. I took another deep breath of fresh air. Before me, across an expanse of flat white snow was the cliff's edge—and beyond that, the endless night of a cold, merciless, black sea. I could hear the waves churning from here, crashing onto the rocks below. Hungry and restless. I stood on a small terrace, bordered by a low stone wall. Slowly, I crossed the snow-covered flagstones, my footsteps muffled, my breath sharp in my chest as I drew in cold breath after cold breath.

When I reached the wall, I lifted a hand, pulling pins from my hair and letting it fall. The wind caught it instantly, whipping it around my face and shoulders, lashing the strands across my cheeks. I lifted my head to the wind, letting it have me. My lungs already ached from the cold, but I still drank in more of it, greedy for something so fresh and so pure, so untainted by Viktor. Free of his scent, his voice, his hands.

I shuddered. The day had been all I'd expected. To think I'd believed myself prepared for it! What a fool I was to think power alone could save me from what Viktor really was.

I forced a laugh; the sound was brittle and cracked. I coughed, the cold wind sliding down my throat, pushing at my back. The wind wanted me. The sea wanted me. I could feel them pushing me, pulling me, drawing me into the darkness.

My first day as queen of the castle. My first day as headmistress of Bloodwing. It should have been such a triumph. So why did I feel as fragile as the flowers covered with snow? Twisted and frozen. Like a corpse.

A corpse.

I closed my eyes.

Viktor had commanded me, and so I'd tried. But I hadn't been able to do it. I had the power. But when I went to summon the thrallweave, nothing would come. The blightborn woman had stood there, blinking, terrified. Waiting. It should have been swift. Practically painless. Nearly merciful. I'd said the words. I'd condemned her. I was her judge. I was supposed to be her executioner, too. But I'd been useless. Paralyzed.

Before anyone could even notice what was happening, Viktor had done my job for me.

I unwrapped my arms from myself, then slowly lifted up the edge of my shirt. I hissed. The bruises there were fresh and ached dully. The marks were red and purple now. Soon they'd darken to green in some places, lighten to yellow in others. There were more on my upper arms, all over the inside of my thighs. More would be bestowed tonight, no doubt.

Pretty little blossoms, Viktor would croon. He'd lay beside me, a monstrosity of scarred, naked flesh, and stroke his handiwork. *Look how beautifully you bloom for me, pretty girl.*

Pretty girl. It was what my father had always called me. I was his pretty girl, his darling.

This was the cost of being pretty. Men wanted you, and it was exciting to be wanted. Flattering.

But when you were a little girl, no one told you that what the men wanted was to devour you whole. To break you apart with their hands. To rip you up into the pieces they found palatable while they threw away everything else.

Shaking, I leaned forward, placing both hands along the rough stone wall. The cold wind scorched my skin. But in a few moments, I'd be numb, unable to feel anything at all.

How had this happened to me? I was supposed to be the golden girl of Drakharrow. Blake's consort. The most popular girl at Bloodwing—and the most powerful. I hadn't needed Viktor to elevate me: I'd already been riding high. Then it had all come crashing down. In the course of one year, my life had somehow become a waking nightmare. I wouldn't say I hadn't gotten what I'd deserved in some ways, or that I had no regrets whatsoever . . . because that would have been a lie.

But that didn't mean I didn't feel sorry for myself now, even though I knew no one was coming to rescue me—and certainly no one else was coming to this little pity party. Not even my own family.

I closed my eyes, letting the snow soak my face and settle on my lashes. Just a few moments, I prayed silently. Please. Just a few.

Better to be out here in the cold than in there with Viktor's weight above me, his hands guiding me, punishing me. Petting me like a dog one moment, beating me brutally the next.

Could the Bloodmaiden hear me? Was she a merciful goddess? Considering how we asked the blightborn to serve us, I doubted it. Highblood ways were cruel and self-serving. Kindness was for the weak.

So did the Bloodmaiden want me to keep carrying on exactly the way I was? Did she just want me to be strong?

I brooded, staring out to sea. I knew what my father would say: that the answer was staring me in the face. It had happened because I'd shown weakness. Because I'd been too soft. Because of *her* I'd lost my place. My home. Blake.

Father had wanted me to kill my fellow consort in the Games. So I'd tried. But by the last trial, something happened. Something... changed. I didn't have the heart. Or was the truth even more humiliating? Medra Pendragon had saved my life that day. Then she'd ended my triad and taken my archon. I'd been discarded like an old gown thrown on the waste heap.

But even then, I hadn't killed her. I hadn't gone straight for her throat. I'd tried to move on, tried to tell myself something better would come along

A great choking laugh filled my throat again, tinged with rage and sorrow. Something better. Gods, just look at me.

Stop. Enough.

I squeezed my eyes shut more tightly. Just one moment of stillness, of quiet, of peace. One moment where no one was watching me. One moment where no one was telling me what to do, who to be. Not even myself. It worked. For a minute at least. I felt slightly calmer. More at peace. When I opened my eyes, I saw a flash of white in the distance. Standing at the far edge of the clearing, near the cliff's edge, was a wolf.

The creature was massive, larger than a horse. Silver fur gleamed in the moonlight, pale and ghostly against the dark, damp with melted snow. The wolf stood, looking out at the sea. Its breath came in slow puffs, so steady and so calm. It was beautiful. So beautiful that I didn't even think about what a beast like that might do to me. The wolf was a part of the landscape. As perfect as the snow itself, as natural as the wind. As I watched it, some of the horror of the day fell away, like snow melting off a rooftop. I expected the wolf to slip away at any moment, to vanish back into the night like some dream I'd conjured up.

I closed my eyes again, half expecting the wolf to be gone by the time I opened them. But instead, when my eyes reopened, the wolf had begun to *change*.

Fur receded. Bones bent and twisted. There should have been gruesome sounds to accompany the horrific sight—sounds of bones snapping, flesh tearing. Because this wasn't natural. Wasn't right. It went against everything I knew.

Instead, the animal form simply . . . unraveled. Became something new. The sleek form of a man. He stood with his back to me, but even from that vantage point, a hot ripple went down my spine. Broad shoulders. Strong arms. A narrow waist. Moonlight shone upon the contours and curves of the man's body, illuminating it like warm golden marble.

I watched, spellbound, as he moved, silent and sure, towards a snow-covered bush and drew out a small bundle of clothing. He dressed with quick efficiency. Dark trousers, a high-collared shirt. A long cloak that fluttered in the whipping winter wind. All black. I stared, fascinated, unable to look away, my heart pounding.

Finally, he turned. For the first time, I glimpsed his face.

I gasped. Hands flew to my mouth, but it was too late. He'd heard me.

Dark eyes locked onto mine, and in an instant, the expression of peace and calm was gone, replaced by something . . . not angry but *animal*. He moved. Launching towards me with a speed beyond any highblood.

I was all alone. Cold, numb. But the door was behind me, just a few steps away. I had less ground to cover, so I might have made it. But I didn't run. I didn't scream. I stood exactly where I was, closed my eyes, and waited.

"You're supposed to run."

I opened my eyes. Dark eyes stared down at me with an expression I couldn't pinpoint. Half-thoughtful, half-bored. I knew who he was: Kage Tanaka. Avari House Leader. Blake's biggest rival. Not that that last one meant anything to me anymore. Kage was also the eldest son of the second-most powerful house in Sangratha.

I knew all of this, had always thought I knew *him*. But as I stared into those dark eyes, I realized I knew nothing. I'd never actually *seen* Kage Tanaka before in my life.

"It's kind of a tradition. People run."

I licked my lips. "Sorry for spoiling the game, but I'm not most people."

"No, I guess not." He tilted his head in a way that was still rather wolflike. "You were watching me."

"I was watching the wolf."

"You weren't supposed to see what you saw." There was anger there, below the surface, a great deal of it. But Kage's anger was nothing like Viktor's. It was tightly controlled, and it wasn't directed at me. If anything, I thought he was angry at himself.

"You weren't supposed to exist," I pointed out. "And you picked a stupid place for your little run." I glanced behind me, but for the first time noticed no windows were on the side of this side of the tower. He must have been used to coming here. He'd taken a risk, but this was the first time he'd paid the price.

"Well." Kage gave a dry shrug. "Shit happens, I guess."

He was playing it cool. But I knew the truth. "You should kill me," I said bluntly. "That would be the smartest move. You have no choice."

He studied me for a long moment—too long.

"You're right, I suppose," he murmured. "It would be the simplest solution."

"The cleanest," I agreed. "We've had students go missing before. I won't be the first or the last." Of course, those had been blight-born. Also, I wasn't a student anymore. I was a highblood girl, not to mention Viktor's consort. But I had no doubt Kage could dispose of my body in a way that led suspicion away from him. Throw me in the sea, make it look like an accident.

I still could have run. Could have planned how to fight.

Kage shook his head slowly. "I don't think so." I could feel my face fall. It would have been a swift ending. Probably far kinder than the one we'd given that blightborn woman that morning. I should have run then, as fast as my feet would carry me, straight back to the castle door. Back to Viktor to tell him the Avari's little secret—but I didn't. I kept standing there, out in the snow with the fucking Avari House Leader, of all people. Pendragon's House Leader.

If Viktor knew . . .

Maybe that was why I stayed. Wedged my feet firmly into the snow and didn't bother turning and trying to make a run for it. A tiny little rebellion.

Kage could have changed his mind at any moment, but he just watched me. The way I'd watched the wolf. He looked different. I couldn't get past it. Not just because of what I'd seen him do—though, Bloodmaiden, that should have been enough. He radiated a calm confidence. He stood like a man who knew who he was and had no doubts.

This, *this* was the sort of man who should have been my consort. The sort of man who was everything Viktor wasn't. The kind of man who didn't need to use cruelty to get what he wanted, because he was enough without it. Not like most of the highbloods I knew—myself included.

The wind tore past, sending snow flying around us, but I barely felt it anymore. Bloodmaiden, what was happening to me? I was the headmistress. I was Viktor Drakharrow's consort. I had been claimed by the most powerful highblood in the land. Yet here I stood, trembling in the cold. Making small talk with the enemy. I looked out at the sea. I was the fool standing on the cliff's edge. And Kage clearly wasn't going to do me the favor of pushing me off.

"Why are you really out here, Regan?" he asked abruptly. No titles. No formalities. No bullshit.

Maybe I should have chided him, demanded the proper respect. Instead, I took a deep breath, my eyes still on the dark sea. "I needed some air." I glanced at him. "So are you going to do it?"

"Kill you?" He shook his head. "It's not my style. Sorry to disappoint you."

I wanted to turn away. When he looked at me, it was as if he saw everything. The thoughts I most wanted to hide. My desperation. He was the one who should have been feeling desperate, not me. Yet here I was, feeling trapped and naked.

"Besides, I know the difference," he murmured, never taking his eyes from mine.

"Difference?"

"Between a monster and the one wearing its chains."

I stared at him. I should have been offended. I should have been cold with rage. I should have demanded he follow me to the Black Keep right then and there, brought him straight before Viktor, and then . . .

I looked away. I was a fool, yes. I knew I wasn't going to do any of those things.

Kage stood there looking at me, and I knew what he must see. To him, I was Viktor's pet, a wretched highblood girl playing a nasty game of power. Or maybe he saw a pawn traded between men. Just another jewel in the dark crown of Sangratha. A woman as shallow and hollow as a gemstone, too.

"Why didn't you scream?"

I let out a breath and watched it mist into a cloud. "I'm tired of screaming."

Kage tilted his head. "Rough day?"

"Not at all," I said, trying to strike a bored tone. "Why would you say that?"

He shrugged. "You're standing alone on a cliff in the snow, talking to a man who was a wolf not just five minutes ago. You didn't run, even though you thought I was going to kill you." He tilted his head. "And that blightborn woman on the balcony this morning. You might have fooled the rest of them, but . . ."

I stared at him. "That obvious?" I finally choked.

"Yeah, a little obvious."

I stood there, feeling like an idiot. "Guess I'm not the only one too weak to kill," I said coldly.

"I kill when there's a need, not simply to impress a crowd. In House Avari, cruelty isn't considered a sign of strength." Without warning, Kage moved towards me, his hand flicking back the collar of my dress. The silk slid aside at his touch, and I let out a gasp.

"Easy." His voice was cool and authoritative. "I'm not going to hurt you."

I froze, not bothering to glance down, already knowing what he'd seen: the dark bruises blooming over my breasts like cruel roses.

"Viktor do that to you?" His face was very still.

I didn't answer. I knew he didn't really expect me to. I gave myself a mental shake. I couldn't stay out here all night, no matter how much I might want to. "What happens now?"

"You're not going to tell anyone what you've seen here tonight. We'll take it from there." He wasn't using thrallweave, and he wasn't asking a question. He was stating a truth we both knew.

I felt unsettled. There he was, cool and steady, while I held his greatest secret in the palm of my hand. I could destroy Kage and possibly his entire house with what I knew.

"No," I agreed slowly. "I'm not."

He nodded. "You'll make the vow?"

Silently, I held out my hand. He drew out a silver dagger and sliced his palm. Then gently, ever so gently, he lifted mine and did the same.

As the blood flowed, he placed his palm against mine and pressed lightly, the briefest of touches. I felt a sudden jolt, like fire, racing straight from his veins to mine.

I snatched my hand back. "What was that?"

Kage gave me a strange look but didn't respond. I'd never made a Vow before; for all I knew this was normal. I looked at my palm, watching the blood well. Highbloods healed fast. This was nothing compared to what I could endure. The mark would be gone by the time I returned to the Keep. Viktor would never see it. He never had to know.

"Now what?" The blaze in my palm was already fading.

The Avari was turning to go. Now he stopped, eyebrows rising. "Isn't that up to you?" He paused. "But do me a favor."

"What's that?"

"Stop looking out to sea like it holds the answers you need. It doesn't."

I stared after Kage as he moved towards the tower door. Like a fool, I almost called after him. Then he was gone.

I stood in the snow, in the dark, a while longer, trying to figure out why the fuck I'd just made an unbreakable Blood Vow with a wolf.

CHAPTER 6

BLAKE

The latch of my door clicked behind me. I walked down the hall, yawning and trying to roll the tension out of my shoulders, then descended the stairs leading down to the common room.

The place was almost empty. Most students had already left to grab breakfast in the refectory. The fire had been stoked recently. I sniffed appreciatively: cedar logs. They were expensive, so they were only used in the highblood towers. *Only the best for the best*, my uncle liked to say when I was growing up. As if blightborn couldn't appreciate a scent just as easily.

Some plates of fresh rolls and carafes of kava, tea, and juice had been placed on a table for students who were too tired, busy, or hungover to make it to the refectory in time for a real meal.

I glanced around. The place was my second home. More of a home than my real home at this point. Weapons from past centuries were mounted on the walls between Drakharrow banners. The crest and motto of our precious bloodline were everywhere: on cushions, tapestries, even carved into the arms of the chairs we sat in. As if any of us needed that many reminders of who we were. *Sanguine Vincti*. Bound by blood.

I shook my head. Kind of ironic when my so-called bonded was over in House Avari right now. I doubted she considered herself bound to me. That headstrong girl would do what she liked—just as she always did. Nonetheless, thinking of Pendragon sent a warm feeling soaring through my chest. Headstrong or not, she was mine. Though, I'd finally learned to stop saying it to her face quite so often.

A few blightborn students sat in corners, sipping tea and reading books, studying up before classes began. The highbloods were all probably either in the refectory or drinking from their favorite thralls in their rooms. I'd recently decided that open feeding in the common room was gauche: Funny how quickly trends changed. My house had quickly gotten the message. This was the new way of things. Shape up or ship out.

Theo was sprawled on a red velvet couch by the fire, a book in his lap and a cup of steaming kava in one hand. He wore one of his favorite sweaters, black with gold thread at the cuffs, absurdly oversized and practically in tatters. It was a family heirloom of sorts. It had belonged to my father when he'd gone to school here.

I walked over and fell into an armchair across from my cousin.

Theo looked up. "You're lucky. You just missed Regan."

I raised a brow. "Really?"

He nodded. "Our new headmistress just came trotting through with her new squad of Bloodguards in tow," he said making air quotes with his free hand.

I choked. "*Bloodguards*? Seriously? She couldn't think of a better name?"

Theo looked thoughtful. "Good point. We should suggest she run a naming contest. Everyone can vote. There could even be a prize."

"Right. I'm sure the blightborn students will love selecting a name for their new tormentors." I frowned. "Who the hell are they, anyhow? Her guards, I mean?"

Theo studied me. He was careful not to let his gaze linger too long on my wasted eye. I appreciated what he was trying to do, but he needn't have bothered trying to be tactful. Most students gawked openly and for far longer than was polite. I'd snarl at them, sometimes add a little display of fangs, and that usually was enough to send them screaming and scurrying. Was I a bastard for doing it to First Years? Sure. But honestly, it never got old. And serve them right for being so rude in the first place, right?

"You don't know? They're alumni. She called in most of Marcus's old pals."

I sat up straighter. "For fuck's sake."

"Quite a few from House Mortis, too."

I shook my head. "I assume they left a trail of testosterone and shitty cologne behind them." I sniffed, but fortunately all I could smell was the cedar smoke.

Theo wrinkled his nose. "Oh, they smelled worse than that. Think more of a training bag boiled in highblood sweat."

I chuckled.

"Your ex-consort is a real piece of work. Walking around like she owns this place."

"Well, she basically does," I pointed out.

"Bloodwing is bigger than just one person. It's better than that, too," Theo protested.

"Really? You think so?" I was dubious. But I supposed I should be glad my cousin still had some idealism left.

"We're going to have to be careful, Blake," Theo said softly. "Those assholes think nepotism, fangs, and muscles equal real authority."

"If Regan purposely brought in some of Marcus's dumbass friends, things could get ugly," I agreed. "They were never too bright to begin with." With the amount of Crimson Ambrosia they drank and other shit they did, it was no wonder. I thought of something: Maybe that was how Regan had gotten them to come. Had she bribed them? "They'll be drunk with power in a few days. Did Regan say anything to you about what she has planned?"

Theo shook his head. "No. And I'm sure it's not her plan—it's Viktor's. Besides, it's not me I'm worried about. It's Vaughn."

Theo's boyfriend was over in House Orphos. "I'm sure Lysander will keep a careful watch on his house," I said.

"Have you talked to him about Lunaya?"

"Only briefly."

"What exactly did you tell him?" Theo asked curiously. "You didn't tell him everything, did you?" He lowered his voice. "You know, about the . . . d-word?"

I laughed. "Is that what we're calling them now? I mean, a fucking dragon is missing from the Dragon Court. Lysander would have figured it out eventually."

Theo looked dubious. "Would he? You didn't tell Viktor or Regan exactly what happened, right?"

"Fuck no," I practically shouted. I cleared my throat. "Lysander is different. He has a good head on his shoulders."

Theo raised his eyebrows.

"What?" I demanded.

Theo snickered. "Just not something I expected to hear you say after the role he played in the Tribunal at the start of last term."

I flushed. Lysander had basically suggested we all let Pendragon walk free. "He's still a little too idealistic for my tastes."

"*Let her lead her life as she sees fit,*" Theo mused. "I believe those were his exact words."

"Were they?" I frowned. "I didn't take notes."

"I have a good memory," Theo said with a grin. "And it isn't as far-fetched an idea as you seemed to think at the time. Besides, isn't that exactly what's happening now, anyways?"

I thought for a moment. Pendragon in House Avari. Pendragon punching me in the face the day before without any repercussions. "There have certainly been some changes," I said carefully.

Theo hooted. "I'd say so—in *you!*"

I rubbed my eyes. Theo didn't know the half of it. "Fine. Laugh it up."

Theo watched me. "You sleeping all right?"

"Define *all right.*" My dreams were all red ones. Full of blood and scales. So no, I wasn't sleeping well.

"Nightmares?" He quickly looked away, setting his cup down on the table. "I've had my share of those."

I examined him. My cousin looked a lot like me in some ways. Same sharply cut cheekbones, same gray eyes, same old blood in our veins. But there were differences. His jaw was softer, his mouth a little less. . . . well, cruel, I guess. His hair was duskier than mine, more like dark honey. He'd grown it out and taken to wearing it in a bun. He had it piled in a messy knot on his head now.

If Viktor could see Theo right now, he'd probably give his nephew a jaw-cracking slap. Thank the Bloodmaiden the old bastard wasn't around. My jaw tightened. *Only his proxy, Regan.*

My gaze dropped to Theo's hand. His fingers gripped the side of the couch tightly.

There was tension in him, hovering in the air between us, unspoken and heavy. And we hadn't even broached the word *wolf* yet.

"Aenia." We both spoke at the same time.

I swallowed. My little sister. His cousin. His kill.

"She always liked this room," Theo said hurriedly. "Remember when you brought her here the first time? She said she'd go to this school one day and be the best student they'd ever seen."

"Then she'd tried to pull the swords off the wall. Said they were hers because her name was Drakharrow and she wanted to take one home," I said dryly. "I remember. The little tyrant princess."

"She was a brat," Theo said softly. "But she was our brat."

I didn't respond.

"She died quickly." The words came out of Theo's mouth in a rush. "I don't think she was in pain. It happened fast. So fast."

I sat up, leaned forward, my hands wrapping around my knees, knuckles white.

"I don't think she even knew it was me who . . . who did it. I think it happened so quickly she didn't even see. I like to think she didn't, anyways." Theo's face was a picture of misery.

My spine stiffened.

"Just let me get it out, Blake. Just let me say the words," Theo begged, rushing on. "Then if you want to hit me or kill me . . .

whatever. It's your right, I know it's your right." His face became stoic. "At least I've already said good-bye."

I choked. "You've what?"

"I've already said my good-byes. Not to everyone, I mean. Just to Vaughn." There were tears in his eyes. "I left him a note. He won't come after you."

I almost choked again. Nearly said I wasn't afraid of Vaughn Sabino. But that wasn't the fucking point, was it? The point was that my little cousin was *afraid* of *me*.

The dragon inside me tensed, sensing opportunity. The chance to kill. I slammed it down hard. "I'm not going to kill you, Theo."

Theo's whole body seemed to sag. "You're . . . you're not?"

"How could you even think that?" I said, suddenly angry. "You really think I'd do something like that? That I'm what—the next Viktor?"

"I don't know," he said slowly. "No, not like Viktor, of course not. Though, he'd certainly like you to be."

"I'm not Viktor," I snarled. "I'm nothing like him. I'd never do that to you. I've stood up for you. I've tried to help you. We're fucking family, Theo."

"I know, I know, all right?" Theo's voice was pleading. "But, Blake, that's the point. Aenia . . . She was family, too. I killed my own *family*."

I stared at him trying to really understand. Trying to absorb the cloud of guilt I now saw hanging over him. He'd done his best to hide it from all of us these past few days as we'd all struggled to process that night, each of us in our own way. Theo had waited patiently, grieving alone. He hadn't even told Vaughn he thought his cousin was going to eventually come for him. No, he'd written Vaughn a letter. Because the words were too heavy, too terrifying to even say aloud.

"You seriously wrote your boyfriend a letter?" I shook my head. "So right now, Vaughn is what—reading it and thinking I'm murdering you here in this tower?"

Theo looked sheepish. "Maybe."

I laughed out loud. Some heads turned towards us, then just as quickly whipped away. "For fuck's sake, Theo." I stood up. Theo shrank back. I held up my hands. "May I?" I sat down on the couch next to my cousin. Then, shocking even myself, I slipped one hand around the back of his neck—not roughly but firmly—and pulled him towards me, tilting my forehead so it rested against his. "Theo, you don't get it. You just don't fucking get it, do you?" I whispered.

"Get what?" he whispered back, his voice trembling a little.

"You spared me. You fucking spared me."

"Spared you? What do you mean?"

I let go of him and sat back, breathing hard. There was water in my eyes, but I blinked it the fuck away. This wasn't the time, not when Regan and her posse could march back in at any moment.

"You did what I'd have had to do. What I knew I'd have to do."

Theo's face was still uncertain.

"There was no hope for Aenia. Don't you think I knew that?" I shook my head. "She was turning feral. I fucked up the moment I saved her life. I ruined things, like I always do." I swiped at my eyes with the back of my hand. *Fuck no. Not in the common room.*

Theo was staring at me in wonder. "Blake, is that what you think? You think you ruined Aenia?"

"Of course I did. You know exactly what I did. You've always known." I'd turned her, made her into one of us. Or some would say something worse—a so-called foulblood.

Theo glanced around. "I know you . . . *made* her." His voice was very low. "But you had to. You had to save her life." He shook his head. "Blake, if anyone is to blame, it's Marcus. It's Viktor. It's me. But it's not you. You tried to save a little girl. You tried to give a child a better life."

I snorted. "And look how well it turned out."

"Don't. Stop it. I am looking. You bought her time. You gave her a new family. You loved her. She lived, Blake. That's all any of us get, the chance to live, the chance to make a few happy fucking memories. No one knows how long they have to make them. It's fucked-up, and it's unfair, yes, but it's not your fault. That's how it all works. You gave her a longer life, a happier life than she would have had. You tried. And you're braver than me for doing it, better than me."

I stared at him. "What the fuck are you talking about?" Theo was the better one, the good one. The Drakharrow who still had an actual heart and—Bloodmaiden help him—even a soul. He'd stood up to Viktor. Chosen a blightborn boy and stuck by that choice, come hell or high water. I was the fuckup. The prick. The asshole. I was the scum. Theo? He didn't even know half of what I was, what I'd become. What I was still becoming.

"You're a good person, Theo," I said stiffly. "I'm the one who . . ."

"You're the one who Viktor has tried to make feel like shit ever since your father died," Theo said bluntly. "And guess what? It's worked, Blake. But you're not like that. I see you, I know you. We're not so different, despite what you may think."

I forced a laugh. "Look at the time. The bell's going to ring any second."

"Fine. No more heart-to-heart," Theo said, immediately getting the picture.

I glanced at him. "You thought I was going to murder you in the common room a few minutes ago. Now you're trying to make me into, I dunno . . . some kind of a fucking martyr."

"You are a fucking martyr, coz," Theo said quietly. "There is absolutely no doubt in my mind about that. Never has been. You martyred yourself for your family. You'd do absolutely anything for the ones you love. It's your greatest strength. Your greatest weakness."

I stared at him.

"I never thought you were really going to kill me," he admitted.

I raised one eyebrow. "So there was no letter?"

"No, there was." He grinned and punched me lightly in the shoulder. "Come on. We're going to be late. Let's get to class."

The stone courtyard that served as the Defensive Arts arena was open to the sky. I glanced up, remembering the time Nyxaris had appeared there, perching on one of the stone walls. That wall was looking a little worse for wear these days.

A cold breeze swept through the training yard, but at least it wasn't snowing on us. Not that snow would make Sankara cancel a class. We'd have to soldier on no matter what the weather was. Just part of our training.

Theo and I were a few minutes late. The yard was already full of highbloods in leather training gear sparring on mats in practiced movements, in pairs or solo. Some had weapons, others were drilling hand to hand. But some were standing around in groups, chatting and doing absolutely nothing.

I glared at them. Sankara wasn't there yet, which explained the lack of order. Then I cursed under my breath. "Oh, shit. I'm supposed to be supervising."

Theo lifted a brow. "Better get started, then."

I marched forward, barking commands and taking pleasure in the way the groups of chattering students immediately broke up. Highbloods ran this way and that, forming pairs and grabbing weapons from the racks. Doing what they were supposed to be doing. Good. I scanned the training grounds as the shirkers got to work. The students who had already formed pairs seemed evenly matched. There were shouts of exertion but nothing unusual. Until my gaze landed on a roped-off set of mats at the far end of the room. A flash of red. My breath caught. Pendragon.

She was holding her own fighting a highblood girl, a Third Year who I immediately recognized: Larissa, one of Regan's old lackey friends. She was a little shorter than Pendragon but thicker, more muscular. She should have been able to hold her own. I'd have said they were evenly matched. Except, Larissa was struggling. Pendragon moved like an unsheathed blade, sharp and relentless. She was kicking the ever-loving shit out of Larissa, to put it bluntly.

Pendragon feinted left, then slammed an elbow into her opponent's ribs, knocking her off-balance as her fist found Larissa's nose. Blood sprayed, and Larissa stumbled backwards, clearly dazed. But Pendragon didn't stop. She surged forward, tackling her opponent to the ground and throwing herself on top of her, driving her fist into her stomach, her ribs, her face, again and again.

Students nearby had stopped what they were doing. Whispers rippled through the yard. A few tried to sneak closer to get a better view.

"Get the fuck back to work," I roared, my voice echoing off the stone walls.

Everyone jumped back into position, and the whispers immediately ceased.

The only pair my voice hadn't seemed to reach was Pendragon and Larissa: They were still going at it. At least, Pendragon was. Larissa was quickly becoming a bloody meat sack.

I marched towards them, my mind racing back to Pendragon's very first day at Bloodwing, when she lay in this same yard with Visha atop her, broken and bleeding, a laughingstock. I'd stood by then, too. Watched her be humiliated and put in her place—on my orders. But now things were completely reversed. Pendragon was half-mortal, half-blightborn. But she wasn't a halfborn like Professor Wispwood. No, her blood was even more unique. She had rider blood. *Fae* blood, she'd told me. I was still trying to wrap my mind around that—her being from another world, one filled with beings called fae. Regardless, from the look of things, she was using all of the advantages of her blood right now, without holding anything back. I'd only seen her like this one before, on the island with the other consorts. She'd had my blood to heighten her senses then, though. Now she was showing me just what she was capable of on her own. She shouldn't have been able to even take on a highblood—not like this. Sure, she'd held her own against Laurent when I'd set him on her in a moment of self-indulgent weakness that I was now ashamed of. But there was a difference between holding her own and pummeling someone to a bloody pulp.

"Pendragon," I yelled as I approached the mats. "Good fight. You're done."

She ignored me. Or maybe she didn't even hear me at all. All I knew was she kept throwing punches. Larissa's face was covered in blood, her cheeks swollen. I didn't like the girl much either, but this was gruesome, even for me. Though, a part of me saw the blood and thrilled at the sight of it. A part of me looked at it and screamed *More, more, more!* I glanced down at my forearms, praying I wasn't about to see red scales appear. I rubbed at my wrists, trying to force the urge away.

"Pendragon," I tried again. "Get the fuck off her. Didn't you hear me? I said you're done."

She didn't stop. Not when I shouted. Not even when Larissa gave a truly pathetic garbled moan. Not even when I noticed Pendragon's own knuckles starting to split and bleed from the impact of the blows. So I jumped in, letting instinct take over. One arm snagged around her middle as I hauled her body up and off the other girl. Pendragon thrashed like a wild animal. Her elbow caught my jaw hard, and I saw stars. But I didn't let go.

Where the fuck was Visha when I needed her? I scanned the courtyard, but she was nowhere to be seen. I owed her a talk. "Theo," I yelled. "Get over here. See to Larissa." Across the courtyard, I caught my cousin's eye. He nodded and ran towards us.

Pendragon was still fighting me, teeth bared, lips pulled back as if she might even bite me. I didn't want to hurt her, but I tightened my grip, tossing her over my shoulder as I cleared the ring and crossed the yard.

"Let me down," she snarled, beating her fists against my back.

I ignored her. Inside, my dragon was roaring his approval of the way I was handling things, struggling to rise to the surface. I could feel my skin heating, the itch of scales just barely hiding beneath the flesh. Not now. Not here, I pleaded.

I made it to the corridor, out of sight of the class. I dropped Pendragon to the ground in front of an arched window, and she stepped back, breathing hard. Her green eyes glowed with fury, her hair whipped around her shoulders in a breathtaking halo of flame. Slowly, her shoulders sagged. Her eyes reluctantly met mine.

"Pendragon," I said slowly. "What the fuck was that all about?"

She blinked. "What?"

I shook my head. "You were beating—" I'd been about to say *that poor girl* but decided that wasn't an apt description when it came to Larissa. "You were beating your opponent senseless. You weren't holding back. At all. What were you thinking? Did you want to kill her?"

Pendragon stared up at me coldly. "Maybe. That a problem?"

"Trouble in class, Drakharrow?" a deep voice boomed.

I glanced over to see Sankara striding up. The professor was a large man, pure muscle and bulk, with at least a few inches on me—and I stood at a decent six feet three inches. He made quite an impression. Now his lips were thinned in displeasure. And Sankara was one teacher I did not enjoy displeasing. He was the kind of teacher who might actually kick your ass if you pissed him off too much.

He frowned. "I thought you were supervising for me today, Blake."

"I am," I said hastily. "I was. Pendragon just needed a break, sir." I scratched my head. "Uh, there's a student who might need to see a healer. I left Theo with them."

Sankara glanced at Pendragon, then back at me. I could see him trying to put the pieces together. "A highblood student?"

"That's the only kind we've got in this class besides Pendragon, isn't it, Professor?" I said through gritted teeth.

Sankara raised his dark eyebrows as he looked Pendragon up and down. "Impressive. Good work, Miss Pendragon."

I wasn't sure he was going to say that when Larissa's family complained to him.

"Thanks, Professor," Pendragon muttered.

Sankara tilted his silver head. His tight curls looked as if they'd been freshly cropped. He'd been growing a beard out. I'd heard some of the girls talking about how much he looked like a pirate. I doubted they knew they didn't stand a chance with Sankara. I wondered if he and Rodriguez were still fucking—not that it was any of my business. "We'll talk later, then."

I nodded. "Professor?"

He stopped in the doorframe.

"I think Pendragon could use a break from class today," I said meaningfully.

Sankara looked a little disappointed. "Very well. If you think that's best."

"I do," I said firmly. "I'll get her back to her tower." Well, to the door, anyhow. I'd never actually visited the House Avari tower, just like Kage wouldn't dare to step foot in the Drakharrow one. When Sankara was gone, I turned back to Pendragon. She gazed out the window at the bright, snow-covered hills. "Hey," I snapped. "Let's go. You're done for the day."

She faced me with a glare. "Fine."

I snuck a glance at her as we walked side by side down the hall. Then I held myself back, giving her a few minutes to calm down. I watched her breathing slow and turn more even. Only when we neared the Avari tower did I finally speak up.

"Now are you going to tell me what that was really about?"

"I wanted to kill her," she said, not even bothering to look at me. "Isn't that enough? Wasn't it obvious?"

"Oh, it was obvious," I agreed. "But it's not enough." I searched for words. "It's not like you to . . . to do something like that."

She stopped. "Why? Because I'm blightborn? Because we aren't supposed to hurt highbloods? I mean, not *really* hurt them."

"That's not what I meant . . ." It was exactly what I meant.

"Why the fuck should I hold back, Blake? Tell me. I really want to know. I should have killed her. She probably deserves it. And at least then she . . ."

"Why? Why does she deserve it?" I demanded. "What happened?"

She looked away. "Just a little blightborn bullying as usual."

"Larissa was part of it?"

She nodded, her face furious. "They can hurt us. They can drink us. They can kill us. So why can't we kill them?"

"Mostly because you can't," I snapped. "You're not capable of it. Well, most blightborn aren't. And if you are, well, good for you. But do I have to remind you there's only one of you and a hell of a lot more of them? If you'd killed Larissa back there, what the fuck do you think would have happened?"

She tightened her lips. "I don't know. Enlighten me."

"They could have surrounded you," I said, a hint of fear creeping into my voice. "Theo and I, we might not have been enough. You wouldn't have been able to take them all on. Not to mention the trouble you'd have been in . . ."

"Another tribunal?" she asked dully.

"Something like that. Or just a really fucking quick execution." I ran my hands through my hair. "I want to protect you. I need to protect you. But if you act like that, then who knows what could happen."

CHAPTER 7
MEDRA

"What about what I need?" I said softly, turning to face him.

He stared down at me. "What you need?"

I nodded. The truth was, I felt like I was going to explode. I could feel myself splitting. Breaking. Ever since the night in the courtyard. Ever since I'd lost Florence. No, not just her. Ever since I'd lost Nyxaris. Lost my mother. Lost my trust in Rodriguez. I felt numb inside. But also on fire. Could both things be true? I wanted to stop holding everything in. Stop pretending. I didn't want to be calm anymore. I didn't want to be good. I wanted to *burn*.

It hit me like a blow to the chest, sudden and absolute. I didn't want to run away from Blake. I wanted to run straight towards him. I wanted his mouth, his hands, his teeth. I wanted him to forget everything with me, forget to be careful.

"Come upstairs with me," I said, my voice low and throaty. "Come back to my room."

His body went still. "What?"

"Come up to my room with me. Right now."

The air between us ignited. No touch. No magic. No blood. Just the mere words. The *thought* of what we could do together. I saw it happen, saw the flicker in his eyes. For a moment, sheer disbelief. Then, the spark. The heat. I drew a shaky breath, watching his jaw tighten—but not in anger. His nostrils flared. He was struggling to breathe. So was I.

He shook his head tightly. "I . . . can't."

I blinked. "What?"

"I can't enter the Avari tower. It would be seen as a challenge to Kage. A huge sign of disrespect."

I stared at him. I didn't give a shit. The thought of Blake and Kage at one another's throats again like in the library that one day was . . . well, kind of fucking hot. But Blake was probably right. I wanted to be reckless. But not in quite that way. "Fine," I said flatly.

He looked confused. "Fine?"

I spun away from him and stormed down the corridor to our right, towards one of the castle wings full of classrooms. Blake caught up, falling in step with me easily. "What are you doing?"

I yanked open a classroom door. A highblood professor looked up from a lecture with a stern glare. Fifty highblood students from House Mortis turned their heads towards us. "Not this one," I muttered, slamming it closed again.

"Pendragon," Blake hissed.

I tried another door. Occupied. This time full of groups of blightborn, working on some kind of a map project involving lots and lots of paint and papier-maché. Another full of First Years, sitting in a circle all holding the same book as Hassan droned on about highblood history.

"Ugh."

"Pendragon, what the hell?"

I ignored him. Then, finally, I found one. The door swung open into an empty lecture hall. Long wooden benches curved in rows around a central platform with a large wooden desk. The air was full of dust and shadows. Filtered light streamed through high arched windows, clouded with dirt on one side and snow on the other. But it was empty. I breathed a sigh of relief. *Perfect.*

I grabbed Blake's wrist and yanked him inside, then slammed the door shut behind us and flicked the lock.

"What are you—" he started.

I didn't let him finish. My lips were on his in a heartbeat. Hard.

Fierce. Reckless. His back hit the nearest wall, and I moved against him, hands in his hair, my teeth tugging at his lower lip. I didn't want slow. I didn't want careful. I wanted to devour and *be* devoured. I wanted to feel something. Something so powerful, so overwhelming, it would make everything on the other side of that fucking door completely vanish. At least for a while.

And when Blake kissed me back—it did. Everything else disappeared. All that remained was fire. All that remained was *us*.

My fingers were already attacking the laces of the sleeveless leather tunic he had on, yanking at them as if they'd personally wronged me somehow. Blake's breath hitched as I tore the leather over his shoulders. There was a thin shirt beneath separating me from his bare skin, but I could still feel the heat of his body, smell the scent of his skin. *So close, so fucking close.* I reached for it; his hand caught my wrist. For a second, Blake looked at me and I saw confusion there, hesitation. His eye flickered. I thought I glimpsed red behind the gray.

Then the impossible moment passed and he was on me again.

His mouth collided with mine, running his hands through my hair, pushing me backwards, up one step, then another, until my hips hit the desk on the center of the platform. I arched into him, his hands already clawing at the lacings of my leather corset. It was a simple kind—worn for sparring, the lightest kind of armor. I'd known I'd be fighting hand to hand today, not using heavy weapons.

Blake tugged the cords, swearing impatiently under his breath, while simultaneously yanking the knots undone with ruthless efficiency. Finally the corset fell open, and I let out a heaving breath. The leather was soft and well-worn. It was tight-fitting but comfortable; I hadn't bothered wearing anything underneath.

"Gods," Blake rasped, staring at my naked body as the corset dropped away. "That's all you wore to class?"

I grinned darkly, breathlessly. "Are you going to lecture me about it?"

His hands were all over me then. Hot, greedy, desperate. I slipped his own cotton shirt off him and felt him beneath my hands, reveling in the warmth of his skin. He was trembling, I realized, something stirring in him beneath the surface.

I'd lit the spark. There was no going back now.

Whatever this was between us was dangerous, and we both knew it. But I was sick of resisting. Sick of pretending. Sick of denying myself what I truly wanted. When what I truly wanted was him. This man—this *vampire*—had promised me everything. Anything. He'd promised to kill for me. But maybe all he had to do was give me himself.

I slid a hand between us, stroking him over the leather, feeling the hard length of him. "I feel so fucked-up, Blake," I whispered.

He nodded tightly. "I know the feeling. You think this will help?"

I let out a sound somewhere between a giggle and a hiccup. "What the hell? It's worth a shot."

His lips descended onto mine as his hands slid over my breasts. I moaned, searching for the lacings of my own leather trousers and starting to pull them loose. His hands covered mine. His one good eye met mine. Stormy and clouded with need.

"Let me." His voice was raw.

Blake undid the laces, then worked the leather down my hips, as if he'd done it a thousand times before. As they reached my ankles, I kicked them off with a grunt of impatience. Blake reached for his own, unfastening the ties and pulling the training gear off. He hadn't stopped trembling. I wasn't sure what the hell was going on, but I wasn't going to ask; his aggression seemed barely leashed but at least it wasn't directed at me. Besides, I had my own fury to contain. Better we attack each other than go on a rampage in Sankara's class.

Leather dropped to the ground in a heap. A linen undershirt followed. We'd kicked off our boots long ago. I took him in: Blake's body was incredibly beautiful. Perfectly shaped in every way. Pale blond hair curling down over his neck, basically chin-length at this point. He raised his hands to push it back off his face, and the black dragon tattoos painted over his skin rippled as his muscles flexed. I followed the lines of ink down his torso, eying the pale hairs that formed a line down his stomach, past his hips . . . My throat felt dry as I took him in.

He grinned. "See something you like?"

I met his eye. Heat. Clawing urgency. We crashed back together, flint striking tinder.

He lifted me, hands rough, breath harsh, then slammed me ass-down on the desk, scattering a tower of parchment to the floor. He leaned into me, grinding his hardness against my core as I gasped his name.

"Want me to stop?" he growled.

I swallowed. "If you stop, I won't be held responsible for your death." I started to slide a hand between us to stroke his cock and bring it closer to where I wanted it, but his hand gripped mine with an iron-tight grip.

"No."

"No?" I challenged.

"I'll think I'll take what I want from you first." Blake's hand slid between my legs, and I gasped as his fingers made contact, slipping between my thighs and into the slick wetness at their center.

"First your pussy," he murmured, leaning towards me. "Then your blood. Then all of it. All of you, given entirely to me."

I narrowed my eyes. "How the fuck did you just make that sound hot?"

But Blake had already moved on. Moving his lips down my neck, biting teasingly but not enough to break the skin, then trailing a string of kisses down my breasts, over the planes of my stomach, and down to the tops of my thighs. My legs were already slightly spread in anticipation. Now he shoved them open wider. A whimper crossed my lips as Blake grabbed my wrists, slamming them down on the desk on either side of me, holding them there as he lowered his mouth and dragged his tongue over me. His tongue flitted across my clit, his forearms pressing my thighs apart while his hands held my wrists firmly against the desk, as if there was no way he'd let me escape now. It was primal. Feral. Fucking hot.

I cried out, feeling my hips lifting as the urge to shamelessly press my center against his face overwhelmed me. I bit my lip, arching upwards against his tongue, as I watched him lave and lick my pussy like a starving lion at a feast.

Blake looked up at me, somehow radiating an inferno yet also steely as ice. I was all over his mouth, shiny slick remnants of my arousal coating him like a second skin. "I'm going to let go of your wrists now. Don't fucking move," he instructed.

I opened my mouth to protest. Then shut it again. This was what I wanted. What I'd dragged him here for. I managed the weakest of nods and did as he said. His hands caressed my thighs, moving down gently. Then his mouth found my clit again, ravaging it with expertise, as he slid one finger inside me, then another. Nothing had ever felt like this. This intense and incredible pull. The pressure in my clit throbbed. I felt myself on the edge. About to come.

Blake buried his face deeper between my hips, and I could feel the explosion rising. I ground against him as his fingers plunged in and out, in and out.

"Please," I moaned.

He pulled his face away and stood up.

I looked up at him in disbelief. "What are you doing?"

"Turn around."

"What?"

"You wanted this, Pendragon. You asked for it. You dragged me here. Need I remind you?"

"No, but you're doing it anyway," I muttered.

He smirked—that glorious, infuriating fucking smirk—and unbelievably, I felt the wetness between my legs grow. Hell, if he wasn't the absolute picture of everything I wasn't supposed to want. A secret thrill went through me. But *mine*. I turned around slowly.

"That's it," he encouraged. "Put your hands down flat on the desk and bend over."

I gritted my teeth but did as he asked. "Really getting into the role-playing, aren't we?"

His voice was suddenly in my ear with vampire speed. "You've been a naughty girl, Miss Pendragon. And now you're about to be punished. Punished for being the most fuckable girl in the entire blooddamned school."

I opened my mouth to make a hot retort just as I felt his cock press against my entrance. I moaned; it felt so good. Blake's fingers expertly strummed my clit.

"Blake, please," I said, clenching my jaw.

"It's Professor Drakharrow, actually," he murmured, his mouth dancing over the soft skin at my throat. "There's so much I want to teach you about the ways of pleasure, Miss Pendragon."

"You're enjoying this a little too much," I whispered, "*Professor*."

"Bloodwing professors aren't technically supposed to compromise their students, you know," he breathed. "And yet . . . here we are." His teeth found purchase, sinking into the tender skin.

"Here we are," I gasped. The gasp turned into a moan as his cock slid inside me.

"I can't believe you came to class dressed like this today, Miss Pendragon," he murmured, sliding his hands over my ass, then gripping my hips as he thrust.

"Yes, stark naked as always," I said through clenched teeth. "I find I can focus better this way." I closed my eyes, losing myself in the blissful feeling of his cock pumping in and out of me. Just when I thought he'd filled me with his length completely, he pulled out, then thrust back in. I screamed.

"I'll take it that was an appreciative sound," he said, lapping and licking at my neck before finally pressing his fangs into me. "You'll receive full marks for this."

I shivered. I'd never get over the—quite frankly—humiliating fact that having his fangs sink into me felt, well, fucking good. Really fucking good. As did the sensation of his tongue licking up the bloody remnants, sliding over the tiny puncture marks he'd no doubt left on my skin. Marks that would quickly heal as they always did, now that I was willing and compliant.

"What's the matter? Are you having trouble taking all of me now, Miss Pendragon?"

"Oh, I can take it," I breathed, as he gripped my hips.

"Good," he whispered. "Now touch yourself. You know you want to."

I whimpered slightly as I slid one hand between my legs, gripping the desk with my other. My clit was already swollen and throbbing from his earlier ministrations. I tilted my head down, letting my long hair cascade around my shoulders, then closed my eyes, imagining how we must look together. I wished I had a mirror so I could see just how incredible Blake Drakharrow looked fucking me from behind over a teacher's desk. But in the meantime, my imagination would have to suffice.

"You feel," Blake growled from behind me, "fucking exquisite, little dragon. And you taste . . ." he snarled and sank his fangs back into my neck as I gasped in delight " . . . you taste even better." He moaned—a sound I absolutely reveled in having elicited. Blake pulled away, and I felt him trembling against me, holding himself back from coming. Simply holding on to the feeling of ecstasy that this—our being together, two bodies united—created. "You taste so sweet, Pendragon," he whispered, nuzzling his mouth against me. "Do you like how I fuck you?"

A moment's hesitation. Then, "Yes. No one's ever made me feel this way. This good."

It was a confession I hadn't meant to make. I felt him go very still.

When he spoke again, his voice was quiet. "You don't know what you do to me. You don't know how much I'm holding back."

I crave everything about you, Pendragon. Your voice, your lips, your body. And the sounds you make when you come? Sheer perfection." He kissed his way down my neck, then slid his hand over mine, rubbing my clit with his finger. "Come for me now, little dragon. Come for me."

And I did. Exploding at his fingers, while his cock filled me up and he thrust hard into me, shoving my thighs against the table so roughly I knew I'd have bruises afterwards. I didn't care. I saw stars. Sparks. Fire. Whatever you want to call it at that moment you reach your climax, I was there, floating, weightless, breathless. I heard Blake cry out, felt him bury his head against me, then lift his hands to cup my breasts—a gesture so perfect, so gentle, it shocked me.

And then I was falling back to earth, my body trembling, tears inexplicably streaming down my cheeks, as I turned towards him.

"Hey, hey, what's this?" he said, sounding startled. He reached a hand up, touching the wetness on my cheeks. "What did I do?"

"Nothing," I said quickly, trying to wipe the tears away.

Blake didn't say anything, just looked down at me for a moment. And then he was scooping me up, lifting me into his arms.

"What are you doing?" I exclaimed. "Put me down . . ."

But it was too late. With one great arm movement, he'd cleared the remainder of things littering the desk behind us. I had a moment of guilt thinking of the poor instructor who'd be cleaning up later. And then Blake was laying me down, carefully, with infinite tenderness, and then climbing up beside me, lying down on the desk next to me and pulling me into his arms, until his chin rested atop my head.

"What is—" I started to say.

"Hush," he commanded. Not meanly, just firmly. He tilted his head a little, and I felt him inhale. He was breathing me in, I realized. Smelling my hair.

"What do I smell like?" I asked, unable to resist. I grimaced, remembering. "Probably like Larissa's blood."

"You smell nothing like Larissa. A vampire can smell your true scent even beneath the filth."

Was he calling Larissa filth? I felt myself smile. "Tell me, then."

He sniffed again. Then sighed appreciatively. "You smell like autumn."

"Autumn?" I said dubiously. "It's winter."

"You smell like autumn even in winter. Like fallen leaves."

"Like decay, in other words?"

He pinched my upper arm playfully, and I squealed. "I told you to hush," he reminded me.

"Oh, are you still playing professor, Professor Drakharrow?"

"Autumn leaves," he repeated, ignoring me. "Jasmine. Vanilla." He took another sniff. "Blueberry tarts."

"I had a blueberry tart at lunch," I said, impressed. "Can you really still smell that?"

I felt him nod his head. "And beneath all of it, the rich scent of your blood. Potent. Powerful."

I waited for the inevitable word. When it didn't come, I felt oddly disappointed. "Aren't you going to say it?" I teased.

Blake was quiet for a long time.

"I'm not sure what you want to hear, but . . . I know I owe you an apology beyond words."

I froze. This wasn't what I'd been expecting. That didn't mean it was unwelcome either.

"I owe you an apology today and every single other fucking day for the rest of our lives." I felt him give a choked laugh as he held me. "However long that might be."

I frowned, disliking the bleakness I heard there. The hint of hopelessness. That wasn't the Blake I knew.

Before I could stop myself, it slipped out. "I think I already have."

I felt him turn his head, trying to look down at me. "What?"

My lips suddenly felt dry. I licked them carefully. "Forgiven you, you idiot. I think I already have."

He stayed silent. *Good.* I kept going. "Besides, I'm not the only one who's lost something, am I? Aenia. I'm . . . truly sorry, Blake. I'm sorry about your sister."

His gaze dropped. The fire was still there between us. But it was calmer now. A fire you could hold in a hearth. Not the raging forest fire it had been a few moments before. "I never expected . . . this," Blake said, his voice low. "With you. Ever again."

I pushed away from him a little, so I could tilt my head up and see his face. One eye was stormy gray. The other was . . . ravaged. He might have chosen to wear a patch over it. But so far, he hadn't. It was just like Blake not to bother trying to put others at ease with the truth of his appearance. I traced the outline of his eye socket with a fingertip, very gently. "I feel like I'm burning alive when I'm with you," I whispered. "And the worst part is . . . I don't care. I don't want it to stop." I shook my head. "Even after all the shit that's happened between us."

Blake nudged my forehead gently with his, his breath mingling softly with mine. The gesture was tender, almost dragonlike. "You're the only part of this place that doesn't feel toxic, Pendragon," he whispered back. "You're the only thing that feels real." He took a deep, ragged breath. "Being with you makes me want to believe I can be something better than what I've been."

My heart ached at the stark honesty in his words. I reached up, fingers brushing along the line of his jaw, lingering on the scars that still marred his face. Every mark a story that had led us here, every scar a sign of how much he was willing to sacrifice for my sake. "You already are," I whispered.

His eyes softened, gray eyes less stormy, and I told myself the red I'd glimpsed in them earlier had just been my imagination. Blake was not Viktor. It was only my fear that was causing me to see a resemblance where there was none.

We lay together, breathing slowly, the moment a temporary peace in a little hidden corner of our chaotic world.

CHAPTER 8

FLORENCE

I was a coward. I knew it. My mother probably knew it, even if she'd never, ever in a million years dream of using the word. Even the fluffin sitting on my feet knew it.

I scratched Neville's head, and the fluffin purred loudly, his entire little body rumbling with contentment. For a moment, I envisioned becoming a fluffin, with all the sunbeams, snacks, and naps I could dream of. But I wasn't a fluffin. I wasn't even me anymore. I was something else now. Something new. A *rider*.

The word felt frightening, even said silently in my own head. It wasn't my word. It wasn't *me*. *Rider* was a word that belonged to Medra. To someone brave and bold and daring. Someone who wasn't afraid of climbing onto a scaled monster who breathed fire.

Books belonged to me. Hot tea belonged to me. Endless projects and extra-credit assignments belonged to me. They were what I lived for. I was supposed to be a strategist. Or a healer. Or preferably both. I'd live my days inside, very safely, in rooms full of books, studying ancient battles or testing new remedies. Of course, I'd venture out to my garden or greenhouse from time to time. Plants and books were far safer than a dragon. *Anything* was safer than a dragon.

I glanced across the room where my mother sat hunched over on a pink-and-green floral sofa, surrounded by a pile of books, nibbling on the tip of a quill. Her cup of tea rested on a small table, still full. Completely cold, of course. I looked at my own cup—also cold, but only half-full.

I had three books open in front of me and a quill in my hand. I was supposed to be writing an essay for Professor Allenvale's class, extra credit to make up for the fact that I hadn't actually attended any classes since . . . since *it* had happened.

I'd made my mother bring notes to my professors, notes in which I'd lied and said I was ill. It was childish and immature and silly. But knowing that hadn't stopped me.

Only Professor Rodriguez knew what had really happened. And Kage. Thankfully, my House Leader hadn't pressed me to come back to the Avari tower; he'd left me alone.

But I knew he would come eventually. I couldn't stay hidden away in my mother's suite of rooms forever. I'd have to return to class soon, unless I wanted to flunk out of Bloodwing entirely. And considering the possible consequences, that wasn't an option.

I leaned forward to ruffle Neville's fur again, and the fluffin lifted his head, opened one eye, and peered at me. He'd been a faithful companion since the incident in the Dragon Court.

If I were to ever write a murder mystery, that's what I'd call it, I decided: *The Incident in the Dragon Court*. It had a nice ring to it. There would be no actual dragons in said book, only murders. Even murders were safer than dragons.

I flinched suddenly as a sensation hit me. A scent. Fresh fish, filling my nose. I supposed I should be grateful it wasn't filling my mouth. I wrinkled my nose, but there was nothing I could do. I hadn't been able to block Nyxaris out. Not completely. He'd reached out to me once. I'd ignored him. Pretended I couldn't hear him. He hadn't tried again since that first time. He hadn't needed to. Because I could feel him there always, sense him even without trying. Even if he wasn't trying to speak to me, I knew where he was. Knew when he was flying over the island, when he was curling up for the night on a ledge on the cliffs above the sea. I could even sense emotions sometimes. Right now, he was content; the fish were delicious.

I might have simply gone on with my life. Pretended Nyxaris was something akin to a dog. But he wasn't a dog. He wasn't a mindless beast. He was intelligent. I knew he wouldn't wait forever. I pursed my lips stubbornly. But he'd have to. I wasn't going to be his rider. I wasn't going to be *his* in any way. I certainly wasn't going to fly on his back at a dreadfully great height without even a saddle or reins to hang onto. I. Just. Wasn't.

"I told you Medra came by to see you last night," my mother murmured absent-mindedly, without looking up from her books. "Didn't I?"

"This is the third time you've mentioned it," I answered, a little peevishly.

"Oh, is it?" My mother smiled down at her book as if relieved. "Good. I was worried I'd forgotten." She lifted her head to look at me and sighed. "She misses you, Florence. You know you—"

"I'm in the middle of an essay." I made my voice chill in a way I hated. "Can we talk about this later?"

Her face fell. "Of course."

The silence resumed, but it was no longer a comfortable one. I was being awful. I knew that. Not only to my mother but also to Medra. But I didn't know what else to do. No one had asked me if I wanted to be pulled back from the brink of death. No one had given me any choice about it. They'd done their ritual and bound me to a dragon, without even thinking about what that would mean for me exactly.

Nyxaris was flying over the island now. I could feel him, practically hear his wings flapping. Sometimes when I lay in bed at night, the knowledge of where he was and what he was doing would keep me awake, trapped by this creature now in my head—probably forever, sharing my personal space. After all, if I could sense this much about him, what did he sense about me and my life? What could he hear? Smell? Taste? A dragon's senses were probably even better than mine.

I knew I was being unfair, even ridiculous. But when I lay there sleepless, all I could think about was how this had all happened because of Medra. If I hadn't gone after her to the Dragon Court, if I hadn't run forward to try to save her life. Which, I suppose, I had done rather successfully.

If she hadn't tried to save me. If I hadn't met her.

I snapped my book shut. I hadn't really been reading it anyway. Neville leaped to his feet and barked loudly.

"Hmm?" My mother looked up. "I supposed it is getting late."

"I'm going out for a walk," I announced. "I'll be back in an hour or so."

"But it's a school night . . ." She trailed off, then smiled. "Very well. I suppose I don't know when you go to sleep when you're back in your own room in the House Avari tower, so I shouldn't worry so much about when you go to sleep here. You've always been very capable of managing your own affairs."

I took a deep breath, resisting the urge to tell her how wrong she was. "Thank you, Mother. I'll be back soon."

"Just . . ." She bit her lip. "Be careful, Florence. With the new headmistress . . ."

I nodded, knowing what she meant.

She gathered up her things, dumped out her teacup and left it on the counter in the kitchen, then carried a stack of three books to her bedroom.

When she was gone, I reached for a cloak hanging near the door and quickly left the apartment. She didn't need to know that I hadn't meant a walk in the halls. What she doesn't know won't hurt her, I told myself. For instance, she didn't know exactly how my life had been saved. Or if she had, she hadn't mentioned it, not once. Not a peep about dragons. I assumed Rodriguez had only told her the bare minimum. That he had saved me—and that Medra had something to do with it. Otherwise, maybe she wouldn't be so grateful to them both.

I closed the door to the suite softly and looked down. Neville had followed me out into the hall.

"Fine, but you'd better be quiet," I hissed. He lolled his tongue out in response, panting happily.

I followed the pull I was feeling. Down the hall, down another hall, down endless halls. All full of stone pillars and frost-covered windows. Through the school towards the door that led out onto the hills. I caught my breath at the chill in the air. The sun had set, but the moon was up. It was easy to make my way down the path towards the greenhouse, then past that to a rocky path that led around the edge of the island, where the cliffs rose higher, rocks climbing towards the sky.

Why was I doing this? Why had I come? Because I couldn't go another minute hiding inside when it felt as if my heart was being dragged out of my body by something vast and terrible. It wasn't a good reason. It was probably a very bad one. Yet here I was.

My footsteps slowed. Neville was still at my heels; he'd been impressively quiet. Something shifted on the rocks at the edge of the cliffs, and I froze. A silhouette rose up against the stars. *Nyxaris*.

The dragon pushed himself upwards, perching on the edge of the cliff, stretching out the massive wings that had been furled at his sides. Black scales caught the moonlight, shimmering like obsidian glass. My breath caught in my throat. He looked beautiful. Ancient. Lonely. Regal.

Completely terrifying.

My instincts screamed at me to run, but I stayed where I was, hidden behind a crag, watching the dragon who had saved my life. My heart pounded—and yet it shouldn't have, because I knew I would never move past this rock. I would never go to him. I would never be enough.

Medra hadn't even been fully bonded to Nyxaris. She'd been able to speak to him mind to mind, but she hadn't been able to sense him, not like I did now. Even so, she'd spoken to him, flown on him, fought from his back. But she was fire and fury. And I was . . . a trembling girl hiding in the dark, wishing she could stay hidden inside a book forever.

Well, I'd had the glimpse I wanted. I'd come closer than I probably ever would again. And I'd gotten away with it. I hadn't been caught. The fresh air was good for me, too, I reminded myself. I turned to go, my boots moving over the pebbled pathway.

You hide as if you were prey. The voice struck my mind like a bolt of lightning.

I froze.

Are you prey, fledgling?

Slowly, I turned back. Nyxaris turned his head towards where I stood, hiding in the shadows of the rock. Glowing amber eyes locked onto me through the dark.

I feel you. Are you so foolish as to believe I could not sense you standing there in the dark?

I felt my face flush hot. *I don't know what you can and can't sense.*

Yet there you are, he observed. *Watching me. Do you have questions for me, fledgling? Why else do you linger?*

I took a step back. Then another. *No. No questions.*

Down beside my ankles, Neville whined. The sound was a plea. Did he want me to run or to stay?

I will not harm you.

I froze again.

The dragon rumbled aloud, a great booming sound that echoed over the cliffs. *You think I would choose one I wished to destroy?*

You didn't choose me. My voice sounded small and pitiful even in my own head.

The little one beside you follows you. He visits me, too.

I glanced down. *Neville?*

Neville, yes. A pause. *He's much more civil than you are.*

I beg your pardon?

You ignore me. You would flee even now. Do you know nothing about what offends dragons?

I shivered. *I didn't mean to offend—*

Silence, the dragon commanded. *You do not listen. Not truly. You do not speak. You do not come. What am I to think of you, a rider who refuses the bond? A girl who would rather hide beneath her mother's skirts than face me?*

Tears stung my eyes. *I didn't ask for this.*

A roar filled the air. I stumbled backwards.

None of us ask for this, Nyxaris bellowed in my head. *You think I wanted this? We are chosen. You were chosen. You were saved.*

Then, maybe you saved the wrong person, I blurted out. *Maybe you shouldn't have saved me at all. Medra is the one who belongs with you. She should be your rider, not me.*

Silence. I was breathing hard, my cheeks wet, my eyes blurry. *I'm sorry*, I whispered.

Sorry? Is that what you are? Nyxaris snarled. *She did not tell me you were such a coward.*

I turned and ran, boots slipping on the slick snow-covered gravel. The wind whipped at my face as I scurried up the hillside and back towards the castle. The ribbon tying my hair back slipped out, flying away in the breeze. I didn't even try to turn and look for it. Behind me, the cliff had become silent once more, but I could still feel him, watching me, listening to me. Judging me.

I blinked away tears as I stumbled back into the warmth of the school. Neville had vanished. I didn't blame him. He'd probably stayed behind to visit Nyxaris. The dragon was probably much better company than I was.

The door caught in the wind and slammed behind me with a bang. I picked up my pace again, boots pounding against the stone floors as I turned corner after corner, blindly retracing my steps back towards my mother's apartment. I'd passed the refectory and was nearing the library when I heard them—students laughing. It shouldn't have been unusual. But the sounds were too loud. Too sharp. Too cruel.

I peeked around the next corner, pressing tightly against the stone wall. A group of highblood students were gathered around something, laughing and talking. Some took swigs from flasks in their hands. I recognized a few of the girls from House Drakharrow.

Quinn Riley was there. And another girl, Gretchen, I thought her name was. A bunch of boys were with them; they looked older than any students I'd seen. None of them were familiar to me. All of them wore matching badges with the image of a blood droplet being pierced by a sword on their uniforms. There was writing on the badges, but I couldn't make out what it said.

The voices were getting louder. The group split up, moving in different directions.

I retreated around the corner, pressing my back to the wall and praying none of them would turn in my direction.

". . . really thought she could say no. Can you believe the nerve?"

"The look on his face when Cade told him to pick up the knife . . ."

"Stupid fucking blightborns."

Quinn, the other girl, and a boy I didn't recognize reached the split in the hall. To my relief they turned left instead of right, moving away from me.

I waited, still hugging the wall. Then I looked carefully around the corner again. That's when I saw them: two bodies, lying on the stone, a boy and a girl. They lay sprawled in the center of the corridor, a growing pool of blood around them. Each one held a dagger in one hand. It looked as if they'd stabbed one another to death.

I pressed my lips together. But maybe they weren't dead. I couldn't just leave them like this. I stepped around the corner.

Stay where you are.

I stilled for a moment.

Go back to your mother's apartment. That's where a fledgling like you belongs.

I can't, I hissed. *Go away. Why are you watching me?*

Whatever you're about to do, stop and do the opposite, little fledgling.

I'm not your fledgling, I said furiously. *If they aren't dead, I have to help them.*

I moved around the corner as quickly as I could. Reaching the girl, I dropped to my knees, stretching out two fingers to feel for a pulse at her throat. Her skin was cold. There was no rise and fall to her chest. Stomach twisting, I moved over to the boy, checking him in the same way. Nothing.

They were gone.

I could have tried to fetch a professor, a healer. Someone, anyone. But if I went searching, who would I encounter? A highblood or a blightborn? I thought of Professor Sankara, Professor Allenvale. I thought of Headmaster Kim. Highbloods had done this; highbloods didn't care if blightborn died.

I saw it then, written on the wall behind where the boy and girl lay—their own blood had been used as ink. The school motto was scrawled like a taunt: *Sanguis et Flamma Floreant*. Beneath it, in sloppier letters, words even more cruel. *Never refuse a highblood*.

My hand flew to my mouth. I choked back a cry, looking around. I was alone; there were no teachers coming to rescue me. Medra wasn't there to save me. Shakily, I got to my feet, looking down at the boy and girl. I didn't even know their names. Would their parents ever learn the truth about what had happened here? Would I? But then, I already knew what must have happened. The boy and girl had been walking down the hallway, probably hand in hand. They'd been talking and laughing. They'd looked just a little too safe, a little too happy—for blightborn, that was. They'd made a fatal misstep without even knowing it. They'd turned a corner and encountered Quinn and her friends. One of the highbloods had probably wanted to feed. The blightborn girl had refused. The boy had tried to protect her. Or maybe they'd wanted to feed from the boy first. Either way, someone had dared to refuse.

Cease your dawdling and return to the safety of your home, Nyxaris growled impatiently.

My legs moved on their own, somehow pushing me forward, forcing me to stumble away. There was blood on my hands from where I'd knelt in the puddle. I wiped it off on my skirt as best I could. Then I ran. I forced myself to stop at every junction, checking around each corner before dashing on. Finally, I reached my mother's suite, unlocked the door, and slammed it shut behind me. The lights were low: I knew she'd gone to sleep.

I fell onto the sofa where I'd been sleeping each night, curled into a ball and let the sobs come. My whole body shook.

Thrallweave.

I paused my sobs. *What?*

That is how the tale ends. Thrallweave.

They . . . used it on them? They made them hurt each other? I hadn't been there on the first day of school, but my mother had returned at the end of the day looking tired and somber. She'd told me what Regan had done to the blightborn woman on the balcony.

Highbloods do what brings them pleasure—they always have and always will. They delight in cruelty. It is their nature. Nyxaris sounded both repulsed and resigned.

My skin crawled. I knew exactly what thrallweave was. It had been used on me my very first year at Bloodwing. I'd nearly died because of it.

Do you know how to defend yourself against it?

I shook my head in the dark. *No. Of course I don't. I'm blightborn.*

You're more than that now. You must be. You need to learn.

There was a long pause. I could almost feel Nyxaris pondering. *You did not listen to me, back in the hall. You did not stay put.*

I couldn't! I had to see if they were . . .

Hmm. Another weighty silence. *Perhaps you are not as hopeless as we both believe you are. If you are willing, I can teach you.*

Oh, I don't think I could . . . The words rushed out.

Silence! Nyxaris said with the force of a roar. It was the second time he'd told me to shut up that night—not that I really blamed him. *For one supposedly quite clever, you do not give nearly enough consideration to your words before they leave your mouth.*

I closed my eyes, wondering if that might be true. I'd never had that problem before, but I supposed there was a first time for everything.

I cannot teach someone who believes themselves unworthy, Nyxaris said coldly. *Who recoils not just from me but from her own essence.* Another silence. *You must choose, fledgling. Continue to fall to pieces and hide away in the safety of your mother's home if that is what you wish.* I could hear the derision in his voice. The weight of the challenge. *Or . . .*

He was silent so long I thought he'd disappeared.

Or? I ventured.

His voice came out of the darkness like a shadowy blade. *Or you rise.*

CHAPTER 9

BLAKE

I slouched on one of the hard wooden benches in the lecture hall for Sanguine Rites. Professor Vane was already hard at work at the blackboard, scratching away at the slate with a white piece of chalk. I scowled at his back, the scritch-scratch of the chalk gnawing at my already limited patience. At the top of the board the lecture topic was written neatly: *Sanguine Rites: The Art and Ethics of Blood Invocation in Modern Sangratha.*

Ethics? Now, that was a laugh.

That fucking bastard. Just how much information had Vane given Marcus? What had he told him? For all we knew, he'd been the oblivious key to everything that had happened, passing on to Marcus everything he and Catherine had needed to enthrall Lunaya and awaken Molindra.

I kept up my glare, clenching my fists, willing Vane to feel my hatred. Vane was one of the oldest professors at Bloodwing. Not as old as my dear old uncle Viktor, though. I shifted on the bench, barely suppressing a growl. My skin itched—didn't take a lot of thought to know why.

It'd been happening more and more lately, the feeling of my blood boiling beneath my skin. Of a darkness stirring.

All vampires craved blood: It was our nature. But this? This wasn't the same kind of craving. It was rage in its purest, most savage form. The desire to kill simply for the sake of it. To shred, to rip, to tear. It had nothing to do with feeding. Everything to do with the desire for destruction. And it fucking terrified me. Because the last time I'd been with Pendragon? I'd felt . . . different. Everything had been incredible, of course. She'd been incredible. But I'd been . . . rougher. I'd felt myself come close to losing control. I'd felt my dragon trying to reach towards the surface. At one point, I'd touched her and even now . . . I wasn't sure if at that moment it had been me or my dragon. It was as if there were two parts to me now, two selves that were irreconcilable in some fundamental way. And the idea that one with scales could take over, even for a moment . . .

I flexed my hands, trying to release some of the tension. Red scales shimmered across my forearms, crawling up from my wrists to my elbows like a disease. A warning. I yanked my jacket off the back of the bench and shrugged it on quickly, pulling down the sleeves to hide the evidence. I kept my head low but scanned the rows around me. Students were still trickling into the hall. No one seemed to have noticed. Then, out of the corner of my eye, I noticed someone slide into the seat beside me. Visha.

I blinked. I hadn't had a chance to speak to her since . . .

She didn't look at me. She tossed a battered-looking notebook on the desk and flipped it open.

"Good to see you," I said under my breath. "Missed you in class last week."

She kept her eyes on the notebook but nodded briefly. "I'm still enrolled. Or so they tell me."

I inhaled. "We should talk." I leaned back, trying to relax, studying her. I wasn't used to seeing Visha like this. She was usually fierce and full of life. Now there was something muted about her. Hollowed out. But I recognized one thing simmering beneath the sorrow: rage.

Stop being a fucking coward, I told myself. Get it done.

I cleared my throat. "I'm sorry about Lace. I've been wanting to say that to you . . . since it happened."

She looked up at me, violet eyes narrowing. She'd razored the sides of her hair recently but was growing the top part out. The silver strands were getting longer. She'd tied them in intricate knots at the nape of her neck. "I see your eye is healing."

I touched a hand to my face a little self-consciously.

"It'll probably grow back," she said, still staring at me. "Fucking highbloods. We lose an eye, we get it back again. But . . ." She stopped.

"It's not fair," I said softly, knowing what she was thinking. "Not fucking fair at all. I agree. And the fact that it was Aenia, my own sister, who did that to Lace." I met her gaze. "The way I see it, and probably you do, too, is I owe you a debt of vengeance."

"Vengeance?" she echoed. She laughed.

Professor Vane was still scribbling on the board. Around us, other students were starting to take down the notes.

Visha leaned towards me, purple eyes narrowing. "Are you saying you're ready to duel, House Leader?"

I wasn't intimidated. "If that's what you demand. I owe you blood. My blood harmed you. As her maker, I was responsible for Aenia. You know that."

Visha studied me. "Theo told me what you did in the Dragon Court. Offering yourself to Nyxaris." She shook her head. "Always knew you were a bold motherfucker. Well-played, Blake. Well-played."

"It wasn't about self-preservation. Not at that moment." I took a deep breath. "It was about protecting Florence Shen."

"Right." She gave me a dubious look. "Pendragon's blightborn friend. You actually cared if she lived or died, huh?"

"Yes," I said bluntly. "I did. I still do. Does that shock you?"

She looked at me for a moment, then shook her head. "You've always thought yourself worse than you were. But be careful, Blake. Don't want to see you going soft."

"Soft?" I growled. "I haven't gone soft."

"I need your edge," she continued, ignoring me. "At a time like this, when everything is going to finally blow up in their faces—"

"In whose faces?" I interrupted.

Visha gave me a look as if she thought I was an idiot. "C'mon, Blake. Read the room. Regan as headmistress? Gangs of asshole alumni patrolling the halls? The entire school is a powder keg. Don't you feel it?" She leaned towards me and lowered her voice. "And Lace? Lace was it for me."

"It?"

"I ended my triad."

I stared. "You . . . what? So Lucian and Evander, they're . . ." I swallowed. "I mean, I support you even if . . ."

She laughed. "Oh, don't worry. They're not dead. At least, not yet."

I glanced around. Behind us, a boy from House Drakharrow stared back at me, wide-eyed. I growled low, in the back of my throat. He quickly got the idea, rose, and moved to a row farther back. "Keep your fucking voice down, Visha," I warned after he'd left. "If we're going to conspire to kill your archon and fellow consort, could we at least be a little discreet about it?"

"Lucian isn't my archon anymore. I'm out, Blake. I'm fucking out." She gave me a funny look. "Didn't Pendragon tell you?"

"Tell me what?"

"Apparently Evander and Lucian thought it would be fantastic to team up with Quinn Riley and her friends. They were bullying a blightborn girl in the halls when Medra found them and put a stop to it. Theo told me all about it."

I thought back to the first day of school when Pendragon punched me in the face. "Now that you mention it, she did seem a little on edge that day."

"Right. On edge." Visha snorted. "On edge is what Evander is now. You should see him, scurrying around the halls like a rat with a hound chasing him."

"I assume you're the hound in that analogy."

She tossed her head. "Good guess. As for Evander, the low-lying scum."

"It was a powerful match. Your family worked hard to arrange it. I thought you were happy except for—"

"Except for the fact that my mates would both have been narrow-minded bigots?" she hissed. "Do you think I've heard a *Sorry* pass their mouths since Lace died?"

I stared at her. "They haven't said anything?"

"Oh, if you can consider laughter something. Evander looked a little sheepish." She dropped her voice to a whisper. "It's like they didn't even expect me to care that she was dead. They thought she was just . . . something to fuck." Her cheeks grew redder. "They thought I'd enthralled her."

I felt horrified. Even while I knew that, for a highblood, the behavior was sadly normal. "I'm sorry, Vish. I know Lace meant a lot to you. And I know she cared for you—of her own free will."

I wouldn't accuse Visha of falling in love. No, I wouldn't go that far. But she'd been . . . well, she'd been in something. She'd felt something more than she usually did, that had been easy enough to see. She'd been happier, too.

Abruptly, I tried to turn the tables. Imagined it was Pendragon who I'd lost. *Hard no.* I did not want to go there, not even in my imagination. It wasn't going to happen. I was not going to lose Pendragon. I couldn't allow myself to think about it even for a moment. I tried to focus on Visha again.

"So no, I don't want your debt of vengeance. I want your blade. I want blood. But not from you. And not from Aenia—even if she were still alive to give it. She was just a product, Blake. A product of this fucked-up, shitty world that we've been brought up to think of as normal. We're not gods, and they shouldn't have to worship us as if we are." Her eyes blazed purple. I'd never seen her like this before. "Don't look at me like that," she snapped.

"Like what?"

"With your eyes bulging out of their sockets. Like you think I might explode."

"Well, isn't that what you're suggesting? Look, I agree with you, all right? You know I do. We're not gods. But thinking that way? We're the minority. So you need to, you know . . . tone it down." I took a deep breath. "We have to play by the rules for now. We need to lie low and blend in. Yes, it's a powder keg, point taken. But don't do something stupid and get yourself killed trying to blow things up, all right?"

"Are we lying low?" She looked at me closely—too close for comfort. I thought about the moment she'd sat down beside me. What I'd just been doing. *Transforming.* "Is that what we're doing? I mean, I'm clearly not the only one stirring shit up." She laughed loudly enough that Professor Vane paused his scritch-scratching and turned to glare at her. Visha held up her hands and stayed silent until he turned around again. She lowered her voice. "I mean, look at your fucking face."

"What about it?"

"Where did you get the wounds, Blake? Who gave them to you?"

"I got in a fight," I said tersely. "I'll tell you more when the time is right."

"Sure." She rubbed her chin. "Let me ask you something. Has Viktor ever used thrallweave on Pendragon?"

She'd caught me off guard. "Yes, he has. But why does it matter?"

"Did she give way?"

"No," I replied. "Rodriguez had been teaching her to shield herself. Headmaster Kim had approved her to learn thrallguard. She was able to resist. She's impressively strong."

"Right." Visha folded her arms over her chest, looking smug. "Thought so."

"What?" I demanded.

"Have you ever heard of such a thing in your life? A blightborn—even if she is a rider—who was able to resist thrallweave when it was wielded by arguably the most powerful vampire alive?"

I frowned. "What do you mean?"

Visha shook her head. "A few lessons in thrallguard and you think Medra's, what, a prodigy? Does that make sense to you? She couldn't even resist Regan, for fuck's sake."

"She hadn't started her lessons back then," I protested. But now that I thought about it, it didn't make sense. It had always seemed too good to be true, but I'd simply been grateful Pendragon had been able to keep Viktor out of her fucking head. Now I wondered what Visha was getting at exactly.

Professor Vane was starting his lecture, but Visha seemed intent on continuing her train of thought. "You can worry about me if you want to, Blake. But I'd be more concerned about yourself if I were you, House Leader. And I mean that genuinely."

"What the fuck is that supposed to mean?" I hissed. "Is that some kind of a threat?"

She shook her head and turned to her notebook. "Not a threat, a warning. You know exactly what I mean. You need to get a handle on your shit, Blake, before it handles you."

By some miracle of the Bloodmaiden, I made it through the rest of Vane's class without incident. It was a near miss, though. The whole time I could feel Visha next to me, alarm bells were going off in my head. She knew. She didn't even have to say it out loud. The way she'd looked at me was enough. She knew what I was. What I was *becoming*. Soon someone else would figure it out. Maybe someone I couldn't afford to lose. Pendragon.

The thought of Pendragon seeing me as a scaled red monster, seeing the beast I was turning into . . . Iron bands seemed to tighten around my ribs. I wasn't Nyxaris. I wasn't some wise old dragon.

Pendragon would look at me the way she looked at Viktor, like I was a freak. A monster. Because it was true. That's what I was.

I shoved my way out into the hall the moment the bell rang, not waiting for Vane to dismiss us. I didn't stop moving. I kept my head down, dodging and weaving through groups of students, then climbing staircase after staircase until I was almost dizzy. All of the fear, all of the anxiety, I hadn't kept it in check. Couldn't control it. And now it was happening again. I could feel the shift in my bones, the itch under my skin. With every step I took, the dragon was trying to claw its way out of me.

I needed space. I needed air.

I stumbled into the classroom, the one I'd walked Pendragon to once for her lesson with Professor Hassan. The room was in a wing of the school few people visited. I'd noticed the room was built right into the cliffside, overlooking the ocean, opening out onto a wide stone landing that must have been used as a dragon perch back in the old days, when Bloodwing had been able to boast about having more than one dragon. Now it was mostly forgotten.

Thank the Bloodmaiden, Hassan wasn't there and neither was Pendragon.

I slammed the door shut behind me, hoping and praying I could turn the tide. But it was too late. The change ripped through me.

I gasped, dropping to my knees, body buckling under the pressure. How could this be natural? There was nothing natural-feeling about it. I fought the dragon at every step. Skin splitting, crimson scales forcing their way up to the surface, gleaming in the sunlight. My fingers twisted, contorting. Bones lengthened, thickened. Nails sharpened into wicked black claws. And then my shoulders burst open, wings unfurling, vast and sinewy, scraping the rough stone ceiling as they stretched outward.

I fell onto my hands. No, not hands—talons. The floor gave a shudder at the sudden increase in my weight. A guttural noise tore from my throat. I barely recognized myself. My body was alien. Too big, I was too big. The classroom was too small. The walls were pressing in on me. The ceiling suddenly became too low, too close.

I staggered towards the edge of the room and out onto the landing. My wings brushed against the walls as I went, scales scraping, knocking pieces of stone down in a hailstorm. I tried to breathe, tried to get control. But there wasn't time—it was too late. There was no room. No space. I had no choice.

I squeezed my eye shut. And jumped.

Birds pushed their young from their nest when they were ready to fly, didn't they? But I wasn't a fucking bird. And I wasn't flying. I was falling. I laughed—or tried to. The sound stuck in my throat. I couldn't even laugh as I died. I supposed that was ironic. I was going to die because I was too stupid to fly. Because I wasn't *made* for this, wasn't meant to be this thing.

Then instinct took over. Ancient. Undeniable. My wings snapped open with a crack, catching the air. Pain lanced through my back as my muscles adjusted. I pitched forward, then up, wings carrying me higher. I didn't even dare open my eye. I just . . . felt it. The air rushing over my scales. The power in the beat of my wings. Open space around me.

Freedom.

Slowly, I cracked my eye open.

I was flying. I was fucking flying.

The sea stretched out below me, glinting so brilliantly in the sunlight it was blinding. Behind me lay Bloodwing. I beat my wings, self-preservation kicking in, knowing I had to get away from the school and out of sight as fast as possible. With the glare from the sun, if anyone had happened to see me, chances were good they'd assume I was just Nyxaris. Black scales might look red in the sun, right?

I tilted my head upwards and spotted a cluster of clouds. I nearly crowed. Looked like Bloodwing was in for a storm, and the timing couldn't have been better. I flew straight towards the cloud clusters. Instinct—it was all I had, and thank fuck it was enough. I angled my wings, banking into the approaching storm front. The clouds swallowed me whole. For a moment, I breathed easy; it was peaceful within the swirling gray and white. The world dropped away. Nothing but mist and the muted sound of my own wings as they cut through the damp air.

The vapor was so dense I couldn't see more than a few feet in any direction. Like being inside a gray cocoon. The perfect hiding place. I was safe. I'd done it—I'd flown. I'd stay under cover until nightfall, then turn back to Bloodwing. Hopefully once the beast in me had gotten nice and tuckered out, I'd be able to land and force myself back into my human form.

I tried hard to ignore the part of me screaming for blood. Not Pendragon's blood—for once. No, the dragon didn't have good taste. Right now, it craved flesh. Meat. A fresh kill. It wanted to hunt.

Feed, the voice in my head snarled, now that it was fully free and had me flesh and bone. *Tear. Rip. Kill.* The whispers had been in the back of my mind for months, but now things felt truly out of control. I could hear it, hear the dragon inside of me screaming. *Kill. Hunt. Feed. Weak. Prey.*

But I wasn't giving in. Not now. Not ever.

I could feel the dragon pulling. Where instinct had just saved me, now it tried to drag me down—back to the earth, to where the dragon knew it would find warm flesh and blood.

Prey below. Spill their blood. Rip and tear.

The hunger was frantic, desperate, but also gleeful. That's what scared me the most—the excitement at the thought of killing. I'd never known anything like it before. I'd never relished acts of violence. Whatever I'd done, I'd always done out of necessity. Or, on rare occasions, anger. But this went beyond any of that.

I squeezed my eye shut as I flew, forcing my mind away. Tried to think of anything else. My classes. Visha. My house. Theo. I latched on to Pendragon. Her face. The freckles on the curve of her hip. The smell of her hair. The sound of her voice as she'd gasped my name the last time we'd . . .

Movement. I sensed it. Warning flashing inside me just before I saw it. A flash of darkness, cutting through the mist to my right. I turned my head, hoping I'd been wrong, every muscle in my body tensing up. Something massive moved through the cloudbank. Not a storm, not a shadow.

Nyxaris.

The older dragon's head came into view as he sliced through the clouds, trying to pull alongside me. My heart hammered. The voice in my head had thankfully shut up. Maybe just as intimidated by Nyxaris as I was. Was I really doing this? Was I really flying alongside a fucking dragon? I pushed the thought away. Everything about the scenario should have been impossible. But it wasn't.

You fly very poorly.

I jerked, wings nearly seizing up from the shock. The voice was in my mind. But this was different from the beast's demands for blood. Was this what Pendragon could hear?

Who are you? Nyxaris's voice was cold.

My thrallguard training leaped into action. My mind clamping down, slamming up mental shields I'd spent years perfecting.

Why do you hide, cousin of scales? Nyxaris murmured in my head.

Cousin. Good, he had no clue who I really was.

Or is it that you've forgotten how to speak? The black dragon's voice was sharper. *Vorago? Is it you?* He veered closer, skimming through the clouds.

I panicked. Wings folding, I dropped altitude in a sickening plunge. Air whipped past me, cold and stinging, burning my eyes.

Vorago. The word was a command. It was easy now to imagine Nyxaris as he'd once been. A leader of dragons. A terror in battle. *You will answer me. That is an order.*

I flew harder, flapping my wings, staying in the cloud cover but flying low, closer to the roiling sea below. But it wasn't enough. It was my first fucking flight. I was a novice; Nyxaris was an expert. I could hear him behind me, wings beating. He was catching up.

Then . . . pain. Stabbing through my head. Screeching like a crow.

The screeching was real, I realized. The pain and the screeching were one and the same. I tried to shut it out, but it was no use. I couldn't cover my ears, couldn't close out the sound. It pierced through my mind as easily as Nyxaris's had. The screeching faded. A word took shape. One single word.

Nyxaris, it called to me. The voice was plaintive. Keening. Unnatural.

A chill went through me. Fuck. I knew who this was. *What* this was: Molindra.

Nyxaris, answer me.

Not Nyxaris, I grunted, pushing the words out of my mind.

Behind me, the sound of Nyxaris's wings were fading. Was he feeling this pain, too? I hoped so. I beat my wings faster. He was distracted. This was my chance. After a few moments of silence, I risked a glance back. Nothing. Nyxaris had been swallowed up in the clouds.

He'd either lost me or changed direction. Or been in too much pain to continue his pursuit.

I flew on, already exhausted, wishing my first flight was at an end. But there were hours to go before nightfall. And when I got back to Bloodwing, simply shedding this body wasn't going to be enough. I couldn't just keep hiding, not when I knew this could happen again.

Not when there was no safe place to go. Not within Bloodwing's walls or outside of them where Nyxaris could find me. I had to deal with this—whatever it was. I had bury it so deep no one could ever find it.

And I knew where I had to start.

CHAPTER 10

FLORENCE

I fell to the floor, sweat pouring down my face.
"Florence!"
Dimly, I could hear my mother's voice.

Pain. Overwhelming pain. Physical, yes, but emotional, too. Sorrow and horror mingled together. Tears ran down my face. No, this was wrong. *This. This* should not be. *Nyxaris*, I tried to scream. But the word caught, tangling in my mind, wrapped in the web of pain.

We paid the price. And a great one it was. Did we pay it for nothing? Nyxaris's voice was urgent. *Tell me, Molindra.*

Nyxaris, I tried again. Pain. Unrelenting pain.

"Florence!" My mother's voice was urgent, panicked. "What's wrong? Tell me what's happening."

I tried to push myself up, palms flat on the floor, but it was no use. My wrists wobbled. Gasping, I fell forward, whimpering.

Who has done this to you? a voice demanded. Nyxaris, but he wasn't speaking to me.

Tell me, Molindra. How has this happened? What have they done to you?

He was speaking to someone else. I wracked my mind. The Dragon Court. The third stone dragon, the golden one—the Luminthar of House Orphos. The one Lunaya, Marcus, and Catherine had ridden away.

Could dragons talk to one another? Of course, they must be

able to. If Nyxaris could talk to a weak and foolish human like me, surely he must be able to speak to another dragon.

I knew Molindra was gone, but the details were hazy. I'd been unconscious when it had all happened. Through the pain, I felt a prick of recognition. I'd shut everyone out. I hadn't even asked. I'd only cared about what had happened to me.

The Veil.

My blood ran cold. The voice was neither mine nor Nyxaris's.

They seek to pierce the Veil, the voice whispered tremulously. So much pain in that voice. So much agony.

No. Nyxaris's voice was sharp.

I felt my body nearly sag in relief. If Nyxaris said it, it must be true. Therefore, whatever horrible thing this other voice was saying was false. Impossible.

No, he repeated, and I froze. *That's impossible. You will not allow it. Tell me you will not allow it, Molindra.*

I trembled, sensing the fear in his voice—the terrible horror.

Molindra's voice was gone. I could only hear Nyxaris now.

Nyxaris, I called, pushing weakly against his mind. *What is it? What's happening?*

A pause. *Something beyond your comprehension. Go back to your life of blissful ignorance, fledgling.* And then he was gone.

The words were contemptuous but no less than what I deserved. I felt weak and dizzy, but the pain was dissipating. My mother's arm was around my waist. Gently, she helped me to a sitting position. She touched my cheek, looked at me with the heartbreaking expression only a mother could have, and bit her lip.

"Florence . . ."

"I'm sorry for scaring you," I managed to get out, my voice raw. "I had . . . a headache."

"A headache?" She looked doubtful, then slowly shook her head. "Florence, please. Won't you tell me what's really happening?"

I stared at her, weighing the choice: Clearly it was mine to make. Medra and Rodriguez hadn't told her what saving me really meant.

"When Medra and Professor Rodriguez saved my life," I said carefully, "it came with . . . a catch."

Her eyes widened. "What kind of a catch?"

I studied her face. Did all children love their mothers this much? She had always been the very best of parents. Ever since my father died, it had always been the two of us. We were lucky. Our temperaments were very similar. We enjoyed the same things. Did I love those things because she taught me to, because I had seen her loving them? Or would I have loved them simply because I was me, and thus part of her?

Knowledge. Books. Wisdom. I weighed them, one by one. All worthy pursuits. Now I had access to a very special archive—for what greater treasure trove of knowledge could there be than a dragon? Nyxaris was a flying remnant of a vanished world. He must have been witness to countless historical events.

I stared into my mother's dark eyes, rimmed by wired spectacles so very like my own. If she could speak to Nyxaris, she would have asked him a thousand questions by now. She wouldn't have shied away from him as I had done. She wouldn't have hidden from her fate.

"A catch," I said slowly, "a catch to do with dragons."

When I was finished speaking, my mother's face was thoughtful.

"What are you thinking about?"

"I'm terrified for you, of course," she said without beating around the bush. "You're my daughter. And you're bound to the most powerful creature in existence."

I shivered. Yet part of me swelled with pride at hearing Nyxaris described in such a way.

"The world is changing, Florence," she went on. "The power balance is shifting."

"Shifting?" I repeated. "Shifting how?"

My mother looked around the room nervously—even though we were the only people in the little apartment. When she spoke, her voice was low. "All of us live to serve the highbloods."

"Of course," I agreed. "It's what we've always been taught."

"Only the most devout are accepted at Bloodwing, you know this. The most obedient. Those with the highest respect for Sangrathan tradition. I hoped you would rise within the constraints of being blightborn. I wanted you to succeed." She touched my cheek. "You've always had such a competitive spirit, Florence. I knew you'd need a place where you could shine. So I taught you as best I could. I *wanted* you to be accepted here, to follow in my footsteps." She bit her lip. "But sometimes I've worried that was a grave mistake."

I stared at her, shocked. But then, who could teach a child anything other than obedience? To do so would be heresy. Treason. Worse. My mother had done the right thing, the only thing she could have.

"Outside of the school, compliance with the highblood way is less of a choice," she continued. "Very few people even realize the systems of control that keep the balance, Florence. Blightborn compliance isn't instinctive. It's compulsion."

The blood rushed to my head. "Compulsion? You mean . . . magic?" Enchantments. Compulsion magic. The implications were instantly clear. Woven through generations, all of us, bred and bound.

"You felt the tug lessening once you arrived here," my mother said gently. "You may not have understood what was happening, but I saw the changes in you, though they were subtle."

Like a weight on my shoulders lifting that I hadn't even known I'd been carrying. And most blightborn carried that burden all their lives—the weight of control.

"I've been speaking to some of the other blightborn faculty. There have been . . . whisperings for a while now. Ever since Medra brought back Nyxaris." She gave me a meaningful look. "Don't you feel it, too?"

"Feel what?"

She didn't answer. Not directly. "There is a very old saying: *The axe forgets. But the tree remembers.*"

I stared at her, uncomprehending—or not wishing to comprehend.

"The chains have bound us all for a very long time, Florence. Dragons *break* chains."

I swallowed hard. Is that what Nyxaris was, an axe? "You're speaking of rebellion."

"Perhaps. All I know is that something is coming. And you, you're going to be at the center of it, Florence. If you're bound to a dragon, you must be." She looked terrified but also hopeful.

It was that look of hope which got to me. "But I don't want to be," I blurted. "I didn't choose this. I certainly don't want to start any kind of rebellion."

My mother's face was sad but stoic. "Don't you?"

"You think I do?"

Her hand found mine and squeezed. "Perhaps you should discuss it with Nyxaris."

I felt numb. The pain from my last encounter with dragons had hardly worn off. I couldn't do this. I wasn't Medra. I wasn't brave.

And yet . . . far off, in the back of my mind, I felt a tug. The pull towards Nyxaris.

My dragon. Watching. Waiting. *A great price*, Nyxaris had said.

Just what exactly was the Veil? And what had Nyxaris paid to keep it shut?

CHAPTER 11

MEDRA

I lay on my bed, staring at the ceiling. I knew I should be studying. But instead here I was, not sleeping. Just . . . lying there. Doing absolutely nothing useful. Nothing but thinking the same thoughts over and over.

The bed beside me was still empty. Florence was . . . well, who knew where she was? Maybe she was out flying on Nyxaris.

I felt a pang of envy as I imagined Florence on Nyxaris's back, speaking to him as the wind blew through her hair. The loss hurt a little. Still, I hoped that was what she was doing—I really, truly did. I hoped she'd accepted the bond and let Nyxaris in. But that didn't mean I didn't mourn any less the absence of what I'd started to forge with Nyxaris. It could have been me—was supposed to be me—out there, riding Nyxaris, training him, learning from him. Now I was a dragonless rider. If Regan and the others knew the truth, how gleeful they would be.

I turned over on my side, wrapping my arms around myself. It was past midnight. If I wasn't going to study, I should try to sleep.

It was at times like these that I missed Orcades the most. One touch of the dagger and we'd have been deep in conversation. If I hadn't used that dagger to stab Molindra, would my mother still be here now, with me? But if I hadn't stabbed Molindra, would any of us be here at all?

I groaned. Why did my brain insist on replaying the worst memories and asking questions that had no real answers? I couldn't change the past even if I wanted to. I'd done what I'd done: It was final. There was no going back. That was just life.

There was a knock at the door, and I nearly leaped out of my skin. "Who is it?" I called.

When no one replied, I guessed the answer. One moment, my heart was in my throat.

The next, I was leaping off the bed and running to the door.

"Florence," I exclaimed as I yanked it open. A wave of sadness hit me like a blow. "Oh."

Blake watched my face fall. He grimaced but didn't seem terribly offended. "Sorry to disappoint."

I gazed up at him. "Not a disappointment. Just a surprise."

He grinned, resting his forearms on either side of the doorframe and leaning in. He wore a black button-up shirt tucked into a pair of black fitted trousers. A gold chain mimicking dragon scales hung around his neck. He looked handsome and very put-together. In contrast, I'd literally just crawled out of bed. I resisted the urge to touch a hand to my hair; I already knew my curls were wild and out of control.

"So? You going to let me in?" He tapped his foot with mock impatience. He looked tired but was evidently in a good mood.

I peered past him into the hall, which was thankfully quiet and empty. "How can you be here? I thought you said—"

"I know what I said," he interrupted. "To hell with the rules, Pendragon. I wanted to see you." His eyes burned into mine. "Fine. Not just *wanted*. *Needed*."

My throat felt dry. It wasn't fair how easily he did that. Made me breathless with even the hint of his want, turning my body boneless with desire.

I tried to get a grip. "Um, sure, come in, I guess."

He raised an elegant eyebrow. "You guess? Your enthusiasm and graciousness are truly boundless."

"I'm ever so sorry," I said sarcastically. "Pardon me. I forgot I had the Black Prince himself on my doorstep." I made a flourishing gesture. "Do come this way, Lord Drakharrow."

Blake wrinkled his nose. "Please. Lord Drakharrow is my uncle."

"Unfortunately, yes."

He stepped inside and leaned down towards me. "The Black Prince will do nicely, however."

I snorted, suddenly remembering something my mother had once said. "Seriously? You want me to call you that?"

"'You want me to call you that, *Your Highness*?'" he corrected. He grinned wider as he saw my expression. "What? You don't think I'm princely, Pendragon? Should I have worn more gold tonight?"

"You're wearing too much as it is." The words slipped out before I could stop them.

He laughed as I flushed red. "Oh ho! The truth comes out." He whistled and looked me up and down. "I could say the same about you. It'd be a lie, though."

I glanced down self-consciously at the silky black nightdress I'd worn to bed. It had thin straps, barely covered my legs to midthigh, and was cut low in the front and back. It was silly. Blake had seen me naked before, and yet suddenly I felt more exposed than ever. I crossed my arms over my chest, which only had the unfortunate effect of making my breasts rise up out of the bodice even more.

Blake looked thrilled. He glanced from my breasts to my neck and licked his lips, showing a glimpse of sharp white fangs.

"You just fed from me a few days ago," I pointed out.

"Yes, but with you, I'm always a starving man, Pendragon. My thirst is unquenchable."

It was shameless flirtation. And it was working.

He stepped closer, reaching out a finger and running it over one silky shoulder strap. "I like this. It suits you. You should wear things like this more often."

"Ah, yes, perhaps I'll wear it down to the Avari common room tomorrow morning," I quipped. Blake's eyes narrowed at the mention of House Avari, and for once it was my turn to smirk. "What, you don't think Kage would appreciate the style?" I ran my hands slowly down the shimmering fabric that hugged my hips.

Blake growled low in his throat. "Mention his name again and I might have to remind you who you belong to."

I tried to quell a shiver. Since when had Blake's overly possessive tendencies stopped being infuriating and become a turn-on? On second thought, did I really want the answer to that question?

I lifted my chin defiantly, the words on the tip of my tongue. Usually I'd say something like *I don't belong to anyone. Certainly not you, Blake Drakharrow.* But . . . something had shifted. Still, I decided I'd play the game.

"Last I checked, little *princeling*, I didn't belong to anyone—no matter what some self-deluded highbloods might believe. Certainly not to you, House Leader."

He stepped closer, his chest inches from mine, radiating heat. "No?" His lips quirked. "And yet your body believes it does."

Arrogant bastard. I should have slammed the door in his smug, stupidly gorgeous face. Instead, I decided to torture him right back. I let my fingers trail slowly up the front of my nightdress, deliberately teasing. His gray eye locked on mine, nostrils flaring—reminding me of a hungry animal.

"You're awfully confident," I said smoothly. "For someone standing in enemy territory."

"Enemy?" He laughed, his voice low and sinful. "Kage is a rival, if that. And you—are we enemies, Pendragon? Is that what we are, even while I stand here, in your bedroom? I don't see you trying to throw me out."

I shrugged. "Fuck if I know what we are, Blake. You did make a career out of tormenting me last year."

He smiled—slow and wicked. "You say that like you didn't enjoy it."

I flushed, hating that he wasn't entirely wrong. Rage, fascination, desire—they'd all been twisted and tangled together from the very beginning when it came to Blake Drakharrow and me.

"Is that why you're here, to torment me some more?"

"Maybe I'm here to collect a debt," he murmured, brushing his knuckles down the delicate skin of my arm. "Maybe you still owe me . . . for all those little sins you committed."

"Sins?" My voice had a telltale hitch to it. "I beg your pardon?" Immediately, I regretted using the word *beg* around Blake.

"Every time you defied me," he said, leaning in, his mouth a hairbreadth from my ear. "Every time you fought back. Every time you looked at me like you hated me—but wanted me anyway."

I shivered. Damn him. Damn him and that wicked, teasing mouth.

He pulled back just enough to meet my eyes. "Maybe it's time to pay up, Pendragon."

"And what, exactly, do you think I owe you, my prince?" I tried to keep my voice cold but feared I was failing. Worried he could hear the ragged need there, just below the surface. We were playing a game again, just like the other day when I'd pulled him into that classroom. But this time he was clearly enjoying being the one in control.

Blake's hand came up and brushed the strap of my nightdress off one shoulder. It slid down my arm in a whisper of silk. "Everything," he said simply.

Before I could retort, his hands were on my waist, lifting me easily, spinning me around and pressing me against the bedroom door. His body caged mine in, all muscle and heat. For a second, we just breathed each other in. His breath was hot on my throat. My chest brushed his own with every rise and fall.

"Say it," he demanded.

"Say what?" I whispered.

"That you want this." His voice was ragged, almost pleading. "That you want *me*."

I swallowed. He was still the boy who had tried to break me. The one who'd sneered at me in the halls. Who'd told me my blood wasn't good enough to mingle with his own. The one who'd pinned me down in the training yard, whispered threats in my ear.

But he was also the man who'd given his blood to save me. Who'd betrayed his house for me, gone up against Viktor for me. Who looked at me as if I was the only thing in the entire world and could tame whatever dark shadows tormented him.

And—gods help me—I wanted to. Wanted *him*.

"I want you," I breathed.

The growl that rumbled out of him was dragonlike, making my knees weak. His hand came up, tracing the slope of my neck, brushing over my bare shoulder, featherlight. His fingers were warm. His fangs flashed when he smiled down.

"You're mine, Pendragon," he murmured. "Always have been. Even when you hated me."

"Who said I still don't?" My voice was a whisper against the heat of his mouth.

He chuckled. "That's the spirit, little dragon. Keep fighting me every step of the way. It only makes it taste all the sweeter when you finally surrender."

"You so sure I'm going to?" I said, breathless now, the way my body was beginning to ignite becoming impossible to ignore.

He tilted his head, lips barely brushing mine. "You already have."

I closed my eyes, barely able to think straight, trying to grasp on to whatever sliver of sense I had left.

"I'll admit it," I said slowly. "I'll admit I'm yours." I didn't dare open my eyes. But I could hear Blake's breath catch—just slightly. I let the pause stretch, made him wait for it. "If," I continued, "you'll admit you're mine."

I felt him go very still. I opened my eyes. Blake's gaze drilled into mine, not moving, not blinking.

Then, slowly, he smiled. A guileless smile that had no malice, no cruelty, only certainty. "All you ever had to do," he said as my heart flew to my throat, "was ask." Blake leaned down, his hands flat on the door behind me, imprisoning me. His mouth brushed my ear. "I'm yours, Pendragon. Every brutal, broken piece. If you want me."

I couldn't speak. Couldn't move.

"And you're mine, here, now, forever," he whispered, brushing his fangs lightly along my throat. Teasing me. Promising me.

His hand gripped my thigh, yanking it up against his waist, pinning me even tighter against the door. I could feel his body, hot and hard against me, even through the trousers he still wore.

I shivered. "Prove it," I whispered.

The bite wasn't gentle. It was a claim. Merciless and possessive. I gasped, gripping the front of his shirt, yanking him closer against me as his fangs anchored his mouth to my skin. The pain was sharp for an instant, then melted into pleasure. Pure need. Blake moaned against my neck as he drank, and the sound went straight to my core. When he finally lifted his head, my blood slick on his lips, I stared at him with nothing but longing, dazed from his fangs, drunk on the intimacy of what we were doing.

"You're playing with fire, Black Prince," I warned him. But my voice was unsteady.

His eye gleamed. "Fire's the only thing that can forge something worth keeping—though, you're already priceless to me, Pendragon."

He was on me before I could form an answer, lifting me off the floor, carrying me to the bed. I didn't resist. I couldn't. He laid me down, following me onto the mattress, bracing his weight on his elbows so he didn't crush me.

"You're mine," he repeated, snarling against my mouth as he kissed me, fangs grazing my lips, my chin, the line of my throat. "Say it."

I gasped as he raked a hand up my thigh, bunching the silk fabric of my nightdress at my hips. "You're mine," I shot back.

He laughed in delight, then caught my lower lip between his teeth. "You're damned right I am, Pendragon." He shifted, sliding the nightdress higher, tracing the inside of my thigh with practiced fingers. "Say it again."

I arched up into him, gasping. "You're mine."

He growled, and the sound vibrated through my whole body, reminding me of Nyxaris. "Say it like you mean it, little dragon."

My hands shot up, grabbing his hair, dragging him down closer until there was no space left between us. My mouth crashed onto his, desperate and hungry. "You're mine, Blake Drakharrow," I breathed against his lips. "And may all the gods of your world and mine help you if you ever try to forget it."

His laugh rumbled against my skin. "I wouldn't dare. Not in this life. Nor in the next."

I froze at the words, trying not to think about them too closely. And then he was kissing me back, as if tattooing me with his lips, branding himself into my blood, my bones, my every breath. I clawed at his shirt, yanking it up, feeling the ripple of muscle underneath, the heat of his skin. Blake tore it off, tossing it aside carelessly. His fangs grazed my throat again, teasing, promising. I gasped, raking my nails down his chest, feeling the way his muscles tensed under my touch. His mouth crashed into mine again, but I pushed him back, hands against his chest, surprising him. He let me move him, pressing him down until he was seated at the edge of the bed. Sliding off Blake, I stood in front of him, watching his face as I slid the other thin strap of my nightdress from my shoulder. The fabric slid down my body, pooling around my feet.

Blake's eye darkened, his jaw tightening with barely contained restraint. "Pendragon," he warned, his voice gritty and raw.

But I was done with warnings. Done with games. The same feeling of being about to explode—the reckless desire to throw caution to the wind and burn everything down that had led me to drag Blake into an empty classroom the other day—was upon me again, urging me on, encouraging me to trade rationality for rebellion. I wondered if Blake could feel it, too, that sense of snapped restraint.

I knelt before him. His breath hissed out from between his teeth.

"My Black Prince," I murmured, sliding my hands along his thighs. They were taut, lean, muscular, like every part of him. I reached for the front of his trousers, unfastening them slowly, savoring the sight of him struggling for control. He lifted his hips to help me, and I tugged the fabric down, freeing him. He was hard and beautiful and mine. All mine. I wrapped my fingers around him, and a low, guttural groan slipped from his throat. Slowly, I leaned in, pressing a kiss to the flushed tip of his cock, tasting the bead of arousal there.

Blake's hands clenched the sheets at his sides, knuckles white. "Pendragon," he rasped, "you don't have to . . ."

But I wanted to. Gods, how desperately I wanted to.

I ran my tongue along the length of him, savoring the way he shuddered, the way his body trembled. He was barely holding onto restraint. Then, without mercy, I took him into my mouth. Blake's breath left him in a ragged gasp. One of his hands shot out, burying itself in my hair. I moved slowly at first, hollowing out my cheeks, sliding my mouth down his length, feeling the tension getting higher and higher.

Blake's head fell backwards. "Fuck. You're going to kill me, Pendragon," he breathed.

I smothered a smile. *Good.* Let him suffer. Let him burn the way he always made me burn.

I dragged my mouth around him, swirling my tongue, then sliding back down. His hips jerked, fingers tightening in my hair. I drank in every broken sound he made, every strangled groan. Blake was losing it . . . and I loved every second of it.

"Pendragon," he hissed, his voice wrecked and shaking. "I'm not going to last if you keep—oh, fuck." His hand froze in my hair, but I didn't stop. His free hand gripped the bed behind him, entire body taught, trembling. The muscles of his thighs quivered with the effort of holding himself back.

I felt it when he started to come undone. The low groan he made. The way his hips arched. His desperate hand clenching in my hair. He came with a hoarse cry, body shuddering, hips jerking. I swallowed every drop, drinking him in like he drank my blood, like a starving woman.

When he finally opened his eye and looked down at me, the expression on his face made my breath catch. Pure. Reverent. I stopped myself before I could think too much about what that expression meant. Instead, I wiped the corner of my mouth with the back of my hand and rose to my feet slowly. Blake caught my wrist and pulled me into his lap in one swift motion, strong arms wrapping around me, holding me tight. It felt . . . good. It felt . . . right.

I leaned against him. He pressed his forehead against mine, still breathing hard. "Fuck, Pendragon. That was . . ."

I smiled, brushing his damp silver hair from his forehead. "Good," I murmured.

"*Good* doesn't begin to describe what that was." Blake had me by the waist and flipped me back onto the bed before I could even try to stop him—not that I would have. He reared back for a moment, looking down at me, his very gaze a flame. "Do you even know how perfect you are?" he said, his voice low, worshipful.

I squirmed at the compliment, reaching up for him. "Get back here, Black Prince," I whispered.

He laughed, then his face sobered. "I mean it, Pendragon. There is nothing about you that is not perfect to me. Inside and out. Nothing you do could ever make me run, make me look away."

I thought of the way he'd seen me pummeling the shit out of Larissa and winced.

He touched my cheek. "No," he whispered, as if he were reading my thoughts. "Not even that. Let me see all of you, even your darkness. Let me be the one who will never, ever look away. I treasure you, all of you. The darkness and the light." He chuckled. "Maybe the darkness a little more."

But below the veil of laughter, his voice was sad in a way I disliked.

"Blake."

He'd already begun to move again. His mouth found mine, his hands roaming everywhere—over my breasts, down my sides, across the curves of my hips. His cock pressed against my thigh, hot, heavy, hard again. I moaned as he caught my wrists, pinning them over my head with one large hand, as his other traveled down my body. When his fingers brushed the slick heat between my legs, he grinned. "So wet for me," he murmured against my throat. "Something you've been dying to ask me for?"

I should have resisted. Should have snarled something mouthy back, but I couldn't. I only arched into his touch, aching for more.

"Say it," he demanded, voice low and edged. "Tell me what you want. Tell me who you belong to."

"I want you to fuck me," I gasped. "Please, Blake." I hesitated, gritting my teeth. Why was it so difficult to speak the truth? Maybe because I'd been running from it as hard as I could for so long. "I'm yours."

He made a sound, half snarl, half groan, and shifted, guiding himself against my entrance. I tensed, afraid and eager and desperate all at once. He leaned down, forehead pressed to mine, his hand still pinning my wrists, his other guiding himself inside. I gasped. Stretched. The feeling brutal but delicious. He didn't move right away, he let me adjust, let the connection and the sudden overwhelming intimacy of him inside me settle between us. Then, slowly, he pulled back and thrust forward. I screamed aloud. Blake swallowed the sound with his mouth, kissing me hard, suffocating the scream. His hips slammed into mine, punishing, possessive. I writhed beneath him, panting and gasping his name like an unholy prayer.

All the while, he was murmuring against my skin, "Mine. You're mine, little dragon. All mine." He freed my wrists suddenly. His hands slid down to grip my hips, hauling me up to meet every one of his thrusts. He was being rougher than he'd ever been. Reckless.

It was perfect.

I clung to him, nails digging into the black ink covering his shoulders as the heat built, pleasure coiling ever tighter in my core. "Blake," I gasped. "Please. Now."

His hand slipped between us, flingers finding my clit, stroking, pressing, demanding. "That's it, little dragon," he whispered. "Come for me. Let me completely possess you."

It took only a few more thrusts, a few more strokes, and I shattered. Pleasure ripped through me, wild and consuming, stronger than it had ever felt before. I cried out, clawing him, clinging to him, my body tightening and pulsing around him. Blake snarled, the sound fierce and bestial, then thrust twice more, burying himself deep and coming with a shuddering, heaving gasp.

He wrapped his arms around me slowly, careful not to crush me, as his body trembled with the aftershocks. Carefully, we lay down on our sides, legs still tangled together, bodies slick with sweat. My heart was still pounding. Blake buried his face in my neck, a gesture so achingly sweet it stunned me.

Then, in the quiet, he lifted his head and looked at me. "I'm yours, Pendragon," he said, his voice rough but strong. "You never even have to ask."

I stared back at him, chest aching. Not because I didn't believe him but because of how much I wanted to keep him, to believe that this was real. "Do you think Viktor had a fucking clue what he was really doing when he put the two of us together?"

Blake's face split into a grin. "Not a clue." He lay back, tossing an arm behind his head to prop himself up. "Oh, he knew he'd be pissing me off, sure. But this?" He shook his head. "No. He thought he knew me too well for . . .well, to ever think that . . ." He trailed off again.

I cocked an eyebrow. "What?"

Blake closed his eye. "I'm tired."

"You're not tired, you big liar," I said, laughing. I swatted him on the chest, watching admiringly as his muscles rippled as he flexed his arms over his head and faked a yawn. "Tell me what you were going to say."

He popped his eye open and studied the room around us. "It

must be strange, being in here, without her." He didn't need to say the name.

I nodded, letting him change the subject. "It is. I miss her."

"She'll be back," he said confidently. "I'm sure she'll be back soon. Florence Shen drop out of school? Never."

"You almost sound like you know her a little," I observed.

"Well, I do, a bit. I know she loves books. Adores libraries. Has good taste in friends. I mean, Neville likes her, so she's all right in my book." He grinned.

I groaned and propped myself up on my elbows. "Neville."

Blake looked at me with confusion. "What? He's a sweet little thing. I thought you liked him."

"I do like him," I said, gritting my teeth. "But he's a demonic imp who thinks he can go wherever he pleases and do whatever he wants. Case in point." I pointed accusingly at the fluffin who had just trotted out of the bathroom and was now sitting on his hind legs, licking his front paws while he watched us with undisguised curiosity. I yanked a blanket off the foot of the bed and threw it over us.

Blake snorted. "He's an animal, Pendragon. Get a grip."

"Well, I don't exactly have nice fluffy fur to cover me up like he does," I retorted. I glared down at the fluffin. "Just when exactly did you arrive, and what did you hear?"

The fluffin tilted his head. Then he swished his large red tail. His eyes widened as if to say *I just got here, I swear.*

I sniffed. "I don't believe you. You were probably sleeping in the bathroom all along."

Blake was still laughing. "He's a fluffin." He slid out of the bed and went over to Neville, crouching down beside him. Apparently completely comfortable in his nudity, Blake scratched the top of the fluffin's head. Neville's eyes rolled back in his head. Even from the bed, I could hear the little animal begin to purr in contentment.

"He adores you," I commented. "You and Florence."

"You're the one who saved him in the first place," Blake reminded me.

"Yes, but he has his favorites. I think he only sneaks in here to see if Florence has come back. But I'm sure he visits her, too, so I'm not sure why he bothers."

"He bothers because he likes you." Blake jumped back up and leaped onto the bed next to me, shaking the entire four-poster. I shrieked as my blanket slid off. Blake ran a hand soothingly over my shoulders, kneading and caressing the tension away. I closed my eyes and tried to relax.

"Florence being gone. And Nyxaris . . . It must be a lot to adjust to," he murmured. "I'm curious . . . Can you still hear him inside your head?"

Reluctantly, I shook my head. "Not anymore. For the first few days, I could still hear bits and pieces, like eavesdropping on a conversation in another room." I'd done my best to shut them out. I knew I wasn't supposed to be privy to Nyxaris's mind—not anymore. I sighed. "I was just getting used to the grumpy old bastard, too."

"To be able to sense a dragon, to speak to one mind to mind, to ride on one's back . . ." Blake was looking at me keenly. "It must be incredible."

"I suppose you'll have to talk to Florence about that," I said peevishly. "She'll soon be the expert."

"She'll talk to you about it herself," he said softly. "And think of all you'll be able to share. She'll need your help and advice. Not many people can say they've spoken to a dragon, let alone ridden one. She'll come back to you, Pendragon. You saved her life. She's smart enough to know that you were just trying to protect her. Give her time."

I nodded, trying to show more faith than I really felt.

"What about Rodriguez?" Blake asked. "Have you—"

"No," I said shortly. "He had the nerve to try to work another justification for what he'd done into one of his Historical Strategy lectures. Can you believe it?"

Blake tilted his head. "Can I believe that Rodriguez is still an arrogant prick after all that just happened? Why, yes. Yes, I can."

I sat up, wrapping the blanket around me like a shawl and leaving Blake naked.

He grinned. "Nothing for me?"

"You don't need it. You don't seem cold." It was true, his skin was warm and flushed. "Besides, you look good that way," I said primly. He stretched out more fully, giving me a better look. "The problem with Rodriguez," I said, determined not to be completely distracted again by Blake's beauty, "is thrallguard."

"Thrallguard?" Blake's eyes lit up. "Right. He was your tutor."

"After what Regan did the other morning . . ." I shook my head. "Seems like some practice might be a good idea right about now."

Blake cleared his throat. "You might not need as much practice as you think. And, uh, if you do, I could always be your instructor."

"What's that supposed to mean?"

"Visha said something recently that made me think. The way you were able to shut out Viktor when he tried to get into your head . . . That was impressive."

"And completely shocking," I said bluntly. "What did Visha say about it, exactly?"

"Pretty much just that. She doesn't think you should have been able to do it, not after just a few lessons with Rodriguez." He hedged. "She thinks something more is at play."

"Oh? What?"

"Me." Blake tried to look humble. "I mean, us."

I laughed. "What?"

"Our bond, Pendragon. You're gaining something from it, things you might not even realize."

"Because I'm letting you feed from me now?"

"Not just that, but yes. I also shared my blood with you."

"That was just once. It has to have worn off by now."

"Sure, but it might have had lasting effects on your own physiology."

I glared at him. "Nice of you to mention that might happen beforehand."

He shrugged. "Well, I didn't know. Not exactly. This . . . what we have, between us . . . it's not exactly a common kind of pairing."

"Right. Triads are the norm. Don't remind me." I thought of Regan suddenly, the former third in our trio—and highbloods didn't usually let blightborn into those exclusive mating arrangements.

"We won't be a triad," Blake said quietly. "At least, not unless that's something you want."

His eyes homed in on me, steady and questioning. I stared back in surprise as I understood his implication. There was only one possible third who I might have considered, and Blake probably knew that.

But Kage Tanaka had never outright expressed his interest in me—nor me in him. We'd danced but done no more than that. He was handsome, of course. Strong, yes. Also annoyingly enigmatic, secretive, and stubborn. And that was all right. I was starting to accept those things about him. Overall, we were better off friends. Our connection had never been anything close to what I felt when I was with Blake. I knew Kage felt a sense of responsibility towards me, a protectiveness, but what he probably didn't realize was that it went both ways. We were allies now, like it or not. Bound by blood, but in a very different way from what Blake and I shared.

I looked at Blake. One enigma was enough for me. Something in my heart twisted hard. More than enough.

"I want this," I said simply. "Let's take things one step at a time."

He nodded, but I caught the relief on his face. "As long as we're clear about one thing, Pendragon." He looked into my eyes. "I only want you."

I flushed and looked away. "You know, before I came to Sangratha, I never thought I'd live in a place more fucked-up than Camelot," I said, shamelessly changing the subject like I'd let him do earlier.

"What was Camelot like?" Blake asked, curiosity written all over his face. "Tell me about it."

I told him briefly about my life in the Rose Court. "I was the sole progeny of Pendrath's king and queen, but I wouldn't have been permitted to inherit the throne. When I . . . left . . . we'd been in a state of war, with my grandfather and his army encroaching on our kingdom. My aunt and uncle had gone to find him and finish things." Little had they known the role I'd wind up playing in that.

"And your mother? Your father?" Blake asked. "Where were they in all this?"

"My mother died in childbirth. She was fae." I touched a finger to one pointed ear. "She'd been a famous general once. She had a long life . . . before my arrival ended it."

"So you never knew her?" Blake shook his head. "I'm sorry."

I didn't bother to correct him, to tell him my mother and I wound up reconnecting after all, from beyond the grave. If I told him that truth, would he think I was mad? Or would he believe me without questioning it?

Suddenly the words were on the tip of my tongue, wanting to take the chance. Was Blake someone I wanted simply in my bed or someone I could tell my deepest secrets? But before I could speak, he'd changed topics again.

"And your father, he was the king of Camelot?"

"Was, yes," I said. "He was mortal, not fae. He died the night I was born, too."

"I'm sorry," Blake said again.

"I wouldn't be too sorry," I said flatly. "He spent his last night trying to find me so he could kill me. He sent his men out into the streets of Camelot, searching for any newborn babies because he had no idea where my mother might hide me. His soldiers were ordered to slaughter any infant they found. It was a massacre."

Blake's eyes were wide. "His people must have hated him."

"Apparently he had a little change of heart towards the end. After he found me. But that doesn't change the fact that he was a fucked-up bastard who would probably have killed my mother and me given half a chance."

"Bloodmaiden, Pendragon," Blake said slowly. "You're one-upping me here. I thought I had the most fucked-up family."

I snorted. "You? Your father was basically a Sangrathan folk hero, from the sounds of it. A vampire they called the Peacebringer? It sounds like a fairy tale. Nothing like the Sangratha I know."

"Sure, but it sounds like Viktor and your dad would have hit it off," Blake said with a twisted grin.

I shuddered. "You might have that right." I looked at him curiously. "What about your mother, Desdemona?"

Blake's jaw tightened, but he nodded. "Yes."

"She's alive . . . right? Do you ever see her?"

Blake looked across the room and out the window where snow was falling. "She's alive, yes. Or so we're told. When my father died, she decided to enter the Sanctum. Supposedly."

I raised a brow. "Supposedly?" From what I'd seen of the Sanctum, it seemed the absolute last place I'd want my mother. But I didn't say that.

"Viktor is our only source of information on her," he said tightly. "She disappeared one night. Viktor said she was in the Sanctum. She'd left a note, a messy one. She'd never been all that devout, but . . . I suppose things change. Especially when one is grieving."

"That's true," I said carefully. "But does being in the Sanctum mean she can't leave? Can't send messages to her children?"

"Oh, we've received messages," Blake said, his voice bitter. "All passed through Viktor, of course. Women who enter become priestesses. It's very exclusive, few are accepted. To become a priestess at the Sanctum is one of the greatest honors a devout highblood woman can attain. But usually they enter when they're a lot older or much younger."

"Not when they're still raising a family," I said softly.

Blake gave a tight nod.

"Do you think she's . . ." I bit my lip " . . . safe? Do you trust Viktor?"

Blake laughed harshly. "Not by a fucking long shot—and that's the problem. He can access her somehow. He can hurt her. Hell, he could kill her." He ran his hands through his hair, hunching over. "Sometimes," he said and shook his head, "sometimes I wonder. For all I know, she's already dead." He looked over at me. "She was a halfborn, you know."

My eyes widened. "Half-blightborn, half-highblood? Like Professor Wispwood? Really?"

"I only found out recently. From Viktor. Well, he didn't tell me so much as I guessed."

"What does that mean—for her, for your family? Is it . . . shameful?"

Blake's lips thinned. "Shameful? Some would probably think so. But there's nothing shameful in being who you are. You're not a highblood, but I . . ."

I sucked in a breath as our eyes met.

"But I would never consider you less worthy than me," Blake finished awkwardly.

I gave a small smile. "Not so worried about polluting your bloodline anymore, huh?"

Blake grimaced. "Fuck. I was such a prick."

"Was?"

He smirked. "I can turn that side back on for you whenever you want, Pendragon."

I couldn't help myself: I visibly shivered.

Blake laughed. "You see? You like it. You like me when I'm bad."

"You're not bad," I said automatically. "Just . . . misunderstood."

Blake hooted. "Sure."

"Do you really think you're bad?" I asked curiously. "Last year, when I followed you into Veilmar, I saw you with Rodriguez. What were you really doing there?"

He scratched the back of his neck. "You saw me. I was feeding."

My face grew hot as I remembered watching him with the sellblood girl. "No, before that. That wasn't the only reason you'd gone into the city, was it?"

Slowly he shook his head.

"Just tell me this. Were you doing something good or bad in Veilmar, Blake?" I took a deep breath. "Because I have this theory."

He cocked an eyebrow. "A theory?"

I nodded. "Yes. A crazy little theory that you were there doing something good."

He waggled his eyebrows. "You know I'm as bad as they come, Pendragon."

I threw up my hands. "All right. Don't tell me."

"Fine," he said quickly. "You're right—kind of. Rodriguez and I . . ." He paused, looking sheepish. "We were passing out food and medicine in the slums. To blightborn families, children especially. Ones who had . . . lost someone."

"Lost someone to highbloods, that is?" I said bluntly.

He nodded. "Look, before my father made some sweeping changes, things were worse than they are now. You need to understand that."

"I'm shocked he was able to make any changes at all, honestly," I said.

Blake sighed. "So am I. He was . . . a very smart, very persuasive person. As was—is—my mother."

"They must have been an impressive pair," I said, studying him. "Though, I don't know how two people like that managed to produce someone like Marcus."

Blake grimaced. "He's the worst of our family. Viktor's true protégé."

"Your father saw something in highbloods. He was able to get them to make concessions, to treat blightborn more as people and less as prey," I said slowly. "But now look at things. Viktor's put Regan in charge of this entire school. She has highbloods roaming the halls, treating blightborn students like shit."

"Or worse," Blake said quietly. "There have been deaths already."

I paled. "Of course there have." I thought of Naveen. "Why kill us? Why not just make us thralls? What's it like to be a thrall, anyways?" With a chill I thought of something—something I'd never stopped to consider. "You feed from me, so why aren't I a thrall? Or am I?"

I sat all the way up and shoved myself across the bed.

"Pendragon, no. Stop. Wait." Blake's hands were up, but he wasn't trying to touch me. He looked tired again. "You're not a thrall."

"How am I not?" I demanded.

"Because I'm not fucking using thrallweave on you, am I?" he shot back. "Do you think I'm in your head, controlling you, telling you what to think? Telling you to—" He stopped.

That word again. We kept coming too close to that word.

Blake was breathing hard. "I wouldn't do that to you. I'm an asshole, sure. I'm evil, sure—"

"You're not evil," I interrupted. "Stop saying that. You went to pass out charity baskets to the poor, for fuck's sake. That doesn't exactly sound like the actions of a coldhearted person. I don't see many highbloods doing it."

"Some do," he said, stubbornly. "And it wasn't enough, not nearly enough. You don't know me, Pendragon. Not all of me. Viktor's shaped me, more than even I want to admit. If you knew . . ." He stopped.

I stared at him. "But I don't know. And you don't know all of me either. Clearly, there are things we don't want to tell one another."

He gave a terse nod. "Maybe."

I started to say something, but he interrupted me.

"I don't think you *can* be made a thrall, Pendragon." He sounded weary and a bit frightened. "And I think if Viktor figured that out, he'd kill you."

I stared at him. "What do you mean?"

"I mean, he doesn't know that you don't have Nyxaris anymore, does he? That Florence is the one bound to him now. But when he figures it out . . ." He shook his head. "Viktor likes to believe he can control you. He's been content to do that through me, in a way. I'm supposed to, well, have you under my control."

I bristled.

"I don't," he said quickly. "Obviously. Never have. But the illusion of it . . . the illusion of it needs to be real to Viktor."

"But once he finds out about Florence . . . " I said in horror, as reality dawned.

Blake's jaw tightened. "It's only a matter of time before he does. You can't protect her. You'll have to trust Nyxaris to do it."

"Blake," I said slowly, "we're always so focused on Viktor. But what do you think Marcus and Catherine are really trying to do? They have a fucking dragon. Them, not Viktor. We don't even know where they are."

Blake nodded grimly. "I know. I've thought about it, believe me. I'll say this, though. Marcus hasn't exactly been known for his genius. He's a thick-skulled, dim-witted asshole who usually can't see past what's right in front of him."

"A thick-skulled dimwit who's now bound to Lunaya Orphos," I pointed out. "And who has Catherine Mortis in his corner somehow." I thought of something. "Are they . . . a triad?"

Blake's eyes widened. "I hope not. If they are, they're a pretty messed-up one. They're up to something bad, that's obvious. But with all that's going on right here, right now . . ."

I understood. I was suddenly obsessing over what was going to happen to Florence. And it was hard to worry about Marcus and Catherine when they'd flown off into the wide blue yonder.

"Maybe Molindra crashed into the sea and they all drowned."

Blake snorted. "That would be too good to be true. For everyone but poor Lunaya, I mean," he added hastily. "That girl . . ."

"That girl is fucked, Blake," I said bluntly. "That's what she is. I wish we could help her. But she's on her own."

He sighed. "You're probably right."

Abruptly, I leaned forward, putting my weight on my hands and sliding towards him. "I think it's interesting that you care."

He looked startled. It might also have had something to do with the fact that the blanket had slipped off me. "Care?"

"You care about what happens to Lunaya. You care about what happens to blightborn. You're not the monster you claim to be." I kissed him softly, my breasts brushing against his chest. There was a need building in me again, a need only he could satisfy. "You've stood up for what's right. You faced a dragon's wrath to save Florence. Give yourself a little credit."

He looked at me, face still serious, even as his hands moved to grasp my hips. "And what about you, Pendragon?"

"Me?"

"You can't tell me you're not the hero of this story. The dragon rider who appeared from another world."

I shifted a little, feeling awkward. "I dropped in, I didn't exactly plan to visit. And I didn't come here to save anyone."

"No?" Blake's voice was low. "But you have."

"There are things in this world that are worth saving," I said slowly. "But I'm not stupid enough to think I can save everyone. All I can do is try to help my friends."

"You brought me hope. You've given me something to live for," Blake said, softly tracing the lines of my shoulder blades.

I shivered, leaning into him, brushing my lips against his jaw. I didn't want to talk anymore. I wanted to feel and to forget.

Blake's arms came around me. He rolled us, guiding me onto my back as he lay over me. His mouth moved over mine, claiming me briefly. Then he moved it down my body. Trailing kisses over my throat, my breasts, my stomach, my hips . . . then lower. I breathed out, letting him take his time. Letting him make me forget the creeping darkness just outside the walls. The danger that was always threatening, always just beyond our reach.

When we finally came together again, we moved with a desperate urgency. Our hearts were bare in those moments, at least. No lies. No fear. Just him and me.

When it was over, I watched his chest rising and falling. I tried to let myself believe that this could last. That this feeling, this sense of happiness, might be real.

Blake slept on, his breathing even, his hand loosely tangled with mine. My mother's words came back to me. *Are you so very different? Are you not angry? Are you not lost?*

I was angry. Anger fueled me as it did Blake; we were similar in that way. I'd always be angry. But lost? Alone? It had been true once. Maybe it wasn't anymore, not with Blake beside me. I smiled, shifting, turning my head toward him.

But something wasn't right.

Blake was looking back at me. And yet . . . wasn't. His good eye was closed, relaxed as he slept. But his other, the ruined one—the one Viktor must have ripped away and left empty—it was open.

And it wasn't empty anymore.

It watched me unblinking. The globe wasn't the gray it should have been. It was red. Red as blood.

CHAPTER 12

REGAN

"Let's continue to the next point on the agenda. The list of revisions to the School Code of Conduct." I stood and faced the faculty seated at the long narrow table. "Let's begin with the dress code. A fairly straightforward point: All blightborn students will return to the standard First Year approved wardrobe. Blue and silver only, no house colors."

A murmur of confusion rippled through the room. I suppressed a sigh: It was almost as if they hadn't bothered to read the agenda in advance. Considering some of these professors had once chided me about failing to read their syllabi, I thought it was rather ironic.

I glanced around the room. It was full of dark polished wood furniture, much of which was covered with rather creepy little carvings of naked women that Headmaster Kim had added in his term. Professor Vane leaned forward, squinting to look over the agenda, and his hand wrapped around a carved blightborn woman's left breast. I bit my lip, repulsed. The carvings would have to go at once. I wouldn't even ask Viktor's approval. This was my suite of offices now, wasn't it?

Though, the truth was it was hard to believe I now ran the school and wasn't still a student myself. I saw Headmaster Kim every time I walked into his office. The ghost of him, scribbling with his quill on parchment or frowning up at me as I approached his desk.

At night, I saw him, too—more often than I'd ever dreamed I would. Saw his mouth slack, head jammed ruthlessly onto a blood-slicked spike, cheeks a mottled grey-blue with frost. Had he still been able to feel when Viktor had slammed his head down onto that spike? At what point precisely did nerves cease to feel?

Professor Rodriguez would probably know—not that I'd be asking.

I tapped my foot. "Highbloods, of course, will retain their traditional house colors. No changes there. Any questions?"

"For identification purposes," a familiar voice muttered from the far end of the table.

I gritted my teeth. "What was that?" Was it too much to hope that he'd shut up and let me continue? Apparently, yes.

Rodriguez slowly rose. "It says here that the blightborn uniform is being changed for identification purposes."

"Yes," I said, as brightly as I could. "That's correct. So much easier this way, and think of the money saved on clothing. Many of our blightborn students come from families of limited means. I'm sure their parents will be thrilled."

There were some titters of laughter from highblood faculty.

"What about the danger this dress code alteration places our blightborn students in?" Rodriguez demanded.

"Danger?" I laughed. "I hardly see a change of fashion as a *danger*, Professor."

More titters of laughter. I tried to relax. I'd been manipulating people my entire life. A group of underpaid, poorly dressed academics was no different. They weren't smarter than me, they just *thought* they were. I was the one with the real power. I could do this. Still, my entire body felt tight and tense.

"Visible markers of being blightborn," Rodriguez said flatly. "If you're going to brand them, why not come out and say so?"

"How ridiculous," I said, my smile still not dropping. "We'd never be so savage. They're not cattle, they're people. No one is questioning that. It's a simple change. Really, what got into your kava this morning, Professor Rodriguez?"

Some staff members laughed, but then came the sound of a second chair backing up.

"I beg your pardon, Headmistress," said a female professor. "But I have to admit, I see Professor Rodriguez's point. This makes blightborn students immediately visible and, as such, much easier targets."

"Targets for what, exactly?" I said coldly. "Professor Allenvale, isn't it?"

"Yes, Vasanti Allenvale, Headmistress. And as for targets of what, I'm afraid the answer to that is systemic harassment and discrimination." She paused, looking uncomfortable. "Or worse."

"Professor Allenvale, you're a visiting scholar, aren't you? You aren't from Bloodwing." I gave her a cool look. She wore a long dress in the typical purple and gold of House Orphos. She was pretty enough for a teacher. Dark-skinned with long braided hair, but she'd done something absolutely ludicrous with her hair. She'd *dyed* it—streaking it with green and purple.

"Yes, that's correct," she responded.

I eyed her up and down slowly, trying to raise her sense of unease. "That explains it, then. Obviously Bloodwing fashions must be very confusing to someone who looks the way you do."

I watched her stiffen, and my smile grew.

"I beg your pardon, Headmistress?"

I gestured to her hair and wrinkled my nose. "House Orphos has always set itself apart from the other houses. I'm not sure what's considered fashionable in the Sable Isles, Miss Allenvale—" I said, purposely dropping her title. I was being an evil, snooty little bitch and I knew it. Why? Because it was the easiest way to get someone's back up. And once I'd rattled this woman, she'd sit down, shut up, and no longer be a threat—to me or to herself. "And I don't care to know, but—"

"It's *Professor*, actually," she said, sounding annoyed.

"Of course. *Professor*. Well, this is how we do things at Bloodwing. You simply aren't in the Sable Isles anymore. House Orphos does not have a greater say at the table than any other house." I smiled sweetly, as I drank down my own cup of lies. Spoken like a true Drakharrow. Or nearly so.

I leaned forward and tapped my finger on the next part of the agenda. "Now, if we may move on?" I didn't wait for agreement. "Next point, curfew regulations. Blightborn students will be expected to return to their towers by nine o'clock sharp each night. Highblood students will retain their current privileges." I sped up, not bothering to wait for any questions. "Next, registration for sensitive school areas. The library and greenhouse, as well as any storage areas that contain potentially hazardous materials, will now require blightborn students to register and sign in before entry. For safety purposes, naturally." I glanced up briefly and saw Rodriguez beginning to open his mouth. But to my surprise, Professor Allenvale beat him to it. Apparently she had more of a backbone than I'd guessed.

"This is outrageous," the Orphos professor said, her voice trembling. "The greenhouse? Why on earth would students need to sign in at the greenhouse? It's a *classroom*."

"You teach about plants, don't you?" I said dismissively.

"I teach alchemy and herbology, yes," Allenvale replied, narrowing her eyes. "So what?"

"Well, some of those plants are poisonous, aren't they? We're trying to limit blightborn students' exposure." I smiled reassuringly. "For their own safety."

"You're treating them as if they're criminals," she exclaimed. "They've done nothing wrong."

"Of course they haven't. It's not punishment, Professor. It's merely precaution. We have a responsibility to those students' families." I clasped my hands in front of me and tried to look maternal. "We must keep them safe."

A snort rang out—Rodriguez, of course. I closed my eyes briefly. That man was going to be a constant thorn in my side.

"Safe? I don't recall anyone caring about blightborn safety when it came time for the Consort Games," Rodriguez said disdainfully. "The loss of life there was despicable. But there was no concern for blightborn students' families then. Let's be honest. This is just the beginning. Next you'll have them chained to the lecture tables. Escorted from their towers in groups."

"How ludicrous. There are no plans for any of those measures at this point in time," I said smoothly. "Now, next matter on the agenda. Some classes are being reassigned facilities." I looked down at my notes, trying to remember which classes were being moved. Some of the changes Viktor had demanded be implemented only this very morning. "Ah, yes. Basic Combat for Blightborn, Intermediate Combat for Blightborn—"

"Basically all of the combat classes for blightborn taught by Professor Stonefist," Rodriguez interrupted loudly. "She's right over there. Why not look at her when you're speaking to her?"

A muscular dwarven woman stood up, clasping her hands behind her back. "Pardon me, Headmistress, but I see you've moved the classes to the old gymnasiums. The walls there were thick with mold the last time I checked. And the ceilings leak and are cracking—"

"They're being renovated," I lied, flashing her a brittle smile. *Dear Bloodmaiden, did the woman have a beard?* "As we speak, improvements are being made."

"Improvements?" Stonefist muttered. "Those will take months of repair."

"Just a few small changes, and all should be fine," I insisted.

The sound of a throat clearing interrupted me. "Headmistress Pansera, if I may—"

I looked across the table where Professor Sebastian Sankara was leaning back in his chair. The tall dark-featured professor didn't bother to rise. I'd always thought him rather handsome. Now he looked at me with stark disapproval.

"*Headmistress Drakharrow*, if you please," I cut him off. "I've decided to take my archon's house name."

It was a very old tradition, one many modern highblood women eschewed. Well, I decided to bring it back. The Drakharrow name held immense power, and I needed every bit I could get my hands on if I were to keep this whole sinking ship afloat. My father had wanted me to wed a Drakharrow for as long as I could remember, but Blake was supposed to be my way into one of the most prestigious houses in Sangratha, not Viktor. Never in a million years did I dream I'd be the consort of the head of the family himself. It was a dream come true, I told myself. Not a nightmare. *Not* a nightmare.

"Very well. Headmistress Drakharrow, I must protest these changes," Sankara said, his expression somber. "The faculty of Bloodwing bear a responsibility to the safety of all students, blightborn ones included. Now, some things are tradition. But the changes you're proposing are starkly inequitable. There's no need to set blightborn students apart in this way."

"No need?" I said coldly. "Well, that's your perspective, Professor. And I must say, your loyalty to your own kind is admirable." There were some murmurs of agreement from our fellow highbloods. "My archon, Viktor Drakharrow, who I'm sure you're all very familiar with, saw a need."

"Was the Board of Directors consulted about all of these changes?" Sankara asked, furrowing his brow.

"Of course," I said, lying through my teeth. "We'd never make such sweeping changes without them."

"So you admit the changes are sweeping?" Professor Allenvale interjected, jumping on my slipup.

Fuck.

I glared at her. "That was the wrong word." I glanced at the clock on the wall. "In any case, I do so appreciate all of the wonderful feedback, but I'm afraid we're out of time. Classes will be starting soon, and we don't wish to keep students waiting, do we?

Any further questions or concerns may be submitted to me at any time—in writing."

Some chairs scraped back as faculty began to rise to their feet.

"Oh, yes—one last thing." Trying to sound casual, I gestured and my new secretary darted forward, handing out small square sheets of parchment, muscles rippling beneath his tight white button-up shirt emblazoned with the school motto, of course. I saw Rodriguez take note of the badge affixed to the secretary's uniform and frown at the symbol: a drop of blood being pierced by a sword.

Silvio Santos was the younger son of a well-off family. He'd graduated a few years ago and had been a wastrel ever since, squandering his father's fortune instead of doing something useful with his life: His father was only too happy to *donate* Silvio as one of my new Bloodguards. I'd added secretarial duties to his assignment, and he'd been happy to comply, seemingly content to lounge behind my waiting room desk every day looking pretty.

"One last memorandum for today. You can read it on your way out," I finished.

Rodriguez grabbed a sheet from Silvio. I tucked back a lock of hair and began to put my papers in the red leather briefcase I'd taken to carrying with me, but from out of the corner of my eye I saw Rodriguez skimming.

"What the fuck is this?"

A ball of paper bounced off my shoulder and landed at my feet. Silvio stepped forward, growling exactly like the protective guard dog he was supposed to be.

"What the fuck is this?" Rodriguez repeated, ignoring my secretary. He held up the sheet of paper and read aloud. *"Bloodwing's Blood Donation Incentive Program?* Have you gone absolutely mad, Regan?"

His voice had risen to a fever pitch, filling the small room. For a mere blightborn professor, he was oddly intimidating. I tried not to flinch. He might have been my instructor once, but now it was I who was in charge, not him. Rodriguez had to get used to it—

for his own safety if nothing else. He either listened to me now, or he'd soon be dealing with Viktor.

"It's very straightforward," I said, noticing how no one had left the room yet. They were all waiting to see how this played out. "Thralls, of course, are automatically enrolled in the program. They'll be receiving extra credit from now on for their loyal service: enhanced privileges, reduced curfew time, perhaps even some other incentives. The program details are still being worked out. We thought it would only be fair to extend similar rewards to all blightborn volunteers."

We being *me*. Viktor hadn't wanted to incentivize the program he created at all. He was sadly shortsighted at times.

Rodriguez's lips curled back. "Volunteers? You mean people being stopped in the hallways easily thanks to the color of their clothing and forced to give a so-called donation anytime a highblood student feels peckish?"

"The privilege extends to faculty, too," I said sweetly. Rodriguez's face froze. "And, of course, it's all voluntary. Don't you see the word right there on the parchment? *Vol-un-tary*."

Sankara spoke up, his face very hard now. "In theory, yes. But in practice?"

I shrugged. "School rules must be followed by everyone."

Rodriguez was practically vibrating with fury. "It's coercion."

"Thrallweave has always been permitted, Professor," I pointed out. "You do realize you live under highblood rule every day, do you not? We all worship the Bloodmaiden. We all follow the same precepts, don't we . . . ?" I let the words linger.

"Of course," Rodriguez snapped. "And the Bloodmaiden cares for all her children."

"Some more than others," I muttered under my breath. I started to move away from the desk, but Rodriguez wasn't finished yet.

"Did you even consult the House Leaders about these proposed changes beforehand?"

I took a deep breath, then wished I hadn't. I wrinkled my nose. When was the last time he'd properly washed and ironed his own clothes? He might have been a brilliant mind, but he dressed like a disgrace. "I didn't see the need."

Rodriguez gave a choked laugh. "You didn't see the need?"

"No," I said icily. "And they are not *proposed* changes, Professor Rodriguez. They are effective immediately." I pointed out into the hallway. "As soon as you step out into that hall. They apply to everyone. Students and faculty alike."

I watched his face pale. To my surprise, Sankara put a hand on his arm and looked down at Rodriguez reassuringly. *So, it was like that, was it? Interesting.* Viktor would appreciate knowing. The man was absolutely obsessed with eliminating what he saw as *unnatural liaisons*. But I didn't share his sentiments on the matter, and I didn't plan on passing on everything that transpired at my school to Viktor.

I glanced down at my hand quickly, then closed my palm. The mark where Kage had cut me had faded, but I could still *feel* it. The memory of his blood mingling with mine as it entered my body. The heat of it, the *power* of it. I should never have made that vow. I should have gone straight to Viktor. What I'd learned might have changed the entire balance of power between the two houses. But that was just it, wasn't it? Viktor had enough power already.

I pictured the wolf, throat torn out, lying bleeding in the snow. *No.* I'd made my choice. I was doing everything else Viktor asked of me. What more could he possibly want?

Everything, the voice in my head said softly.

The room was quiet. I licked my lips, sensing the tension. Good, let them be angry. Fear and anger would keep them all in line. It certainly worked on me. "This meeting is adjourned," I said abruptly, turning away from the horror on their faces before I could see my own fear reflected back there.

In the corridor outside of the boardroom, four members of my Bloodguard were waiting: all in prime physical condition, all alumni, all wearing their identifying blood-and-sword badges that marked them as loyal enforcers of my new regime. As I began to stride down the corridor, they flanked me, Bloodguard badges flashing, boots echoing alongside my pointed high heels as we crossed the stone floors.

I kept my chin up, my stride quick but steady. I should have felt powerful. Instead, I felt nauseated. As if something inside of me was rotting away.

Kim's decapitated head flashed behind my eyes again. Mouth gaping. Maggots crawling along his blackened lips. Eternally silent.

I pushed the image away, only to have it replaced by a new one. Dark, intense eyes staring into mine with the fierceness of a wolf.

I shoved that one away, too.

I had a school to run. I was doing this for everyone's good, whether they knew it or not. I thought of Persis, far from his family, helpless and afraid, and I steeled myself. There could be no room for regret. I was my brother's only way back home.

A soft scritch of claws made me glance to my left. My eyes widened: Blake's pet. I'd seen the tiny fluffin marching through the Drakharrow Tower last year, looking as if he owned the place. Much like Blake did, I thought sourly. Now the fluffin sat between two tall pillars, not yipping or scampering away but simply watching me. His wide golden eyes followed every step I took. I swallowed. No one else seemed to notice him sitting there, and yet I could swear the creature was looking right at me, judging me. That he could see straight through the silk and bravado, right to the rot beneath.

I missed a step, my heel clipping the stone. Tearing my gaze away, I faced forward. Behind me, I thought I heard the fluffin give a faint, reproachful chirp. The creature was far smaller and quieter than Rodriguez. Yet his outrage rang for much longer in my ears as I walked away.

CHAPTER 13

MEDRA

The halls of Bloodwing Academy had started to feel like home to me not long ago. Now they were simmering with something ugly. Anger radiated off blightborn students like heat from a stove, and it was easily attributed to the new programs our headmistress recently put in place. The extreme force of the Bloodguard had pressed in on the student body all at once, but no one quite knew how to fight back without facing extreme consequences.

I stood with my back against the wall, flipping through the pages of my essay for Professor Allenvale's alchemy class, while I waited for my Intermediate Combat class to begin. We'd been moved to an older part of the castle and were using a gymnasium that was in a sorry condition. I knew Professor Stonefist wasn't fond of the new space, but she'd managed not to complain too loudly in front of the class.

I'd decided I'd either imagined or dreamed Blake's red eye. Because when I woke up the next morning, he looked exactly the same as when we'd fallen asleep the night before: one eye perfect and gray, the other still wrecked but slowly healing.

The corridor was full of students arriving from their previous classes, most wearing blue and silver. A few highbloods strolled through, looking like they owned the place as usual. Most of us pretended not to notice them. A sound from across the hall caught my attention. I looked over to see a highblood boy leaning in close to a familiar-looking dwarven girl and swore under my breath. Dani had her head tilted up obediently, her body relaxed and pliant as he sank his fangs into her throat, drawing out her blood. The bliss on her face was unmistakable, which would have been fine if she'd managed to stay quiet. Unfortunately, she let out a loud, throaty whimper of pleasure that had more than a few heads turning.

I forced myself to look away, feeling uncomfortable. The scene had too many parallels to my own existence. But Blake didn't use thrallweave to coerce me, I reminded myself. No, I was a willing participant now. Being fed from . . . and being fucked. Was that any better? I felt a disturbing twinge of guilt. Usually, a feeding like that would have been done in a more private space, tucked away in an alcove or behind a closed door. Not because it was shameful but because highbloods had some sense of, well, discretion and tact. But apparently, not anymore. This was open. Blatant. Deliberately provocative.

The highblood boy—someone from House Mortis, from the look of his red and white attire—pulled away lazily from Dani, his mouth wet and gleaming red. He wiped the back of his hand over his lips carelessly, then tossed a smirk over where I stood with the rest of the blightborn students, and walked away.

I muttered a curse under my breath. What a fucking fool to leave his thrall there like that, if she even was his thrall. The last time I'd seen Dani, she'd been with a highblood named Brocklin. The enthralled girl stayed where she was, eyes half-closed, swaying slightly, clearly still caught in the haze of thrallweave and the highblood's bite. At first, I thought it was over. That the crowd of students around me would just ignore her. Maybe they would have, if Professor Stonefist hadn't been late that day.

The buzz of chatter in the hall started to shift. A group of blightborn boys—four or five of them—broke off from the rest of the crowd of waiting students and moved over to Dani. Their faces were tight, angry. I recognized one of them, a tall burly boy I'd encountered a few months back. He was from House Avari. Kage had told him off once for harassing me. I was pretty sure his name was Lochlan.

Now he sneered down at Dani. "Slut," he spat.

The crude comment stopped me in my tracks.

The other boys began to close in. "Highblood whore," one hissed.

"Disgusting," muttered a third. "You're throwing yourself at them. For what? A moment of their attention."

A blightborn girl marched up. I recognized her long braided hair from a previous encounter. "She's not even dressed right." She yanked at Dani's dress. "Look at her—House Mortis colors."

My heart sank: She was right. Dani's dress was red and white. A silver cloak had covered it so I hadn't noticed at first. Now the dress was like waving a flag in front of a herd of rampaging bulls. A symbol of favor.

Before I could even think to react, the girl with braids drew back her arm and slapped Dani full in the face. "That's what you get, whore," she hissed, then followed the slap up by spitting full in Dani's face.

I watched the dwarven girl blink rapidly, horror dawning as she finally realized what was going on. The boys around her laughed and jeered, quickly following up with mouthfuls of spit of their own.

I'd had enough. Dani had been through enough.

Disgusted, I pushed through the circle of students that had formed around Dani and her tormentors. As I made my way to the front, I heard the sound of fabric ripping and saw Lochlan holding up a piece of red triumphantly. Behind him Dani was sobbing and clutching at the bodice of her dress.

"Hey!" I snapped, feeling a ridiculous sense of déjà vu. I shoved through the last of the crowd and snapped my fingers, loudly. "Hey! That's enough."

The girl with braids looked at me. "Look, Drakharrow's pet is here, Lochlan." She sneered at me. "Going to defend this one? That makes sense, you're no different. Part of a special highblood sluts' club, aren't you?"

I could feel my blood boiling. "That's enough. Back off. You have no idea what this girl has already been through, believe me."

Lochlan stepped forward. He was taller than me, brawnier. But if I had to, I knew I could take him. I tensed my body.

"What? You think you're better than us because Drakharrow feeds from you?"

I decided not to point out that this was exactly what the Sanctum taught, what every blightborn had been brought up to believe. The only reason these two felt so feisty right now was because the compulsion magic woven through this world was faltering. Funny how I'd originally thought that would be a wonderful thing.

"So do many other blightborn. And they do so willingly." I tried to lower my voice. "This is different. Dani wasn't willing. I understand why you're so upset, but you need to leave her alone."

"Not willing?" one of the boys behind Lochlan hollered. "She looked pretty fucking willing to me. Let's take her back to the First Year tower and see how willing she is with us, hey, Lochlan?"

To his credit, Lochlan looked a little repulsed by that proposition. But he didn't back off.

"Your friends are mostly First Years, aren't they?" I said to him quietly. "You're going to get them all expelled, Lochlan. Or worse. You're interfering with a highblood thrall." Immediately I knew I'd said the wrong thing.

Lochlan's eyes blazed. "Fuck that. They act like they own us. Own our women."

"*Your* women?" My hackles rose. "We're not your women, you prick. She should be able to make her own choices. But that's just the point, she didn't get to make one. You know how hard it is to say no to a highblood," I pointed out. "So please. Just leave her the fuck alone."

"You're not one of us." The girl with braids pushed in between Lochlan and me, her voice raised. "You let one feed from you, too. You're no better than her."

I stood my ground, heart pounding—not from fear but from

rage and frustration. "Look, it's not about that. It's about consent. It's none of your fucking business what I do or what Dani does—as long as we're all right with it. But what that highblood just did to her? He did it with thrallweave. You and I both know that. She doesn't deserve to be attacked just for being manipulated." I raised my voice so the students around us could hear me. "Because we all know the same thing could happen to you or to me."

The girl blanched a little but her lips were still set in a stubborn expression. "Fuck that. It's not happening to me."

I rolled my eyes. "Fine, then I won't bother talking to you. If you want to be naïve about things, go right ahead." I turned to face the students behind me. "But the rest of you—you think tearing each other apart like this is going to help anything? Change anything? You think it's going to stop *them* from doing what they want to us? This isn't the way."

Some students looked away, suddenly uncertain. Others moved off to the side, clearly deciding they weren't going to get involved.

A tall skinny girl wearing a blue dress stepped forward. "Easy for you to say. You belong to a House Leader."

"I'm not Blake's property, and I assure you he'd say the same thing," I said firmly. The way Blake and I talked to one another when we were alone? Absolutely none of their fucking business. "I am my own person. Otherwise, would I really be speaking to you all like this?"

She ignored me. "You've got a dragon! That's real power. If you really hate the highbloods so much, why not use it? Why don't you stand up for us?"

My heart sank; I should have known it would come down to that. It was, of course, an excellent question. And with the way things had been going at Bloodwing, I was reaching the end of my rope. If Nyxaris had truly been mine, I might have been reaching out to him—begging him to intervene. But he was not mine. He was Florence's.

A chorus of murmurs followed the girl's questions. Obviously many agreed with her.

The weight of responsibility that those murmurs placed upon me was heavier than anything I could have imagined. Even without Nyxaris, I was burdened by their expectations. I wasn't even from this world, and yet I felt a horrible awareness of letting them down.

Another student shoved forward. "Forget the damn dragon, Isha. There are bigger things happening than our little problems at school. Haven't you heard the rumors? There's a plague. A highblood plague. And it's spreading."

The girl he'd called Isha scoffed. "Rumors? Lies, more like. Highbloods don't get sick."

"No one is sick in Veilmar," someone protested. "We'd have heard if there was a plague."

"That rumor came from a little town thousands of miles away, Alain," another called.

Alain set his jaw. "So what? Doesn't mean it can't still be true. A thousand miles, a hundred. Plagues spread, you idiots."

"We're talking about dragons not plagues." Isha's eyes were back on me. "This girl has power no highblood could dream of possessing, and she's done absolutely nothing with it to help us."

I decided not to point out that highbloods absolutely could dare to dream. "Dragons have minds of their own. Nyxaris isn't a weapon to be controlled. But I assure you, he's not fond of the way highbloods rule Sangratha either." I glanced behind me at where Dani cowered against the wall, still holding her ripped dress. "Regardless of what Nyxaris chooses to do or not do, this isn't the way, Isha. Hurting this girl won't fix anything. She's already been hurt enough. We have to stand together, help one another. If we don't—"

Lochlan gave me a shove as he came to stand beside Isha, crossing his arms over his broad chest. I took a step back towards Dani, pulse racing. If they attacked, if I fought back . . .

"Call him," Lochlan demanded. "Prove you're one of us. Otherwise, shut up and get out of here."

Where the hell was Professor Stonefist? A few words from her and these idiots would scatter. Then I had a terrible thought: Maybe

Regan had gotten rid of her. Was that going to be the next step, eliminating all of the blightborn faculty? I wouldn't put it past our new headmistress.

A beefy hand shoved my shoulder—Lochlan again. I let out a gasp as I stumbled and nearly went sprawling backwards.

"Keep your hands off me," I snapped. "And keep them off this girl. I'm taking Dani back to her room now. If you know what's good for you, you'll stay the hell out of my way."

"Or what?" Isha challenged. "You'll sic your dragon on us? You've basically already said you can't. He doesn't listen to you."

A tremulous high-pitched voice rang out through the hall. "No, but he'll listen to me. Leave Medra alone!"

The mob of students slowly parted. A girl stepped forward slowly, outfitted in a knee-length dress of royal blue, her black hair pulled into a long black ponytail. Her cheeks were flushed with emotion. Her glasses had slid slightly down the bridge of her nose. I could tell she was nervous because she didn't bother to push them back up. Her shoulders were squared like someone about to step onto a battlefield.

In that moment, I knew I'd made the right choice to save her, no matter what the price—not that I'd ever doubted it.

Florence was a bookish, quiet girl, far too kind and reserved to ever intentionally *choose* to be a dragon rider—and yet, there was fire in her blood. Once she realized it, gods help the ones she wielded it against.

Still, I knew *this* wasn't the time. I stepped forward, knowing what I had to do.

CHAPTER 14

FLORENCE

"Florence, stop," Medra called. "Stop and leave now."

The tall boy near her turned, face red with rage, his fist already swinging.

"Medra!" I screamed. But I needn't have worried. She already had it under control.

Medra moved—quickly dodging, then darting forward, landing her own fist hard in his chest and following it up with a brutal kick first to one knee, then his other. He sank to the floor with an *Oomph*, looking dazed, and Medra stepped past him, coming towards me.

She positioned herself between Lochlan and me. "Florence, don't say another word," she shot over her shoulder. "I know what you're trying to do, but please. Don't."

"What's she talking about?" The girl with long dark braids came up behind Medra, looking angry. "What do you mean the dragon will listen to you? Why would he listen to you but not the rider?"

I opened my mouth. Medra's eyes were pleading. But if I didn't speak up, what would they do to her?

Some of the students moved in closer, eager to hear what we were saying. A shoulder bumped into mine, deliberately rough. I gasped, suddenly aware of how many people were watching me. I felt hot, claustrophobic.

What is happening? Where are you? Why is your heart beating so fast?

I just about jumped out of my skin.

"Nyxaris," I squeaked.

"Florence," Medra warned. "No."

Your heart should not be beating so quickly. Not in a greenhouse. Precisely what is it you do in this class? Botany should not be this exhilarating.

"Nyxaris?" Isha repeated.

"What?" I asked stupidly.

She leaned forward. "What are you hiding? What aren't you telling us?"

Part of me wanted to tell Nyxaris that botany could actually be quite exhilarating. And part of me was all too aware of everyone staring at me. My mind raced, thoughts all a jumble. It might have been funny—if Lochlan hadn't suddenly rushed at us again. His arms locked around Medra's neck, hauling her off her feet and choking her.

"Medra!" I cried.

Horrified, I watched as she clawed at his arms, struggling to break free. But he was so much bigger than she was. Stronger. His thick forearm was locked so tightly around her throat. Medra's face turned red, her boots scraping against the floor as she fought him, kicking at his ankles, stomping on his feet.

I couldn't help it. I screamed.

I must insist you clarify the nature of this class immediately, fledgling. Nyxaris's voice was commanding, insistent.

But there was no time to talk. "Let go of her!" I shouted.

Medra tried to shove her hand between the vise of the boy's arm and her throat. I could see her gasping, choking, and there was absolutely nothing I could do. I'd made things worse. So much worse.

Lochlan grinned at me and squeezed tighter, the muscles of his forearm bulging against Medra's windpipe. I'd never hated anyone so much.

The girl, Isha, leaned in, her eyes triumphant. "Florence, isn't it? You're in Avari, right? Tell us what you were going to say, Florence, or Lochlan here is going to hurt your friend." She glanced at the boy and nodded. "Tell us or he finishes her here and now."

Medra's eyes were on me. I could feel her silent plea. I knew she didn't want to hurt the boy, but he was hurting her.

If I said nothing, she might die. Medra had saved my life. I wasn't going to let that happen. Lochlan's grip seemed to tighten.

"No!" I screamed. "Stop! Nyxaris is mine. He—" The words left my mouth just as Medra exploded.

There was no other word for it. It was like something had been building in her and suddenly she snapped. With a feral snarl, she twisted her body, angling her elbow up and smashing it into Lochlan's ribs. Hard. I heard the cracking of bones and gasped. Lochlan stumbled backwards, his grip loosening. Medra wasn't through yet. She pulled her head back as far as she could go, then drove it backwards, hitting his nose with a brutal blow. Blood sprayed. Lochlan let out a howl, and his grip faltered. And then my friend moved faster than I'd ever seen her move. She pulled out of his grip, dropping back down to the floor, grabbing Lochlan's wrist as she went and twisting it with her full weight, slamming him down. Medra staggered back, coughing and gasping—as if the impact of what Lochlan had done was finally taking effect. But the boy on the ground wasn't finished. He pushed himself up, violence flashing in his eyes. His mouth twisted savagely as he yanked a knife from his belt.

Medra was breathing hard, but she'd stepped back. I could tell she didn't want to hurt him. She just wanted him to *stop*. But he wasn't going to stop. This was going to end badly.

Tell me where you are. You are not at the greenhouse. Nyxaris's voice was urgent.

Isha was suddenly moving to join Lochlan, fists clenched, teeth bared. There was no time to do anything. To even shout. It all happened at once.

A shadow tore through the crowd. A blur of red and black.

Blake.

I hadn't even seen him arrive. But one second Lochlan was standing, dagger poised, and Isha was rushing up behind Medra—and the next . . . the next, Lochlan went sprawling backwards again with another sickening snap of bone. His head twisted at a grotesque angle. An unlivable angle. His body hit the ground. He didn't move again.

A sob choked my throat but never made it past my lips. Isha screeched and reached for Lochlan's blade, but Blake was faster. He lunged, fangs bared. He was beside Isha in a flash, seizing her wrist and twisting the knife out of her hands. It fell to the floor with a clatter as she cried out in pain, stumbling back and falling hard onto her knees, as she cowered beneath him. The Drakharrow House Leader loomed over her, his mouth still twisted in a ferocious snarl.

I closed my eyes. There was no doubt in my mind that he was about to finish her with his teeth.

"Blake! Stop!" Medra's voice cut through the air.

I peeked through my half-closed eyelids. Blake was breathing hard, still leaning over Isha, fangs bared, his body vibrating with tension. He was a predator poised to kill. His chest heaved with the effort of holding himself back. I held my breath. Around me, no one dared to move.

"Blake, stop it," Medra commanded, the only one brave enough to address this terrifying man.

The highblood slowly straightened, turning his head to face Medra, his fangs still out.

And that's when I saw it. His eye—the one good one that should have been gray—was red.

Blake's gaze flickered, and suddenly his eye was gray again. The tall highblood scanned the crowd of blightborn students, now so still and silent, many backing away, faces pale with horror.

He growled. "No one," he snarled, his voice echoing down the hall, "*touches* her."

Medra didn't look away. She moved towards him carefully and placed a hand on his chest. "Blake," she whispered. "Stand down. It's over."

Only then did his fangs recede, like blades being sheathed. The rage and violence that had seemed to possess him completely now drained. His shoulders sagged. I took a deep breath, realizing for the first time I was shaking from head to toe.

Blake exhaled, looking my friend up and down, his eyes suddenly soft, unguarded. "Are you hurt?"

Medra shook her head, but I could see the red marks still around her throat from where Lochlan had strangled her. She touched a hand to her neck self-consciously, and Blake's mouth hardened. A whimper came from nearby, and I realized Isha was still there, crouching on the floor near Lochlan's body. She stared up at Blake, wide-eyed, tears running down her cheeks.

I didn't blame her for being afraid. Blake ignored her, his eyes fixed entirely on Medra. I swallowed, unable to help but wonder how it must feel to have someone look at you like that. As if you were their entire world. As if the entire world and everyone in it were worth destroying for their sake.

Then I caught sight of Medra's stricken face, and any thoughts I'd had of what Blake had done being romantic were wiped away.

"That's quite enough of that, I think," a cool, clipped woman's voice announced from behind me.

The crowd parted, students scrambling back. Professor Amina Hassan stepped forward, her cane clacking against the stones. She looked past me with distaste at Lochlan's still form, but otherwise paid it no more mind than she might to a dead bird that had crashed against a window pane.

"Professor Stonefist will not be coming today," the instructor declared. "I was assigned to replace her, but I now see my time will be better spent elsewhere. Class is therefore dismissed. All students will clear the halls."

No one moved. We were frozen, all of us transfixed by the sight of Lochlan's still body.

There'd been deaths in Bloodwing's halls before. Blightborn losses. Naveen hadn't made it past First Year. But this? All of this felt different. I'd found two students dead in the hall just a few days before. Now Blake had killed another, trying to protect Medra. Everything was changing. Everything felt wrong.

"Perhaps your ears are not working," Professor Hassan snapped, raising her volume to a higher pitch. "Students will clear the halls. *Immediately.*"

Slowly, the mob of students began to move. I turned to go with them, hitching my bag of books over my shoulder. I'd been planning to do some extra work in the greenhouse. I'd had my essay for Professor Allenvale on my mind all morning, and I wanted it to be perfect. Suddenly I wondered how Nyxaris had even known I was headed there. I hadn't spoken to him in days—not consciously. Just how much of me and my life could he see? Could we not shut each other out completely, even if we wanted to? Based on the impressions I constantly received of him, the answer seemed to be a clear *no*.

Before I could take another step, a hand grasped my arm, nails digging in, pulling me to a halt.

"Oh, no, no. Not you, Miss Shen." Hassan's expression bordered on gleeful. "You're not going anywhere. You and Miss Pendragon will both be coming with me."

I looked over at Medra helplessly.

"See to Dani," Medra quickly said to Blake. He nodded and turned to the dwarven girl still huddled by the wall. She looked confused and dazed. But as Blake approached, she didn't shrink away.

Medra came up beside me, and we followed Hassan down the hall. Though I tried not to look back, I couldn't help it. Lochlan's body still lay there, but Isha had vanished. Blake was crouching beside Dani. His face was calm as he helped her to her feet. The transformation between what he'd done just a few minutes ago and what he was now doing seemed incredible. I touched a hand to my collar, feeling for the silver pendant that dangled around my neck—a small silver fluffin sitting on a stack of books. Blake had given it to me, just a few weeks ago. Before . . . well, before everything had changed.

For the first time, I wondered if things had changed for everyone. Not just for me alone. I'd been so wrapped up in myself, in my own cares and worries. I'd been selfish. I glanced at Medra guiltily, but her eyes were fixed on Hassan's back.

"Where are you taking us?" my friend demanded after we'd turned a corner.

The professor didn't bother to reply. But our destination was clear within a few minutes: the headmistress's office.

Belatedly I realized Professor Hassan must have been in the hallway observing things for quite some time. She'd watched Lochlan choking Medra, but she hadn't intervened. She'd seen Blake appear, and still she'd done nothing.

She'd heard me speak about Nyxaris, I realized with a chill. She knew. And in a few minutes, Regan would know, too. And if Regan knew, Viktor would soon know.

I stopped as a wave of dizziness washed over me. Medra's hand touched my elbow encouragingly.

"Keep moving," Hassan barked, turning to glare at me.

We arrived all too soon. Hassan didn't bother to knock. Lifting her cane, she shoved open the door of the antechamber. Inside, a tall young highblood man lounged at the secretary's desk with his feet up, a telltale blood-and-sword badge visible on his uniform. The whole school knew about this group of alumni who'd been called in to form Regan's new so-called Bloodguard.

He looked up in surprise as Hassan marched in. Apparently, Hassan's reign of terror stretched back to this highblood's time, because he gulped nervously and immediately took his feet off the desk. "Professor Hassan! I know the headmistress would be happy to see you, but she's already in a meeting . . ."

It was pointless. Hassan didn't even pause. Under any other circumstances, I might have admired the woman's nerve—and her skills with that cane. She knocked open the set of doors leading into the headmistress's office, the heavy wood banging against the walls. The Bloodguard boy rose from behind his desk, wringing his hands. But it was too late; Hassan had already swept inside. Medra and I glanced at one another. There was no choice but to follow.

I'd never actually been to the headmistress's office before, even back when we had a headmaster. I'd never been one to get into trouble. I wasn't a rule-breaker. I was a model student. I kept my head down. Got good grades. Was well-liked by all my teachers. I shouldn't have been there. The thought appeared once and then, like a tainted piece of coin, wouldn't go away.

I shouldn't be here. I shouldn't be here. This wasn't my life. This wasn't who I was. The sharp chill of cowardice was on me again.

I thought suddenly of my mother—safe in the library, with no idea any of this was going on. With no idea her daughter was about to be marked as a troublemaker, a rebel, a dissident.

I'd already put her in danger once when I'd been targeted for being friends with Medra.

Dragons. It all led back to dragons, I thought in panic.

My heart pounded like a drum, and my palms were sweaty. My life had been saved in a deal with a dragon, but was anything worth this?

Sunlight streamed in through a huge arched window along the left side of the room. In the center, Regan sat behind an ornate wood desk. Each of the desk legs depicted a naked blightborn woman, their faces rapturous. *Thralls.* I felt sick at such a clear reminder of what the highbloods really thought of us. Of what even Headmaster Kim—a man I'd retained a modicum of respect for—had really thought of us. We were just objects to them, each one of us a potential thrall.

And then I stopped thinking about the desk as my blood turned to ice. Because Viktor Drakharrow stood to one side of it, leaning over Regan. They'd obviously been arguing, I could tell from the tight set of Regan's shoulders, the flush of red in her cheeks, the way her lips were pressed tightly together. Now, as we entered behind Hassan, both of them looked up.

If Hassan was put off by the fact that she'd now be speaking not just to Regan but to the most powerful highblood in Sangratha, she gave no indication of it. In fact, as I glanced at her, I realized she looked even more pleased. She jabbed her cane in my general direction without looking at me, then stepped forward boldly, her eyes locking onto Regan's. "I've discovered something you'll wish to hear about, Headmistress." Something meaningful passed between them, swift and wordless.

"I can see that," Regan said coolly. "But you've interrupted a private meeting."

"I assure you, Headmistress, my lord Drakharrow, you *will* want to hear what I have to say." Hassan's eyes moved to Viktor, as if assessing her chances of getting what she desired.

Viktor straightened, lifting black-gloved hands from Regan's desk. He wore a heavy, long red velvet cape—a mantle fit for a king. But he wasn't our king, he was a regent, one of four. Not that you'd ever know it by the way he acted. As Viktor's red eyes landed on me, I wished the floor would open and swallow me whole. Would it really have been too much to ask? I could feel myself backing up, cowering, just like the girl Medra had been trying to protect. What was her name? *Dani.* I'd seen her before in one of my classes, I suddenly realized. Dani Parks. Her older brother went to Bloodwing, too; he was studying to be a scout. I wondered if he'd been in the crowd back there.

"We'll hear what Professor Hassan has to say, of course," Viktor said smoothly, his eyes sliding over to Medra. "After all, if the dragon rider is involved, it must be important." He came around the desk, and I held my breath. But instead of approaching me, to my shame and relief, he went straight to Medra.

"Could this have anything to do with why our rider has failed to meet her assigned targets with you this month, Professor? Nyxaris has been sighted more than once over Bloodwing and the surrounding lands. And yet I don't believe our rider has been seen once upon his back."

Medra stared back at Viktor with a coolness I found admirable, not backing away or backing down. She said nothing.

Hassan inclined her head respectfully. "My Lord Drakharrow, this pertains directly to the dragon—and thus directly to the matter we've previously discussed." She paused significantly, eyes shifting back to Regan. "Perhaps what I've brought you today could influence . . . other matters."

Regan stiffened slightly. Viktor smiled faintly. "Yes, Professor. I remember our arrangement clearly. You have my full attention. Do continue."

Hassan idolized him, I realized. Where I saw a monster, she saw something else entirely. In Viktor Drakharrow, she saw something truly divine: the Bloodmaiden's image herself. But something else was clearly at play, though I wasn't sure what.

"Go on, then," Regan said coldly from behind the desk. "Say your piece, and get on with it. I have a school to run."

"Nyxaris, the dragon." Hassan paused, clearly savoring the moment.

"Yes, we all know the beast's name. What of it?" Viktor demanded impatiently.

Hassan looked over at me and smiled gleefully. "You know a great deal, Lord Drakharrow. And yet, did either of you know *this*?"

I held my breath, waiting for the axe to fall.

"The dragon is not bonded to Medra Pendragon after all," Hassan announced.

"That's a lie," Medra declared, moving forward before I could even think. "Nyxaris is mine. Everyone knows this."

Hassan's eyebrows arched. "Is it? I was there. In the hall just now. I heard everything."

"I don't know what you think you heard," Medra countered. "But Florence never said that. Not once."

Viktor was frowning.

"She said the dragon was hers," Hassan argued. "I heard her clearly."

"You misheard," Medra said promptly. "But that's no surprise. You were hanging back like a coward. You didn't give a damn about the students turning into a mob right in the hallway. You could have defused the situation. But when that student tried to strangle me? You didn't do a thing about it. Aren't the teachers here supposed to at least *pretend* to give a shit about what happens to us?" She was being purposely melodramatic, trying to get Viktor's attention, trying to keep it off me. I knew that. I also knew it wasn't working.

Viktor paced towards me, his boots soundless. "There's one way to easily clear the matter up," he said lightly as his shadow fell over me, blocking the light from the window.

I forced myself to lift my chin and look at him. To look into those horrible red eyes.

"What did you say this girl's name was?" Viktor said carelessly, waving his hand in Hassan's direction.

"Shen. Florence Shen. Her mother is a librarian here," Hassan quickly replied. "They've both been friends with the rider from the very start."

She made it sound as if that was some kind of a crime. I could feel my chin wobble slightly. Why had she brought my mother into this? The horrid woman.

"Miss Shen," Viktor said, his voice deceptively soft, "why don't you tell us the truth—is the professor correct, or did she mishear you?" He laughed lightly, as if it made no sense to him. "It does seem rather strange for you to claim the dragon belongs to you."

I took a deep breath. Was I really going to do this? I had to. "She's lying," I said, trying to hold my voice steady. "I never said he was mine. That would be silly, just as you say. I'm no dragon rider. Just look at me."

Viktor did just that, his eyes scanning me from head to toe. I held still. I was a mouse, he was a hawk: One wrong move and I'd be his next meal. I was defenseless. Vulnerable. I'd always known that. I was blightborn. But never had I felt it quite like this.

Viktor's eyes lingered on my face. I tried not to flinch. "Miss Shen," he murmured. "You have quite lovely ears."

I blinked. "Th-thank you, Lord Drakharrow."

"They have such fine points to them. Very few people have such a distinctive shape of ears. Have you ever noticed?"

I couldn't help it, my hands shot up, touching my ears. My fingers fumbled around their edges. Desperately, I wanted to look at Medra. I forced myself not to.

"Her ears are the same as they've always been," Medra said. I could tell she was trying to sound bored. "They've looked precisely like this ever since I met Florence." But there was a panicked look in her eyes.

Viktor smiled thinly. "Pardon me if I don't consider you a reliable source of information any longer, Miss Pendragon."

I forced myself to lower my hands, but it was too late. My face must have given away everything I was feeling. Because when I raised my hands to touch the tips of my ears, I'd felt it—a sharpness that hadn't been there before. They'd changed. *Were changing.* Angling into points like Medra's. I'd been hiding in my mother's apartment for weeks; I hadn't even been looking at my ears. I hadn't been attending classes regularly enough for anyone to tell me about them either. Now I realized hiding had been pointless. Lying had been pointless. The truth was literally being written onto my body. How long before they looked exactly the same as Medra's? What else about me would change? I touched a finger to my hair without thinking, and Viktor's smile widened.

"Miss Shen is lying," Professor Hassan spoke up. "Of course the girl would lie."

"Of course the girl would," Viktor murmured. "Fortunately, there's a very easy way to find out the truth." He smiled at me. There was no kindness to that smile.

Suddenly, claws were stabbing into my mind. Raking through my thoughts. My knees buckled, and I fell to the ground, gasping and clutching at my head. The pain was indescribable. I'd led a fairly sheltered life, I'd never been badly injured, never been in a real fight. I'd had headaches, a toothache once or twice. This put every pain I'd ever felt together in one bundle of agony and then put all of that to shame. It was as if my mind was being peeled open, flayed while I was still alive. As if from a distance, I could hear someone screaming.

It was me.

Farther off still, I could hear voices. Medra shouting. Hassan yelling something back. The scrape of a chair. But everything was very far off, muffled under the misery coming from my skull. Viktor was in my head. He was in my head, and he was tearing things apart.

Nyxaris, I thought desperately—even though I knew I shouldn't. The highblood's claws sharpened, pouncing upon the thought. My hands covered my face, trying futilely to get the pain to stop.

Let me in, girl, Viktor's voice called in my mind. I could feel his voice—permeated with cruelty and rot. *There's no sense in hiding. There's nowhere to go. I hold your mind in the palm of my hand. I will find the answers I seek. Give them to me now and perhaps you'll come out of this whole.*

I screamed aloud.

"Stop!" Male. Loud, authoritative. Familiar. "Stop this at once, Lord Drakharrow. This girl is under my protection."

I couldn't open my eyes. Couldn't move.

Viktor was rifling through my thoughts. Cherished memories of my mother. Books I'd recently read. The idea I had for my next essay. He threw them aside one by one, searching deeper, looking for things I didn't wish to share—shouldn't have to share. Things that were mine. Private parts of me. He dug deeper, claws scraping through the layers. My screaming intensified with the search.

The day I'd met Medra.

The day Naveen had died.

This boy cared for you, did he? Such a pity he died. But he was a weakling, Florence. Bloodwing purges the weak. You're still standing, though. Interesting. Very interesting.

This was nothing like hearing Nyxaris—this was a violation, a nightmare. Viktor's voice in my mind left a trail of decay and gore behind. I felt filthy, soiled by his touch.

"She's Avari! She's my house," Kage thundered from somewhere nearby. "You have no right to do this. Let her go!"

Viktor didn't answer, not aloud, anyhow. But he didn't let go. The pain only intensified. I tasted blood in my mouth. Then suddenly the room was full of wind and glass. I heard screaming—from someone else this time. Hazily, I forced my eyes open, feeling wetness on my cheeks, the taste of iron still in my mouth. The window had burst open. Outside the office window, a huge shape loomed, dark against the pale blue sky.

Nyxaris.

Fledgling. The word rumbled through me, filling me with warmth and hope.

You're here, I thought back. *How did you know where I was?*

In future, fledgling, you will answer me when I make inquiry of you. The voice was cold with anger, yet I wasn't afraid. I knew instinctively that his anger was not directed at me.

Y-yes. I will. I'm sorry.

You spoke of the bond between us, he observed. *That is why they have brought you here.*

I nodded weakly through our connection. Unable to even form words.

They would have learned of it sooner or later. Nyxaris sounded resigned.

The room spun with each flap of his wings. Pieces of broken glass littered the floor. Hassan crawled through the wreckage, blood running down her face. I watched as she reached Regan's desk and scuttled beneath it. Regan stood against one wall, her face pale but composed, her hands pressed flat to the stone. Medra and Kage stood by the wall nearest the window, their arms still lifted to shield themselves from the burst of glass. Medra's eyes were on me. She looked afraid for me.

Nyxaris hovered just beyond the ruined frame. His massive wings churned the air, obsidian scales gleaming. His amber eyes fixed on me. *This highblood has threatened you? He has entered your mind, searching for signs of me?*

I nodded. The jerk of my head caused a residual wave of pain to wash over me, and I moaned.

Viktor stood nearby. He held very still, his red eyes moving—first to me, then Nyxaris, then back again. He must have known we were talking about him. But all I cared about at that moment was that he was gone, his claws retracted from my mind.

I know this man, Nyxaris snarled. *We have met before.*

Viktor? I stared at the dragon stupidly. *You know him? Yes, I suppose you would have encountered him at the Tribunal and when they tested you and Medra.*

No. Nyxaris's voice was grim. *Long before that. Many years ago, I remember. Look at his face. He knows me, too.*

I glanced at Viktor cautiously, wondering if it were true. His face was tight, his body tense—as if he were contemplating his next move.

Move to the door, Nyxaris commanded, his voice in my head so much gentler than Viktor's had been. Then, in a completely different voice—one I had never heard him use before—I heard him say *I see you, you highblood bastard. I see you seeing me, and I know you. I know your true name.*

Beside me, Viktor . . . shifted. His bearing changed subtly, his body stiffening. I blinked at him, then looked around. The door had been left ajar in Hassan's haste to enter. It was only a few feet behind me.

Move to the door now, Nyxaris demanded.

What are you going to do? I whispered back, fear creeping up my spine.

I'll do what dragons do, he answered, his voice surprisingly calm.

And what's that?

Reign fire and devastation down upon all those who threaten you and stand between us.

A chill went through me. Not everyone. Not Medra.

She is no longer my rider, he answered calmly. *You are.*

She was your rider. She saved me.

She is not my concern, fledgling. Besides, she has proven repeatedly that she can care for herself.

I looked over at Medra. To my surprise, she gave me a subtle nod. Did she know what Nyxaris was planning?

But Kage . . . I thought desperately. *My House Leader. He came here to try to help me.*

The highbloods are of no concern to me, Nyxaris growled. *Only you. Now, stand back.*

I moved—not because I was fast like Medra or brave like Kage. I moved because I was afraid, and Nyxaris had told me to jump in a way that brooked no refusal. I moved just in time as fire blasted forth from Nyxaris's jaws. My shoulder brushed something as I staggered, my feet landing just outside the office doorway. Everything happened at once.

The room exploded into flames.

Dragon fire burst from Nyxaris, flooding the room with light and heat so intense the air was suddenly searing in my lungs. Medra dove into a corner of the room, shielded from the blast. But I needn't have worried about her at all, for Nyxaris had a target in mind: the desk in the center of the room.

As flames engulfed the desk, Regan screamed, "Amina!" I'd have expected her to call Viktor's name, but either way, it wasn't her archon who came to her aid.

Kage moved like a bolt of lightning. One second he was beside Medra, the next he was at Regan's side. He grabbed her by the waist, half lifting, half yanking her across the room, her high heels skidding over the floor. Pulling her to the opposite end of the room from the window, he grabbed hold of a huge bookcase and drew it away from the wall, shoving Regan and himself behind it.

Hassan wasn't so lucky. No one came for her. She died screaming alone beneath the desk—a scream that lasted only a brief moment before being cut short as the flame hit her full-on, melting her like fat dripping from roasting meat.

And Viktor? He was already gone.

"Holy Mother of Blood," a voice beside me breathed.

I turned. Regan's secretary stood beside me, a crossbow in his hand, his eyes wide and shocked. For a second, he actually pointed the thing at Nyxaris. Then the dragon's eyes narrowed, and a split second later the crossbow had clattered to the ground.

I will not destroy him, Nyxaris said, almost lazily. *Simply because he is too close to you. You may tell him he has been spared.*

I cleared my throat. *I won't, if you don't mind. I don't think he'd take it the right way.*

As you wish.

"Florence!" Medra had me by the arms. She raised a hand to cup my cheek, reminding me of my mother. "Are you all right?"

I started to nod, but Nyxaris interrupted. *You were fortunate. Your mind will heal. Your body, too.*

"Nyxaris . . ." I cleared my throat again, tasting smoke and ash. "Nyxaris says I'll heal. Where is Viktor?"

Together Medra and I looked back at where Regan stepped out from behind the bookcase. Kage came after her, his eyes wary as he looked at Nyxaris.

I tire of this. Nyxaris beat his wings, and the room was filled with the echoing gusts.

Regan screamed, covering her face as ashes from the desk flew into the air. Nyxaris's great lizardlike snout pushed into the ruined chamber. I trembled as I regarded him. His maw opened, breath still swirling with smoke and heat. Then his head dipped low, and I could see nothing but midnight-black scales and molten-orange eyes.

This has gone on long enough, the dragon growled into my mind. *There is only so much time one may avoid the inevitable. My patience is at an end. You will come to me now.*

I stood frozen, the heat of his fire still clinging to my skin, and the smell of scorched wood, burned parchment, and melted flesh still filled the room. Beside me, Medra stood quietly, simply watching. Nyxaris had spoken. Deep inside, I knew I had no choice but to obey. I took a long breath and moved to the window, my shoes crunching on shards of broken glass. The world outside was all scales and wings. The world outside was my future.

Up, Nyxaris murmured, not unkindly. *On.*

My knees trembled, but I took a step forward. Then another.

Nyxaris clung to the tower like a sculpted gargoyle, claws anchored in the stone. He turned his head, showing me the base of his neck and massive shoulder blade.

I stumbled back, my heart stammering in my chest. *I can't. Please, I'll fall.*

You will not fall, he growled impatiently. *Mortals and their endless fear of falling. I assure you, you will not come to harm. You are my rider now. Rise, fledgling, and become the rider you know you must be.*

My eyes lifted, meeting his. The moment belonged only to us. *I'm coming*, I whispered, my mind to his.

He rumbled, a sound of satisfaction, deep and possessive. I could feel the shudder inside my chest, echoing like a second heartbeat. I reached out a hand to touch his shining black scales. He was hot—as a creature of air and flame should be—but not unbearably so. I climbed up, one hand gripping the edge of a scale as gently as I could, the other clutching the ridge of his shoulder. And then I was on, flattened against him, face buried against rippling scales and rising muscle.

The wind swelled. Nyxaris let go of the stones. His wings stretched wide. Together, we took flight.

CHAPTER 15

BLAKE

The dwarven girl, Dani, didn't say a word when I left her at the door to the First Year common room. She just stumbled over the threshold, her hands still clutching at the ripped bodice of her dress, swaying like she wasn't sure where she was or what day it was. Her eyes were wide. Too vacant.

I understood all too well—she was still caught in the web of someone else's will.

Not *someone*, multiple *someone*s. I'd counted three distinct pairs of bite marks on her neck, neither fresh nor healing. There was only one reason that would have happened: She wasn't a single highblood's thrall, she was being passed around like a shared drink at some horrific feast. Her body was suffering the consequences. Slower healing, lingering marks, disorientation. She didn't deserve that shit. No one did.

I made a mental note to send a House Drakharrow healer down to the First Year tower to check on her later that night. And if Dani wasn't there when the healer arrived, I'd follow up personally.

As soon as the common room door was closed, I turned and stalked down the hallway. My senses were still buzzing, heightened from the blood I'd shed. I'd snapped that blightborn boy like a twig, Lochlan, whatever his name had been. I hadn't cared who he was, what he was. He'd touched Pendragon. Threatened her. That had been enough. I'd seen red.

I closed my eyes for a moment trying to breathe. Willing myself to calm down. But it wasn't so easy these days. That red haze was always with me, in the back of my mind. Behind my eyes like a veil of blood. The ripple of scales always just beneath my skin. The dragon pacing inside me.

To tell the truth, I couldn't even remember the moment I'd done it—not clearly. I could remember the *feel*, if not the sound, of snapping bone and tendon. It had felt fucking good. Then, Pendragon was shouting my name, telling me to stop. And I had, thank the Bloodmaiden, I had. I'd stopped on the edge of killing again—of ripping out the throat of that blightborn girl. But the next time, and the time after that? Would I even hear Pendragon when she called? When she begged me to stop?

I skidded to a halt, pausing in the hallway. Closing my eyes, I forced myself to imagine it was Pendragon's throat in my hands. What if I lost control of myself the next time I was with her, the next time she was bare and vulnerable beside me? Could it happen? Would I do that? Did I even know myself well enough to answer those questions right now?

I started walking again. What I'd done to the blightborn boy I'd done for *her*. Everything I'd done so far—well, almost everything— I'd done in service of her. It was different. I tried to convince myself, but fuck me if those weren't the kinds of lies Marcus would have told.

The truth was that the first time I fed from Pendragon, she hadn't even wanted it. I'd told myself our bond made it all right, that her blood was mine by right. That *she* was mine by right. I'd told myself exactly what I'd wanted to hear so I could sleep at night. I still remembered the taste of her, how vivid and sweet she was that first time. The feel of her, thrashing in my arms. How I'd pinned her, held her still. How the moment her blood hit my tongue, I'd nearly gone blind from the rush of it. She'd tasted as good as she'd felt. Like flame and rebellion. Like pure defiance. Like something I'd never be able to let go of again.

Back then, knowing she hated it, hated *me*? It only made it better. Sweeter. Hotter. I loathed myself for it now. No matter how good it had felt, that was the past. I wanted Pendragon to *want* me. The way she'd felt back then, fighting me? It was sick.

I wanted her the way she was now—willing, fighting, but giving. Letting me take but taking in turn. Still defiant, still stubborn, still pure fire under my hands and mouth. But the kind of fire that burned without completely destroying everything it touched. Because I knew one thing for certain now: I didn't want to destroy Pendragon. I'd rather destroy myself than hurt her.

Which was why I now found myself standing in the hall outside of the Avari Tower. I needed help, and there weren't many places I could go to get it. I hated this. Hated needing help. Hated that I had to ask *him*, of all people, for it. But the alternative was much, much worse.

So I knocked politely on the door like a guest the Avari had invited for dinner. And I smiled when a blightborn Avari boy opened the door, still laughing at whatever conversation he'd been in the midst of having. I ignored how his mouth practically fell open as he recognized me.

"Blake Drakharrow to see Kage Tanaka," I announced. "At your House Leader's pleasure."

The student continued to gape, frozen into stillness. I waited one moment, then another.

"As soon as possible," I snapped.

That sent him scurrying. Must have been a Second Year. A few minutes later, the door opened again. This time it was a highblood with short, cropped hair and a ring in her nose. "I'm Evie," she announced. "I'm the House Leader's Second. I'll escort you to his suite."

Thank the Bloodmaiden, this girl actually had a clue what she was doing.

I followed her into the common room, tried to pretend I hadn't seen it all before. Followed her up the winding stairs, pretending

I didn't recognize Pendragon's door as we passed by it. When we reached a door larger than the others and inlaid with a silver moon glistening with pearls, I knew we'd arrived.

Kage's Second knocked once and stepped back. "He's expecting you. I'll be waiting outside."

I guess that was supposed to put me on guard. I nodded and forced a tight smile. The door opened. Kage stood on the threshold. I'd never seen him look so disheveled. His hair was tousled, and his clothes were rumpled.

I sniffed. "Is that smoke I smell? Is something on fire?"

"Drakharrow," Kage said, his voice dry. "To what do I owe this pleasure?"

I gritted my teeth. "I need to talk to you." I glanced at Evie. "Alone."

Kage leaned against the doorway. "You came here for a little private chat? Why, Drakharrow, I'm honored. But next time, make an appointment in advance."

"Just let me the fuck in, Tanaka," I snapped, starting to lose my tenuous thread of patience.

The Avari leader smiled but stepped aside, gesturing for me to enter. The room was spacious and exceedingly neat with multiple rooms leading off the main sitting area. The furniture was rich and well-made, everything in shades of black and gray. I had to give it to the Avari, they had good taste. The decor was more understated than in the Drakharrow Tower but no less luxurious.

"Is it bigger than yours?" Kage asked, as I looked around. There was a glint in his eyes.

I glared at him. "Fuck off, Tanaka. Let's not even go there. You won't like how that little competition ends." I fell onto a black velvet chaise and threw my feet up, trying to look more relaxed than I felt. "So, what's up with you? You look like you've been through the wars."

"Had a little encounter with Nyxaris this afternoon."

I swung my feet off the sofa. "What? When?"

"Just before you arrived." He came over to a small side table and started pouring himself a drink. He downed it, then gestured to me. "You want one?"

I shook my head. "What the hell happened?"

He shrugged, pouring out another glass. "Oh, you know. Nyxaris lit up our new headmistress's office like a beach bonfire."

"Holy shit," I breathed.

"Pendragon was there."

I growled, already halfway to my feet.

"Calm yourself, Drakharrow. She's fine." He took a sip. "Professor Hassan didn't have the same luck, though."

"Hassan? Professor Hassan who hauled Pendragon and Florence away this afternoon?" I stared at him. "Are you kidding me?"

Kage shook his head. "Apparently, the dragon doesn't like tattletales. Hassan hid under the desk, a fat load of good that did her."

I whistled. "And Florence?"

"She's all right, too. At least, I think she is."

"You think?"

"She left by way of dragon." Kage came over to a nearby armchair and sat down, another drink in his hand. "The headmistress survived."

"Regan? What a fucking relief," I muttered. Was it my imagination or did the Avari leader's body tighten at the sound of my former consort's name?

"Your uncle was there, too. Not that it did our new headmistress much good," Kage said coolly.

There was definitely a story there, but I decided it wasn't a good idea to ask. I snorted. "You're telling me Uncle Viktor didn't throw himself between the dragon and his new bride? I'm shocked. Really, I am."

"Your uncle disappeared leaving Regan at the dragon's mercy. For a moment, I thought she was to be the target of Nyxaris's wrath—not Hassan."

I stared at him. "And I take it you did something about that?"

"I may have," he said, a little stiffly.

I whistled. "Feeling a little sympathy for the headmistress tyrant, are we?"

"She's not the tyrant," Tanaka snarled, reminding me of just who and what he was. "Last I remember, proximity to a tyrant or even a family connection didn't automatically make you just like them."

"I appreciate the vote of confidence," I said, staring at him. "But I'm not sure Regan warrants such a strenuous defense."

"The woman was once your consort," he reminded me coldly. "You don't believe you owe her any loyalty or care?"

I laughed lightly. "I think Regan can take care of herself. We grew up together, you know. I think I know her well enough to say she's probably very happy with her lot in life."

Tanaka's eyes narrowed. "I wouldn't be so sure."

I shrugged. "Anyhow, you're saying Viktor disappeared. Like, highblood-style ran away, or literally vanished in a puff of smoke?"

"There was no smoke besides the dragon's. But he vanished, yes." Kage leaned forward, clasping his hands. "Did you know he could do that?"

I stared at him. "Hell no. But then, I'm also not surprised. Viktor has a lot of secrets up his sleeve. None of them fucking good ones." I thought of something. "So Nyxaris knew where she was? Florence, I mean."

Kage nodded. "Apparently. He seems . . . rather possessive."

"Something you and I wouldn't know a thing about," I deadpanned.

Kage ignored me. "You've heard about the new school rules?"

"I know House Leaders weren't consulted. Are you as pissed about that as I am?" I chuckled. "Not that I expected Regan to be a great headmistress."

"I assume these rules came straight from your uncle's lips," Kage pointed out. "I doubt they were her idea."

I scowled. "Curfews for blightborn. A blood donation program with perks? That sounds a lot like the Regan I know."

"The point is they're being implemented. I've already had to shut down altercations in my own common room." His lips thinned. "Blightborn students are scared."

"Understandably so." I leaned forward. "We'll each protect our own."

Kage nodded. "That goes without saying."

"We should speak to Lysander about this. But I have no doubt he'll be with us."

Look at the two of us, I thought. Consulting like real leaders. Then I felt a chill. Not consulting. *Conspiring.* Talking about protecting blightborn instead of going along with Regan's new bigotry? It went against what most highbloods believed. But if anything seemed amiss to Kage, he didn't show it. Maybe things were different in his house. Or maybe the Avari just wanted blightborn protected because they were more complacent the safer they felt. Easier to control.

"Lysander will protect Orphos," he agreed. "He's always been a forward thinker. But Mortis still has no House Leader. Not since Catherine . . . disappeared."

I frowned. "I've noticed Mortis is where Regan's been finding some of her best enforcers."

"I've noticed the same. Catherine wasn't quite who we thought she was."

"No, she wasn't," I agreed. I'd always thought Drakharrow was the strongest house—and perhaps the cruelest. But Mortis was coming up as a strong contender. "I've heard some things."

"We've probably heard the same things. But we're not here to discuss Mortis today. That house isn't our responsibility."

I sighed. So that's how Kage wanted to play it? I supposed that was fair. We did have enough to worry about. "Speaking of protecting those in our own houses," I said, "you do realize Florence Shen is vulnerable now, more than Pendragon ever was? If Viktor wants a soul-bound rider, she's his new target."

Kage nodded. "Are you thinking what I'm thinking?"

"Shockingly, I might be. I'll talk to Pendragon. Explain the danger. Get her to talk to Florence. If that doesn't work . . ."

"Then I'll talk to the girl myself," Kage finished. He shook his head. "You know, it was strange, Drakharrow, watching Nyxaris with his new rider today. Like watching a courtship unfold between a girl and a volcano."

"Courtship?" I wrinkled my nose. "I wouldn't have called it that when Pendragon was involved."

"Well, Nyxaris never actually bonded to Medra," Kage pointed out.

I ignored the fact he'd used her first name—as if he were her friend. "Good point," I forced myself to say.

Kage smiled slightly. "Now, why are you really here? Is it to ask my permission this time?"

My hackles rose. "Permission?"

"Oh, you thought I didn't notice?" Kage's eyes narrowed. "How cute. You're fast for a highblood. But you're not exactly subtle."

So he knew I'd been sneaking into Pendragon's room. I hid a smirk; I guess we had made a fair bit of noise. At least Kage hadn't made a big deal about it. Not yet. I sighed, sinking back into the chair. "Look, I didn't come here to fight."

"A pity," Kage murmured. "But I suppose I am a bit tired."

I ignored him. "You once said that if I survived my . . . transformation, I should come see you. That you could help me."

Kage rubbed his chin. "Did I? I don't recall."

The fucking asshole.

"Yes. You did." I breathed in deeply, trying to tamp down my annoyance. "Look, you know what I am."

"A dragon," Kage said bluntly. "Unless I'm much mistaken. An Infernus."

Great. As usual, Kage knew more than I did.

"I can become a red dragon, yes. But I don't have great control. My dragon . . . he's bleeding through more often. I feel like I'm losing control, not gaining it."

"He?"

"What?"

"You said *he*. As if your dragon was someone else. He's not. He's you."

My lips twisted. "Well, it sure doesn't fucking feel that way."

Kage's brow furrowed. "My wolf is me. There is no distinction."

"And you have great control. Good for you. Can you teach me?" I asked.

"Just what exactly is happening?"

I ran my hands through my hair. "I can't control when I shift. I can't control the dragon even when I haven't shifted. Like I said, it's as if there's someone else inside of me. And he takes control sometimes. He's . . . violent. Twisted."

Kage looked skeptical. "That doesn't sound too different from the Blake Drakharrow I know."

"Well, it is," I snapped. "I killed a boy in the hall today, a blight-born. He was threatening Pendragon. I just . . . snapped."

Kage frowned. "If he was threatening your consort, that doesn't sound completely unreasonable."

"No," I agreed. "But I nearly killed another girl, too. She hadn't laid a hand on Pendragon. And it's not about that. It's about the fact that I can hardly remember doing it. And that's when it's someone I *don't* care about." I met Kage's eyes, willing him not to make me say the words.

"You're afraid you'll hurt someone who's more important to you," he summarized.

I nodded. "Yes."

Kage was quiet for a moment, brow furrowed, arms crossed over his chest. I watched him in silence. He was a handsome bastard, I guess I'd give him that. And he'd been fairly gracious in letting me into his private space. That didn't mean I didn't still plan to get Pendragon out of his house as soon as I could.

"Look, Drakharrow," he finally said, "you're not wrong to be scared. I can see you're cracking."

"Cracking?" My blood pressure rose. "I wouldn't put it quite like that. But you admit it, then. I'm dangerous." I forced a laugh.

"You always have been," Kage said dryly. "All of you Drakharrows are wildfires waiting to happen. That's nothing new. Just look at your brother."

I tried not to take offense—especially as he might have had a point. "I think you're forgetting my father. Besides, you try being practically raised by Viktor Drakharrow and we'll see how you turn out."

"Sure. Point taken." He stood up and stretched. "I told you I might be able to help. But I'd assumed things would go the same way for you as they did for me."

I blinked. "And you don't think that now?"

"No. My wolf is myself. You seem to see the dragon inside you as some other entity completely. And you're talking as if that dragon is trying to, well, harm you. Harm people you care about."

"Well, he fucking is," I hissed. "He could."

Kage nodded. "All right. Look, I've trained other Avari before. But what you're describing . . . well, it's not shifting. You're not just having trouble changing and changing back again. You're splitting apart at the seams."

I sat there, silent. Feeling strangely ashamed.

"You don't need me," Kage said, not unkindly. "You need someone who knows the history of what you are."

I narrowed my eyes. "Don't say Rodriguez. Please don't say Rodriguez."

Kage had the decency to actually try to look sympathetic. "He might have answers. We already know he knows a hell of a lot more than he should."

I thought about how Rodriguez had saved Florence's life by suggesting something none of the rest of us even knew was possible. "You're right about that," I said gruffly. "But can we trust him at this point?"

"He fucked up. I think he knows that. You can't say you haven't made mistakes, done things you regret."

"No, I can't," I said coldly. "And you? I suppose you're perfect, Wolf Boy."

Kage held up his hands. "By no means. I make mistakes all the time." He gave me a meaningful look, and I knew he was thinking of the way we'd betrayed Nyxaris. "I've done things I regret. Things I've had to apologize for."

Had he apologized to Pendragon? She hadn't told me that. I thought of how he hadn't tried to stop me from seeing her. Almost as if he'd, well, conceded her to me. He wasn't trying to get in the way anymore. I wondered why.

Kage watched me and frowned. "Don't even go there, Drakharrow."

"What?" I said innocently. "I was just thinking."

"Don't think," he said icily. "Not about that. It's none of your fucking concern. Pendragon remains in my house, lest you forget that so easily. This is where she belongs."

"But she's my consort. My . . . mate," I said, a little stiffly.

Kage smiled thinly. "Is that what she is?"

"What the fuck is that supposed to mean?" I said, leaping to my feet like a dragon about to defend his lair.

"I mean Pendragon will decide exactly what she is or isn't in relation to you. That doesn't mean I've relinquished all of my claims," Kage said, smiling in a way I didn't appreciate.

"What the hell does that mean?" I snarled.

Kage rose to his feet and gave me a gentle shove in the chest, just enough to warn me, not enough to actually piss me all the way off. "Relax, Drakharrow. I don't want to join your little triad."

"There is no triad," I said without thinking. "It's just the two of us. Me and Pendragon. For good."

Kage raised a brow. "Really? Interesting."

I looked away, suddenly feeling a little awkward. "Fine. I'll go to Rodriguez."

"Good call, Dragon Boy." I was moving towards the door when Kage spoke again. "And, Drakharrow?"

I paused. "What?"

"If you do lose control of your dragon completely, don't let it be her you hurt. I wouldn't want to have to put you down." He met my eyes.

I nodded tightly. "Believe me, Tanaka—if that happened, I'd fucking beg you to do it."

CHAPTER 16

BLAKE

I still couldn't believe I was doing this. Pendragon would kill me. And honestly, after everything we'd done to her, she'd probably be fully justified.

Rodriguez had treated us all like chess pieces. But that didn't erase the fact that Kage and I had made a choice to behave like pawns. Rodriguez had fucked up, sure, but he was still the only person who might understand what was happening to me. So yeah, I was doing this.

The hallway leading to his office was empty; classes were finished for the day. Dinner was probably half over by now. I stood outside the door and rapped my knuckles against it, hoping he'd still be around. I knew he kept a place in Veilmar, but that was a longer trek. I also knew he spent half his nights sleeping at his desk.

No answer. I knocked again.

A clattering sound. Then the breaking of glass.

"Rodriguez?" I called. "I know you're in there. I need to talk to you."

A muttered curse came through the door. "Shit."

Rolling my eyes, I twisted the doorknob. I paused in the doorway: The office was a mess. If Rodriguez was trying to hide the fact that he basically lived at the school half the time, he was doing a poor job of it. Books and clothes littered the floor. The desk was piled with parchment and empty bottles. Kneeling beside it was Rodriguez, picking up the pieces of a shattered bottle.

A red, shimmering liquid pooled on the carpet. It only took a second for the scent to hit me: Crimson Ambrosia. A narcotic-infused liquor—an expensive one, frequently consumed for fun by wealthy highbloods. I knew Theo and Visha enjoyed its effects from time to time. But when taken by a blightborn, the reactions were more pronounced. Ambrosia could unspool a blightborn's mind into nothing.

"Seriously?" I exclaimed. "You're drinking that shit?"

Rodriguez glanced up. His eyes were bloodshot. Cheekbones sharper than they'd ever been. His shirt was half-unbuttoned and his dark hair looked as if it hadn't been combed in days.

"Well, well," he said, slurring his words slightly. "The highblood prince returns."

I stepped inside, shutting the door behind me. "Who else has seen you like this? Dammit, Rodriguez. Regan's running the school, and you're pulling this shit? Do you want to get fired?"

He laughed. "Only a matter of time, isn't it? I can always find my true calling." He yanked at the collar of his shirt, pulling the material aside, and I froze.

"Fuck," I hissed. "You've got to be kidding me." Bite marks. Still healing.

"Did they . . . ?" I cleared my throat.

"Larissa was kind enough not to enthrall me," Rodriguez said dryly. "She only took a few sips."

"I'll fucking kill her." I curled my hands into fists. The girl was in my house, therefore she was my responsibility. "When was this?"

Rodriguez waved a hand and sat back on his haunches looking tired. He'd given up trying to pick up the broken pieces of the bottle. "Don't bother. It's all part of the new Blood Donation Incentive Program after all. Or, as I like to call it, *B-DIP*."

I blinked. "Bee—what now?"

"Bee-dip," he said, stressing the first letter. "Doesn't it have a wonderful ring to it?"

"Not exactly." Was Rodriguez losing his blooddamned mind?

"I agree with you. Regan didn't think through the acronym when she came up with the program name. Now, if she'd put it to a vote, I might have suggested something like *DIB-P*."

I stared blankly.

"*Donation Incentive Blood Program*," he elaborated.

"Ah. Much better." I came over and started picking up the pieces of the bottle of ambrosia, tossing them in the nearby wastebasket. "So what the hell is really going on? You're just going to lie back and let Regan and Larissa and every other highblood walk all over you? That doesn't sound much like the Rodriguez I know."

"The Rodriguez you know is a monumental fuckup." He picked up a piece of broken glass and stared down at it. "I made a plan. It went to shit. I failed. I thought I could steer this place away from the fire. Instead I poured out the oil and lit the flame myself." The shard was cutting through his finger, but he didn't seem to notice. "I gambled. Thought I could outmaneuver Viktor. Thought I could keep people safe. But that's life, isn't it? You can't keep your hands clean and try to play the hero."

"Look, it wasn't just you. We all made mistakes." I gently took the piece of glass out of his hands and tossed it away, then pulled a handkerchief out of my pocket and passed it to him. "To soak up the blood."

He stared at the blood welling up on his hand as if he were just noticing it but pressed the cloth against the cut. "You're still standing."

I clenched my jaw. "Barely."

He raised a brow. "Is that so?"

"Why do you think I'm here?" I said quietly. "You're not the only one whose life is going to shit."

Rodriguez didn't answer right away. Instead, he hauled himself up, leaning against the desk for support, then slumped into the chair behind the desk, looking a little green. I took a seat across from him warily, half expecting him to pass out.

He looked at me, his eyes—bloodshot as they were—focusing and assessing. "I'm going to go out on a limb here and take a wild guess. You're changing." He leaned forward. "Tell me, Blake. Do your eyes go red when it happens?"

My back stiffened. Even though I'd planned to tell him, I hadn't actually expected him to figure it out on his own. At least, not this quickly. "What makes you say that?"

He didn't answer right away. Just studied me for a long moment. Giving me a look that said he knew. *Knew.* More than about just me.

"Well, shit," I said finally.

"You know, back in the good old days—" he was clearly being sarcastic "—there were two kinds of dragons. The ones who were born," he paused and I found myself holding my breath, "and the ones who were made."

My throat went dry, even though I already knew where he was heading. "Made?"

"Blood," he said simply. "The wrong kind. Or the right kind." He shrugged. "Depends on your perspective, I suppose. Throw in a little light blood magic, and there you have it."

I thought of Pendragon's blood. The way it burned through me, filling me with a sense of power, making me feel invincible.

Dragonlike.

"For some, rider blood isn't just powerful. It's catalytic. Especially when you were already bound. Something inside you wanted to change."

"I didn't want this," I said swiftly.

"But there are some perks," Rodriguez said meaningfully. "Aren't there?"

I wrinkled my nose. "Power?"

He nodded. "If you can get it under control, learn to work with Nyxaris . . ." For a moment, he looked almost optimistic.

For a moment, I let myself believe it was possible. Then I blanched. "Bloodmaiden . . . Am I going to have dragon babies?"

Rodriguez blinked at me, then laughed. No, full-on howled, his entire body shaking. "Oh, Blake," he wheezed. "Not unless you're planning on fucking another dragon."

I scowled. The pickings were rather slim in that regard. "No, thanks."

Rodriguez wiped his eyes, still chuckling. "I don't think you need to worry about it, then." He shook his head. "Fuck, I needed that." He was still smiling.

"Glad I could be of service in stopping your existential spiral," I muttered. Then I thought of something. "Wait. You said there were two kinds of dragons . . ."

Rodriguez's smile turned grim. "That's it. Put the pieces together."

Part of me didn't want to.

Rodriguez leaned forward, clasping his hands. "Blake, the answer is literally staring you right in the face."

"Nyxaris, Molindra, the others . . ."

"Molindra hatched from an egg. We have her birth records." He sighed, taking in my expression. "You don't want to go there yet? Then, we won't. So tell me, how'd you lose your eye?"

I didn't answer. My mind was still tossing over the last revelation. I didn't want to put the horror I was feeling into words. Didn't want Rodriguez to confirm what I'd just guessed to be true. Because if it were true, then what were the implications for me?

"Viktor," Rodriguez guessed. "I take it he didn't offer any help on how to deal with your new . . . condition." He shot me a look of admiration. "Of course, you didn't exactly leave him unscathed. He looks like shit. Good for you." He tilted his head. "Almost makes me pity Regan."

"Don't," I snapped. "She got what she wanted. All she cares about is power and rising to the top. As for Viktor, he thinks I'm fucked. He couldn't take me down, and I couldn't kill him, so we're at a standstill. For now. And the way things are going . . ." I shook my head. I wanted to destroy Viktor. But first I had to get control before I took another stab at it. "It's not looking good. Either I'm going to lose control and wind up accidentally offing myself, go feral, or . . ."

"Or?"

My face hardened. "Or maybe it'll all work out. I'll become something powerful. But if Viktor manages to control me first . . ."

Thrallweave wouldn't work if I was in dragon form. I suddenly wondered if the bond that Pendragon and I had offered me any similar protection. But based on how easily Viktor had managed to manipulate me the last time, it didn't seem like it.

"A fleet of dragons with you at the helm," Rodriguez mused.

Belatedly, I remembered something important. "Of course, you could always put me down yourself," I said coldly. "After all, you said your order turned Nyxaris and the others to stone."

Rodriguez smiled. "I wondered when we'd circle back to that."

"I suppose I'd better watch my back," I said bitterly. "I was an idiot to think—"

"To think what—that I might help?" He leaned back. "Blake, I'll tell you a little secret that it seems even Nyxaris has forgotten. When those four dragons were turned to stone, it was done willingly."

I stared at him. "What?"

"The Emberwatch had their consent to do what they did. It was done for a reason."

"What possible reason could those dragons have had for allowing that to happen?"

"We all come to a place of sacrifice in our lives one way or another. You can't tell me there aren't things you'd willing give your life—your freedom—to save."

I thought of Pendragon. "Fine, maybe you're right. So what were they saving?"

"All of us," he said simply. "Everything. They were holding back the Veil."

"The Veil? What's that?"

Rodriguez got to his feet. He walked over to the floor-to-ceiling bookshelves that lined the wall next to his desk, then pulled one out and tossed it onto the desk. The book slid to a halt in front of me.

I leaned forward, scanning the title. *"Chronicles of Sangratha: An Official History."* I looked up. "It's a textbook. What's this got to do with anything?"

"All highbloods and blightborn learn the official history. The Great Famine. The Blight of Shadows. The Dragon Cataclysm."

I shrugged. "Sure. I remember the basics."

"No official history is ever true. Perhaps you've learned that already."

I thought of my uncle's journal I'd found in the Black Keep. "So, what part of this isn't true? That the highbloods weren't the saviors of the blightborn? I figured that out a while back. I think a lot of us did."

Rodriguez grimaced. "Not just that. Think back on the Cataclysm."

"A time of monstrous creatures. The dragons arose. Dark forces threatened Sangratha. The highbloods and the dragon riders forged an alliance and vanquished them."

"Right. But where did they come from in the first place?" Rodriguez had shoved his hands into his pockets and now was pacing back and forth, in full-on professor mode.

"Uh . . ." I tried to think.

"Have you ever been to the borders of Sangratha?"

"I've been to the coast before, sure." Sangratha was a massive island, surrounded by ocean waters. A few scattered islands lay close to shore. Past that, there was nothing.

"No." Rodriguez took a deep breath. "To the true borders of

the Thralldom. You can't say yes, no one can. Except maybe your brother."

"Marcus? What do you mean?" My heart sped up.

"Haven't you even wondered where he's gone?"

"I've been a little self-absorbed the last few weeks," I admitted. "Can you blame me?"

"I suppose not." He sat back down in the desk chair. "Sangratha isn't the only world. There are many. But one in particular used to connect to ours."

I was stunned but tried to hide it. "Used to? And I suppose the dark creatures came from there? The dragons?"

"The creatures?" He shrugged. "Perhaps. The riders? Almost certainly."

I stared. "The riders? What the hell are you talking about?"

Rodriguez looked satisfied. "Ah, I knew that would get your attention."

"You always had my attention," I snapped. "I came here looking for answers. As usual, you're full of the ones I *didn't* want." The list of things Rodriguez knew that I didn't want to suddenly seemed much larger.

"Your problem is bad, Blake. But it's not the only problem. We have a bigger one than you being unable to shift on command."

"It's more than that, Rodriguez," I almost shouted. "I fucking killed someone today."

"Who?"

"Does that really matter? A blightborn. They were threatening Pendragon. He'd . . . hurt her."

Rodriguez relaxed slightly. "Justified homicide."

"Sure, this time. But next?"

"Finally growing a conscience, are we? You've killed before, Blake. You didn't seem to care so much then."

"That was different." I clenched my jaw painfully. The difference was I'd known exactly what I was doing. But this time? It was like my body had been taken over. Like thrallweave . . . but worse. Because the monster was inside me. If Kage was to be believed, he *was* me.

"There's no easy solution for your dilemma," Rodriguez said, sounding impatient. "Time and practice."

"I've had time. I've tried to practice. It's not fucking working," I hissed. "Tell me something I don't already know. Teach me, dammit. Otherwise, I could shift in class one day and do a little more damage than to just a single blightborn."

He looked at me. "Is it really that bad?"

"It's bad. Really bad." I rubbed my face. "I want to talk about Marcus. I want to learn about this Veil. I mean, I don't *want* to. It sounds like an absolute fucking mess. But I can't help you with the world's big problems if I can't even control my own body and keep from . . ." I took a deep breath " . . . from killing my own consort by accident."

Rodriguez's expression turned serious. "Understood." He looked towards his bookshelf. "But the only answer I have is one you won't like."

"Try me." I suddenly realized Rodriguez's expression was a little too somber. "Why are you looking at me like that?"

"Like what?" He was trying to sound innocent, but I fucking knew better.

"Like I'm about to fucking die, Rodriguez." He was quiet far too long, and so then I knew. "Because I am?" I choked out. "I'm *dying*?" He looked away. "You knew as soon as I walked in."

He shook his head. "Not that soon. Suspected. But if it's as bad as you describe . . ."

"There's another *being* inside of me. And he's a fucking animal who wants to kill everyone. So yeah, it's bad."

Rodriguez sighed. "What you've described sounds like soul-splitting."

"That doesn't sound good."

"It's fairly self-explanatory," he agreed.

"So, what do I do? How do I fix it?"

He stood up again, walked across the room, and reached for a book high up on the shelf. Even from where I sat, I could tell it was ancient, the black leather cover cracking with age. Yet the tome was a beautiful one—embossed with silver, a serpentine dragon embedded in the center. Rodriguez studied the book, looking faintly amused.

"What's so funny?" I demanded. "Does that book have the answers or not?"

"Answers? Many. To your problem? It might have one. Will you like it? Decidedly not."

"Just give me the fucking book, Rodriguez," I snapped.

He held it out. *The Dark Art of Eternal Bonds*, I read, as I grabbed the old book.

"Listen, Blake," Rodriguez started to say, just as the door swung open.

"Visha," I exclaimed as my Second walked in. She looked just as surprised to see me as I was to see her.

I stared. Her short platinum-blond hair was swept back in a messy twist. She was dressed to kill—wearing a sleek crimson sleeveless corset-top paired with tight black trousers.

My brain stalled for a second, then finally caught up. "Visha," I managed to squawk. I looked behind me at Rodriguez. He had a sheepish look on his face.

The instructor cleared his throat. "We'll talk more later." His eyes flicked to the clock like he'd lost track of the time. "Miss Vaidya, I assume you're here to talk about your essay?"

I blinked at him. "You're kicking me out? *Now?*"

Visha stepped in front of me without looking me in the eye. "Absolutely, Professor. I'd love to have you look over my thesis."

"Really? You're not carrying any notes," I pointed out.

Visha turned, staring down her nose at me coolly. But her face looked a little flushed. She tapped the side of her head. "Don't need notes. It's all up here."

Rodriguez pinched the bridge of his nose. "Blake, you have the book. Take it and go before I feel the urge to pull out another bottle."

Behind me, the door clicked shut. I stumbled out into the hallway, clutching the book as if it could do more than save me—as if it might be able to block out the mental images I was absolutely, definitely not having.

CHAPTER 17

FLORENCE

Neville was following me, trotting at my heels since I got back. Since I *landed*, I should say.

I shivered, half in fear, half in delight. I'd landed on the back of a dragon. Neville had been sitting on the wide expanse of grass down near the greenhouse waiting for me, with a look on his face that one could only describe as *smug*.

"Wipe that look off your face," I hissed down to him now. "You've been wearing it long enough. It's absolutely ridiculous." The fluffin made a happy mewing sound. With a sigh, I bent over, letting my heavy bag slide down onto the ground. Then I scooped the little furball up into my arms and rubbed his head gently. "I suppose you think you're coming inside."

He made a soft barking noise.

"Fine," I said with resignation. "But you'd better be quiet." I shifted my grip on the fluffin and nudged the heavy door to the Avari Tower open with my boot.

It was strange to be returning like this. It felt like I'd been away much longer than I really had. The common room was dimly lit, cozy, and quiet. I inhaled. Someone had been burning sage. I stepped in, only realizing then that it was *too* quiet. Then I heard it—weeping. A girl was curled up on a sofa near the fire, sobbing into her hands. A small cluster of students surrounded her. One rubbed her back. All of them were blightborns.

Across the room, a group of highblood students stood together, talking in low voices. I recognized one of them—Evie, one of the House Avari wardens.

I walked over slowly. "What happened?"

Evie glanced at me. "Shen. Nice of you to join us. You're back, then?"

I nodded awkwardly. "Yes. What's going on?"

"Lysa's mother died."

"That's so sad," I murmured. It was rather kind of the highblood students to stand to one side so respectfully.

But Evie wasn't finished. "She was murdered."

My stomach dropped. "Murdered? How? In Veilmar?"

Evie shook her head. "No, back in her home village. Somewhere on the eastern coast." She gave me an assessing look as if debating whether to say more. "A highblood did it."

My eyes widened. "That's awful." I looked over at the crying girl. Her life would never be the same. I understood: I'd lost my father at a much younger age.

Blightborn murders . . . There was a time when such a thing wouldn't have been so shocking. Highbloods used to hunt with abandon, and it was accepted. They were superior to us, after all; they deserved everything—apparently, even our lives. But there was no reason for it. Not when they had thrallweave. Not when they could simply take what they wanted without killing. It made no sense.

"The highblood was killed," Evie said. "If that's what you're wondering."

I blinked. "They were?"

She nodded. "He went after three other people in the village, including another highblood, before he was stopped. A group of highbloods took him down."

I felt oddly relieved. "If he went after his own kind, then it must have been madness. A fluke. A terrible accident."

Evie shrugged. "Maybe."

"What do you mean?"

She turned, as if to go. "I mean this isn't the first story I've heard like this."

I stared. "More murders?"

"Highbloods murdering blightborn—and other highbloods—for no real reason. Highbloods who had gone . . . berserk." She'd lowered her voice, but the other highbloods around us were listening in. They didn't seem shocked, however. Clearly they'd heard this rumor before. "I'll see you around, Shen. I'm going to talk to Kage."

I watched her go, remembering that she was Kage's Second now, then gave Neville a little boost in my arms.

A highblood boy approached me, Andrew, a Second Year. He was in one of my classes. "That fluffin." He looked at Neville curiously. "He's yours?"

"Sort of," I said cautiously. "He's not really anyone's."

"My sister's always wanted one as a pet. They're hard to find these days. I wonder if I could take him home. If he's just roaming around the school, I mean." Andrew leaned forward, reaching out a hand to pat Neville's head. Before he could finish the gesture, Neville growled. The boy quickly yanked his hand back.

"I'm not sure Neville likes that idea. And now that I think about it, he does have an owner," I lied. "Blake Drakharrow."

"Blake?" Andrew took a step back. "I didn't know that. He lets you what—borrow him?"

"Something like that," I called over my shoulder, already marching towards the staircase. "Good night, Andrew." To Neville, I whispered, "Don't worry, no one is going to take you home with them."

Neville gave another little growl, as if to say *I'd like to see them try.*

"Besides, you don't really belong to Blake or to me, do you?" I murmured.

He is his own person. Not a pet.

Neville made a high-pitched yipping sound as I jumped.

You need to stop doing that, I complained. *It's called eavesdropping.*

A pause. *Very well. Good luck.*

I frowned, realizing Nyxaris knew exactly what I was about to do. *Thank you*, I said reluctantly.

You rode well today. And then he was gone.

I sighed and raised my hand, knocking on the door gently. Then I waited. Wondering if she'd open it. Wondering what I'd see in her eyes when she did.

The door flew open. Medra stood there, her red hair loose around her shoulder and extremely fluffy, as if she'd just been brushing it. I glanced down, and sure enough, there was a silver brush in her hand. "Florence!" And then her arms were wrapped around me, she was pulling me inside, and we were both talking at the same time.

"Nyxaris! I couldn't believe he—"

"I know! And when he—"

"Did you see the look on her face before he—?"

"I'll never forget it."

We burst out laughing, beaming at each other.

"I suppose it's terribly heartless to be laughing at the death of a teacher," I whispered, putting a hand to my mouth. Part of me still hadn't taken it in. That Nyxaris had actually *killed* someone. For me.

"Are you kidding? I don't think Hassan deserves any of your civility or sympathy after leading you straight into the jaws of that snake Viktor." Medra scoffed. "If anyone was heartless, Florence, it was her. Besides, I thought we were talking about Regan!"

I stared at her for a moment. Then we erupted in laughter again. Finally, the sides of our faces sore from smiling, we calmed down. Medra grabbed my bag from where I'd dropped it, hauling it across the room with a grunt of effort.

"I see you packed light," she joked.

I blushed. "I brought back . . . well, everything."

She looked at me, her eyes soft. "So you're back for good, then?"

I nodded, then knelt down so Neville could jump out of my arms. He padded straight over to a bowl of water Medra had left on the floor for him. Apparently she'd still been receiving fluffin visits.

"I mean, it's all right if you aren't," she said quickly. "You can stay one night, see how you feel. I know being around highbloods all day is a lot. If being closer to your mother is more reassuring, I'll understand. I—"

"Medra," I interrupted. "I'm back. If you'll have me back."

She bit her lip, then nodded eagerly. "Of course. I've missed you so much. This place isn't the same without you."

I glanced around the room, looking to see if she'd made any changes. Everything seemed much the same. Except . . . "Is that Blake's shirt?" A white button-up hung over the back of an armchair.

"Um, no. I mean . . ." Medra blushed. "I guess he left it here, and I haven't given it back yet."

"Oh, Bloodmaiden," I whispered in delight. "Don't tell me you smell it at night when he's not around."

"Florence!" she shrieked. "How dare you. Also, how did you know that?"

I shrugged. "I've read a lot of romance books, remember? Typical girl-in-love behavior . . . Oh, I'm sorry, Medra. I didn't mean . . ."

She'd frozen, her eyes wide. Like a moth caught in a flame. "It's . . . all right."

"I didn't mean to cross a line." How could I have said something so stupid? My face was red. "Maybe I should go."

"Don't be absurd!" She looped her arm through mine, then leaned down to kiss Neville on the head. "You're my best friend. If anyone is allowed to tease me, it's you. I'm just being silly. It's just . . . That word. It's such a heavy one, you know? And we . . . Blake's never . . . I've never." She stopped. "I mean, I don't know what I feel for him." She looked at me, helplessly. "I guess I don't hate him anymore, though."

I giggled. "I mean, you wear his shirt, so I guess not."

She sniffed. "Speaking of scents, you smell like a dragon. How was your first ride?"

"I do not," I said, horrified, lowering my nose to smell my sweater. "Do I?"

"It's not a bad smell," she assured me. "Smoke and scales. A little like the sea. I've never figured out exactly what Nyxaris eats. A lot of fish, maybe a few sheep?"

"He steals sheep?" I said, horrified.

Medra snickered. "Well, I doubt he pays for them first. Can you imagine?"

We fell onto her bed side by side, howling at the image of Nyxaris offering a purse full of coins to a terrified-looking farmer.

"I suppose not." I hiccuped. "He's r-rather . . . intimidating, Medra."

She sobered. "He is, isn't he? I was afraid he'd kill me more than once." She saw the look on my face and quickly added, "But he won't hurt you, Florence. I'm sure of it."

I sat up, drawing my knees to my chest and wrapping my arms around them. Neville was sitting on one of the desks by the window, licking himself like a cat, his ears perked up as if he was listening to every word we said. For a moment, I sat waiting, then realized Nyxaris had taken my complaint seriously—he wouldn't be confirming or denying what Medra had just said.

"He's in my head a lot, Medra," I confided. "He just pops in and out, whenever he wants to. At first I ignored him, but now . . . Well, I guess I'm starting to get used to it. Was it like that for you? I can sense him. Sometimes, I can see what he sees. Smell what he smells." I grimaced. "I've tasted raw fish." I didn't tell her the taste was starting to grow on me. Or that the crunching of bones could be oddly satisfying.

Medra's eyes had widened. "No, it wasn't like that for me. I could hear him, of course. When he wanted to be heard, but we weren't always connected. Today, in Regan's office, he found you. How? Had you told him where we were?"

I shook my head. "No. I haven't quite figured out how to, well, juggle what's happening around me while speaking to him. He was asking me things, but I hadn't responded. I was too distracted." And frightened, I added silently. "I was as surprised as you when he appeared."

"Well, it's a good thing he did. He saved both our skins."

"For now," I said softly. "But Viktor . . ."

Medra bared her teeth. "That old highblood bastard will be back, I'm sure. But you have a dragon to protect you now. You'll be all right." She glanced away. "Look, there are snacks, if you want them. A plate of muffins. My half-eaten sandwich." She grinned when I wrinkled my nose. "I made tea. It's cold now, but you're welcome to it."

There was something wrong, something she wasn't telling me. But it could wait. I wanted to enjoy this—being back in our room, together, just talking.

"Medra, there's something I need to say," I burst out. "You saved my life. Again." *There. It was out. It was done. Better late than never.* "I didn't even thank you. In fact, I did the opposite—I ran. I've treated you so badly. I've been an awful friend. Really, I have. I'm sorry. Can you forgive me?"

She half smiled. "It's fine, Florence, really. I know what we did to save you was . . . extreme. And we couldn't exactly ask your permission first." She'd gotten right to the heart of the matter.

Medra hesitated. "Does your mother understand what happened?"

I nodded. "Most of it. She knows I'm connected to Nyxaris now. Not exactly how much or how closely, though."

"It must be frightening," Medra murmured. "So many changes."

"I've been frightened, yes," I agreed. "That's why I hid. Not just from you, but from *him*. I'm a coward."

You are not a coward.

I froze. *You called me one yourself.*

That was . . . before, Nyxaris said magnanimously.

I furrowed my brow. *Are you saying you were wrong?*

The answer came instantly. *Dragons are never wrong.*

Medra looked at me curiously, but she stayed silent.

I'm trying to have a private conversation, I reminded him.

And I am trying to reassure my rider that their bravery is no longer in question. He was quiet for a moment, but I knew he was still there. *You are not the same as she is. You are different.*

There was a lump in my throat. *Bad different? I'm sorry. I know I'm a disappointment.*

Not a disappointment, he rebuffed me. *You are a very clever girl, a scholar with a brilliant mind. When one lives their entire life expecting to be a scribe, it is understandably difficult to adapt to becoming a rider. You rode well today, as I said.* A brief pause. *Better than I expected you to.*

Is that . . . a compliment? I said in surprise.

It is not a compliment if you must ask if it is a compliment, he grumbled. *Take it or leave it, fledgling.*

I smiled at Medra. She smiled back. She was waiting patiently. Obviously, she'd figured out what was going on.

You did not scream, Nyxaris added, apparently still considering all that might have gone wrong. *Or faint. Or toss the contents of your belly onto my back.*

I bit my lip, trying to hold back laughter.

Which is more than I can say for some of your kind the first time they ride a dragon, he continued.

I'm not sure that not vomiting sets the bar very high, I pointed out.

You held steady, he went on, ignoring me. *You are used to excelling, to receiving the best marks. To earning your teachers' praise.*

I sensed him watching me. The strange mental weight of his attention pressing against my skin. My cheeks warmed self-consciously. *Yes, I suppose that's true.*

You will have to earn your admiration from me, he chided, almost teasingly.

I'll work hard to do so then, Professor Nyxaris, I teased back.

What was this? Was I really bantering with a dragon?

You're my rider. Not simply because your life was spared thanks to me.

No one could ever accuse Nyxaris of having low self-esteem; he was rather full of himself, and yet it wasn't intolerable. If anyone had earned the right to an ego, it was a dragon.

You remind me of someone I lost. The words were said almost reluctantly.

I blinked hard. *Who?*

No one you need worry about, he said gruffly. *She is long dead. You are not her.*

There was a pain in my chest. *Do you . . . wish I were?*

No, Nyxaris snapped, his voice like a breaking stone. *No. I do not.* He hesitated, then spoke again. *You are different. Calmer, quieter. But there is fire in you.*

My breath caught. Was this a compliment? It felt like one.

Do not let anyone put that flame out. Let it blaze within your heart. And then he was gone.

Medra touched my shoulder lightly. "Are you back?"

I nodded. "I'm back."

"What was that?" she breathed. "Was he talking to you?"

"Yes. Apparently, he couldn't stay away." I should have been annoyed that he'd interrupted yet again, but oddly I wasn't.

"You look . . . happy," Medra ventured. "Does talking to him feel right?"

I looked at her. "It didn't at first. But it does now. Is that strange?"

She shook her head. "I don't know. I've never been bonded to a dragon. Our connection was different than this. Remember at the beginning? Nyxaris would only talk to me because he hoped I'd be able to get him information."

There was a knock at the door. We looked at each other.

"I wasn't expecting Blake," she said. "But that doesn't mean he hasn't decided to just show up."

"He can come into the Avari Tower?"

"Well, no, but that doesn't mean he doesn't sneak in anyways. He usually waits until it's night, though."

I stared at Medra. Of course she'd had company while I was away. She must have been lonely. Now here I was, disrupting her new routine. "I can leave," I offered. "I can go to the library, start working on my next essay for—"

"No," she interrupted. "Absolutely not. Not another essay. You probably have five on the go already."

I blushed. She wasn't far off. "Six, actually."

She laughed. "I'll tell him to go away." She smiled mischievously. "It'll be fun to say no. He needs to hear it now and then."

I smiled as she hopped off the bed. But when she pulled the door open, it wasn't Blake standing there after all, but Kage.

"House Leader," Medra quipped. "To what do we owe this great honor?"

He looked right past Medra and directly at me. "I'm afraid that I need Miss Shen to accompany me." His voice was strained.

"What? Why? Not back to Regan's fucking office again!" Medra exclaimed hotly. She crossed her arms over her chest. "We're not going back there. Florence is not going back there. Unless everyone wants another taste of dragon fire."

She is very protective of you. Nyxaris was back.

She is, I agreed, feeling happy. *She's a very good friend.*

Of course she is. She gave you me, Nyxaris said with shameless self-centeredness. *In any case, I've been expecting this. Don't overreact.*

Overreact? What do you mean, "Don't overreact"? I hissed back. *I like to be prepared for everything. You know that! Tell me, Nyxaris.*

But he was gone again.

"No, not back to the headmistress's office," Kage responded. "My grandmother is waiting. She'd like to speak with us."

I looked at Medra. Kage had said *us.* What did that mean?

My friend was frowning. *"Us?"*

"With Florence and me," Kage said stiffly. "Florence, will you please accompany me back to my room? She's waiting there."

I got to my feet slowly. "Of course."

Medra glared at Kage. "She'd better be back here in an hour or I'll be banging at your door. In one piece, do you hear? And not crying." She glanced at me. "Will you be all right? Do you need me to go with you?"

I shook my head. "I'll be all right. But thank you. I'll see you back here soon."

I followed Kage into the hallway. He led the way up the next flight of stairs, down a narrow hall. Finally, we stopped in front of a door etched in silver.

"What's this really about?" I whispered to him.

But he just shook his head and flung open the door. "Grandmother, may I present to you Miss Shen." He gestured for me to step into the room. "Miss Shen, may I present my grandmother, Lady Elaria Avari."

Lady Avari stood on the far side of the room, near a white marble hearth. With the firelight flickering against silver hair pinned up with diamonds, she looked like a portrait of highblood royalty come to life. Slowly, she turned to face us. She was dressed in a long black velvet dress with a silver jacket overtop. The motto of House Avari, *Luna Sanguinea Surgit*, was stitched across her left breast. A silver crescent moon pendant hung from a pearl choker at her throat. Her eyes were dark like her grandson's. They found mine instantly—sharp, assessing. Not unkind exactly, but not completely warm either.

"Miss Shen." She came across the room and stopped halfway near a cluster of comfortable-looking armchairs and sofas. "It's so good to finally meet you. My grandson has told me how eager he was to make sure you were recruited into his house. I understand you're something of an academic prodigy." She sat down in an armchair and gestured for me to come take a seat.

I selected a sofa across from her and sat down slowly, feeling ill at ease. "It's an honor to meet you, Lady Avari. But I assure you, I'm no prodigy. I just work hard."

I glanced up as Kage crossed the room. He took a seat by the window, stretching his long legs out in front of him.

Lady Avari was watching me. "You've led a very eventful life these past few weeks, haven't you, Florence?"

"I suppose so," I said carefully. How much did she know? I wondered.

Everything. Nyxaris's voice was grim. *The Avari boy will have told her everything. There is no point in hiding, fireheart.*

Fireheart?

A pause. *I have decided it is no longer fitting to address you as* fledgling. *You are not a hatchling, after all. You are a rider.*

Thanks, I guess, I stumbled.

Do not thank me yet. You are in the wolf's den now, remember. Tread warily.

That was a little alarming. I sat up straighter.

"And yet you've come through intact." Lady Avari tilted her head. "You're clearly resilient. I understand you nearly died."

Kage had been there, witness to everything. What had he really been thinking that night as Medra offered to give up her dragon for my life?

I took a deep breath. "Yes. That's true." I didn't offer more information. What was the point if she knew everything already?

"You've bonded with Nyxaris," Lady Avari observed.

I smiled slightly. "So they tell me. It wasn't exactly a choice."

It was for me.

I tried to hide my surprise, but of course, Nyxaris was right. He had chosen to save me.

My throat was dry. *I'm grateful for what you did. I didn't mean . . .*

It is of no consequence. Nyxaris's voice was wry. *Listen to the highblood woman now.*

"I mean, it was not intentional," I clarified. "Medra would have made a much better rider."

Lady Avari smiled. "Perhaps. But intention is irrelevant. What matters is what is done." She touched a ring on her finger, twisting the diamond-laden band. "You know, Nyxaris was once bound to House Avari. He was loyal to us for many years, before events forced his long slumber."

"Of course. I'd forgotten that."

I have not. Nyxaris's voice was cold.

"I'm not surprised. It's to the advantage of House Drakharrow that we all forget. But your bond to Nyxaris is a revival of that ancient tie, for you are a member of our house. Your bond is thus one we would like to honor—and protect."

Protect. There was a weight to the word. "What kind of protection?" I asked carefully.

"I propose an arrangement," Lady Avari said smoothly. "A formal bond. Viktor Drakharrow has already made his interest in you known. I have no doubt he'll try to exploit you for his own gain. We cannot allow that to happen."

My fingers curled around my knee. "So Kage told you what happened today."

"It is a miracle that the dragon arrived when he did," Lady Avari said directly. "Florence, have you ever heard the term *soul-binding*?"

Slowly, I shook my head.

"It is not a pleasant thing for a blightborn. Soul-binding describes the process in which a dragon rider's soul is merged to a highblood's—forcibly. It allows a highblood to bind a rider as a living chain."

"So they can ride a dragon," I whispered.

"Yes. Highbloods are not riders. *You* were never meant to be a rider. And yet, here we are."

I licked my lips. "And Viktor . . . You think he knows how to do this? That he wants to do this to me?"

"There is absolutely no doubt in my mind that Viktor Drakharrow knows precisely how to perform the ritual. We know he intended to use it upon Medra Pendragon." She shrugged elegantly. "Now, whether he intended to be the soul involved or whether he would use another, I cannot say. He has recently taken a bride, after all."

"Regan." I stared at Lady Avari in horror. "Are you saying he'd bind my soul to hers?"

"I cannot say for certain, but we have reason to believe the soul involved would not necessarily be his own. There is a risk for the highblood involved in the ritual. It does not always succeed, you see. Viktor Drakharrow has safeguarded his own life over that of others for centuries. He is the most risk-averse man I know." Lady Avari sounded disdainful.

"And this is allowed?" I whispered again.

"It's forbidden," Kage cut in quietly. "But that doesn't mean it's not possible."

Lady Avari waved a hand. "Viktor sees himself as above every law, we all know this. He believes dragons should be controlled, bound like weapons, like slaves."

In my head, Nyxaris growled. I touched a finger to my temple. I could feel Lady Avari's and Kage's eyes upon me.

"You are the key, Florence." The old highblood woman's voice was gentle. "You are the most vulnerable piece on the board."

Nyxaris stirred in my mind. *She is speaking the truth about Viktor. About the soul-binding.*

Why didn't you tell me this before? I hissed.

"Viktor will come for you," Lady Avari went on. "Because you are the key to Nyxaris."

I swallowed. "So, what do I do?"

She smiled faintly. "You let us protect you."

Try not to panic when you hear what comes next.

What is that supposed to mean? I hissed. *I am already panicking.* But I didn't have to wait long.

"The solution is clear," Lady Avari said calmly. "You and my grandson must be betrothed at once."

"I beg your pardon?" I squeaked.

I blinked. I stared at Kage. His shoulders had stiffened, but he didn't speak, didn't exclaim in shock. It was obvious he'd known exactly what was coming.

"It would be a great honor, Miss Shen," he said slowly, "if you would consider becoming my consort."

"This is a very generous offer," Lady Avari pointed out, as if I should be jumping up and down on the sofa with glee. "And a very strategic one. Someday Kage will take a second consort—a highblood, of course. Together, you will form a strong triad. Together, you will protect the bond you have with the dragon. Not to mention safeguarding your very soul."

I found my voice. "It also brings strength to House Avari. You'd have a dragon on your side. It's politically brilliant, isn't it?" I was training to be a strategist—my education hadn't completely evaporated despite my anxiety.

Elaria didn't flinch. "Of course it is. We hope this will solidify Nyxaris's allegiance, not to mention showing him our good intentions. We wish to protect his rider, after all."

Nyxaris snorted derisively.

You don't believe them? I ventured.

I believe they want my allegiance. As for whether they'll protect you . . . they will as long as it is in their best interests. It is . . . a wise arrangement.

You really want me to do this? I asked in disbelief. *Become betrothed to Kage?*

He is a highblood, Nyxaris replied contemptuously. *You could do better. But in terms of power, you could do no worse.*

I stared at Kage. *If we did this, he might expect to feed from me.* I'd never felt a highblood's bite before. But Medra had. She'd survived. She'd even started to seem to, well, like it.

That is the downside, yes, Nyxaris said coldly. *Of course, you may be able to negotiate a marriage contract that excludes feeding.*

A contract? My throat felt tight. This was all happening so fast.

"I would treat you with kindness and respect, Florence," Kage said stiffly. "You would be an honored consort and part of the Avari family."

Do you believe the boy?

I . . . I don't know. He's my House Leader. He's always been true to his word. He's shown me kindness before, yes.

Then, it might not be so bad. Nyxaris sounded remote.

"It is an engagement, Florence, not a marriage," Lady Avari pointed out. "Not yet. But it will make a powerful statement. And it will be a shield—one which you desperately need within the walls of this school where Nyxaris cannot always protect you."

Nyxaris growled, but I could hear the frustration in his voice. *I could burn the walls down to powder right now, if I chose.*

Yes, but I'd be powder, too, I pointed out. *And Medra. And Neville. And . . .*

The point has been made, he snapped. *She is not wrong. It is not an ideal choice. But it is the least foolish one.*

You think I should do this, then? I whispered.

I believe you should live. If this will help you reach that end, then it is the most logical choice.

"What about Kage?" I asked, nodding towards my House Leader. "Has he had a say in this?"

Kage's grandmother arched a silver brow. "My grandson is the future leader of this house. He will do whatever is necessary to protect it—and to protect you."

"She's right, Florence." Kage leaned forward.

He had very nice eyes, I suddenly noticed. Dark pools of obsidian. Full of strength and intelligence. He was strong and stalwart, and he'd been kind to me, especially for a highblood. But I'd never thought of him in this sort of way—as my archon, as my betrothed. As someone to share my bed—because that's what it would come down to eventually, wouldn't it?

"You'd have my protection," Kage continued. "Not just my name. You'd be under House Avari's protection for as long as you lived. Not just you, your mother, too. No one would be able to harm either of you."

I hesitated.

It will not be forever, Nyxaris said quietly. *I have my own plan.*

My heart sped up. *To deal with Viktor?*

Yes. All of this has gone on long enough. I did not return from the stone to become a pawn to highbloods—nor to have my rider become one herself. I will end him. But there are . . . complications.

What kind of complications?

A pause. *The kind which would put you in more danger to know.*

Dragons and their cryptic natures. I wanted to say no. I wanted to *scream* no.

"Yes," I said. "I'll do it."

I walked back to our room in a daze. I'd knocked before even realizing I'd done it. Medra opened the door almost instantly. She wore a long loose blue tunic over black leggings, her hair now tied up in a messy knot, little curls popping out around her face. She looked amused.

"You live here, Florence. You don't need to knock."

"Right," I said, my voice hollow.

She narrowed her eyes. "What happened?" She ushered me inside. "You look like you've seen a ghost."

I dropped onto the nearest object, which happened to be her bed, unable to answer right away.

"Florence?"

"There's good news and bad news," I said finally.

"Oh goody," Medra muttered. "Go on."

"The good news is—" I tried to make my voice bright and plastered a smile on my face "—there's going to be another ball!"

Medra blinked suspiciously. "A ball? That's the good news? Have you forgotten what happened after the last one?"

"Oh. Right."

"And the bad news?"

I hesitated. "Well, the Avaris made a proposal." I snuck a glance at her face. So far, so good.

"All right," she said cautiously. "What kind of proposal?"

"I mean, it was Kage who made the proposal. Well, I mean his grandmother did the actual proposing, but it doesn't really involve her."

"It doesn't?"

"I mean, it does," I said hastily. "But not directly. That would be really weird. Can you imagine?"

"No, Florence," Medra replied. "I can't. Because you're dancing around what really happened. Just tell me."

I took a deep breath and said the words as quickly as possible. "I'mbetrothedtoKage."

"You're what?" Medra looked exasperated. "Say it again more slowly, less mumbly."

I bit my lip, hesitating. "I'm betrothed. To Kage."

There was a stunned silence. Medra sat down slowly on my bed, across from where I stood. "You move back in here. You're here for less than an hour. I let you go off with Kage to meet his grandmother. And now you're . . . betrothed?" She put her head in her hands and moaned. "Florence, your mother is going to kill you. Or me. Or both of us."

"Is she?" I tilted my head. "Maybe she'll just be happy I can't be soul-bound."

Medra's head jerked up. "What?"

"When were you going to tell me?" I asked quietly. "You already knew, didn't you?"

"Yes," she whispered. "I'm sorry. You've been so afraid, I didn't want to scare you more. Especially when you'd finally come back."

I nodded. "That makes sense."

"But I was going to tell you, probably as soon as tomorrow. I had to. Especially after Hassan told Regan and Viktor. He knows now."

"Lady Avari might be a match for Viktor," I said thoughtfully.

"Maybe. She's certainly an imposing woman. She impressed me during the Tribunal." Medra sighed. "How do you really feel about this?"

I chewed my bottom lip. "Nyxaris says it won't be forever. He has a plan."

Medra raised one dark red brow. "Oh really?"

"Yes, but he won't share it. He'll only say that Viktor's more complicated than he looks."

"Not precisely encouraging," Medra said dryly.

When the time comes, I will unmake him. Piece by piece, Nyxaris growled.

I shifted on the bed. "Nyxaris says he'll destroy Viktor. Eventually."

"Eventually," Medra echoed. "And in the meantime we're just going to have another ball and pretend everything's fine while you're what—fake engaged to Kage fucking Tanaka?"

"*Pretend*, yes. *Engaged*, also yes."

"Do you . . . feel anything for him? Is it possible this could just . . . work out somehow?"

In my mind, Nyxaris had gone very silent—and yet, I knew he was still there, waiting for my answer. "He's . . . very handsome. He's always been kind to me. He's noble. Wealthy. Powerful," I listed obediently. "But those things have never been important to me before. I don't even know if he reads books."

Medra snickered. "I'm sure he knows how to read."

"But does he read as homework, for pleasure, or because he craves knowledge?" I threw up my hands. "I don't really know him at all, do I? So do I *feel* something? No, I don't think I feel anything. I don't think Kage feels anything for me either. I don't think he wants this, he's just . . . doing his duty."

"This is not what I want for you," Medra said softly. "Someone who will just do their duty. You deserve so much more than that." She lay back on the bed. "I can't fucking believe this is happening again. Another betrothal to another highblood—one neither of us wants."

"Well, things turned out all right for you and Blake," I pointed out.

She sat up. "Is that what we are, *all right?*" She shook her head. "We're a dangerous mix together, Florence. Tinder and sparks. He still scares me. But you're right, at least when I'm with him, I feel something. Something so intense, it's—well, terrifying sometimes."

"I'm not sure I want that," I said thoughtfully. "To feel that terrifying feeling. It sounds awful."

Medra giggled. "It's not all bad. I promise."

"Still, maybe I don't want to ever fall in love. It's so scary. I'm already bonded to a dragon. Can't that be enough?"

Medra smiled sadly. "Maybe it'll have to be. For now." She looked at me thoughtfully. "Or maybe things will change. Kage isn't so bad."

"I knew you'd say that eventually," I said, laughing.

"He's not hard to look at, all right? I won't deny that. He certainly has charisma, though he can be infuriating, too. Not as infuriating as Blake, though," she said, tilting her head in consideration. "Maybe you could come to have feelings for him. At least you don't hate his guts and want him dead, right?"

I suddenly wondered which was the better foundation for a relationship: a total absence of affection or emotion of any sort, like what was currently between Kage and me, or the tempestuous hatred that Medra and Blake immediately possessed for one another when they first met.

"Try to dream about him tonight," Medra suggested, only half teasing. "Maybe it won't be so bad." She winked.

I curled up in my bed after Medra had put out the lamps. We'd talked until late into the night; now I needed to fall asleep. I had to get at least a few hours of rest or I'd be a mess in the morning. I'd missed a lot of my classes, but my professors had been surprisingly understanding. It helped that I'd continued turning in all of my assignments, and some extra-credit ones besides. Tomorrow would be my first full day back, attending all of my regular classes.

Neville was already snoring. He lay at the foot of my bed, his little paws twitching as if he was chasing something in his dreams. Probably a rabbit.

Try to dream about Kage, Medra had said.

I closed my eyes and tried to picture my House Leader. But when I drifted off to sleep, Kage never showed up. Instead, the dream crept in like fog across glass. Warmth spread over my body, heat coiling and spreading beneath my skin. My breath caught. I was dreaming. But it was so vivid. So real. My body arched, hips pressing into the phantom weight above me. Hands—broad, clawed, impossibly strong—gripped my thighs, spreading them open. Not hurting, but unmistakably possessive. And the heat. There was so much heat.

I twisted, sweat beading along my collarbone. I was naked. I could see the rise and fall of my breasts.

A low voice wrapped around my ribs, hard as stones but far more intimate. *Open your heart to me, rider. Show me that heart of fire.*

I gasped. My dream-self whispered a name. *Nyxaris—*

This is a dream, another part of me said reassuringly. *Just a dream.*

Of course it is, he murmured, hands sliding up to grasp my hips as he ground against me. *I would never touch you like this when you were awake.*

My eyes flew open. My pulse thundered. The room was dark. Moonlight spilled like milk across the carpeted floor. Neville was still snoring. Medra was in her bed, a peaceful lump beneath the blankets. And I . . . I was burning. My skin was flushed, covered in a sheen of sweat, my legs tangled up in the sheets. I'd clenched my thighs so tightly I was cramping. I lay still, trying to calm my breathing.

It was just a dream. Just a dream.

I had ridden a dragon for the first time the day before. Maybe this was some weird side effect that Medra had forgotten to tell me about.

Except . . . except I could still feel him on top of me.

I squeezed my eyes shut, desperate to fall asleep again. This time determined not to dream.

Then, maddeningly . . .

Interesting.

I froze. *You'd better not be awake right now. Go away.*

I did not do anything came his smug, infuriating reply. *Did I?*

I groaned aloud and rolled onto my stomach, hiding my face in my pillow. *Please tell me you can't see my dreams.*

I cannot see your dreams.

I popped my head up, sucking in breath. *Wait. Are you saying that because I told you to or because it's the truth?*

Which would you like it to be?

Nyxaris, I hissed.

Was I in your dream? Is that why you are acting so bizarrely?

I'm not answering that, I said hotly, my face flushing with shame.

The bond is a two-way corridor. I have had to suffer through your mortal cravings before. I am sure it will not be the last time.

Cravings? My face felt hot enough to melt a candle. *Before?* Oh, Bloodmaiden.

Of course. The strawberry scones. The time you cried over that painting of the bird with a broken wing.

That was sad, you monster. And it was a masterpiece.

Nyxaris ignored me. *The way you looked at your new betrothed this evening . . .*

I did not look at Kage any which way, I protested. *I was assessing him, that's all. Besides, I thought you wanted me to do this. To be safe.*

A pause. *I do wish that.*

Then, what's the problem? I grumbled. *Or are you jealous?*

There was no reply.

Nyxaris?

He'd probably gone to sleep. Or was chasing down sheep. Poor, pitiful sheep. They had no hope in hell of escaping that dragon—and neither did I.

I turned over again, lying on my back. But all I could think of was the way it had felt. To be *desired* like that. In the dark, every inch of my body betrayed my rational mind, my hand moving slowly between my thighs, and my eyes closed tightly.

Bloodmaiden . . . I was in so much trouble.

CHAPTER 18

MEDRA

Florence was back. Florence was home. And so I fell asleep with ease. In my dreams, the forest outside the castle in Camelot was just as I remembered it. Sunlight spilled through the tree canopy. A gentle breeze stirred the aspen trees. The sound of the wind in the leaves might have been my favorite sound in the world. In the clearing ahead, Odessa stood waiting, pulling her long, black braided hair up into a heavy knot.

"You're dawdling." She wore a gruff expression, but the teasing tone of her voice belied it.

"I was picketing the horses," I protested. "Someone had to do it, after you stalked off to do your hair."

I studied my mentor. In some ways, she was the closest thing I had to a mother. Her features were lovely, even delicate, but the dark skin of her face was lined with countless scars. Two formidable blades were strapped to her back, hilts wrapped in worn leather. Now she slid the sword belts off her shoulders, reaching down to pick two wooden practice swords up off the ground.

She grinned. "Catch."

Moments later, our blades clacked together. The rhythm was familiar and comforting, just like Odessa herself—yet how I'd hated her at first! As a child, I was used to hating everyone, trusting no one.

Duck, twist, spin. Strike!

Odessa was faster, far superior in skill, but I still possessed the surety of youth. I believed I'd catch up someday, perhaps even surpass her. I wasn't afraid. I wasn't nervous. I was just *there*. Happy.

The forest changed, trees shifting closer together. The canopy overhead suddenly dimmed, no light spilling through the leaves. The colors of the woods melted from warm greens and browns into a palette of black and gray. The colors of death.

Medra.

I froze, my sword half-raised. "Did you hear that?" I asked Odessa.

She blinked. "Hear what?"

The birdsong faded. An unnatural wind rustled through the now-leafless branches.

Medra. The voice came again. *Can you hear me, child?*

"No," I whispered. "That's not possible."

But Odessa was suddenly gone. I stared at the place she'd been standing.

You didn't think you'd be rid of me that easily, did you? The voice chuckled.

I gasped. *Mother?*

That's certainly one name for what I am—and the one I'm most fond of, Orcades said dryly.

My knees nearly buckled with shock. But beyond the shock there was joy, painful and aching, but wonderful.

What other names might there be? I asked nervously.

She sighed. *I suppose you might call me Scorched, Scaly One. Or Queen of Carrion.*

I snorted. *Good to see you haven't lost your sense of humor.* I hesitated. *So you're still . . . inside Molindra, then?*

I am. Her soul is shattered. She sleeps now, but her dreams are scattered things.

My heart surged with relief. *I thought when you vanished with Marcus and Catherine that you were gone . . . for good.*

Still with those two idiots, not that they know it. Orcades sounded shockingly cheerful for a disembodied voice inhabiting a corrupt dragon raised with necromancy.

I thought I'd failed you. I was so stupid when I used the knife.

Stupid? How were you stupid? You didn't fail me, she chided. *You're still alive, aren't you?*

Apparently.

And Florence?

She's still alive, too, I conceded.

Well, then. Orcades sounded satisfied. *All is well.*

I swallowed. *Is it? Where exactly are you?*

A forest of some kind. Those two egomaniacal dolts have been calling it the Bonewood.

The name made me shiver. *That doesn't sound pleasant.*

It's certainly not the place I'd have chosen to reside. An utter mess of mist and cobwebs. Not much room for a dragon the size of Molindra between all of the trees either. But apparently it's the perfect place for this nefarious little project.

The clearing I stood in had become a stone ravine, half-swallowed by mist. I took a few steps forward. Something vast shifted beyond the haze: a golden, ruined shape, wings webbed with dark veins. A dragon, massive and decaying—Molindra. I recoiled, stepping back quickly, twigs snapping beneath my feet.

Is Molindra . . . alive?

She's . . . something. Something more like me, Orcades mused. *Old bones, even older rage. She can be difficult. But I think we've reached an understanding.*

I assume that means she gave up in the face of your stubbornness, I said, half laughing.

I do pride myself on my determined nature. You should, too, considering you've inherited it. In any case, I've been able to get through to her, in a sense. We've spoken—if you can call it that. A pause. *I pity her, really. On some level, the poor old girl knows what's been done to her.* Orcades was silent for a long moment. *Well, on the positive side*, she said eventually, *Molindra may be mostly dead, but her power is enormous. Why, her breath can melt stone. That said, one must wonder why our two fearless leaders chose a dragon whose specialty is drawing strength from the sun when they planned to bring her to such a sunless place. I suppose we should simply thank the gods they are such fools. Really, it's difficult to take villains seriously when they make such fundamental mistakes.*

I suppose they chose Molindra because she belonged to House Orphos, I said cautiously. *It must have had something to do with Lunaya.*

Oh, Lunaya, my mother sighed. *Don't get me started on that poor dear girl.*

Poor dear girl? My heart sped up. *So Lunaya's alive, then? You've seen her?* I thought of Lysander. I could tell him. But would he even believe me?

Seen her? My dear child, she's ridden atop my back. A pause. *Not very well, but I suppose it can't be helped in her condition.*

In her condition? What does that mean? What's happening to her?

Oh, horrid things. The poor girl is not entirely herself, just like the old scaly one here. I could practically picture her patting Molindra's rotting scales.

You're a strange trio, I murmured.

Another sigh. *Yes, aren't we? But never fear. I have a plan.*

My heart hammered. *A plan? Mother, please. Perhaps it would be best if you kept your head down. Metaphorically speaking, I mean. They don't know you're even there.*

Keep my head down? Oh no. That isn't my style at all, dear heart. Orcades gave a tinkling laugh that reminded me she was a fae princess. My heart clenched. How I wished I could have seen her in all her glory! If my mother was this vivacious as a disembodied voice, she must have been truly something in the flesh. *I'm going to save her, you know. I've absolutely committed myself to that.*

I could almost see her nodding emphatically. My heart soared and sank. I'd heard that tone before—I'd used it myself. When anyone said that, it usually meant someone was going to die.

All right, I sighed. *I wish you luck. How can I help?*

Help? Ah no, Daughter. It is I who shall be helping you.

How can you help me? I said, a little amused.

By delaying the inevitable, of course. Stalling tactics. Sabotage. Molindra is on board—at least, I think she is.

Of course the dead dragon is in your corner, I muttered. *How reassuring.*

Well, it should be. Don't look down on her simply because she's necrotic, Medra. Someone should have taught you better manners than that.

I rolled my eyes.

Now, you know of the Veil, of course, Orcades went on.

The what?

A pause of disbelief. *By the Three, child. Didn't they teach you anything back in Aercanum?*

They taught me a great deal, not that I was there all that long, I said, a little grumpily.

Very well. I shall enlighten you as best I can, she said with a sigh. *Now, I do take it you know what a portal is? You may know them as archways?*

Of course. I saw them in Camelot. We traveled by them sometimes.

Excellent. Think of the Veil as a portal. But one which connects worlds.

I stiffened. *Marcus and Catherine are trying to get to another world?*

I don't believe travel is on their mind, precisely. Think of the Veil as a wall between realms. A pause. *Sangratha is a very strange place, you know. Different in so many ways . . . and yet, familiar in others.*

My stomach did a somersault. *What do you mean? Familiar how?*

I haven't quite put my finger on it yet, but you'll be the first to know when I do, she said cryptically.

Fine, I said impatiently. *And this Veil? Why does it matter what Marcus and Catherine do to it?*

Use your head, child, she scolded. *It wouldn't have a guardian if it wasn't supposed to be locked.*

A guardian? This is the first time you've mentioned a guardian.

No, I'm sure I mentioned her before, she said, a little peevishly.

I suddenly wondered something: If my mother was in Molindra, was Molindra also in her? If Molindra was truly, well, *dead*, then was she also decaying? How long could Catherine keep the dragon in this in-between state? Would she eventually crumble and rot? When that happened, where would Orcades go? What would she be?

Of course you've heard of the guardian. Everyone has. Why, they stole her name, the Old One. You've visited her temple, for heaven's sake.

I frowned. *Her temple?*

The Sanctum, my mother said, impatiently.

I sucked in a breath. *Holy shit, Mother, are you saying that the guardian of the Veil is the fucking Bloodmaiden?*

Such unnecessarily foul language, Orcades tsked. *But yes, the Bloodmaiden, precisely. An odd title, but there is no accounting for these vampire tastes.*

Have you actually spoken to her? I hissed. *She's supposed to be a goddess.*

I don't know what she is exactly, only that Marcus and Catherine are hammering on her door, and she's not willing to open.

Well, thank the gods for that, I muttered. Hammering on the fucking door of a goddess? That couldn't be good.

Regardless, the fools aren't giving up. And what's worse, they're making inroads.

I groaned. *Inroads?*

Cracks. In the Veil, she continued. *These two see themselves as dark prophets, heralding a reclamation.*

A reclamation? What do you mean?

They want to bring back part of Sangratha they believe was lost. But none of that matters right now.

I rolled my eyes, finding that hard to believe.

What matters, she went on, *are the cracks.*

Right. The cracks.

Do not mock me, child, she said, hearing my sardonic tone. *I may be mostly dragon, but I am not senile yet.*

I'm sorry, I said and meant it. *You know, I really have missed you terribly, Mother.*

I've missed you, too, my love. She sighed. *How I wish sometimes I were still in that silly little knife. Who would ever have imagined I'd miss it? Now, listen, something is happening—not just here in the Bonewood, but out in the rest of the world. Perhaps you've noticed things. Signs, warnings. Tiny cracks. I fear those cracks will build and build.*

I tried to think of anything strange, but all I could think of was Viktor and Regan and their new regime of blightborn cruelty. *Things are pretty normal here at Bloodwing,* I said carefully. *All things considered. But I'll keep an eye out.*

Very well. In any case, my mother went on, *do what you must to stay alive. Protect Florence. When whatever happens happens, I need you standing.* Orcades became hurried. *I must go. She's waking now. We'll speak again.*

A wave of mist swirled around me, and then she was gone. I realized I was awake—truly awake. I pushed back my blankets. In the other bed, Florence slept on, her face still and peaceful. Neville lifted his head lazily from the end of Florence's bed to glance at me. He gave a wide yawn, then lowered his head again, tucking his tail over his eyes. I turned over on my side, watching the two of them sleep. I wasn't alone. Not here, not even in my dreams. The thought was comforting.

But I suddenly wished Blake were with me. Not only because I wanted his arms around me, but because of the solid weight of him, the unshakable strength he carried about with him, without even realizing it.

Orcades was still out there. Alive—well, sort of. That was something to be grateful for. But what she'd told me was strange and terrifying. She'd given me the pieces of a puzzle. Cracks in a wall, a dreaming dragon, a sleeping goddess. But I wasn't sure I'd be able to put the pieces together. Not until I knew more.

Part of me wanted to tell Blake about the dream, the Veil, my mother's soul riding a half-dead dragon through the Bonewood. But something held me back. Maybe it was the knowledge that he was holding back, too. Blake was holding too many secrets of his own. I wouldn't add to the weight he carried until I had something we could act on.

Still, I knew one thing: If the cracks split wide and the world fell apart, he'd be beside me. Once his darkness had frightened me, but

I'd seen his rage and reached for him anyway because I'd glimpsed what else lived beneath his skin: loyalty so fierce it scorched. The desire to do better. He'd seen the shadows in me, too. He hadn't turned away. I knew he never would.

Once, I'd thought him dangerous, a monster. But that was our bond. Not clean, not easy. But unbreakable.

Book 2
Springrise

CHAPTER 19

REGAN

The wind from the sea tugged at the skirt of my gown, fingers of ice trying to drag me over the side of the cliff on which I stood. I was too close to the edge. The ground beneath my feet was slick with melted snow. One wrong step and I'd be down on those jagged rocks in pieces. But I didn't move back. Blades of grass forced their way up through the melting snow. Sangrathan folklore said the first day of Springrise was a special time of renewal, the time for new beginnings—for hope and rebirth.

But standing there in the dark at the close of the first day of spring, with the salt-heavy wind slicing through me, I didn't feel a sense of renewal. I felt *old*. Hard. Tired. In the mirror, my face looked much the same as it always had. As long as you didn't peek beneath the high-collared gowns I'd taken to wearing, you'd never know. Never know how battered I was under all the silk and satin. Never know how ancient I felt inside, as brittle as the frost that was now vanishing to make way for the birds and the flowers.

I folded my arms over my chest; I'd come outside without a cloak again on purpose. The cold was punishing, but at least it was a punishment I'd chosen for myself.

I'd thought things with Viktor couldn't get any worse. I'd been wrong.

After Nyxaris's appearance in my office, I'd returned to our chamber that evening flushed with righteous rage, for once feeling too angry to be afraid of my archon. I'd gone to him with my voice raised, demanding to know why he'd vanished, why he hadn't stayed to protect me. I'd called him a coward, accused him of running away. What a fool I'd been, demanding things like a woman who still thought she had the right to expect something from the man who held her whip.

It had been a mistake. I'd have been better off biting my own tongue off. I should have gone down on my knees and praised him for saving me with his absence. That was what he really wanted: to be worshipped, adored, feared. Never, ever questioned. But I'd never been good at controlling my temper. As a child, I'd been spoiled and pampered, rewarded for my tantrums.

Now, with Viktor, it was the opposite. Control meant *everything* at any cost. I'd always been proud of my boldness, but Viktor didn't want me to be bold, he wanted a shadow of the girl he'd once watched from afar. A pretty thing who smiled on cue and bled when asked. He wanted me subdued. Obedient. With Blake, I'd mostly been able to play that part. Blake never asked much of me. He'd always been . . . distant, never interested in closeness, no matter how hard I tried. We'd never had that kind of connection. Not the kind he seemed to have with *her*.

With Viktor, I was learning I wasn't very good at obedience after all. Maybe the part of me that had happily followed orders had died the day Blake dissolved our triad. Or maybe it was that Blake had never really ordered me at all. He'd certainly never beaten me, never bruised me. Never hurt me, not intentionally.

With Viktor, I thought I was already broken, that it couldn't get any worse. But that night, he'd showed me I had far more to learn about pain. He'd shattered me. Not like a porcelain plate accidentally dropped on the floor. No, this had been slower. Longer. I'd woken the next morning in silk sheets, my skin scoured raw in places it had no right to be. I hadn't raised my voice to Viktor again since then.

I took a deep breath, air stinging my lungs. I'd told myself that was all I'd need, air, that it was the space I missed, the freedom of the cold. But deep down, I knew I'd been hoping to see him. I'd caught myself scanning the halls for him more than once. It was stupid. Utterly pathetic. A schoolgirl crush on someone who should have been my enemy.

If Viktor had even an inkling of what was going through my head when I thought of Kage Tanaka, he'd have killed me already. It wasn't in his nature to merely be jealous. He'd be vicious, brutal. He'd drain me dry. But maybe it was precisely because Kage knew what Viktor was that I couldn't stop thinking about him. He'd seen the bruises. He'd seen Viktor's cruelty carved into my skin, and he hadn't flinched. He was the only one who knew the truth.

A muffled thump broke the hush of the evening. I spun around just in time to see the little fluffin come racing across the lawn, his ears flattened back, a comet of orange fur skimming over the patchy, melted snow. And two bounds behind him loped a wolf. Silver, huge, with a grin full of teeth. For a moment, my heart flew to my throat. Then I relaxed; the wolf wasn't hunting, he was playing—letting the little fluffin dash just out of reach, then resuming the chase.

The smaller creature doubled back as the wolf skidded to a halt on a drift of crusted snow. He shook wet flakes from his coat like a dog, then cantered after the fluffin again, tail wagging back and forth.

My chest tightened. They looked absurdly happy. A feeling of warmth slipped beneath my ribs, sweet and unfamiliar. For a split second, I was ten again, chasing my brother through fresh snow. I closed my eyes, the memory hurting more than any blow. That was then, before duty spoke in bruises. When happiness— real happiness—had still sometimes felt possible.

I opened my eyes, and the fluffin had disappeared. There was a crunch. Heavy footsteps on snow. The wolf approached, coming to sit beside me, sleek and massive, his fur damp with melted snow. He was breathing hard, his tongue still lolling out a little. He'd obviously been enjoying the fresh night air. He sat close but not touching, eyes fixed not on me but the sea. I stared at his paws, each one as big as my face, then swatted away a few strands of hair that the wind had pulled loose from the braid coiled around my head like a crown.

"So what's it like, being a wolf?"

He couldn't answer, of course, but he looked up, his gaze holding mine for a moment. Then, just as silently as he'd arrived, he raced off, vanishing into a cluster of trees.

"Good talk," I called, knowing I was being ridiculous. I watched him go, hating the strange, hollow ache his absence left behind. What had I expected? He'd seen me standing there, and he'd come as a warning, to remind me of my Vow. Nothing more.

Another minute passed. I told myself it was time to go, that I hadn't come out here for him. But the lie broke as I turned around. The wolf was gone; he was a man again. Tall and broad-shouldered, long legs clad in silver wool. A black cloak wrapped around him like a shadow. His hair was still damp with snow, pale strands curling at the ends and falling slightly into his eyes, eyes as dark and silent as a night sky.

He came to stand beside me as I turned around again to face the sea. We didn't speak, just stood together in silence, watching the waves as they crashed on the rocks below.

Finally I broke a silence that felt too weighty. "So is this all it is to you? Running in the woods? Escaping from your real life? Hiding away?" There was an envious edge to my voice. I didn't bother smoothing it away.

But Kage didn't bristle like I'd expected him to. He looked down at me, his size hitting me all over again. Even when he wasn't a wolf, he could block the light so easily, could crush me with ease. "There's nothing wrong with wanting an escape. Life can be cruel. Reality can be harsh and painful. Isn't that why you're standing here right now, after all?"

I wanted to say I doubted his life was all that hard. But I bit my tongue, staying silent.

"Does it bother you, Regan?" he said softly. "To think that others may have a way to escape that you lack?"

I looked up at him quickly.

"Is Viktor still hurting you?"

The words landed like a slap. I stiffened. "How dare you."

"How dare I? Your archon—" he said the word with disdain "—fled from a dragon's presence, leaving you unprotected and exposed. Did he apologize when you returned to him that night?"

I trembled. "You have no right to ask me that."

He crossed his arms over his chest. "I'll take that as a *no*. No, I doubt Viktor apologized. And if you dared to ask him why he fled, if you called him a coward and asked him why he hadn't treated you as you deserved, as a consort should be treated—treasured and protected—then, I'm sure he met your accusations with cruelty. Tell me I'm wrong, Regan. Tell me there aren't still bruises underneath that high-collared dress you're wearing."

He moved a hand as if to touch me, and I flinched. "I don't see how it's any of your business, *Avari*," I hissed, taking one step back. "Why do you even care?"

Kage didn't back off. "Someone has to."

I threw my head back and laughed. "Oh, come off it. You don't get to stand there and pretend this is about concern. Highbloods aren't taught to *care*. We're taught to conquer, to exploit each other's weaknesses. You shouldn't be caring, you should be gloating." My lips twisted. "And maybe beneath that calm front, you're doing exactly that."

"Is that what you think?" Kage's eyes were calm and composed.

"I think if you were a true Avari, you'd be on your knees thanking the Bloodmaiden that I've fallen. That Viktor's broken me."

Kage's eyes narrowed. "Is that what he's done? Funny, I don't see it."

I turned away from him and stared out at the roiling sea. I shouldn't be here. I should be walking away. If Viktor could see me now, speaking to an Avari—to Kage Tanaka, of all people—he'd kill me. Kill us both. But I didn't walk away. I stayed.

Kage was quiet for a minute. Then, "I'm not pretending. I'm not gloating."

"Then, you're lying." The wind tugged at my hair again. I'd had enough. I reached my hands up, pulling out the pins that held my braid and letting it fall behind my back. "Or worse—you're pitying me."

"Would that be worse? To know someone cared enough to have pity?"

"I'm not worth your pity." The words were out before I could stop them.

He shook his head slowly, jaw tightening. "You're being hurt by someone older, stronger, and far more powerful than you. No one's stopping him. No one's even trying, not even your family. Do they know, Regan? Have you told your father?"

I took a gulping breath, trying to hold back the sobs that threatened. I lifted my chin. "Of course not. There'd be no point. Father arranged the match, and it's a fine one." I paused. "Besides, my little brother . . . Persis is being held somewhere as leverage against my family. He's only eight. He's basically a captive." I swallowed, thinking of what had happened to Blake's little sister, Aenia. She'd always been . . . different. But she'd been family. I'd watched her grow. She and Persis had played together; they'd been friends. I'd thought one day they'd attend Bloodwing together. Only now . . . Aenia was gone.

That wasn't happening to Persis. Not to my brother.

"Why would Viktor take Persis when you'd already agreed to be his consort?"

I laughed. "Compliance. To ensure the honor of the Drakharrow house. Because he can do whatever he likes, Kage. He told my father this was once a highblood custom."

"It was. But the children weren't hostages, they were exchanged to forge bonds between families," Kage said shortly.

"A scholar of history, are we?" I could hear the teasing tone in my voice. What was happening here?

He shrugged. "I like to read."

"Anyhow, Amina—Professor Hassan, I mean—knew about Persis. She tried to help me. And you can see how that turned out."

Kage stared. "Professor Hassan? Why would she do that?"

"She was my tutor when I was a child. She lived with my family for years. She was there when Persis was born. Even when she became a faculty member at Bloodwing, Amina would come back for visits. I made a mistake, told her what happened. She must have talked to Viktor, believed bringing him the new dragon rider would persuade him to let Persis go." *Why am I telling Kage this?*

"Then, it's Viktor's fault she's dead, isn't it? She gave up Florence Shen in a futile attempt to placate him. But he doesn't have to be doing any of this, Regan." Kage sounded disgusted. "Viktor isn't a leader. He's a monster. And what he's doing to you? It should matter to someone."

I looked at him, not with thanks but with rage and shame. "You don't understand anything," I said, my voice cracking. "I let him do it. Don't you understand that? I stand there. I don't run. I don't fight. I never do."

Kage's gaze didn't waver.

"I let him break me." Each word cracked my heart open like a stone. Telling him this, standing in the shadow of his judgment. "I go back each day, and I smile, and I play my part. I make it easy for him."

"I'm sorry." The words were gentle. Tender. Real. They gutted me.

"What?" I whispered. I stepped back from the edge to flee, and my foot slid on the icy ground. My balance was lost in an instant. I pitched sideways, already starting to fall to the rocks below.

In half a breath, Kage was there. His hands gripped my upper arms, strong and unyielding, his cloak swirling around us as he moved faster than I'd ever thought possible. I was back on the cliff as if it had never happened. I crashed against his chest, breathless, fingers curling into the front of his shirt, his heartbeat steady and strong under my palm. Everything went very still. I could feel every point of contact between us. My shoulder digging into his ribs. His gloved hands clasping me, holding me in place. It was the second time he'd touched me—the first when we'd made a vow, mingled blood.

Something had changed in me that day. But had it changed from the moment his hand touched mine or from the moment I first saw him as the wolf?

An ache formed in my chest as I looked up and saw the concern etched into his face. It couldn't be real. None of this was. I broke free, stepping back, carefully moving away from the cliff.

"So that's what this is about," I said bitterly. "You shouldn't have done that."

"Done what? Stopped you from falling?"

"Touched me," I hissed.

His hands fell to his sides. "Forgive me."

I was being ridiculous and unfair, but I didn't care. "The Blood Vow. Is that it? You think I'll break my word? That you have to earn my trust?"

Kage looked amused. "The Vow is unbreakable. I have no fears in that regard. If that were the case, I could have let you fall to your death just now."

I flushed.

"No, that isn't what this is about."

"Then, what is this about?"

"For a girl who's always seemed so confident, you seem to have a shocking disregard for your own self-worth lately."

I took another step back, everything in me fighting to just lean into his warmth again.

"Why would you be sorry for me? Why?"

"Let's call it a responsibility towards you." His voice was tight, as if he were finding it difficult to get the words out. "One I feel more and more strongly by the day." The words were dutiful and should have landed coldly. Yet to me they were full of meaning. They were the words I'd been waiting for someone—anyone—to say.

My pulse stuttered. "That makes no sense. We've hardly spoken." I gave a mirthless laugh. "Half the time, you've been a wolf."

He didn't laugh with me. Didn't let me use humor as my shield. Instead, he took a step closer, closing the space between us I'd tried to create.

"I've done awful things," I whispered, trying not to look into his eyes. "You shouldn't even be talking to me. You know what I've done. I've hurt people. I've manipulated—"

"Stop," Kage's voice commanded. "It's pointless. None of that will work on me. I see you, Regan. Not just what you show the world. I see it all. What you hide. The strength it takes just to stand here, to survive the day. You think I don't see it? You think that's a weakness?" He shook his head. "You're at war."

I swallowed, unsure of where to look.

"You've done what you had to do to survive," Kage said, his voice low and rough. "You know he'd kill you if you tried to stop him. That doesn't make you weak. It makes you strong. Sometimes simply surviving is a rebellion."

My breath caught. "I *serve* him. I do what he tells me to do. That's not rebelling. The responsibility is mine. You say you know me? Then, look into my heart. It's icy, empty. I'm just as cruel as he is."

Kage's eyes darkened. "No."

"No?"

"He holds the blade. You're the one who's bleeding."

I shook my head. "You can't shield me. You can't absolve me."

"Maybe not." The amusement was back in his eyes—but also something harder. Flintier. "But I won't let him break you."

Hope cracked my heart open, painful and terrifying. "I'm not a good person," I whispered. "You don't understand."

For a long moment, he said nothing. Then, "You deserve to be protected. You deserve to be safe. If you were so terrible, you wouldn't be standing out here in the cold, hating yourself for what you've become, hating everything about the life you lead."

I looked up at him, heart thudding.

"You matter. More than he ever will. More than you think."

The more he spoke, the more I was at risk of believing him.

Then the moment was broken. Something flickered across his face. "I'll walk you back to the castle."

Before I could respond, he'd stepped forward and taken my arm, his fingers closing around my elbow without asking. "It's slippery," he remarked, as if this were mere courtesy. As if his touch wasn't burning through to my skin like a brand.

I could have pulled away, but I didn't. We walked on in silence for a few paces, the sound of the waves slowly receding behind us.

"Well, Avari," I said lightly, breaking the silence, "when can we expect the announcement of your own triad? I suppose your grandmother is shoving a line of pretty debutantes your way." It was the worst possible choice of topic. And yet something in me wanted to pull at the wound, rip it open, and pour in salt. Wanted to try to hurt him before he could hurt me. Still, I'd expected him to laugh, but he didn't. Not even a twitch.

Instead, he shocked me by saying. "So you've heard, then."

"Heard what?" He suddenly wouldn't meet my eyes. My body clenched. "It's Medra, isn't it."

"Medra?" His eyebrows shot up. "Medra Pendragon is a friend, an ally. Nothing more." He shook his head. "No, I meant heard about the ball."

I blinked in confusion. "The ball? What ball?"

He hesitated. I felt his fingers tighten. "A ball to announce my betrothal." The words scraped out of him.

I froze, shock coiling in the pit of my stomach. "You're . . . betrothed?"

"It was arranged only very recently." He paused. "I'm sorry. I should have told you before."

I latched onto that word. *Arranged*, not *chosen*.

I forced a laugh. "Why would you apologize? You don't owe me a thing. So who is the lucky highblood?" I said, making my voice bright. "Anyone I know?"

He hesitated, then met my gaze—his eyes pleading with me to understand. "Florence Shen."

I kept my face steady. "The new dragon rider. She's bonded to Nyxaris. Of course, what an excellent match. Your grandmother must have selected her for you."

He nodded slightly, the motion wooden. "She did."

"Lady Avari is nothing if not pragmatic," I said, trying to keep the bitterness from my voice. "What a lovely couple you'll make."

"Florence needs my protection." His voice cracked on the last word, as if it hurt him to say.

I froze.

"The protection of my house," Kage added, a moment too late.

"Of course she does," I said coldly. "And I'm sure you take your *responsibility* towards her very seriously. How sweet of you to provide your protection." I gave a hollow laugh—making sure to fill it with a hint of cruelty. "And how wonderful for you, House Leader, to gain a dragon for your family's honor. Why, it seems you're just as much a pawn as the rest of us."

Something in me was tearing apart like wet parchment, yet I bared my teeth in a smile anyway. I couldn't stop imagining it. Scenes flashing in my head. Florence Shen in his arms. Her name on his lips. His hands upon her naked body as she lay in his bed. Would it be her first time when he entered her? Would she cry out his name, grateful and adoring?

I closed my eyes, hating the visions, hating myself for caring at all. Then I yanked my arm free from his grasp, turning aside, needing to flee before the pain in my chest turned into something that showed on my face.

Kage's hand shot out, catching my arm—more roughly this time. "Regan."

I tried to wrench free, but he wouldn't let go. His fingers curled around my arm, not hard enough to hurt but enough that I was reminded of his strength. Slowly, I looked up. What I saw there stole the air from my lungs. Guilt, longing, and something close to panic mixed in his eyes. The mask of composure was gone, and what was left was raw and helpless and inevitable all at once.

"Tell me you feel it, too," he demanded. "This pull between us."

The wind howled around us. I refused to answer.

Kage's eyes narrowed, sharpening with pain. "When a wolf finds his true mate, he knows."

It was the most unfair thing he could have said. Every word was a knife twist—for the Bloodmaiden knew how desperately I wanted to believe it. How much I wanted his certainty to cover me like a shield. How much I wanted to accept his strength, his heat, his absolution. But he wasn't offering any of those things, was he? Not truly. He was Florence Shen's shield now. And I was still standing in the dark, cold and alone.

I tore myself free of his grasp, the absence of his touch more bitter than any winter wind, hope shattering like smashed ice. Then I held his eyes for the span of one long breath before saying, in a voice flat and cutting, "It's a good thing I'm no wolf, then."

I turned on my heel and walked away—back to the castle, to the prison of my own creation.

CHAPTER 20

FLORENCE

A feeling of wonderful contentment filled me as I reached the greenhouse. I shoved my shoulder against the cool iron door, pushing it open and letting the humid air from inside roll over me like a warm blanket. The great glass house, covered with its arched cage of green-black iron, always felt like a world away from the castle's clanging bells and intense school politics. Here, surrounded by raised beds of dirt overflowing with fragrant herbs and colorful flowers, I could just *be*.

I moved to a wooden table in the last row, dropping the heavy stack of books in my arms with relief. I'd come a little early, but Professor Allenvale didn't usually mind. I glanced around and peered at the back of the greenhouse. In fact, she didn't seem to be here yet. I quickly went back up to the desk at the front to sign in—a new step that I was trying to get myself used to. I wrote down my name, my house, and the time I'd arrived. Then I went over to the supply cabinet and grabbed the materials I needed for my experiments, carefully logging every item I took from the cabinet in another new book that had been placed there. Some items—deemed too unsafe for blightborn students—were kept in a separate, locked cupboard. Fortunately, the things I needed hadn't been deemed prohibited or unsafe . . . yet.

I returned to my seat, arranging everything carefully in front of me, just the way I liked. Just as I finished, the door to the greenhouse swung open, and Professor Allenvale marched inside, her purple- and green-streaked braid swinging behind her purple House Orphos robes. To my surprise, Professor Rodriguez was with her. He didn't usually visit the greenhouse. His portions of the class were always taught in his usual lecture hall inside the castle.

I raised a timid hand to wave, but neither of them noticed. They were deep in conversation and seemed to be arguing.

Professor Allenvale dropped the papers she was carrying onto her desk at the front of the greenhouse—I assumed she'd marked our essays over the weekend and would be handing them out today. I chewed my lower lip and leaned forward as if by doing so I'd somehow be able to see the mark I'd received.

". . . cannot believe you'd have the audacity—" Allenvale's voice floated back to me "—no, the *stupidity* to act this way. You're jeopardizing. . ."

Blushing a little at overhearing my two favorite teachers arguing, I eyed Rodriguez. He did look rather awful—collar askew, eyes bloodshot. The sharp tang of cheap brandy drifted through the sweetness of the herbs lining the sides of the greenhouse. But I decided it was none of my business. I tried my best to ignore them as they continued to raise their voices, opening one of my books and hunching over it. I scanned the page, double-checking a few details, then opened my notebook, carefully labeled *The Synergistic Applications of Emberfern and Mirthleaf*, and scribbled some quick notes.

Next, I pulled on a pair of gloves and reached for a pair of tongs. Carefully, I pinched a frond of emberfern from the plant in front of me. The fern's edges glowed orange, and a single drop of sap hissed as it struck the hard metal surface of the worktable. I pulled my hand back quickly. Emberfern was volatile. Lunaya Orphos had warned us about this months ago—in fact, she was the reason my interest in the plant had been piqued. I could still remember her voice softly describing the herb's potential. She'd mentioned how emberfern was often paired with mirthleaf to stabilize it. But when I'd gone to look up more about emberfern later, I had to question her use of the word *often*. There was very little literature in the Bloodwing library about emberfern or its use in conjunction with mirthleaf.

Not for the first time, I wished Lunaya was still with us. I could ask her about the plant, perhaps even share my ideas for my end-of-term project with her. I swallowed the lump in my throat and tried to focus. I'd been far luckier that night. I'd had friends there to protect me. I knew they'd tried to save Lunaya as well. But, well, that had been impossible.

A sharp crash yanked me out of my reverie, and I dropped the tongs. Rodriguez had knocked a tray of glass flasks off Professor Allenvale's desk. He stood there looking sheepish as she exclaimed loudly and reached for a broom.

"We'll discuss this more after your class, Vasanti," I heard him mutter as he rubbed his temples and headed towards the door.

Students slowly drifted in. A few gave Rodriguez strange looks as they passed him.

Allenvale looked around the greenhouse as students began to take their seats. "All right, class, we'll spend today as we previously discussed. All of you should have some idea of your topic for the end-of-term project by now. If you don't, this is your last chance to run any ideas by me or ask for my help in choosing one. Please approach my desk if you're struggling. I'm happy to help." She looked down at the stack of parchment in front of her. "Professor Rodriguez and I have also marked your exams from Wintermark. You may come and receive your marks at the end of today's class."

I'm not sure little fireheart can wait that long.

I scowled. *Don't be ridiculous. I'm perfectly capable of waiting*—I checked the clock on the wall—*fifty-nine minutes.* I stared at the second hand as it ticked slowly.

Nyxaris yawned. *How interminable the hour will be.*

Less than an hour, I said automatically. *Fifty-eight minutes.*

The dragon laughed, a great, rich rumbling sound that echoed in my mind.

I'm so glad I amuse you. But my voice had no real ire.

Amuse, yes, but also frustrate. To waste an hour in the greenhouse when you could be practicing your riding . . .

Now who's impatient? I'll meet you as soon as my class is done, just as we arranged.

Fooling around with plants and herbs. A pause. *Do you truly find such things interesting?*

I do. It's peaceful here. And the work I do could be important someday. Much more important than helping highbloods to some far-off military victory. Alchemy and healing arts could save lives—blightborn lives. I'd recently decided that was a far nobler calling than becoming a strategist.

As important as learning how to guard your mind? He sounded peevish. *You are already far behind where I would like you to be in your thrallguard lessons.*

I need to pass my classes, Nyxaris, I reminded him. *Emberfern is a very important plant. In fact, it's been sadly understudied. Actually, I'm surprised you haven't . . .*

"Miss Shen."

I nearly jumped out of my skin. Coloring, I looked up at Professor Allenvale.

"You seemed half a world away from here." She touched my shoulder gently. "Are you worried about your paper?" She glanced around, then lowered her voice. "You needn't worry, Florence. It's a very fine mark. You continue to impress me. In fact, would you ever consider a scholarship semester in the Sable Isles?"

I stared at her. "A semester?"

She nodded. "I'll be returning to my own school at the end of Springrise."

My face fell. "I'm sorry to hear that."

"Well, you knew I wouldn't be able to stay here forever. But perhaps you might join me for the Summerfell session? I take on a few students every summer for an intensive research retreat."

"Me?" I squeaked.

Nyxaris snorted. *Yes, you, little scholar. You cannot tell me you are surprised by this.*

"You're a brilliant student, Florence. I can't help but feel, however, that you do not belong at Bloodwing."

I stared at her. "What do you mean?"

Allenvale leaned down. "This school is a battlefield. It's meant to prepare you all for potential war."

War between houses was the only kind of war there had ever been—at least, for the past five centuries. Which was why I'd always thought it rather ironic that all of us were trained at the same school. I supposed it meant that no one house could claim a large advantage over another militaristically.

"To defend the highblood houses, yes. Isn't that what your school is like?"

She shook her head. "The Somnaria Institute isn't a war college, not like Bloodwing. It's primarily a research academy. No combat classes, just gardens, laboratories, and libraries that never close." She smiled as my eyes widened. "Yes, I thought you'd like that last bit."

"But your school does exist to serve House Orphos," I said carefully. "Doesn't it?"

"The knowledge we discover at Somnaria supports House Orphos, and the school receives grants from the Orphos family, yes. But that doesn't mean we don't also do work that is beneficial to blightborn."

But that wasn't their main focus. It never was.

I picked up my pair of tongs and fiddled with them. "I'm House Avari, though, not House Orphos. I'm not sure how it would work," I said regretfully.

She shrugged. "Sangratha is at peace. There's nothing in our school charter that precludes an Avari student from visiting or even enrolling. Apply for the summer scholarship. Spend one term in the Isles. Who knows? Maybe you'll decide that's where you really belong."

My heart pounded with excitement, but I knew what she suggested would never be possible. Not now that I was betrothed to Kage and bonded to Sangratha's only dragon. I nibbled my bottom lip, not sure how to respond.

You wish to go to this place? To spend your summer studying instead of spending your days in leisure like other students?

I'd like nothing better than to study under Professor Allenvale all summer. It would be a dream come true. But you know it's not possible. Lady Avari would never let me go—or you, for that matter.

If you wish to see these Isles, we will go. If your new archon objects, he may travel with you.

It would put me far from Viktor. Perhaps Lady Avari would see the benefits of that.

Allenvale was watching me.

"Think about it, Florence. We'll discuss it again next class. Regardless of what you decide, I think you have a very bright future ahead of you as one of Sangratha's foremost scholars in alchemical research."

"I've enjoyed your class immensely, Professor Allenvale," I blurted out. "In fact, it's made me decide to drop the strategist path and focus on the healing arts next year."

She smiled warmly. "I'm so glad to hear that. You certainly have an aptitude for them. Now, remind me of the topic you decided on for your final term paper?"

"The properties of emberfern and mirthleaf in relation to one another. They're truly fascinating."

"I'm sure they are. Well, you'd need to have your project wrapped up in the next three weeks. We'd have to submit your thesis as part of your scholarship application. Do you think you can work more quickly than the other students?"

I bobbed my head quickly, ignoring Nyxaris's low groan of disapproval. "Absolutely."

"Excellent. Well, I look forward to reading about your discoveries." Professor Allenvale walked away to another table.

You'd really do that for me? I said quietly, after she'd gone.

Do what? Insist upon you being able to fulfill your ambitions? the dragon rumbled. *You are my rider, fireheart. Wherever you wish to fly, I will clear the skies.*

A warm feeling spread in the pit of my stomach. I tried to focus on my note-making. The rest of the class went by in a blur as I jotted down observations and conducted small experiments combining varying ratios of emberfern and mirthleaf. Emberfern was unstable, yes, but it wasn't *unusable*. If I could harness the best properties of the plant, I knew I'd be able to make a minor but very useful mixture that could be used as a sun-sickness tonic. In the village I'd grown up in, I recalled how blightborn laborers often grew sick after working long shifts in the fields under the baking hot sun. This could be a cure for that—a tincture that could be made freely in any village stillroom, from very easy-to-grow ingredients.

When Professor Allenvale dismissed us, she pressed my graded essay into my hands; I'd received an Excellent. What was more, the mark was perfect with no deductions. I floated out onto the sunny hillside, beaming with pride.

Nyxaris waited at the bottom of the hill, near the edge of the cliff. *Finally,* he grumbled. *Mount.* But I sensed his pride, feeling his quiet approval.

I quickly climbed up and swung into position between his shoulders. As we leaped into the skies, I couldn't help it. I screamed.

Will you ever cease doing that? Nyxaris complained.

I'm so sorry, I said lamely. *I never intend to do it. It just . . . happens. I'm not sure I'll ever get used to this feeling. One minute I'm safe on land, and the next, well, we're up here.*

Below us Bloodwing was shrinking away, already the size of a child's dollhouse. Cold air knifed past, yet sitting on Nyxaris, his scales radiated a furnacelike heat that I could feel from head to toe.

Adjust your seat, he instructed. *Knees tighter. Anticipate the next pitch. You must work on this, or those delicate thighs of yours will be aching.*

His voice was matter-of-fact, yet I blushed at his mention of my aching thighs. Quickly, I did as he said, squeezing my thighs tighter, trying to ignore how the heat of his scales bled straight through the fabric of the split skirt I was wearing, warming my skin. *Better?* I asked dubiously.

Good. Now, thrallguard, he said gruffly. *Walls up.*

I was caught off guard. Nevertheless, I quickly threw up the walls I'd been practicing, picturing my mind as a garden, surrounded by thick hanging vines of mirthleaf.

Plants, Nyxaris snorted. *You ward me off with plants.* His mind stroked over mine like thorns upon silk, and I shivered despite his heat.

Plants can be very dangerous in the right hands, I said with dignity. *Even our new headmistress knows this. Otherwise, why would she be forcing us to sign in to the greenhouse?*

Nyxaris snorted, mentally clawing against my barricades. I twined my vines around cores of emberfern, trying to push him out. When he finally allowed me to take a break between drills, I began to broach a question that had been on my mind for a while.

Dragons are excellent at both thrallweave and thrallguard, I said carefully.

We are masters of both, Nyxaris agreed.

No one can penetrate a dragon's mind, I continued. *So why did dragons need riders in the first place? When you can already do everything?*

Why does the most powerful animal in existence require a weaker one?

Well, yes, I said, flushing. I knew I was weak, far weaker than my dragon.

His wings beat steadily, once, twice, three times, before he finally answered. *I have wondered the same thing. I have a theory . . .*

What sort of a theory? I asked, curiously.

My mind is still fragmented. Many memories lost, he reminded me. *And yet, I theorize that dragons required riders as interpreters. We may speak mind to mind only with other dragons or with a single rider. Most humans cannot hear us. They feel only awe and terror in our presence. As it should be*, he added.

So, I'm basically your translator? I said with delight. That was much more to my liking than trying to believe I could actually direct a dragon in any meaningful way—especially as some sort of a warrior team.

You have pacifist tendencies, little scholar. Do not let them get out of hand. His voice was stern yet gentle.

I suppose I just don't see how having me as your rider could possibly make you a better fighter than you already are alone. If anything, having me on your back might be a distraction. A weakness.

He dipped a wing, and for a moment I gasped, clutching his scales, my whole body pressing tight against his spine. Then we slid through an updraft, every motion perfectly synchronized. Still, I could sense something troubling him.

A dragon's talons are built for rending, not for the finer points of warcraft, he pointed out. *In close sieges, riders might leap from our backs to deliver firebombs or to shoot a volley of arrows down with precision. I once—* He broke off.

Yes?

I once had a rider leap from my back with a rope-hook to open enemy gates from within. He paused, and the memory of what he described ghosted through our bond. Another body, sitting where I now sat, bracing herself against Nyxaris's shoulders. Something in me rose up, hot and quick, put off by the image. Jealousy.

Strength is nothing without focus. You, small as you are, give an edge to my claws. I carry you across the sky. I deliver fire upon your enemies. You carry my will where I cannot.

Highblood enemies, you mean, I said uncomfortably. *We're both in service to highbloods in the end. I don't understand that part of things either. Why did the dragons even want to work with highbloods?*

He was quiet for a long time. I tried to be patient, thinking about my project, admiring the view.

I have had . . . highblood riders.

I stiffened. *What? You mean . . .*

Soul-bound, yes. Just as the Avari woman described.

So . . . I began to tremble.

A highblood soul in a blightborn body, yes. Nyxaris sounded as if the idea troubled him, too.

And you . . . accepted them as your rider?

I had no choice.

There was something missing here. Something he wasn't saying.

You were loyal to your house, to House Avari, over your rider, I stated, trying not to make it sound like a judgment.

I continued to carry my rider, he said stiffly.

Their body, you mean. Where did their soul go? What happened to it once they were soul-bound?

Their own soul was . . . suppressed. Yet present.

That sounded horrible. *And the new soul? The highblood's? You grew to accept it.* This time his silence stretched so long I began to wonder if he'd speak again at all. *Nyxaris?* I prodded tentatively.

A low growl vibrated through him. He banked so abruptly my stomach lurched. *Enough questions,* he snapped.

His show of temper surprised me. He was often stern, but rarely angry. *I'm sorry,* I murmured. I tightened my knees again, trying to remember to hold to the position he'd taught me. Even so, my thighs were beginning to ache a little.

My memories, he said grimly, *they are intense. Confusing. At times I see things from perspectives that . . . should not be possible.*

What do you mean? I asked cautiously.

He didn't answer. The air seemed to crackle with frustration.

I tried a new tactic. *What's the last thing you remember . . . before being turned to stone?*

It was as if I'd fired a crossbow at him. He stiffened, his wings locking. For one terrifying instant, we began to plummet. Wind tore at my hair. I wrapped myself around him, heart slamming against scales. I screamed, clutching at his neck, the ground spinning up in a blur. Then, at the last second, he caught himself. Wings beating rapidly, we leveled out, meters above the water.

My heart hammered as loudly as the wind in my ears. *We don't have to talk about it. I'm sorry for asking.*

Too late. His voice was ragged.

I swallowed, a chill spreading through my veins. *Nyxaris, what is it? What did you remember?*

He flew in silence for several moments. *I killed my rider.*

I stilled. *What?*

Not in the way you are thinking. She was killed because of me. I recall it. I recall . . . everything.

I'm so sorry, I whispered.

Afterward, he went on, ignoring me, *I began to question . . . everything. The house I served. Our cause. All that had been demanded of us.*

We reached the shore and began to cross over a forest of pine trees.

Molindra . . .

Yes? I encouraged, my heart beating faster.

She came to me. She offered me a new purpose. But in return . . .

I touched his scales gently, my throat tight. *Yes? In return?*

In return, I gave up everything.

A chill came over me as I finally understood. *You mean you sacrificed yourself? Is that it? You and the other three dragons?*

His only reply was a low rumble—half grief, half rage.

You don't have to tell me, I said quickly. *We don't have to talk about it anymore.* But I couldn't help myself. *Do you remember why you decided being turned to stone was, well, worth it?*

It was meant to change things. And yet when I awoke, the dragons were gone, and the highbloods still ruled. I was quiet for a while. Nyxaris stayed silent, too, clearly brooding about what we'd just discussed.

Had my dragon been a rebel? I thought of the soul-bound highblood rider he'd had before; she must have been his very last rider. The one whose death he felt responsible for. He must have cared for her very much to make such a drastic sacrifice. Of course a soul-bound rider would have been preferred by highbloods—no wonder Viktor wished he could do the same to me. A highblood would be able to use battle magic in ways I wouldn't. They healed faster. They'd have numerous advantages. Or did they lose some of those advantages when they stole a blightborn body?

I touched my ears. The points were becoming sharper, more fine. Was my body changing in other ways? I thought of Medra's fingers and toes. They were longer than a typical blightborn's. I considered asking Nyxaris and decided to take the risk.

Medra has the red hair of a rider . . . I began to say.

Red, yes, he rumbled. *The other dragon was red.*

Other dragon? What other dragon? I assumed he'd remembered something else from his past.

I saw another dragon the other day.

My heart sped up. *Molindra?*

No, not Molindra. He sounded peevish, irritable.

Another dragon? How is that possible? Where? I said in disbelief.

While flying. It was . . . unsettling. And yet, I know what I saw. For a moment, I believed he was Vorago.

He? You could tell it was male?

I felt his assent rather than heard it.

Did you speak to the dragon? Where did he go?

He vanished before I could receive any answers as to his identity. He fled from me. Nyxaris sounded shocked and even a little hurt. *From me. When we are so few.*

I'm so sorry.

For a moment, I believed I knew him. For a moment, I truly thought he was Vorago, Nyxaris said again. *And then . . .*

And then?

And then I thought he might be the other.

The other? What other?

No answer.

Do you mean Molindra?

Indeed. Molindra. Nyxaris's voice was tight. *How are your thighs?*

I jolted. *They're . . . they're fine.* I shifted a little, trying to relax the sore muscles.

You lie, he rumbled, a faint hint of smugness there. *I can feel their tremor. They ache as you sit upon me. We have pushed you hard enough. We will return now. We will continue to work on your endurance. You must be able to ride me without trembling.*

Heat flooded my cheeks; I thanked the Bloodmaiden that he couldn't see their crimson color. *Very well,* I said a little primly, sitting up straighter and trying not to writhe against him as I'd just been doing. *I'll be ready.*

Good, he said, sounding amused, as he flew back over the school. *We'll meet at dawn. I intend to push you hard. Recover while you can.*

I slid off his back when he landed, careful not to show him my face, which was beet red. *Sounds wonderful,* I said carelessly. *I'll see you in the morning.*

Ice your thighs.

I paused. *I beg your pardon?*

Ice. Or cold pads. My riders used to tell me it helped.

Thank you for the kind suggestion, I said, trying to gather up the little dignity I had left.

I walked back to the castle, doing my best to ignore the feeling of the dragon's eyes on my back, as I moved stiffly up the hill, sore from our flight, aching where my body had met with his.

CHAPTER 21

FLORENCE

The day had come much too soon. I felt trapped. Out of time. Sunlight spilled across the courtyard. I squinted, adjusting my stance, then pulled back and let the next arrow fly.

Whoosh. Thwack. It hit the target. Dead center, again. I smiled, and a hand slapped my lower back.

"Good work, lass." Professor Stonefist's voice was gruff. She stood beside me, stroking her beard. "Pretending the targets are highbloods, mayhaps?"

I looked down at her in surprise. "Well, maybe a few in particular."

Her mouth twitched. "Not your betrothed, I hope. He seems decent enough, for one of them."

"He does," I agreed. "I'm . . . lucky."

"Lucky, are you? Let's see if your good fortune continues with your shooting." She folded her arms over her chest and stalked back to the sidelines, being careful to stand in the shadows, avoiding the sun.

Stonefist had been evicted from her former classroom, forced into an older part of the school. But after too many blightborn students had come down with coughs and other illnesses from the mildew and mold in the decrepit classroom she'd been moved to, the dwarven instructor had had enough. She'd made a deal with Professor Sankara, arranging to use the outdoor training courtyard whenever it was free. I didn't think the headmistress knew about it, otherwise she probably would have put a stop to their little arrangement.

Meanwhile, Professor Stonefist's original classroom sat empty, as far as anyone knew—the school had moved her for absolutely no reason. No reason except for the fact that she was a blightborn instructor teaching blightborn pupils.

Setting my jaw, I reached for another arrow. The old training longbow felt natural in my hands, the string settling against the callus on my knuckle. I'd quickly learned hand-to-hand combat was not my forte. Even Medra's patient coaching hadn't changed that. But when they'd put a bow in my hand? The world had faded away, narrowing to a clear steady line: my eye, the arrow, the target.

Whoosh. Thwack. Another arrow hit, slightly off-center this time.

I frowned. Still, it wasn't as if I was exactly an expert archer yet.

"Adjust your hips," Professor Stonefist bellowed.

She reminded me of Nyxaris. I grimaced but nodded and did as she said, shifting my body, then wiping at the sheen of sweat off my forehead with the back of my arm. I'd lost track of how long I'd been here. I'd warmed up first with at least an hour of stretches and laps. The old Florence hated running laps. The new Florence loathed laps with a passion but did them anyway. The extra conditioning paid off when I rode Nyxaris. My thighs no longer screamed in quite the same way by the time I dismounted.

Swoosh. Smack. My arrow flew wildly off target, and I grumbled. I was distracted, and it was easy to figure out the reason. Tonight was the engagement ball. The thought was at the edge of my mind, constantly intruding. How had it arrived so quickly? Springrise term was nearly over. My project for Professor Allenvale's class was finished. The essay needed a little more proofreading, and then I'd be turning it in. If only I could spend the evening working on my essay or riding Nyxaris instead of attending this ball.

I smiled to myself. Things had certainly changed when I found myself looking forward to dragon riding more than I did to donning a silk dress. The closer the ball came the more I wanted to run far,

far away. I felt like I was constantly choking on the weight of expectations. Not just from being a dragon rider but from being *their* dragon rider. After tonight, the Avaris would practically own me.

I'd seen how Viktor had treated Medra. Being linked to Kage would protect me from him—at least, that was the plan. But were Lady Avari and her house really any better? The Avaris would still expect things of me, want things of me. And not just of me—of Nyxaris. They'd expect me to be able to deliver his obedience.

Right now the engagement was mostly for show—at least, that was what the Avaris had claimed. But after tonight, it was going to feel all too real. After Kage and I were officially betrothed, the next step would be an actual wedding. And if that happened . . .

I took a deep breath, trying not to imagine a passionless, awkward wedding night with a man I didn't love and who didn't love me.

Nyxaris was quiet in my mind, but I could sense his restlessness. Was he on the fence about this, too?

"Florence!"

I whirled around at the sound of Medra's voice and saw her marching across the courtyard.

"You're not supposed to be here," she said, looking exasperated but amused.

"I'm not?"

"No, you said you'd meet me back at our room to get ready for the ball."

I glanced up at the clock. Somehow time had flown by. I was half an hour late. "Oh my goodness. That's right. I'm so sorry. But . . ." I bit my lip.

Medra put her hands on her hips. "But?"

"But I don't want to go, Medra," I groaned. "Please don't make me."

Her lips twitched. "Is it the gown, the dancing, the people, or the entire thing?"

"The entire thing. Definitely the entire thing." I covered my face with my hands and moaned. "This was a terrible idea. All of it. I should never have said yes."

She was quiet for a moment. Then, "I don't like it either. You know that."

"I know."

"But you're doing it for a good reason," she reminded me. "A very rational, logical one. And this isn't a bonding—not like what I was forced into that day in the Black Keep. You won't be, you know, making a vow or exchanging blood or anything like that. It's just a ball. Just a very . . . public . . ."

"Spectacle," I finished. "Where I'll be on display as Kage Tanaka's future consort. And after tonight, most people will consider me bound to him."

"Right," she finished lamely. "See? So simple." She shook her head. "I'm sorry, Florence. I really am. But didn't Nyxaris agree this was the best course of action?" She stepped forward, lowering her voice. "If he could protect you—fully and completely—from, you know, Viktor, then he would, right? You wouldn't need Kage."

"Right," I said hollowly. "But it seems that he can't."

Medra linked her arm through mine, and together we walked to the weapons rack where I put back my bow and quiver.

I glanced at her as we walked out of the courtyard. What would my best friend say if she knew that night after night, a shadowy version of my dragon prowled into my mind and did unspeakably sinful things to my body. I'd tried to dismiss it the first few times, but the dreams just kept coming. Vivid, lush visions that left me tangled in my sheets, skin fever-hot and pulse humming fast. Eventually, I stopped *wanting* them to stop. I went to bed each night, hoping to see Nyxaris. He'd circle me, his hot breath skimming my neck, lowering his head to graze my skin, and then . . .

I could feel a flush creeping up my neck and forced my thoughts away. The dreams had made one thing terribly clear: Whatever I was supposed to be trying to feel for Kage Tanaka just wasn't there. I felt nothing for him, nothing like what unfurled in my belly at night when Nyxaris's voice coiled like smoke through my dreams, all velvet and flame.

If ridiculous dreams could stir me like that, what did it say about the loneliness that awaited me when I stood at Kage's side, possibly for the rest of my life? Still, Medra was right: I'd made my choice, and it was too late to back out.

"You're right," I repeated out loud. "I promised Nyxaris I'd go through with this, and I won't shame him tonight."

A low growl rippled in my mind. *Shame does not enter the equation. You will carry yourself with grace and dignity, as you always do. Are you prepared?*

My guilt spiked. Had he sensed the images that were just simmering in my thoughts?

Almost. Medra's here to help me get dressed.

His growl softened into a sigh. *If I could spare you from this pageantry, I would. Forgive me.*

I know. There's no need to apologize, I said quickly.

Regret pulsed through our bond. *For now, the Avari boy's name is the best shield we may wield.*

It's all right, I answered, even as my throat tightened at the lie. *I'll be fine. I'll manage. Just . . . stay close tonight.*

Always. The word rumbled like thunder, Nyxaris's voice warm and possessive.

Forcing my thoughts away from my dragon and back down to ground level, I followed Medra down the corridor, and together we headed to the tower.

CHAPTER 22

BLAKE

I bent over my desk and flicked at a page in the book with one hand while buttoning my waistcoat with the other. The book was a fucking joke; I'd lost count of how many times I'd stared at the same page in *The Dark Art of Eternal Bonds*. Because I now knew, after reading the damned thing from cover to cover at least three times, that there was only one spell in the entire tome that could possibly apply to my situation: The Spell of Twin Hearts.

I scanned the page, as if I hadn't already memorized most of it.

In the furnace of one soul, bind name for name, flame for flame. If will should falter, ash devours ash.

My stomach lurched, also not for the first time. At first, the words had held no meaning. They were like a cryptic poem, one I'd had to read again and again. But now I understood all too well what they meant. The spell was meant to complete a merge with another dragon. A second dragon caged behind my ribs when I couldn't even leash the fucking first.

I rubbed my temples, barely resisting the urge to hurl the book across the room, then touched the piece of parchment I'd taken to using as a bookmark. It was a note from Rodriguez. He'd sent it in an envelope and had someone stick it under my door the morning after he'd given me the book.

Blake, the note read, *I was a drunk idiot when I handed you that book.*

Well, on that we could both agree.

The Twin Heart spell hasn't been attempted in living memory.

Considering all of the dragons had been stone until a few months ago, that hardly needed to be said.

There is a chance it could grant you control. But chances are higher it would simply tear you apart.

I'd figured that out on my own, too—thanks, Rodriguez.

Forgive me for not being more helpful. I'm sorry.

It went without saying what he was sorry for. He was sorry that I had a clock counting down over my head, each day inching closer to my last. I snorted, pushing the piece of parchment aside, and reading the last line of the spell.

If heart-fire answers heart-fire, two may become one. Mastery forged anew.

Gods, that sounded good. *Mastery.* How I longed for that. But two becoming one? I didn't want to become one with anyone or anything else. The oneness I felt with Pendragon when we were fucking was the closest thing to being *one* with another person I ever wanted to experience. In fact, I felt weirdly guilty for even thinking of doing a spell that involved *twin hearts*. As if it were cheating on her or something.

And yet, you don't feel guilty for not telling her you can turn into a fucking dragon, a voice in my head reminded me. I clenched my jaw: I knew I was in denial. Hoping she'd never find out. That she'd never need to know. She had enough on her plate, especially tonight. I knew how worried she was about Florence and this engagement. I pushed away from the desk and crossed over to the mirror.

Twin hearts. How did that even make sense when it felt like there were already two beings inside of me warring for dominance? One mortal muscle, one invisible and scaled and furious. But if Kage was right, we weren't two—we were one and the same. Try telling that to the red-eyed demon who was constantly trying to surface.

I looked in the mirror, smoothing my hair off my face. I was an unlucky bastard in some ways, but a fucking lucky one in others. The socket where Viktor had scooped my eye away was whole again— miracle of highblood regeneration. I'd had an inkling something was happening, an itchiness that never went away, especially when I was trying to fall asleep at night. And then one morning, I woke up and it was like a plant blooming overnight. An iris was there, shimmering with the familiar slate-silver.

Until it didn't. I blinked into the mirror, and the iris of my left eye flashed scarlet. The color pulsed like the heartbeat of the monster inside me.

"Not tonight," I muttered. "I don't fucking think so." I pinched the bridge of my nose tight, until I saw stars behind my eyes. *Go the fuck away.* I looked back in the mirror. My eyes were both gray again. For now. Still, I seemed to have some control over it. In fact, these past few weeks, since I'd picked up the book from Rodriguez, things seemed to have plateaued, almost as if I were finally gaining some of that control Kage claimed I should have. Or almost as if the red demon inside me knew I was thinking of doing a suicidal ritual that could kill us both.

I decided tonight I'd go with optimism. I hadn't killed anyone in a few weeks. That had to count for something.

I tugged on the sleeves of the black jacket I wore, then pinned on my cuff links. Small ruby red circles engraved with tiny dragons. Ironic, yes. The linen shirt I wore was snow-white, cuffs stitched with crimson silk. I glanced at the clock: half an hour. Half an hour until the Avari engagement ball would throw open the doors of Bloodwing's Great Hall—the same vaulted refectory chamber the Frostfire ball had recently been held in. And look how well that had gone.

Apparently there had been a fight over whether or not the Avaris would be permitted to use the refectory for tonight's festivities. Lady Avari had gotten the Board involved, and things had gone her way.

Viktor wouldn't be in attendance tonight; he was at one of our Drakharrow estates in Veilmar—one of many. One I never visited. Viktor had turned the entire city manor house into his own private den of blood, filled it with his several thralls. Did Regan know? Surely she must by now. Viktor had always had a lascivious, greedy appetite, one which he'd managed to keep mostly hidden from his rivals. But within our family, it was common knowledge that Viktor didn't just *use* thralls. He spent their lives like they were coins, drinking so much they never recovered fully or even draining them completely. And he'd taught Marcus to feed in the same way. Just one more reason why Theo and I hated them both so much. And just one more reason why Viktor looked down on me for not following precisely in his footsteps.

I smirked at my reflection as I realized something: Tonight could be seen as a twisted victory, of sorts. One in which the Avari one-upped the Drakharrows, claiming Sangratha's only dragon and a rider for their own.

I still had pride in my house, but if Kage becoming betrothed to Florence meant Viktor was left feeling furious and impotent, then I was all for it. Poor, poor Viktor. He'd barely had time to try to sink his claws into Florence Shen. And now, with this betrothal, hopefully he'd be forced to back off for good.

I let myself imagine, just for a moment, how sweet it would have been to raze Viktor's throat with my dragon's fangs the night of the Frostfire ball. What if I'd been able to end it all right then and there? But as usual, dear old Uncle Viktor had a card up his sleeve that I hadn't seen coming. One that I was bound and chained to keep a secret. One that made him even more fucking dangerous than I'd ever imagined. I'd wounded him badly. We'd reached a standstill. Me with one eye missing, him looking even more fucking awful than usual. I suppose it had been a shitty wedding present to give Regan, but she'd survived.

Still smirking, I picked up the blood-red cravat from the little table by the mirror and began to tie it. The door rattled with a knock. I checked my reflection: both eyes still gray. I exhaled. "Enter." I already knew it wouldn't be Pendragon; she was meeting me at the reception.

Theo slipped into my room first. I eyed his ensemble. He skirted the boundaries of House Drakharrow colors in dark gray tails and a silver waistcoat. I raised my eyebrows.

"I'm supporting the groom," he informed me.

"Are you, now?" I shook my head. "Well, I doubt Viktor is coming tonight, anyhow."

Behind him, Visha entered more slowly. She wore a strapless crimson satin gown that hit a few inches above her knee. Gold bands in the shape of dragons swallowing their own tails wrapped around her upper arms. I whistled, but she ignored me, moving straight towards the fireplace, and sinking into a chair, wrapping her arms around herself.

"What's the problem, Vaidya? Rodriguez turned down your invitation to be your date tonight?" I joked.

Theo looked at me nervously. He already knew about Visha's little dalliance with our professor. "I wouldn't do that if I were you."

"Why?" I lowered my voice. "Did they break up?"

"I don't think you can break up when you aren't technically together, but no. It's family news. She got a letter this evening delivered by a special messenger. Straight from the Vaidya estate."

The Vaidya estate bordered a small town a few hours outside of Veilmar. My smile vanished. "What happened?"

Theo glanced at Visha's back, then beckoned me over so we were standing just inside my bathroom. "Her nephew, Arjun. He's eleven. He . . . fell sick. At first, they thought it was just a fever. But then, he got worse. Got . . . strange."

"*Strange*? What does that mean?"

Theo swallowed. "He went feral. Attacked his parents, hurt his little sister. Tried to feed from them. They restrained him, but he managed to break loose."

My heart started pounding. This sounded painfully familiar. I knew this story; it didn't have a happy ending. Sure enough . . .

"He ran into the village, attacked blightborn. A blightborn merchant wound up being forced to kill him in self-defense."

A spike of horror. The memory of Aenia, her fangs bared as she held a little blightborn girl in her arms. "And the fallout?" I asked grimly.

"Bad. Visha's family hung the man on the gate leading into their manor. Now the whole village is on edge. The place is mostly blightborn workers, farm laborers who the Vaidya family employs. They're fortifying, preparing for the worst."

"The worst has already happened," I said coldly. "They strung up an innocent man."

"I know that. Visha knows that. Why do you think she feels so awful?" We both glanced over at her. Maybe she was listening to us; highbloods had good hearing. But if she minded us talking about her, she wasn't showing it. And she was still here. Theo looked at me oddly.

"What?"

"We both know few highbloods would consider that man *innocent*," Theo said.

"But he was. If Arjun attacked him—"

"I know," Theo said quietly. "But highblood lives come first. They always come first. The Vaidyas were just following custom."

"Doesn't make it right," I muttered. "Maybe just even more fucked-up."

I thought of the blightborn boy I'd killed, weighing if it were the same. But it wasn't. He'd struck Pendragon first. She'd defended herself. Then I'd made it so he'd never touch her again. Seemed like simple justice to me. I'd have done the same to a highblood; it had nothing to do with the boy being blightborn. If anything, I'd stayed my hand against the other girl because she was also blightborn. I'd have gone harder against a highblood—used more cruelty, knowing they'd do the same. Take Larissa: She was still recovering from the week-long blood fast I'd forced upon her for biting Rodriguez. I'd seen her slinking around the tower, looking pale and pissed off. She wouldn't be fucking with blightborn teachers again. At least, not anytime soon.

Outside in the corridor, a bell tolled, the signal for guests to begin filing toward the hall.

I crossed over to Visha and touched her shoulder. "Why not just stay here? You don't have to come to this thing. Hang out at my place. We'll be back soon."

It went without saying that we'd been to a ball much like tonight's just a few months before—and it hadn't gone well. Visha had lost her girlfriend, Lace Ironstride, that night. Visha looked up at me, and I knew we must both be thinking the same thing.

"I'm sorry, Vish," I said uncomfortably.

She nodded. "Thanks, but I'm going. Need a distraction." She glanced past me at Theo. "Did you tell him the best part?"

Theo looked uncomfortable. "No."

"What's the best part?"

"She means *the worst*," Theo said.

"His sister is sick," Visha said hollowly.

"Whose, the merchant's?" I said stupidly.

"Not the merchant. Arjun's little sister, my niece." Her face clouded. "He bit her. And his mother. And his father. Before he . . ." She choked.

"Shit," I breathed. "What's happening? Is this some sort of a plague?"

But we must have all been thinking the obvious. Highbloods didn't get sick.

She shrugged. "Who the fuck knows. If it is one, maybe it's been a long time coming. Maybe we brought this on ourselves."

I stared at her. I'd never heard her speak so darkly. "Well," I said slowly, "I think it's good you're coming with us. Theo and I, we'll distract you."

"Should be easy. We've all seen Blake's dancing," Theo quipped.

I punched him in the shoulder, just as another knock came at the door.

Theo's face lit up. He had the door open before I could even make a move. "Vaughn!" he exclaimed.

The tall blightborn boy stepped into my room looking a little awkward. He was in Orphos colors, dark gold trousers and a bright purple silk shirt. His voluminous, tightly curled black hair had been combed back and pulled into a short ponytail. "I told the warden I was here with your permission so she'd let me in. I hope that's all right."

"Absolutely," I said enthusiastically. I glanced at Theo and raised a brow.

"He's my date," Theo said coolly.

I shrugged. "The more the merrier."

Theo linked his arm through Vaughn's, leaning into the lanky blightborn. He looked happy and excited, just like he deserved to be.

Viktor won't be there, I reminded myself, trying to relax. Theo would be all right. What was one more blightborn? Florence Shen was blightborn. Everyone's eyes would be on her tonight, not on Vaughn and Theo. *As long as we could keep them safe*, a nagging voice in my head said. Safe even from ourselves. But one night wouldn't cut it. We didn't just need a few nights of freedom from Viktor's threatening presence—we needed a lifetime.

I thought of the book on the table, belatedly realizing something. Was that what Rodriguez had drunkenly been hoping? That if I did the spell, if I merged with Vorago, I'd finally be strong enough to stop Viktor?

Would it be worth the price, if I were?

The refectory hall was already mostly full when we got there. Swaths of jet-black silk looped between pillars. Silver lanterns in the shape of crescent moons had been hung from the cavernous ceiling. Avari midnight and moon-gray silver were the reigning colors, relieved only by the warm gold shimmer coming from the hundreds of candles in the cast-iron chandeliers dangling overhead. Even the bloodwine being handed around had been poured into silver flutes.

Black dragons were displayed everywhere: embroidered on banners alongside the Avari motto, decorating the napkins, even appearing as tiny black sculpted sugar candies decorating each table. A dragon—that bore no resemblance at all to Nyxaris—sat in midsnarl atop a massive cake displayed on the stand. Blightborn musicians wearing shiny black suits played on a raised stage at the back of the hall. It was clear Lady Avari had spared no expense on the spectacle.

We'd barely cleared the threshold when my friends vanished. Vaughn pulled Theo towards the dance floor, while Visha snatched two goblets of bloodwine from a passing waiter's tray and muttered something about getting some air. I watched her stride towards the terrace doors, nearly bumping into Lady Avari walking with Kage's mother, Natsumi. The younger Avari woman was draped in a long gown made to resemble silver scales. Elaria glared after Visha, then turned back to murmuring with her daughter-in-law.

As Visha disappeared onto the terrace, I threaded through knots of chattering guests, making my way towards the bar. I was trying to catch a bartender's attention when Kage Tanaka stepped up beside me, clearly intent on doing the same. I side-eyed him. He looked as if he'd been carefully crafted to match the same monochrome palette as the decor: black jacket, silver satin vest, collar fastened with a curved sliver of silver. His white-blond hair was swept back, and the sides had been freshly razored. His dark eyes looked more brooding than usual.

We regarded each other like rival blades laid out side by side. "House Avari certainly knows how to throw a party." I reached for the drink I'd ordered. "Congratulations, by the way. Florence Shen is . . . well, she's brilliant, isn't she?" I finished lamely.

I should have been used to this. Most highblood matches were arranged affairs. And yet there was something especially awkward about this one. Maybe because Kage and I both knew blightborns typically married for love. They also didn't do triads.

"She is. But you congratulate me as if the choice was mine," Kage said shortly. It wasn't like Tanaka to sulk. I looked at him in surprise as he grasped a flute of smoky champagne and tilted it back.

"It's a good match," I said uncomfortably. "Shen will benefit from your house's protection." I lowered my voice a tad. "Gotta say, it's a weight off my shoulders knowing you'll be shielding her from Viktor."

"Well, if it's benefiting you, Drakharrow, then that changes everything," Kage drawled.

I smirked. Now we were back on more familiar ground. "Seems to me we've been here before." I gestured to the bar. "Last time was a little different."

"It was," he agreed, taking another sip.

"Was that invite back then just to make me jealous?"

He looked at me. "Why don't you tell me. Did it work?"

I chuckled. "Abso-fucking-lutely."

"Good. Maybe I'll try it again."

I eyed him coldly. "Don't even joke about that. Besides, you have your own triad to worry about now."

He winked. "Sure do. And there's room for one more."

I knew he was just messing with me. I sighed. "Look, let's cut—"

But before I could say more, a fanfare sliced through the air, and conversation came to a halt. Everyone pivoted to face the entrance of the hall.

Florence Shen appeared, stepping slowly into the room from the hallway. Her black hair was swept up with silver half-moon combs. Her gown was a sleek affair, all satiny liquid moonlight that clung to her slender curves. She looked every inch the startled, timid fairy-tale princess whose carriage had suddenly turned into a ravenous beast.

Behind her, a step back and to her right, came Pendragon. I sucked in a breath. Pendragon wore Avari black, but it wasn't the black of the night sky. This was a starlit river. The gown shimmered as she moved, covered with tiny glimmering pearls. A plunging scooped neckline revealed the freckles that dusted her collarbone like scattered flecks of autumn leaves. She'd left her hair down, and it fell loose around her shoulders in a riot of brilliant copper. A circlet of onyx lay across her brow, nudging her hair back just enough to reveal the tips of her pointed ears.

And at her throat gleamed the black dragon pendant I'd given her a few months ago—marking her as unmistakably mine.

Ours, something inside corrected. My newly healed eye pulsed.

I gave a low, possessive growl and felt Kage looking at me strangely. I cleared my throat, shutting my eyes for the briefest moment until the sensation had cleared. I looked back at Pendragon: She was fucking radiant. Brilliant as a falling star. I felt dizzy just looking at her. Beside me, Kage set down his glass. I glanced at him, noticing the tension in his shoulders; he wasn't so cocky now. No, the Avari leader looked like a man about to step off a cliff.

"Good luck," I murmured.

He nodded as he stepped past me, moving towards where Florence waited nervously by the door. Across the hall, Pendragon turned her head, and our gazes met. Something lit up in her emerald eyes, hot and secret. She smiled slightly, and my chest tightened. For a moment of reckless whimsy, I considered sending her a new pendant the next day. A red one, to match the beast that slept beneath my skin. Then I pushed the idea aside. Pendragon's smile was pure sunlight, warm and fearless. But the dragon inside me didn't know light, he only knew the darkness of eternal hunger. If I let him slip out, he'd destroy me, destroy her. He'd shatter everything in blood and fire.

Pendragon started walking across the grand hall towards me, the crowd parting, and all I could think of was the dragon fighting to get out. If I let that happen, my girl would be in the arms of a monster, not a man.

Kage reached Florence's side, offering her his arm and leading her onto the dance floor. For a moment, I envied him; he might have two bodies, but at least he and his wolf shared a single soul.

Then Pendragon reached me. She put her hand on my arm, and I looked down at it, frozen for a heartbeat. Slender, freckled, so beautiful—and I remembered the truth that kept me standing. I'd rather burn myself to ash than ever let that hand tremble in fear because of me.

So if the Spell of Twin Hearts was the only thing strong enough to leash me, I'd swallow my fear and risk my death. Better to carry another dragon under my ribs than to watch the first one devour her light. Because she was it. She was everything. She was the line I could never, ever cross.

CHAPTER 23

REGAN

Wind rattled the window panes as I walked slowly through the castle halls. The Avaris had gotten what they wanted. Kage's engagement ball was being held this evening in the school refectory. When Viktor tried to refuse them, Lady Avari attacked him with the full force of the Bloodwing Board of Directors. The Board demanded an explanation for all of the recent—and completely unauthorized—changes at Bloodwing. They wanted most to be rolled back. Viktor refused, deeming them all necessary for student security. Even so, he was treading a little more lightly now. So Lady Avari had got her ball.

To be honest, it was a relief. Not the ball, but the fact that the Board had been able to intimidate Viktor in any way whatsoever. Oh, I didn't kid myself that he was actually *afraid* of them, but perhaps they might be able to slow him down a little.

In the meantime, here I was, decked out in a dress of black netting over scarlet satin, the whalebone stays digging into my ribs, preparing to go to the Avari ball. Not because I wanted to, but because I was an invited guest and Bloodwing's headmistress.

I paused beneath a flickering torch on the wall to gather myself. Outside the doors of the refectory, four of the Bloodguards were gathered. They were supposed to be a kind of peace offering—extra security for the most exclusive highblood event of the season. I gritted my teeth. My Bloodguards lounged around as Avari guests waltzed past them into the refectory. They were supposed to be checking each guest against the list Lady Avari had provided. They were supposed to be doing their fucking jobs.

Instead, it seemed they had brought a little snack. A young dwarven woman lolled between two of them, her pupils blown black, her throat covered in bite marks both old and new. And standing before them, his voice already raised with dramatic flair, was Professor Rodriguez. He'd obviously come straight from class, carrying a leather satchel and wearing a heavy brown overcoat—not exactly dressed for the ball.

I quickened my pace as I noticed some guests stopping to watch. "Please go into the ballroom," I said brightly, urging them inside. "I'll handle this matter." Moving to stand beside Rodriguez, I hissed, "Lower your damn voice."

"Lower my voice? *Lower my voice*, Regan?" He'd begun refusing to address me as *Headmistress*, preferring to treat me as if I were still one of his students. "I'll lower my voice as soon as your fucking Bloodguard sends this *child* to the infirmary."

One of the Bloodguards snickered. I whirled around. "Something amusing, Silvio?" I asked coldly.

The House Mortis guard held up his hands innocently. "I was just telling the professor here that everything's fine. This girl is my personal thrall." He leered. "Believe me, she's no child."

I glanced past him at the girl. She was dwarven and a blightborn, of course. All dwarven were. She was also young but not a *child* as Rodriguez had claimed, though she was obviously a First Year.

I frowned. The girl was a thrall, obviously. But I didn't have to be a healer to see that she looked a little worse for wear. Her skin was pale and clammy, and she was breathing strangely—each breath a shallow flutter, the bodice of the royal blue dress she wore scarcely moving.

Rodriguez's voice dropped to a vicious whisper meant only for me. "Look at the girl. She's one fainting spell away from going into severe shock. She's dwarven, which means she's even more susceptible to blood loss—" his voice rose "—and these assholes are draining her dry. Can't you see it?"

"Hey, back off, you blightborn bastard. Unless you want a taste of my fangs. I hear you like that." Silvio stepped forward with a nasty grin, put his hands on Rodriguez's chest and gave the professor a shove. "Now, get the fuck out of here. I already told you, she's fine."

My temples were already throbbing. I didn't need this. The Board was breathing down my neck. Viktor's shadow was at my back. And now this, right outside the ballroom doors.

I'd heard Rodriguez had been fed from. I didn't know which student had done it, but I suspected it was one of my former House Drakharrow friends. Maybe Quinn Riley. Funny how the higher I rose, the fewer friends I seemed to have. For a while the number had actually spiked to a pitiful one, but it had been a mistake to count a wolf as a friend.

I looked between Silvio and Rodriguez. I'd warned Viktor that the blood donation program could result in the total disrespect of our blightborn faculty. He hadn't seemed to care, so I'd done his bidding and pushed the program through. He was cruel to me even when I obeyed him, but he was much, much worse when I challenged him. I had a scar on the back of my thigh still left from that specific conversation . . . and it took a lot for a highblood to permanently scar. No one could say my archon wasn't hardworking.

I stared at Silvio, suddenly filled with dislike. He was just like Viktor. He was a bully. They were all bullies. At first I'd thought Viktor's plan was a good one, that the Bloodguards would be a symbolic presence, nothing more. But things had gotten out of control. My Bloodguards had done terrible things—and they kept getting away with them. There was no one to stop them, no one but me. I knew if I tried to rein them in, there'd have been hell to pay with Viktor. Still, I'd enabled them. Now they needed to remember who was in charge here. They didn't need to know I was just as much of a pawn as they were. They were supposed to be intimidating the blightborn students, but killing them was going too far. I knew Viktor wouldn't care about the loss of a few students. It had happened even under Headmaster Kim's watch—just look at the Consort Games.

But as I stared at the girl, I felt something. *Revulsion.* Was this really the highblood way, treating a thrall like this with no concern for her safety whatsoever? Passing her around like a bottle of wine? It was disgusting. It was uncivilized. It was *wrong.*

Something else followed hard on the heels of my sense of revulsion, something far worse: recognition. I looked at the girl. She was dwarven. She was blightborn. But she was *me.*

I felt dizzy with a wave of terrible understanding. An awareness of a similarity I wanted to reject—but knew I would never be able to deny again.

"Mind your tongue," I snapped at Silvio. "You're addressing a faculty member. You'll keep your hands off him and step back. Now."

Silvio looked at me as if he couldn't believe his ears. Then he bowed in a mocking way. "Yes, Headmistress."

I turned to Rodriguez. He didn't look shaken. If anything, he looked even more furious. For a moment, I rather hoped his fist would fly and he'd deal Silvio the blow he deserved. Instead, he looked back at me grimly. "It's textbook depletion. See her eyes?"

"The professor exaggerates," Silvio declared. "A few mouthfuls and she always swoons. She's fine. Aren't you, sweetheart?" The girl moaned.

"You keep saying *she*. Do you even know your own thrall's name?" I hissed.

"Sure I do." Silvio cleared his throat. "It's . . . Dari."

"It's Dani, you dumbass," the Bloodguard beside him said, bursting out laughing.

"Thank you, Cade," I said coldly.

"Whatever. Dani. I knew that." Silvio looked annoyed. "Whatever her name is, she's my thrall. The law is clear. You wouldn't trample over highblood custom, would you, Headmistress? Not after all you and Lord Drakharrow have done to uphold tradition."

I glared at him. *Tradition.* It was tradition for an archon to be the final authority in a triad, too, to have total control over his consorts. Tradition. The word suddenly tasted like iron chains.

Rodriguez rounded on me. "If you leave this girl another hour, I assure you it will be too late. You'll be trying to resuscitate a corpse. Custom be damned."

A clear, sweet voice rang out. "What's going on here? Is something wrong?"

I whirled around as Medra Pendragon and Florence Shen emerged from the nearby stairwell. Florence's eyes were wide. She looked demure and innocent. Medra, on the other hand, assessed me from green flashing eyes. I wondered if Blake was far behind.

Wonderful. More witnesses I absolutely did not need.

I drew myself up a little taller. Silvio had stepped back. Now his fingers tightened on Dani's arm. The girl swayed, her eyelids fluttering.

Rodriguez swore under his breath. Then he leaned down. "Do you even know who this girl is?"

I stared at him blankly. "A First Year, I assume."

"She's Professor Stonefist's niece," he hissed. "Do you want to tell the professor, who I might add is already none too pleased with you, how her niece died in your halls because you refused to send her to a healer?"

I stared back at him thoughtfully. The fact that Professor Stonefist was dwarven did complicate things—in a way I could use to my advantage in this situation. We'd already had dwarven deaths. Viktor had received a missive from the Dwarven Council demanding that there be no more this year. I knew he didn't want to have to worry about the threat of their involvement as he continued rolling back blightborn freedoms above the surface. I reached a decision swiftly.

"Professor Rodriguez, escort this thrall to the First Year infirmary, if you please," I declared. "Silvio, she may be your thrall, but you will feed from her only if and when a healer decides it is safe. And as she is a pupil at Bloodwing and you have caused what may be permanent injury already, you will do so only under supervision." This was pushing things a little, but I didn't care. I felt suddenly reckless.

Anger flashed across the Bloodguard's golden face. "Is that an order, Headmistress?"

"It certainly fucking is," I snapped. "Now, clear out. You've behaved like a fool. You've embarrassed me and this school instead of doing what you were supposed to do this evening and guarding the blooddamned doors."

Silvio stalked off. I knew he'd be trouble later. Resisting the urge to rub my temples, I turned to the other three guards. "Are you blind? Don't you see Miss Shen standing here waiting to enter? She's our guest of honor tonight. Open the fucking doors."

Rodriguez put his arm around Dani and gently led her down the hall. As I watched, he turned his head and looked back at me. He nodded. *Was that meant to be thanks?* Stiffly, I nodded back.

"Miss Shen," I said quickly, before she could move past. The blightborn girl's dress was a fanciful concoction of silver. She looked pretty and pristine and pure—my opposite in every way. As I spoke, she paled and looked up at me as if she were afraid. But I'd become used to such reactions.

"Yes, Headmistress?"

I took a deep breath. "You look lovely this evening. Congratulations on your engagement and best wishes on your future union to Kage Tanaka."

"Th-thank you," she stuttered, her brown eyes widening.

Medra said nothing. I could feel her watching me, but I refused to meet her eyes. A trumpet played, announcing Florence's arrival. Medra swept in after her.

The doors shut behind them. I stood there for a moment, trying to regain my bearings. I hadn't meant to say that. I wasn't even sure where the words had come from. It wasn't like me to be gracious or bother trying to be kind. That wasn't who I was—or who anyone expected me to be.

"Headmistress." It was Cade, one of my Bloodguards. He stepped forward and looked me up and down appreciatively, his eyes lingering on certain parts of my body a little longer than was strictly appropriate. "Are you attending the ball alone?"

I raised my chin. "I am."

"If you'd like an escort, I'd be happy to accompany you." He grinned at me.

I stared up at him, still feeling off-kilter. My archon, a wretched specimen of a highblood, was in Veilmar, no doubt drinking his fill from his trove of thralls and fucking half of them senseless while I stood here alone, doing his bidding, the obedient consort as always. Inside the hall . . . my breath hitched. Inside, Florence Shen was no doubt being swept into Kage Tanaka's waiting arms.

And this was how it would be. Now—and forever. This was my life now. This was what I had chosen for myself.

I forced a crisp smile. "That's very sweet of you, Cade. But I'll be fine."

I pulled open the doors and entered the hall.

I worked my way around the ballroom like a drowning woman treading water. I smiled, I nodded, I held onto my silver flute of bloodwine like a lifeline. I was cornered by highblood nobility. First by Quinn's mother, Lady Riley, who asked if she could use the refectory for Quinn's betrothal ball. I told her no—politely. She didn't take it well.

At dinner I was seated with the Sylvains. Lord Sylvain commended me for instituting more restrictions on blightborn freedom, while his son, Evander, sat silently listening. I'd heard about what happened to Evander's little triad, how Visha Vaidya had decided to walk away from both him and Lucian Aleron in a fit of pique. As I listened to Evander's father spouting about the need for greater dominance over the blightborn, I wondered if there was more to it than what I'd been told.

After dinner, I drifted about the room, refusing offers to dance from lecherous old highblood men. Not that Viktor would have cared if I danced; he would only have cared if I enjoyed it. A soft melody began to drift through the hall, and I turned my head to the dance floor where Florence Shen, looking pale and ethereal in her silver gown, began a waltz with Kage. The Avari House Leader steered her unhurriedly, his hand steady at the small of her back, as if he'd been born for the ballroom instead of battle drills and highblood house intrigue. But I knew better—there was a wolf inside Kage Tanaka. He'd been born for the wild. For the open air and freedom. For something better than stifling ballrooms and cruel gossip.

How I envied him. If I could turn into a wolf, I wouldn't have been standing there, I'd have my teeth at Viktor's throat.

Florence smiled up at Kage. I studied her face, wondering how much she cared for him already. Probably a lot. After all, he was a highblood, and she was a blightborn. It was like something from a fairy tale: the blightborn girl who married the wolf-prince.

My stomach twisted as Kage smiled back at her. Was it my imagination, or did his smile seem a little forced? I reached for another glass of wine. Dessert was being served—a rich chocolate cake trimmed with bloodberry frosting—but I knew I wouldn't be able to taste it.

Viktor had promised me power. Promised I'd rule this place. Instead, I was the ghost haunting the castle. Everywhere I moved, conversations broke apart, re-forming only once I'd moved away. I was the youngest headmistress Bloodwing had ever had. I was also the most despised. Everyone knew how I'd gotten the position—by sleeping my way to the top of the Sangrathan food chain. Would they care if I told them I regretted my choice every day? Would they care if they knew the real reason why I'd done it? They were highbloods, so of course they wouldn't. They'd be gleeful.

I thought of Persis. He was so small, so young. There was no use in asking if he'd do the same for me someday. Of course he would—if he ever had the chance to grow up. I thought again of Kage as the wolf, how strong he was, how fast he could run. If I were a wolf, could I save Persis? Would I be any match for Viktor then? Or would he tear me to pieces just as easily?

Somewhere between the hallway and the refectory, I realized something had happened. A cascade of unrelenting self-knowledge and unwanted truths. Viktor was never letting Persis go, not so long as I was his consort. It didn't matter that I was obedient. It didn't matter that I was doing everything he wanted. He enjoyed the leverage too much to ever relinquish it. Another man might have tested my loyalty and then honored his agreement and let Persis go. But somehow, I knew—Viktor never would.

Persis was trapped—but so was I. I couldn't save him any more than I could save myself.

I decided this self-torture had gone on long enough. I'd made an appearance. I'd congratulated the happy couple—well, one of them, at least. I'd mingled and played my part. No one would notice if I slipped away. When the musicians struck the notes of the next set, I headed for the doors. I was almost there.

"Leaving so soon?" Kage stepped into my path. The Avari leader towered over me. I wore heels—I was always wearing heels—but even those hardly made a difference with him. His eyes locked onto mine, rich and dark, with a touch more warmth than usual. His pale hair gleamed like polished silver against the rich black of his formal jacket. There was an elegance to him tonight that made him look both refined and fiercely commanding. Beneath his dark brows his gaze was intense, focused—as if he could read the turmoil swirling about beneath my carefully constructed mask.

"Dance with me."

I smiled coolly. "No, thank you. I was just leaving. I've stayed long enough to fulfill my obligations."

"Not all of them."

My mind went straight to the last words he'd said to me the last time we'd been alone together: *When a wolf finds his true mate, he knows.* What the hell was that supposed to mean? How could I be his mate when I was trapped with Viktor and when Kage was about to take Florence Shen as his consort?

Kage was still standing there waiting. "One dance is all I ask. Then you can go." He held out his hand. "You don't want to make a scene, do you?"

I glanced around. No one was watching us yet. Continuing to refuse would be too revealing, too much of an admission of my own vulnerability.

I tilted my head in assent and let him take my hand. Kage's fingers closed around mine, and all the intentions I'd had of remaining restrained and poised fled. His grasp was firm and warm. As our palms met, I shivered, remembering the feel of his blood flowing into me. I should never have made the Blood Vow. There was something far too intimate about the highblood tradition. I'd let a piece of Kage Tanaka enter my body and slide right into my soul. Now I wasn't sure I'd ever be able to get him out again.

The orchestra shifted so seamlessly into the next waltz that I wondered if Kage had asked them to play it. The song was slower, with a melody that seemed sad to me. He led me onto the dance floor, then firmly clasped my waist with both hands. For a moment, my entire body stiffened. But the next, I found myself leaning into his touch. I inhaled slowly. He smelled so good, the opposite of Viktor. There was no death and decay here; Kage smelled like the earth, like fresh fallen snow and cedarwood.

"This is an unusual waltzing position," I murmured.

One hand should have been at the small of my back, the other clasping my hand. There should have been distance between us, just like when he'd danced with Florence. Instead, his hands were practically wrapped around me. I imagined them slipping lower, grasping my hips as he pulled me tight against him.

"Would you like me to move my hands?"

I cleared my throat. "I didn't say that."

I closed my eyes, letting myself drink in the moment just for a few seconds. This was dangerous. *He* was dangerous. I should have walked away when I'd had the chance, even if it had meant causing a scene. Because now that Kage Tanaka had put his hands on my body again, I didn't want him to take them off. His hands made me want to do bad things. Selfish things that were just for him and me alone.

Around us, guests whispered and stared. Kage studiously ignored them. His movements were confident, assured, fluid, guiding me effortlessly. His grip tightened slightly around my waist, and my breath hitched.

He leaned down, speaking near my ear. "You seem tense. What's wrong, Regan?"

So many things, I wanted to say. So, so many things were terribly wrong. His engagement to another woman being one of them.

"Everyone's staring at us," I said breathlessly instead.

"And why do you think that is?"

I forced a laugh. "Isn't it obvious? Everyone hates me. If they don't hate me, then they're afraid of me."

He raised a brow. "Is that what you think? Perhaps they're simply staring because you're a beautiful woman."

I flushed. "The world is cruel to beautiful women. I learned that long ago."

He was quiet for a moment. "I'm sorry for that."

"It's fine," I said, trying to sound casual. "I learned the solution to that problem a long time ago, too."

"Oh? And what's that?"

"Make the world afraid." I bit my lip as he studied my face. He seemed disappointed. "What?"

"You think these people are staring at you because they're afraid? I promise you, that's not it."

"Then, what is it?" I demanded, lifting my chin.

"They're all looking at you because you're the only thing in this room worth possessing—and because you're in my arms." He lowered his mouth to my ear. "Tell me, when's the last time your archon said that to you?"

Kage was deluded, I decided. Maybe that's what becoming a wolf did to a person. Still, I swallowed. "Never."

"I thought not. You're trapped in a lie, but it doesn't have to be that way, Regan."

I shook my head in disbelief. "And you? You think your life is any less of a lie? Look at where we are right now!" I glanced at the stage. Would this waltz ever end, or had the musicians begun playing the same song a second time?

Kage moved us through the next turn before answering. "You make a fair point. Which is why I've decided to end my engagement."

The ballroom dissolved. I felt the floor sway beneath my heels. "You've what?"

"My betrothal ends tonight," he repeated, his voice unnervingly calm. "I misjudged what I could live with—and without."

"And your fiancée? When were you planning on telling her this?"

"As soon as we've finished dancing."

"You'll humiliate her," I hissed, feeling some odd measure of sympathy for the blightborn girl. "Not to mention your grandmother. Your entire family! What will they say?"

"They'll understand—if not tonight, in time. This engagement was never real, it was meant to shield Florence from Viktor. You know this—and I think you know what will happen to her if Viktor is able to get a hold of her." His eyes bore into me, suddenly cold.

My throat felt dry. "I have . . . some idea."

I knew Viktor fantasized about something called soul-binding. And I knew he was too much of a coward to do the ritual on himself. "I'd never have let him do that to me," I whispered. But I also knew I didn't have a hope in hell of stopping him if he'd tried.

Kage nodded. "I knew you'd say that. Regardless, I've realized I can still offer Florence the protection of House Avari without chaining her to a future with me that she doesn't want."

My heart thudded. "How do you know she doesn't want it? That she doesn't want you?"

"I know," he said simply. "Is it really so hard to believe?"

I couldn't give him an honest answer to that, so I didn't reply.

"Why can't you accept that the world isn't always forged from fear and cruelty, Regan?" he said softly. "Who taught you those were the only coins worth spending?"

I gave a brittle laugh. "My family. Not to mention years of experience." I looked across the room at where Blake and Medra were dancing. "Maybe even him."

"You cared for him so much, then?"

I shook my head slowly. "No. Not like that. But it would have been a good life. A better life . . . than the one I've ended up with."

Blake had humiliated me. Rejected me. And while I stood alone and disgraced, licking my wounds like a dog, Viktor Drakharrow had swooped in. For a little while, I'd truly been flattered by his attention. What a naïve fool the old Regan had been.

Blake leaned down to speak into Medra's ear. I should have been filled with hatred and jealousy. But suddenly, all I could think of was that I was glad at least one person here tonight was truly happy.

Kage watched me watch them. "I heard what happened earlier, out in the hall. You sent that thrall to the infirmary, even though your own Bloodguards mocked you for it."

I stiffened. "That was nothing. You know Rodriguez. He's like a dog with a bone."

"Nothing?" He drew me a little closer. "Professor Stonefist's niece is going to wake up tomorrow because you intervened and saved her life. I wouldn't call that *nothing*. Would Viktor have wanted you to do what you did?"

Heat pricked behind my eyes. "Of course not. But one small choice won't change anything. It won't change all the things I've done. Blightborn students die at Bloodwing all the time. We both know this."

"Maybe not," he conceded. "But I think it shows there's more kindness in your heart than you want to admit—even to yourself."

I stared up at him. "This talk of ending your engagement . . . Don't do it. Not if it's . . ."

"Not if it's what?" he asked.

"Not if you're doing it for me. I'm not free—I'll never be free. And I am who I am. I can't undo what I've done." There was a lump in my throat. "The blightborn girl . . . Florence. She's probably a good person. Better than I am." Not to mention she had a fucking dragon as her dowry.

The waltz was ending, but Kage didn't let me go. Instead, he leaned down. "I'm going to speak to Florence now. But I want you to meet me later tonight."

"Meet you?" I hissed. "Are you insane? You know I can't do that."

We'd already met alone, but that had been different, completely accidental. Well, mostly.

Kage's breath was hot against my cheek. "I won't keep watching you drown behind that mask. You saved a girl tonight. I want to talk to the woman who did that—not the headmistress, not Viktor Drakharrow's consort, not Blake's ex-consort. Just you. Let me show you that you don't have to live like this, Regan. Let me help you."

I closed my eyes. "Where?" I wasn't promising anything. I was just asking a simple question.

"The Dragon Court. Come at midnight. You know the state it's in. It's always empty now."

"So simple," I said hollowly. I already knew I wasn't going to show up. I couldn't. Viktor would kill us both. I wouldn't let Kage waste his life this way. And while I might not have valued my own life very highly, I still had Persis to think about.

Persis—who Viktor was never, ever letting go.

Kage flashed me a smile that showed his canines. "Simple enough. I just want to talk. That's all."

But if talking wasn't all I needed?

His hands left my waist, their warmth gone in an instant. Immediately I yearned to have them back. If his hands felt that good over the satin of my dress, how incredible would they feel on my bare skin? I stood there silently for a moment and watched him walk away, his back straight, his stance confident; I knew I couldn't change his mind. Kage Tanaka was about to go up against the second-most powerful highblood in Sangratha. More than that, he was about to risk a dragon's wrath.

And he was doing it all for me.

CHAPTER 24

FLORENCE

Kage's palm settled on the small of my back as the waltz began. The contact was perfectly respectable. Two layers of satin separated us. I could hardly feel the warmth of his hand.

Your heartbeat has risen. Is the wolf touching you? Nyxaris's voice coiled through my mind, a low rumble.

Has it? I was surprised. *We're dancing, but I feel quite calm.*

Hmm. Nyxaris sounded suspicious. *A strange human custom. He should not be permitted to touch you until the wedding night.*

The wedding night? I choked. *That seems a little . . . extreme. And far-off.*

Precisely, Nyxaris agreed. *It may never come to pass.*

Kage moved through the steps of the dance with crisp efficiency . . . and not an ounce of heat. His steps were sure. He danced gracefully. But as he held me in his arms, there was nothing pulling us closer. No sense of passion or urgency. Not like there was when I so much as brushed a hand over Nyxaris's scales or slid my hips along his back. My pulse sped up as I thought about it.

What is happening? If the wolf dares do more than dance with you, I swear I will shred his intestines.

I cleared my throat hastily, shifting a little.

"Sorry." Kage misread the gesture. "Too tight?"

"No, it's fine. My slippers are hurting," I lied awkwardly.

He nodded, his expression polite but distant. We'd tried to keep up polite small talk all through dinner. But now I got the impression that he was tired. If he noticed my pulse was beating a little faster all of a sudden, he gave no sign of it.

Round and round we went, turning in meaningless circles while the sea of bored highbloods watched. Did they approve of this, a blightborn girl in one of their most favored son's arms? Perhaps what they approved of was keeping Nyxaris within highblood control; that was something everyone could get on board with.

The waltz finally ended, and I couldn't help it: I breathed a sigh of relief. Kage looked amused. He released me and bowed. I awkwardly curtsied. Relieved to get away, I moved over to the refreshment table that had been set up along one wall. Fortunately, the servants had set out some punch and lemonade alongside the vats of bloodwine and champagne. I took a sip of lemonade—and then nearly choked.

Kage was dancing again, and this time, Regan was in his arms.

The young headmistress's black and scarlet gown glittered like embers. Kage had both hands wrapped around her waist in a way that seemed overtly possessive, even to a novice like me. He leaned in close to murmur something in her ear.

I turned away quickly, deciding this form of eavesdropping wasn't for me. Kage and I might have been engaged, but he wasn't bound to me, not truly. Of course he would still take lovers. I lifted my chin. And so might I. I took another sip of lemonade, walking around the ballroom slowly, and then nearly choked a second time when a finger tapped me on the shoulder.

"Florence? I was hoping we could talk."

I turned around to see my fiancé.

Kage looked uncomfortable, which was unusual for him. "Would you mind joining me on the terrace for a moment? There's something I'd like to discuss with you in private."

Could he not have spoken with you while you danced? Why is he here again? The wolf reeks of guilt, Nyxaris muttered.

Hush, I rebuked him. But he had a point. Kage was looking a little, well, cagey.

I followed him onto the terrace. No one else was out there: The spring night was too chilly to linger outside.

Kage walked up to the railing, then turned to me. "I won't keep you long. Florence, this engagement—"

The traitorous bastard, Nyxaris growled without warning. *I shall snap the pup's neck.*

There was only one thing that could make Nyxaris react in such a way. Instead of shock, I felt a flood of relief. I knew exactly what Kage was about to say.

"You wish to end our engagement," I interrupted.

He blinked. "I do. Does that mean . . . you agree?"

"I agree that it was a mistake. I never wished to tie you to me like this, even for my own protection."

"And I would not have you tied to me," he said quietly. "I've been rehearsing apologies all evening. None of them seemed adequate."

Because they are inadequate. He is a coward and a traitor.

Nyxaris, behave, I warned.

I am behaving. Do you see me in the skies? No. Because I have not roasted him yet.

Nyxaris, I hissed. *Hush.*

He is a spineless pup, Nyxaris grumbled. *And I was a fool to entrust you to his care.*

I tried to shut him out. "So we're free, then?" I said hastily to Kage. "You'll speak to your grandmother?"

He nodded. "At once."

"I hope it goes well."

He smiled slightly. "It won't. But before I go, please know that I won't leave you unprotected. We may be ending our engagement, but House Avari will continue to stand between you and Viktor Drakharrow. I give you my word on that."

I could feel Nyxaris's temper flare. *His word? Did he not give you his word when you became betrothed? I scoff at his word. His word means nothing. I shall protect you. It was idiocy to trust a highblood. We will no longer count on this silver wolf cub.*

"Thank you," I said, ignoring Nyxaris. "That's generous. And very kind of you."

Kage gave me a rueful half smile. "Kind? Maybe. Or selfish. But I've come to realize that a life of lies will poison everyone who tastes of it." His gaze drifted towards the ballroom windows. "I'll go and speak to my grandmother now."

"Good luck," I said and meant it.

Kage disappeared back into the refectory.

Wolves who break their word deserve neither mercy nor luck.

Please, I said. *Stop that. I know you won't hurt him. He's not our enemy. Besides, I'm relieved. Truly, I am. I never wanted this.*

A grudging pause. That does not absolve him.

Very well. But he set me free. So forgive me if I'm grateful.

I stifled a yawn, then realized something. *This means I can go home. I don't have to be here. I can proofread my essay for Professor Allenvale.* I started to smile.

The little scholar is nothing if not predictable. Nyxaris sounded amused, but I didn't care.

I hurried back into the ballroom, careful not to make eye contact with anyone in Kage's family.

"Florence." It was Medra.

I sighed in relief. "I need to talk to you."

"And I need to talk to you." She glanced across the room, then lowered her voice. "Kage just came back in. He went straight over to his grandmother. She does *not* look happy."

I held up a hand to shield my face. "Don't tell me. I don't want to know. You know I don't like drama, Medra."

She looked amused. "Is this drama? What's happening exactly?"

I nibbled my lip. "Kage and I have ended our engagement. I mean, he mostly ended it. But I agreed."

My friend's eyes widened. "Well, that was fast."

"You don't sound surprised," I said indignantly. "Why? You didn't think I could do this?"

She sighed. "Sustain a relationship with a highblood you have absolutely no romantic feelings for in an effort to gain some sort of shield from Viktor Drakharrow? No, Florence, I was pretty sure you wouldn't be able to do it. In fact, I expected *you* to end things. If not tonight, then soon."

"But you let me go through with all of this. Why, you dressed me and did my hair," I hissed.

She smiled gently. "Would you really have listened to me if I told you I thought it was a terrible idea? If I tried to convince you *not* to do it? When you came back after that meeting with Lady Avari, your mind was already made up. Why? Because Nyxaris had told you this was the answer. You respect him, you listen to him. And I understand and respect that. After all, he's very wise."

I suppose you can hear Medra singing your praises, I grumbled to Nyxaris.

Indeed, quite gratifying. As well she should. I was nothing but gracious to her.

I snorted.

Medra laughed. "You're talking to him now, aren't you?"

"I told him what you said," I admitted. "He's very pleased." I glanced around. "Can we leave now? In a few minutes everyone will know."

"You mean Lady Avari will realize she just paid a fortune to host a ball for the most elite highbloods in Sangratha, only to be made a fool of by her grandson?" Medra whispered innocently.

"Yes." I pulled her towards the door. "Goodness," I said, raising my voice and hoping someone would overhear. "Will you look at that. I fear I've twisted my ankle. I simply must go to the infirmary. Please take me, Medra."

She giggled. "I think you're overdoing it slightly."

"I doubt that. Please, can we go?" I begged.

We reached the door and were soon in the corridor. Fortunately, Regan's goons were no longer guarding the entrance—not that they'd been doing a good job of that in the first place.

"Oh dear," I said, smacking myself on the forehead. "I just realized I need a book from the library. I have to double-check one of my citations."

"The library already, hmm? Good to see your heart isn't too, too broken by Kage's throwing you over," Medra teased.

I grimaced. "I think I'll be fine. You know, you said to try to feel something for him, but . . . I never really could."

"Because he isn't the one," she said softly, touching my arm.

I almost told her then. But logic or fear held me back.

Blake suddenly appeared. "Are you all right?" He looked at me anxiously.

I blushed. "I'm fine. Really."

He scowled suspiciously. "The whole room is talking about it. Apparently Kage has ended your engagement."

"Yes, that's right," I confirmed.

"And Florence is absolutely fine with that," Medra said, stepping up to Blake and putting a hand on his chest as his eyes narrowed.

"She is? Because if you tell me otherwise, Florence, I swear I'll go back in that ballroom and pound the shit out of him." Blake looked eager.

"That won't be necessary," I said hastily. "But thank you for the . . . very sweet offer." He seemed disappointed.

Medra looped her arm through Blake's. "He'll be fine," she mouthed and grinned. To Blake, she said aloud, "Let's go, Drakharrow. Florence is going to the library. And we're going to change."

Blake was still frowning. "We are?"

"Yes, out of these clothes. Into something more *comfortable*," she emphasized.

"But I thought Florence hurt her ankle." He eyed the bottom of my dress. "Should I carry her?" he asked hesitantly.

Medra rolled her eyes at me. "Look at her. Does she look injured? She's perfectly fine. Blake, you can't believe all the gossip you hear."

I snickered as she pulled him down the hall towards the Avari tower, arguing with him about the best way to remove a corset. I headed in the opposite direction towards the library. The halls were dim at this time of night. Most students were already in their towers. Belatedly, I realized I was breaking my curfew. I was a blightborn, and it was past nine o'clock. I bit my lip, trying to decide if the correct citation was worth breaking a school rule. I knew precisely where the book was located. Lord Ryan Bryan's *Botanical Index*. West Annex. Third tier. Stack M72. Shelf 4. Also, all of the librarians knew me. They wouldn't think twice if they saw me sneak in. Besides, they'd be busy, tidying up for the library's closing at eleven. I doubted they'd even notice me. I'd sneak in, quiet as a mouse, and go straight to the shelf.

I'd already survived a ball and a broken engagement. Surely I could check a citation and get back to my room without being expelled. After all, Regan was probably still back in the ballroom. And her guards hadn't exactly seemed committed to doing their jobs.

It all went as planned. At least, on the way to the library. Finding a secluded table, I wound up poring over the *Botanical Index* for nearly an hour. But I dawdled. The library was closing as I left. I walked back to Avari tower slowly, the excitement of the evening finally catching up with me. Feeling bone-weary and ready for my bed, I'd only gotten a little ways away from the library when a thin yip shattered the stillness.

I stopped. A growling sound came from up ahead. Nothing like Nyxaris's. Nothing like anything I recognized.

But that yip? I already knew who that was.

The hairs on my arms stood up. "Neville?" Another yip—this time higher, more frantic.

"Neville, I'm coming," I shouted.

When I tried to speed up, my satin slippers, well, *slipped* against the stones. I paused to yank off the ridiculous little things, then the silk stockings underneath. I didn't have a satchel to put them in, I realized. My gown didn't even have pockets. Women's formal clothing was an absolute disgrace. I threw the slippers to the side of the hallway and began to run, my bare feet slapping against the flagstone floor.

Turning a corner, I looked down the next hall. There, wedged against the wall, his fur puffed out in all directions like a cat, was an orange-and-red ball of fluff. Neville was backed in between two ancient suits of armor. The fluffin's huge tail swished back and forth like it did when he was upset or scared or angry. His mouth was open, tiny teeth bared in defiance.

"Neville!"

A tall young man stood over him. There was a blood-and-sword badge affixed to his uniform: one of Regan's Bloodguards.

He must have gotten the wrong idea. Maybe he'd mistaken the little fluffin for some kind of a pest. Usually Neville scampered through the halls without even being noticed. The fluffin must have drawn attention to himself somehow.

"Come here, Neville!" I called, hoping the fluffin would shoot through the boy's legs and we could run off.

What is happening? Where are you?

I was headed to my room after finishing in the library, I said, my heart speeding up. *But I heard Neville cry out. A highblood boy has him cornered. Neville is scared. I'm trying to get to him.*

Stay where you are. I'm coming.

There are no windows here. What can you do?

I'll tear the roof off if I have to.

I was about to tell him not to worry, not to bother coming. Then Neville bolted, speeding straight towards me.

I opened my arms in relief, preparing to scoop him right up and run. I'd head straight back to the library so one of the highblood librarians could sort this out for me. They all knew Neville and his antics. Some of them thought he was a nuisance, sure. After all, he loved to run through the stacks knocking books off the shelves. All right, so technically, he was banned from the library.

But in the end, it didn't matter. Because nothing went according to plan. The highblood moved with vampire speed, snatching Neville up by his scruff and holding him aloft. Neville's paws batted helplessly against the air, his desperate growls and snarls echoing uselessly off the walls.

"Let him go!" I cried, stepping forward.

The highblood lifted his face and looked at me. I could see he'd been very handsome—until now. His skin was fissured by a web of soot-black veins. His eyes had gone a murky white. Dried blood rimmed his mouth like rust. My stomach crawled. What *was* this?

"What's going on?"

I whirled towards the voice as Regan Pansera stepped forward, a pair of red high-heeled shoes dangling from one hand. She frowned, looking at the Bloodguard.

"Brocklin, is that you?" She glanced at me. "Isn't that Blake's pet?"

"Yes," I said, my voice almost breaking. "That's Neville. Please, help me get him back."

"Is this what you've come to, Brocklin, you dolt? Hurting little animals?" Regan sounded truly disgusted. "I never authorized this. You've gone too far. You're out of the Bloodguard, as of tonight. I want your badge turned over immediately." She stretched out her hand as if expecting instant compliance. But Brocklin didn't move.

"Regan," I whispered. "Look at him."

"I am looking," she complained. "He's an idiot. I should never have appointed him to the Bloodguard. I can see that now. You don't—"

She broke off as Brocklin growled, opening his mouth, revealing his fangs.

"You aren't seriously about to bite that little creature, are you?" Regan shrieked. "Brocklin, I'm warning you."

I side-eyed her, wondering what exactly she planned to do. "Regan, there's something wrong with him. I think he's . . . infected somehow."

"Infected?" She wrinkled her nose skeptically. "Highbloods don't get sick."

"I know, but look at him," I insisted.

She studied him. "Shit. You might be right."

Neville was still squirming in Brocklin's grasp. I was terrified the highblood would squeeze too tightly and break the fluffin's tiny neck. I let out a choked sob, reaching slowly for the dagger hidden at my thigh—the one Medra and Professor Stonefist had insisted I start carrying, even though I was terrible at handling it. I suddenly wondered if Regan was armed. Did a highblood girl like her even need to be?

Nearly there, Nyxaris vowed.

Neville's terrified yap sliced the air again as Brocklin's grip tightened. The web of veins beneath his skin seemed to crawl, moving, almost as if something were burrowed there.

"Regan," I sobbed, "we have to do something."

Nyxaris's roar thundered in my skull. *Hold fast.*

A scarlet blur rushed past me as Regan moved first. She crossed the space between us in a heartbeat, her skirts whipping around her legs, making me wonder how much faster she might have moved if she hadn't been hindered. She held one shoe in her fist. Angling it downwards, her hand flashed out, the stiletto heel punching through Brocklin's wrist with a wet, cracking sound. Bone gave way, and Neville tumbled free.

I dove as he scampered towards me, catching him and cradling him against my chest. "Neville!"

Brocklin howled—his voice sounded neither highblood nor blightborn. He moved towards Regan, fangs bared, swinging his good arm. Regan was swearing, the heel of the shoe she'd used dangling uselessly, broken. She dropped it, hefting the other, and drove the heel into the soft meat beneath Brocklin's jaw. Viscous black blood ran out, dripping to the stone. Brocklin wobbled but stayed standing.

"Florence, run!" Regan shouted, never taking her eyes off the other highblood.

I am here. Shield your eyes and get back, Nyxaris commanded.

"Regan!" I screamed. "Get back! Nyxaris is here!"

But it was too late. The ceiling above us exploded in a boom of mortar and stone. I staggered back as ancient beams sheared apart, and slate rained down like hail.

A wedge of night appeared overhead. Nyxaris forced his head through the gap he'd created, ember eyes burning hot, smoke curling from his nostrils. Brocklin had slowed after Regan's second attack. Now he looked up at Nyxaris, clearly confused and enthralled. Regan seized the opportunity and, screaming like a warrior on a battlefield, she vaulted forward, clutching her stiletto like an ice pick and driving it into the soft hollow where neck met skull. Brocklin lifted his arms, flailing pathetically, wet black blood spraying. I gagged as a foul smell wafted towards me.

Nyxaris roared aloud, the sound shaking the hall. *Get the girl back. Now.*

"Regan!" I shouted.

Heat began to flood the hall. Regan's eyes widened. She dove forward, driving both her palms into Brocklin's chest and hurling him towards the ancient suits of armor. He slumped against them as she darted away, her skirts twisting beneath her. The heat became flame as Nyxaris struck, a cone of fire spreading from his jaws, brief but blinding. As the flames guttered out, Brocklin disappeared. All that remained was a smoking pile of ash and a heap of melted steel. Regan pushed herself to her feet. She came towards me, face pale.

"Regan," I whispered, stepping forward, Neville still clutched in my arms. "You're hurt."

Her eyes lifted to mine, wide and suddenly filled with something very familiar: fear. "Brocklin tried to bite me." There was a tremor in the words.

Whatever this is, it cannot withstand dragon fire, Nyxaris murmured grimly. *Yet take no chances. Cleanse her of his blood—and yourself, little fledgling.*

But I barely heard him. Regan started to stagger. "Regan," I gasped, trying to clutch at her with one hand while holding onto Neville with the other.

A black and silver streak rushed past. Kage. He caught Regan before she could hit the floor. Blood coursed from Regan's scalp. One of the falling stones must have hit her when the ceiling caved in.

I watched Kage press a hand to her slick hair. Then he looked up at me, his face grim. "Shen, report."

I gulped at the uncustomary command but did as he asked, speaking quickly. "I was coming back from the library. I heard Neville. He sounded scared. I found Brocklin—" I glanced at the pile of ash. "I found Brocklin standing over him, threatening him. Regan arrived. And then, Nyxaris arrived—" I tried to catch my breath.

"Right," Kage said, his voice like ice. Mere hours ago, this man had been my betrothed. Now I hardly recognized him. He was my House Leader. No, more than that—he was a highblood commander ready for war. "We're heading back. Are you armed?"

"I have a knife strapped to my leg, but I'm holding Neville, so I don't know how I'd use it," I babbled.

And you have me, Nyxaris reminded me grimly.

"Nyxaris says he'll stay with us."

"It won't help us if he knocks the ceiling in again. He could kill us all," Kage said shortly.

I swallowed hard, nodding. "Where are we going?"

"The Avari Tower. We'll take her to our infirmary." He frowned, looking around the hall. "Something's wrong in the castle tonight. I can smell it." I glanced at him curiously. Of course I knew highbloods had heightened senses, and Brocklin had certainly had . . . a stench.

Kage glanced up at where Nyxaris was still peering through the ceiling. "Tell the dragon to follow."

"I think he'd follow even if I didn't tell him," I said shakily.

You are correct.

Kage shifted Regan gently against his chest, and we walked away from the rubble.

CHAPTER 25

BLAKE

"You look happy," I observed, tousling Pendragon's hair. "I never knew you hated Kage so much."

She looked at me in surprise. "I don't hate Kage . . ." Then she saw my grin. "Why, you—" she exclaimed, punching me playfully on the arm. "I'm happy Florence isn't going to be trapped in a loveless arrangement, that's all."

Loveless. The word hung in the air between us for a moment.

"So my place or yours?" Pendragon finally said.

"If Florence comes back and doesn't find you, will she be, you know, mad or hurt or worried?"

"So much concern for Florence tonight," she teased. "Who knew so much softness was hiding under that hard exterior?"

I felt my cheeks heat. "She's your friend, so she's under my protection."

Pendragon smiled. "I know. And I love that. Anyways, Florence should be fine. She'll know I'm with you if I'm not in our room." She laughed. "She'll probably stay up all night working on her essay. It's all she could talk about when we were leaving."

"Good. Come to mine, then." I slung my arm around her shoulders as we walked down the hall, then pulled her in tighter and kissed the top of her head.

"What was that for?"

"For being you," I said gruffly. "I missed you."

"We see each other almost every day," she said with a breathless laugh, but she looked pleased.

I tucked her hand into the crook of my elbow as we walked down the quiet corridors, the ballroom music fading into the background. Every few steps, Pendragon would nudge my hip playfully with hers. I'd answer by brushing my knuckles down the inside of her wrist. When we reached the Drakharrow Tower, I pulled her up the stairs, taking them two at a time, her laughter trailing behind me.

Inside, I shrugged out of my jacket, throwing it onto a chair, and turned back towards her.

Our eyes met. My hand rose, brushing a curl from her cheek. She leaned into the touch, as I traced the dusting of freckles along her jaw. When our mouths found each other, the world shrank away. There was nothing but this—our lips and the intake of breath. Pendragon's palms flattened over my chest while I angled closer, tasting the faint tang of wine still lingering on her lips. I nipped, feather-light, at her lower lip. She sighed, parting her mouth, inviting me in. Heat flared between us. I cradled the back of her head, threading my fingers through the mass of red curls as I drew her nearer. Our bodies aligned, pressing together with eagerness. I kicked the door shut behind us with my heel.

"Lock it," she breathed.

I grinned, moving to slide the latch home. No interruptions. Then I was back, holding her, feeling her hands fumble for the buttons of my shirt. She made quick work of it, her palms leaving traces of heat wherever they touched me. Then she dragged my shirt free from my trousers, her nails scraping greedily over my stomach.

I shivered. "Bloodmaiden, Pendragon."

"Say my name."

"Your name?"

"Yes. My real name." Her green eyes gleamed playfully. "Just once."

I remembered when she'd told me not to call her by her given name. I'd respected it. *Pendragon* had taken on a life of its own. I'd come to love the sound, the taste of the word.

"Medra," I breathed against her lips. I kissed the syllables along the curves of her throat. "Medra, there is nothing I won't do for you. Nothing I won't give you."

There was more I wanted to say—three small words specifically. But I was scared. Afraid I'd overwhelm her. Afraid she wouldn't say them back. Most of all, afraid she'd run.

"Then, give me everything," she whispered. "Right now."

My fangs lengthened with enthusiasm, throbbing with need. I grazed them gently over the spot where her shoulder met her neck, silently asking the question. She turned her head slightly, granting me better access; the answer was *yes*. I bit down deeply, and she arched against me with a cry. Her taste flooded my mouth—rich and heady and full of power. I lifted her, carrying her over to the bed as I drank, her fingers tightening on my bare back, her breathing even and trusting. Her black gown pooled like ink as I laid her down, breaking away from her neck for a moment as I stripped her dress off, the shimmering fabric sliding down freckled curves until it gathered at her waist.

"Fuck, you're gorgeous," I whispered, bending over her to suck one perfect red nipple. She gasped as it puckered in my mouth. I stroked her other breast, so soft, so full and lush. "You want this, don't you? For me to fuck you, fill you, feed from you?"

"Yes," she breathed. She writhed her hips, grinding them against me. "Do it. Don't hold back."

I pushed the skirt down the rest of the way, laying her bare, and tossing the silken fabric halfway across the room. I could smell her scent, sense the wetness pooling between her thighs. She was all dark heat and rich, lush blood. She was everything I'd ever wanted. Everything I never believed I deserved. I still didn't deserve her, but that didn't mean I wasn't going to claim her if she'd let me. I lowered my mouth, tasting the hollow of her throat, feeling the delicate tremble of her pulse beneath the skin. As she arched, nails sliding across my shoulder blades, I gasped—the dragon inside me rose.

It started tickling beneath my ribs. Then it flared, red and ravenous, spreading like fire through my veins. Scales spread across my forearms, gleaming just above where her hands roamed. In the low light, she didn't seem to notice, but I felt ridges forming as the beast in me tested the limits of my skin.

Down, I commanded. She's mine. Not yours. Mine.

But the command bounced uselessly inside my head. The red dragon never spoke back, only a darker hunger pressed forward—demanding and possessive. A draconic grin spread over my face. I flipped Pendragon over on the bed.

She gasped in surprise but wriggled her hips. "Is that how you want it?"

"Mmm," my dragon murmured. "Hold onto the bed." I lifted her hands, placing them on the wooden surface, then gripped her hips tightly, rougher than I'd ever touched her before, dragging her flush against my body, letting her feel my hardness. She moaned, and I sensed the dragon purr, utterly delighted by her eagerness.

This is how we take a mate.

I froze. Then shuddered, fighting as if for air, willing the scales to fade, praying Pendragon wouldn't open her eyes and see them. They rippled, half obeying. Then the beast moved, commanding my body like a hand inside a glove. My hips rolled forward, and I slid inside her.

Sensation overwhelmed me, powerful and intoxicating. I cried out, driving myself into her hard. Except it wasn't *me*. It was him.

Pendragon gasped as I thrust again, rocking against her hips. Her hair hung like a heavy scarlet curtain around her shoulders. I pushed it aside, kissing her back.

"Harder," she begged, her voice raspy with need.

Something inside me snarled in agreement. My grip tightened, bruises blooming beneath my thumbs. Medra only arched, crying out my name like a prayer in the Sanctum.

She wants me, the dragon hissed.

She wants me, not you, I snarled back. *Me, not the monster wearing my shape.*

The dragon laughed and gave an answering thrust that was anything but gentle.

"Gods, Blake, what are you doing to me?" Beads of sweat pearled over her neck. Stray curls stuck damp against her skin.

My dragon pushed the curls away, then licked Pendragon's nape, the tang of salt sliding over my tongue. I brushed my lips along the column of her throat, my fangs sliding into the skin just below her left ear before I'd even realized the dragon had bared them. I tried to force them back down, but my desire and the beast blurred together. I slid my hands beneath her, cupping her breasts.

Pendragon's gasp became a broken moan. Her blood raced through our veins—the dragon's thirst and her answering pleasure going round and round like a carousel until the room began to blur.

Enough, I roared. But the command was futile.

The dragon drank deeper, thrust again and again, more and more roughly, tugging her hips against his, staking his claim. His mouth was greedy at her throat, drinking too deep.

"Touch yourself," my dragon commanded.

She moaned, thrusting her hips back towards me and sliding one hand between her legs to stroke her clit, oblivious of the welts on her hips, of the hurt I'd already caused her body. My hands slid higher as she touched herself, wrapping around her throat, squeezing, choking. Her knuckles tightened as she clutched the bed frame one-handed, and I sensed her arousal increase.

"Blake!" she gasped hoarsely through the vise my dragon had wrapped around her, and I groaned, low and deep, as my seed spilled inside her. We climaxed together.

Stop. Stop now. I felt panicked, desperate. Pendragon's pulse was fluttering under my mouth. A distant part of me realized it was slowing. I tried to tear myself away, but the dragon clamped down harder.

Somewhere beyond the haze in my head, the pounding in my skull, I heard furniture splinter. My body seized up, swaths of scarlet bursting from my shoulder blades, filling the room with a rush of wings. Shelves crashed from the walls, books and ornaments smashing to the floor. I heard the shattering of glass as one wing hit a window, sending the pane flying from the frame.

Pendragon moaned beneath me, still lost in the haze of pleasure and sensation, as the dragon drank, his thirst for her unquenchable.

I felt the precise moment everything tipped. My hands squeezed, my fangs pulled blood from her veins, and her pulse . . . stuttered. I caught sight of my reflection in the broken mirror across from the bed. My eyes were burning red. My hands were covered in scales as they grasped Pendragon's slender throat.

I. Am. Going. To. Fucking. Destroy. You, I snarled. *Let. Her. Go!* With a surge of my own will, I wrenched the dragon back, ripping my fangs free.

"Pendragon," I gasped. "Medra!"

Her body slumped forward over the headboard. I pulled her into my arms, turning her over and gathering her close. She sagged against me, lips parted, eyes dimming. Her breathing was shallow. Her skin was cold and pale.

"Stay with me," I whispered, my voice breaking as I cradled her, my wings sweeping back and forth in desperation, sending gusts of wind through the room. "Stay with me. Please, don't leave me."

Her head lolled against my arm, as I pressed trembling fingers to her throat, feeling her pulse, faint but there. I had no healing draft. Knew no curative spells. I had only myself. Only instinct. Lowering my head, I slashed my fangs along my own wrist, scarlet beads welling. I willed the healing power of my kind to the surface, stretching it out between us like a fragile golden thread. Tilting her head, I let my blood drip into her mouth, gently touching my fingertips to her throat and willing her to swallow.

"Come on, Pendragon. Take it. Take me."

Crimson drops slid over her tongue one after the other. I held myself there, for one agonizing heartbeat after another, pouring everything from me into her, not caring how much it took.

Finally, she coughed, her lashes flickering. I pressed my thumb to her pulse, feeling an answer beneath my fingertips. She gave a thin, ragged breath, then another. Relief crashed over me. I let out a raw cry, holding her gently against my chest, my wings spreading out around us like a cloak.

"I love you," I whispered. "I love you, and I'm so fucking sorry. I will never hurt you again. Never betray you. Do you hear me?"

But I knew she didn't. Would I have said the words if I knew she would? Her lashes fluttered, but she didn't open her eyes. Maybe it was for the best. I couldn't bear to have her see me this way, still in the shape of a monster. I bowed my head, heart hardening, the weight of guilt crushing and unbearable. Then I wrapped her carefully in blankets and laid her back on the bed. A chill wind blew through the broken window. I pulled the curtains down and tied them over the hole as best I could.

I willed my wings back into my body, every muscle tensing as I forced myself to shift. Pain wracked my frame as bones cracked and realigned. But the pain had changed. It was less agony and more *intensity*. I gritted my teeth, clenching my jaw as my body convulsed, wings furling back inside in a strange and terrible way. The dragon wasn't fighting me now—maybe because he had gotten what he wanted. If so, it would be the last time.

I crept out into the hall, pulling the door shut behind me, Rodriguez's book tucked under my arm. I'd come within a heartbeat of killing the woman I loved. The one who meant more to me than anyone else in this entire godsforsaken world.

Now I was going to end this, end *him*. Even if it killed me.

CHAPTER 26

MEDRA

I woke from a dream of wings and blood. Cold air prickled my bare shoulders. For a moment, I lay there, tangled in blankets, blinking at the starlight that slanted through the tower window. Then the wind gusted again, carrying the scent of spring rain and blowing straight in through the casement.

I sat up, shivering. The glass in the window was gone. The curtains billowed in the wind. I looked around the room. Shelves had been toppled, the wood cracked and smashed, books splayed open in heaps all over the ground. A lamp lay broken on the floor. The mirror across from the bed was cracked, and the table in front of it had been knocked over. Pieces of glass were spread beneath the open window where the pane had shattered.

What the hell had happened here, and how had I slept through it? My memories slipped and slid. Flashes hovered behind my eyes. Red eyes. The scrape of scales. I shivered. It must have been a nightmare, a dream of Molindra in the Bonewood. I pushed the sense of foreboding away. Sliding out of the bed, I hunted for my gown. I found it beneath the overturned writing desk. As I started to wriggle back into it, a voice interrupted.

Medra, can you hear me?

I touched a hand to my temples. I'd slept like the dead and only for an hour, yet I felt surprisingly good. Strong. Energized. *Yes, I'm here.*

If you're sleeping, you need to get up. Get prepared. Wherever you are, whatever you're doing, get ready.

Get ready for what? What's going on?

I don't know. Orcades was usually composed. Never desperate. Yet now she sounded almost panicked.

You don't know?

All I can see is a wave of red. An unstoppable wave. And it's headed your way.

I glanced out the window. The sea was calm. *I don't see any waves, Mother.*

Not a literal tsunami, child, she said, sounding annoyed. *Goodness, I speak in symbols.*

Now it was my turn to take a breath. *All right, so the wave is a symbol. A symbol of what?*

A symbol for danger. Are you armed? Are you with Florence?

I frowned. *No, I'm not. I was with Blake, but . . .* I walked over to the bathroom *. . . he's disappeared.*

Very inconvenient timing, I must say, my mother snapped.

I smiled. *I'll be sure to tell him you said so.*

Medra, you're not taking me seriously enough. She didn't sound angry. Just desperate. Whatever was happening, it was enough to scare my mother. My mother who hadn't even been afraid of Molindra. *I need you to listen. Find your friends. Warn them. Arm yourself. Do you understand me?*

I understand. I'm listening. I'll find Blake, and we'll take a look around, gather the others. Try not to worry.

I'm your mother. It's my right to worry, she said, sounding more like her imperious self for a moment. *Find Florence. She shouldn't be alone.*

Agreed. I'll find her as soon as I've figured out where Blake's gone.

Good. Please, darling, try to be safe. May everything good watch over you.

Then she was gone. I stood there for a moment, a little surprised to hear that my mother believed in any kind of force of goodness. I looked down at myself. If something bad was about to happen, did I really want to be wearing a ball gown? I crossed over to Blake's dresser, miraculously still standing, and began yanking drawers open. Finally, I found what I was looking for: a pair of leggings I'd once left behind. They were neatly folded and freshly laundered. I yanked off the gown and pulled them on, then found one of Blake's sweaters—one that wasn't quite as huge on me as the others. Rolling up the sleeves, I looked in the broken mirror, frowning at my reflection. Not exactly armor, but at least I'd be able to move my legs. I had no choice but to put on the slippers I'd worn to the ball, as all of Blake's footwear was far too big.

I rifled through his armoire next and found two sheathed daggers at the bottom, beneath a mess of crumpled parchment and graded papers. Grabbing belts, I strapped them to my thighs, then moved towards the door.

The door clicked. Instantly I was half-crouched, a dagger in each hand. Blake stepped inside and shut the door quietly behind him, clearly thinking I was still asleep.

He turned towards where I crouched, and his eyes widened. "Holy shit, Pendragon. Ambushing me, are we?" He smirked. "I mean, sure, if you want to play, I'm up for a little role-play." But the smirk didn't reach his eyes. He looked tired. Worn-out. *Different*.

"Where were you?"

He shrugged. "Just down in the common room. Look, I'm wiped. Mind if we talk about this later? I need to sleep."

"Later? I thought you were full of energy and ready to play," I said in disbelief. "I mean, you clearly played with this room. Or someone did. What the hell happened to it?"

He didn't answer.

I stood up and stepped towards him. Moonlight from the open window behind me spilled over his face. "Blake, what happened to your eyes?" His pupils were gray, but the irises? Where the moonlight hit them, I could see they were tinted a dark crimson.

He frowned at my expression, then crossed over to the broken mirror, peering at his reflection. "Nothing," he said finally, rubbing a hand over his face. "I'm just tired. They're bloodshot."

"Bloodshot?" I shook my head. "Tell me the truth. What's going on? Where were you really?"

He turned towards me. I saw his throat tighten. "Pendragon, I—"

The door banged inward. Visha stormed in, still in the short scarlet dress she'd worn earlier that evening. Her violet eyes were wild. There was a knife clutched in her hand. Theo stumbled in behind her. I gasped: Blake's cousin's shirt was soaked with blood.

"It's not mine," he said hastily, raising his hands. "I'm fine, really."

"Something fucked-up is going on," Visha declared. "And I mean *very* fucked-up."

"What happened?" Blake crossed over to stand between me and the door protectively.

Visha slammed the door shut. "Theo, Vaughn, and I stayed late at the engagement party. Or whatever we're calling it now. The breakup ball?" She shrugged. She was playing it cool, but I could see her shoulders trembling. She kept clenching and unclenching her hand around the dagger. "We dropped Vaughn off at House Orphos. Got back to the tower. Were coming through the common room, and the little bastard came at Theo like an animal."

"Little bastard?" Blake interrupted.

"Everett Cavendish," Theo said quietly. "He was a First Year. A highblood."

Blake glanced back at me. Was. Theo had said *was*.

Blake looked at Visha. "You killed him?"

"Yes, I killed him," she snapped. "He was about to sink his teeth into Theo's neck, and not in a sweet, romantic way."

"She had to," Theo said hurriedly. "Blake, you should have seen him. He was like an animal. Bursting out at us with no warning, fangs bared, eyes white. His skin . . . Blake, he wasn't . . . normal. Something's wrong."

"Oh, something is most definitely wrong," Visha agreed. "And I know exactly what it is."

Blake and I stared at her. "You do?" I said.

She nodded grimly. "The plague."

I caught Blake and Theo looking at one another. "Plague? What plague?"

"A highblood plague."

"Highbloods can get sick?" It was news to me.

"No, we can't," Visha said. "That's why this is really fucked-up. There have been reports and rumors spreading from the outskirts of Sangratha. Just a few here and there. I thought it was all bullshit at first. Just rumors. But then," she said and cleared her throat, "my nephew caught it. He attacked his own family."

"It's true," Blake murmured. He looked at Visha. "Have you heard anything from them tonight?"

She shook her head. "Not another word." Her face hardened. "And I don't expect to."

"But that's your family's estate. It's not just your uncle and his family. Your mother and father and . . ." Theo stopped himself, seeing Visha's face.

"Maybe they're fine. Maybe I'll get another letter. But I won't fucking hold my breath."

"This was just one student. You took him out," Blake observed.

"Blake, she's right. It has to be a plague," Theo said. "There'll be more."

"You need to arm yourselves, and I need to get to Florence," I said suddenly. "She's all alone back in House Avari."

"I need to get back to Vaughn," Theo said. "There's no way I'm leaving him in House Orphos by himself while this is going on."

"No one is leaving this tower," Blake declared, looking at us. "Not yet. Our responsibility lies here, first and foremost. We'll get the wardens, seal off the tower, count heads, post guards, and have all of the other students stay in their rooms. They can barricade their doors if necessary. Then we'll discuss the next move."

Theo looked reluctant but nodded his head slowly.

"I'll give you half an hour. Then I go find Florence," I said stubbornly.

Thud. Something slammed against the door.

"What the fuck was that?" Theo whispered, already backing away from the entrance.

"You two get back," Blake ordered Theo and me. "Visha, to me." He moved towards the door as Visha flattened herself against the wall to one side, her dagger up in a reverse grip, ready to plunge downwards. Meanwhile, Theo looked around for something to arm himself with. He dragged a chair over, smashing a leg off with impressive strength, and lifted the sharp, jagged piece of wood like a club. He looked over at me and nodded, his knuckles white. And me? I had my daggers strapped to my thighs. I was ready. But for what exactly, I had no fucking clue.

Blake yanked the door open and sprang aside.

A girl in scarlet-trimmed pajamas toppled through the gap. She hit the floor sideways, one arm stretched out in front of her. Blood was pumping from a huge wound in her throat. I recognized her: Marta, a Fourth Year warden. Her glazed eyes found Blake. "T-tried to . . . You . . ." Her lips had barely formed the words when her entire body went slack.

"Fuck," Theo whispered.

"Quiet," Blake hissed.

Two shapes loomed out of the corridor. Highbloods. Males. I'd seen them around the common room. They were Second Years. I gasped as they stepped into the light. Their skin was gray, laced with branching, blackened veins. Murky white filmed their eyes. Dried gore crusted their mouths—Marta's blood. One of them lifted his head and sniffed, nostrils flaring. He looked down at Marta, and a hungry growl echoed from his chest.

"Let's do this," Blake barked as the boy closest to him began to lunge. "Vish, on me. Pendragon, stay back."

It was sweet that he wanted to keep me out of it, but that wasn't happening. Still, I did as he said for the moment because Visha was already on top of it. She slid in low, slashing up beneath the boy's ribs. Blackened blood splattered with a wet, sickening sound, filling the room with a horrific smell that left me gagging.

Blake reached for the second attacker. His hand clamped around the boy's throat, muscles cording along his forearm. With a roar, he threw the boy across the corridor where his body smashed against the wall.

The first boy was still coming, I realized. Visha's attack had slowed him down but not stopped him. Not that he was moving with typical highblood speed, exactly. In fact, one might have even called him slow—at least, slow for a highblood. He rushed for Theo, and I sprang forward, daggers already drawn, as the boy swiped. Ducking beneath his arm, I jammed one blade up into his skull, then wrenched it sideways, listening to the sound of cartilage snapping. The boy spasmed, then dropped to the floor.

"That seemed to do the trick," I said quietly.

Theo nodded tightly. Moving past me he went into the hall where the boy Blake had thrown against the wall was already starting to rise. Wood and bone crunched as Theo swung his chair leg down on the boy's head. The body convulsed, then was still. We stood there, waiting, chests heaving.

"How many do you think there are?" Visha asked finally. "How many are infected?"

"And how did they get infected?" I added.

"They want to feed," Blake observed. "They don't seem to care from who. That must be how it starts, a bite."

"They're slow, too," Theo noted. "At least, slow for highbloods."

"About the same as a blightborn," Visha agreed. "Which makes them easier for us to take down. Still hard for blightborn."

I thought of Florence. She could still barely defend herself. Kage had ended their engagement. Now who would be there to stand by her side? "I need to go find Florence," I said shortly.

"You're not leaving this tower without me by your side." Blake's voice was iron. "Florence is House Avari. Kage will have things under control."

"We don't know that," I snapped. "She could be all alone. She could be—"

"The girl has a fucking dragon," he cut in. "She's not defenseless. But if you go out there, alone . . ." He shook his head. "You're staying here. We're sticking together. No one goes out by themselves. That's an order." He looked back and forth between Theo and Visha. They nodded. "Now, we sweep every level of the tower. We knock on every door. We check every room. We count the healthy students. We find any who are infected."

Visha interrupted. "And then? Do we kill them all? What if we can save them?"

We all looked at her.

She crossed her arms over her chest. "Well?"

"I don't know," Blake said, his face weary.

Was I the only one who had noticed his eyes? The change was subtle. The dark crimson was almost mistakable for black when he stood in the shadows. But I knew what I'd seen.

"If they're trying to actively attack us, we have no choice but to eliminate them." He frowned. "But you make a good point. We'll keep the injured in the infirmary under close supervision. Let's begin. We'll go door-to-door down the second floor hall first, then make our way there." He glanced at me. "Medra, Florence will be all right."

"You don't know that," I said bluntly. "You're just hoping you're right."

"We'll go to her as soon as we've secured the Drakharrow tower, I swear it. Until then, you're by my side. Tell me you understand. Tell me you'll listen."

I bit back the questions I was burning to ask. Whatever he was hiding I would drag into the light later. I glanced at the clock on the wall—twenty minutes left. "For now."

CHAPTER 27

FLORENCE

My heart pounded as I hurried down yet another hallway behind Kage, Regan's limp form draped across his arms. Where was Medra? Had she gone back to our tower or to Drakharrow? If she was with Blake, I'd be less worried about her. Yet part of me hoped she'd be there in our room, waiting for me to get back.

I reached for Regan's wrist, counting the throb of her pulse.

"How is she?" Kage asked, sounding tense.

"It's faint, but it's there," I answered.

We turned a corner, and I froze. Here, curtains had been ripped down from the hallway windows. Someone had smashed the hanging lanterns off the wall. A small fire was burning in the spilled puddle of oil.

Kage's jaw tightened. "Keep your eyes on my back, Shen. Move fast."

I tried, I really did. Until a boy's scream broke through the silence. Five paces ahead of us, in an alcove off to the side, a group of girls in torn purple-and-gold gowns crouched low over a supine blightborn boy. Their shoulders jerked. Their heads dipped and rose. They were feeding. The boy's scream cracked, sliding into a gurgle.

"Shen," Kage said, his voice low. "Move. Now."

I realized I'd stopped, frozen in horror. The girls' backs were to us. They hadn't seen us yet. "But—but that boy . . ."

"He's gone. We can't save him. I can't help him. All I can do is get you and Regan out. Now move!" Kage barked.

The Avari is right. Listen to him.

But maybe if you just . . .

Nyxaris roared. I jumped. *Go now. Listen to the wolf. Get to your tower. I'll meet you there.*

"Not a sound, Shen," Kage commanded, looking at me as my lip trembled. "Eyes on my back. Follow me. Don't look." He started moving again.

But as soon as we'd passed by and turned the next corner, a sob ripped free from my throat. Kage paused at the next junction, shifting Regan a little in his arms. He glanced at me. "There was nothing you could do. You can't save everyone."

"I know," I said, hiccupping. "But their clothes. The girls were in gowns. They'd come from our . . ." I trailed off.

Kage's eyes were hard and resolute. "If we fall here, the same thing that happened to him happens to everyone in Avari. You're our only rider. We need you." He started moving again, then threw a last command over his shoulder. "Steel yourself."

I nodded, choking on guilt and grief, but doing as he said. They needed me? How could Nyxaris and I possibly help with . . . whatever this was?

We took the next corner at a trot—and nearly collided with Professor Rodriguez. He was holding someone in his arms, too. The dwarven girl I'd seen the Bloodguards feeding from earlier. Behind him streamed at least thirty blightborn First Years, disheveled and bleeding. Some were being carried, others leaned against a friend's shoulder. Most were wearing nightclothes. Some clutched candlesticks. A few had knives. One brandished a battered, sharpened broom handle.

Kage halted. "Rodriguez."

"What the fuck is going on here tonight, Tanaka?" Rodriguez snapped, blunt as a brick as always.

"Something bad," Kage retorted.

Rodriguez's lips twisted. "Bit of an understatement, but I suppose that sums it up."

"Where are you headed?" Kage asked. "What's the state of the First Year tower?"

"The First Year tower?" Rodriguez shook his head. "The First Year tower is lost. It's been overrun."

"Overrun with what?" I asked, my voice small.

The professor looked past Kage to me, then back to Kage. "Surely you've seen what we've seen. Students. They've all been infected with . . ." he shook his head " . . . with something."

"Infected how?" Kage demanded. "Some of these students are highbloods. How is that possible?"

"I have no idea how it's possible. But it's obvious, isn't it? Something is stripping away their rationality, heightening their hunger. They're like animals." He glanced behind him, then lowered his voice. "I think the ball may have been where the outbreak began. The infection spread from there."

Kage's face hardened. "Which means it either came from or has been carried back to Veilmar. Where my family is."

Rodriguez nodded. "Seems that way. Look, I need to get to an infirmary—now. Several of these First Years were injured in the attack. The girl in my arms was already wounded. She's lost a lot of blood."

"What happened to the First Years' healer?" I asked.

Rodriguez shook his head grimly. "He's gone."

Kage's jaw tightened. "Follow us. The Avari tower has an infirmary—and reinforced doors." He raised his voice. "First Years, stay close and stay silent. We move as one. Form pairs. Those of you with weapons, eyes sharp. Let's move."

Rodriguez took up a position at Kage's side, angling Dani higher. The two men started forward, and I followed, the crowd of frightened First Years shuffling behind us. My tears were drying to salt on my cheeks. As we funneled through the castle, into the darkness, I prayed we could find some safety in this night of horrors.

The Avari tower doors slammed shut behind us, and two stern-faced Fourth Year wardens took up positions in front of it immediately on Kage's command.

"All uninjured First Years—common room, now!" Kage's voice boomed.

The First Years who had crowded around Rodriguez like chicks to a hen scuttled away, piling onto couches and sinking down onto the floor. When only the wounded remained with us—four trembling First Years, three girls and a boy, Rodriguez with Dani in his arms, and Kage carrying Regan—we hurried up to the second floor and into the Avari infirmary. The fact that each house had their own infirmary was a blessing from the Bloodmaiden. Even though the First Year one had been overrun—a description that didn't bear thinking about in too much detail—at least every house had their own facilities and healers.

As we entered, Healer Elycia, her silver hair coiled in prim braids around her head, looked up from where she stood mixing a draft and paled as she saw our procession. "What's happened? Here, put them here—quickly." She pointed to empty cots along one wall. A lone patient already occupied one of them, a curly-haired highblood girl with a bandage on her arm. Elycia had clearly been tending to her before we barged in. Now she sat up, swinging her legs over the side of her cot and peering with interest at the First Years, who began to sit down on chairs in the waiting area.

Kage laid Regan down gently on a mattress. Rodriguez put Dani on another, then immediately went over to one of the supply cupboards and began rifling through it.

I moved to his side. "Iron-wort tonic?"

"It's the easiest thing to give her, yes. We need to boost her blood production over the next hour as much as possible. Healer Elycia should help the other students. I know she's skilled in coagulation charms."

"Regan's lost a lot of blood, too," I murmured. "Will she heal on her own?"

Rodriguez glanced at the headmistress. "I'll talk to Elycia and take a look. She's highblood, but some iron-wort might not hurt."

I nodded. "Let me mix the draft for Dani. I know what to do." I wasn't a healer, but I'd recognized the ingredients and knew the right ratio to use. It was a simple-enough mixture. "You help the healer and see to the other students."

I was still holding Neville. He'd been dozing in my arms, no doubt recovering from his earlier ordeal. Now he jerked awake, his fur bristling. As I went to put him down, his muscles tightened, and he wriggled from my grasp. Jumping down to the floor, he trotted over to where the injured highblood girl now stood beside her cot.

Elycia hurried over. "Jacklyn, get back in bed. I'm not finished examining you."

"I feel fine," Jacklyn protested, sounding slow and sleepy.

"Neville, what's gotten into you?" I walked over as the fluffin kept growling.

Before I could even begin to process the way the highblood girl's eyes were hazing over to a milky gray, she lurched forward, not at Neville but at Elycia. In a split second, her fangs were out and her jaw was open.

Things happened in the blink of an eye. One moment Elycia was opening her mouth to scream. The next Jacklyn was crumpling to the floor, with Kage behind her. He'd crossed the room and leaped the cot to get in behind her. Now he held a dripping dagger in one hand. The blood on the dagger, I saw, was a dark red, nearly black.

For a heartbeat, no one breathed.

"She'd been bitten," Elycia whispered, staring at Jacklyn's body. "I thought it was a random attack, someone playing some sort of horrible prank after drinking too much bloodwine. She'd been walking back from the library. She managed to ward her attacker off and get back here. The injury was on her upper shoulder. She would have been fine. Should have been fine . . ." The healer trailed off, her eyes still on Jacklyn's body.

Then Kage looked over at Rodriguez. "You understand what this means? Anyone bitten is infected. We cull them or the tower falls."

I looked over at the First Years, still waiting to be triaged. Their eyes were wide. One girl began to cry.

Rodriguez was between them and Kage in an instant. "We don't know that. There may be a cure, an antidote—something to slow this down. We have no idea what we're even dealing with yet."

The Avari didn't look convinced.

"Kage, please," I pleaded. "Look at them."

His eyes blazed. "I am looking. You think I want to do this? Did anyone even notice what was happening to Jacklyn? She changed in an instant. I won't risk the tower. Another hour and they'll all be just like her."

"You can't kill everyone who's injured. We don't even know for certain that they were bitten," I said desperately. "What about Regan?"

Kage's eyes flew to the headmistress's bed, his expression instantly one of horror.

"She wasn't bitten," I said immediately. "I was there. She was injured but not bitten."

His shoulders seemed to sag in relief. "Fine. Only the bitten."

One of the First Year boys began to cry. "Please, my lord, don't do this."

Neville had begun padding between the First Years, pressing his nose to their ankles and sniffing.

"Get out of my way, Rodriguez," Kage said roughly. "I'll do what I have to in order to protect my house."

My eyes widened. "Wait—look!"

Neville had plopped down on the floor amongst the First Years and begun licking one paw. He was purring.

"He's not afraid of them. What if he can smell it? The sickness. He growled at Jacklyn. He must have known she was infected."

Kage looked skeptical. "He's an animal."

I shot him a look of disbelief, and he crossed his arms.

"That's different."

"Fine. But fluffins have healing abilities," I insisted. "They can sense things we can't." I turned to Rodriguez. "Tell him."

The professor looked doubtful. "You seem to know more about these creatures than I do." He looked at Kage. "But we were both there when . . ." They exchanged a glance.

"When what?" I demanded.

"When Neville told Nyxaris to save you," Kage answered.

I stared. "He what?"

"That's what it looked like to me, too," Rodriguez agreed. "I think that fluffin spoke to your dragon."

Medra hadn't told me that. *Nyxaris, did Neville tell you to save me? To bond with me?*

I am well, thank you for asking. The dragon sounded cross and slightly bored. *I am perched at the top of the tower. Not that anyone has bothered to ask after my whereabouts.*

I'm well, too, I said quickly. *We're in the Avari infirmary.*

Yes, I can tell you are not in mortal danger . . . at the moment, he said dryly. A pause. *The fluffin did play a part. He . . . sang to me. Reminded me.*

Reminded you of what?

That it would be good to have a rider. That you were worthy of life.

Thank you for listening to him, I whispered. I took a deep breath and looked at Kage. "Lunaya once told Medra and me that there were stories of fluffins appearing in times of great upheaval." I raised my arms and gestured. "Look at what's happening here."

"That's not exactly evidence, Florence," Rodriguez pointed out.

"You want evidence?" I said, my voice rising a little. "Let's take Neville down to the Avari common room. So far, all of the infected have been *highbloods*, not blightborn. Haven't you noticed?"

Kage and Rodriguez looked at one another.

"She's right," Rodriguez said finally. "The ones who attacked the First Year infirmary had broken into the tower. They weren't blightborn."

"The Bloodguard who attacked Neville. The girls who were . . . feeding back in the hall," I listed. "They were highbloods, too."

Kage's eyes narrowed. He seemed to be weighing possibilities. "Fine. Let's go. You and the fluffin. Down to the common room. If the infection is in this tower, we need to find it."

I swallowed hard. "Right." I went over to Neville, scooping him back up. I ran my hand over his head. "You're up, little one," I whispered. "We need you. Please help us. I'm counting on you."

Kage's boots pounded down the stairs. I followed, still barefoot; I hadn't even had a chance to run back to my room and fetch shoes yet. In my arms, Neville had gone tense and still. His nose was raised to the air as if he were tracking a scent.

The Avari common room was packed shoulder to shoulder. I could tell many students had come out of their rooms to see what was going on. The moment Kage strode in, all talk died down.

"You can do this," I whispered to Neville. "I know you can."

The fluffin gave a tiny yap. Kage nodded to me. I set Neville down on the carpet. For a moment, he stood there, sniffing. Then, he gave a low growl and padded straight towards a lanky Second Year standing by the hearth talking to a friend. I recognized the boy—it was Andrew, the same highblood who'd asked if he could take Neville home for his little sister. I bit my lip, hoping Neville wasn't simply holding a grudge.

Kage marched over. "Injuries?"

Andrew stared at the House Leader.

"Are you injured?" Kage demanded.

Andrew shook his head, but his hand, I'd noticed, had crept up his sleeve. Neville's growl deepened to a snarl. Kage seized the boy's wrist, yanking the fabric back. A piece of gauze, hastily knotted, was wrapped around Andrew's wrist, dark with blood.

"I was with Jacklyn," he stammered. "Jacklyn wanted to see the healer, but I told her I was fine. It's just a scratch."

Kage's eyes were hard. "A scratch? Or a bite?"

Andrew said nothing.

"When did this happen?" Kage asked.

"A few hours ago. I'm fine, really." He glanced at me, as if seeing me standing there for the first time. "Is Jacklyn all right?"

"Jacklyn's dead," Kage said shortly. His dagger flashed—clean, merciless. A single thrust beneath Andrew's jaw and he toppled, like a puppet with cut strings. Screams tore through the room. Someone began to sob. Kage wiped his blade, then turned around and raised his voice. "If anyone else here is hiding a bite, step forward now. To hide a bite is to endanger this house. Come to me now, or I'll let the fluffin find you, and I promise you, things will not go so quickly as they did for Andrew."

Kage's Second, Evie, stepped forward. "Jacklyn and Andrew were the last ones back. After that, there was just you and the professor and—" she gestured at the First Years "—the rest of them."

Kage nodded grimly. "Good. Inspect them for bites." He looked around the room. "Listen to me carefully. House Avari is now in lock-down. There's a plague."

Immediately highblood eyes swept towards the blightborn students who'd entered with us accusingly.

"It is not a blightborn plague," Kage said immediately. "Highbloods are the ones in danger of infection." He looked at me. "Shen, tell them what we know."

I stared at him. "Me?" When he nodded impatiently, I quickly cleared my throat. "Bites seem to be the catalyst. Based on what we just learned from Andrew and Jacklyn, it can take hours before the infection sets in. A person's eyes go milky white. Then they . . . well, attack. Go berserk."

"Is there a cure?" someone yelled.

I glanced at Kage. He nodded very slightly. "There may be," I said, trying to make my voice carry. "If you're bitten, you need to come to the infirmary at once." I was sealing their fate either way. Either we would find a cure or some kind of a treatment or . . . or Kage or someone else would finish them.

Still, I knew the House Leader was right. The infection was

spreading too rapidly. We had to contain it, even though the means of doing so might have to be terribly ruthless. Otherwise there'd be nothing left of Bloodwing to save.

Kage spoke briefly to his Second and the wardens, then I followed him back to the infirmary. When we got there, Rodriguez was tying a bandage around Regan's head. She was sitting up in bed. Her long blond hair had fallen out of its pins and hung around her shoulders. She looked very young and frightened, far too young to be a headmistress of a school like Bloodwing.

Kage moved so quickly. One moment he was by my side, the next he was crouched down beside her bed. "How are you feeling?" he asked her, his voice surprisingly gentle.

"Like a brick fell on me," Regan complained, frowning and touching a hand tentatively to her bandage.

I gave a little laugh, not quite hysterical. "That's because one did. Maybe more than one." I walked over, and she looked up at me. "You saved me. You saved Neville. Thank you."

She glanced away, looking uncomfortable. "Brocklin was being a complete idiot. What on earth could have come over him?"

"A plague," I said. "He didn't know what he was doing."

As Kage began to tell her what was going on, I moved to where Rodriguez and Elycia were standing together at a table, talking in low voices. "Do you think there's a cure?" I said directly as I approached them.

Rodriguez looked up. "Well, certainly not yet. And who knows how long it could take to find one. In the past, blightborn plagues haven't been solved overnight. It can take weeks, months. Years."

That didn't bode well. "We need something quickly. People are panicking. Kage has sealed the tower. But the rest of the school . . ." Medra. I still had no idea where she was. "I'm going back to my room," I announced. "I have to check for something."

Kage looked up as I moved towards the door.

"I'll be right back," I promised. "But Medra . . ."

He stood up. "She's not here, Florence."

"What?"

"I already spoke with Evie. Medra's not accounted for." Kage looked sympathetic. "I'm sure she's with Blake. She's probably fine."

"What about my mother? She'll be in her quarters all alone."

"Your mother's smart. I'm sure she won't open the door unless she knows it's safe. As it is, I'm sending out a small group of Avari to check the halls. They'll also do a sweep of staff quarters. If she's still in her chambers, they'll bring her back here," Kage promised.

It was the best I could hope for. I nodded, a lump in my throat.

"Florence," Rodriguez called. He beckoned for me to come over.

They'd shifted Jacklyn's body onto a table. Linen sheets had been placed over her head and lower torso. He and Healer Elycia had cut open her chest. I stared down as thick, treaclelike blood oozed slowly out, glistening like dark oil.

Elycia touched a glass rod to the substance, watching as threads of clotted gore stuck to the tip as she lifted it away. "I've never seen blood behave like this."

"The blood isn't this thickly clotted when the victim is alive. It can't be," I said in disbelief. "That would kill them."

"No," Rodriguez agreed. "It's only when the blood is exposed to air—or upon death. Of course, we'd need more victims to tell for sure."

I grimaced. "I'm fairly certain you'll get your wish."

"This isn't an ordinary illness, that's clear."

Elycia was nodding. "I agree." She looked afraid. "There's something magical in origin here. There hasn't been a plague capable of infecting a highblood in . . . well, I can't think of when."

"A cure may be beyond us," Rodriguez muttered. "But if we can slow down the clotting, keep the victims from reaching the stage in which they turn rabid . . ."

Elycia opened a drawer and began laying out bundles of herbs. Silver lamium, red sap, iron-wort. All anticoagulants.

"We'll need to sedate anyone infected immediately," Rodriguez said.

"And restrain them." It was Kage. He'd come up to stand behind us.

Elycia nodded. "I'll mix some sleeping drafts. Heavy ones."

"What about mirthleaf?" I blurted out.

Rodriguez's brows drew together. "Mirthleaf is an antitoxin. Not a coagulant."

"I know. But what if the plague isn't a real sickness at all? What if it's a toxin, something alchemical that spreads by bite?"

Rodriguez hesitated—long enough that I knew my idea wasn't completely absurd. "You'd need samples. And to test reactions."

"We may as well throw everything we have at this," Elycia said quietly. "It won't hurt."

He nodded. "True. Very well, Florence, prepare a mirthleaf tincture. If anticoagulants don't work, you'll test it and see if the mirthleaf has any effects."

Neville purred at my ankle, as if he approved. Squaring my shoulders, I set to work, determined to focus only on the task at hand as I desperately tried to put my fear for my mother and Medra from my mind.

Easier said than done.

CHAPTER 28

MEDRA

*A*re you safe?

I'm safe, I told my mother. *For now.*

The Drakharrow tower felt too quiet now that the screaming had stopped. We'd gone through the entire tower, checking every room, securing it top to bottom. Blake had stationed Fourth Years on every stair landing, and another group were convening in the common room to receive orders and work out a rotation schedule. Anyone who wasn't a guard or a warden was to remain in their room with the door locked and barred. Things had calmed down a little—and yet there was still a sense of panic in the air. All of the students had families outside of the school, whether in Veilmar or in other parts of Sangratha. And right now, no one knew just what was going on out there.

Now we were down in the common room, and I was about to take another stab at getting Blake to let me leave. One way or another, with or without him, I couldn't stick around. I had to find Florence. Theo was equally desperate; I could see it on his face. He'd left Vaughn at the Orphos tower not knowing what was about to happen, and now he was filled with regret. Theo and I would leave together. The House Orphos tower was closer. We'd find Vaughn, and then we'd find Florence.

What's happening on your end?

Oh, you know. Orcades sounded weary but also bored. *Blood sacrifices and all of the usual.*

Blood sacrifices? I tried to focus. *That doesn't sound good. What exactly is going on?*

The typical things that happen when two fools try to break down the barricade between realms and anger a supernatural entity.

I hadn't realized blood would be involved. Though, immediately, it made sense. Catherine Mortis was clearly an experienced necromancer, and Marcus had been studying up on sanguimancy, the specialty of House Drakharrow.

It doesn't need to be. There are other ways. But these idiots don't know that. Blood magic and necromancy are their weapons of choice. They're all they seem to know. Watching them is like watching children throw a tantrum. Like trying to stab a door with a knife and expecting it to open, instead of using a lock-picking kit.

Well, whatever they've done is really fucking up the rest of Sangratha, I replied. *They've unleashed some kind of a plague.*

The wave.

Yes, the wave. Except it's a wave of infected highbloods, every one of them trying to kill us.

She was so quiet I thought she'd disappeared. *Orcades?*

I'm here.

What is it?

What you describe . . . a plague that spreads mindless violence. There was a similar plague once in Aercanum. In Valtain, where my father once ruled.

I felt a chill go over me. *Grandfather?*

Yes, your grandfather unleashed it. Purposely, of course. She sighed. *Do terrible things with magic, pay a terrible price. How easily history repeats itself, even across worlds.*

Except, the ones doing the terrible things don't pay the price, I pointed out, bitterly. *Ordinary people do.*

Yes. In the case of your grandfather, children did.

My heart sped up. *Children?*

Yes. Fae children. It's a long, sordid tale. Do me a favor and please remind me to never tell you about it sometime.

I thought for a moment. *Orcades, I'm fae. Well, half. So far, the plague here has only infected highbloods. But could it infect me? Am I as susceptible as they are?*

I was quick like a highblood, stronger than a blightborn. My body was physiologically different in subtle ways, from my ears to my elongated fingers and toes. What marked me as a dragon rider in this world marked me as half-fae back in mine.

It's a different plague than the one that was set loose in Aercanum, she replied slowly. *Still, yes, I suppose you're right, and that could be the case. You'll need to be vigilant, Medra. Make sure Florence is, too.*

My blood had gradually changed my friend's physiology. Had I made her more susceptible to this plague as well? I hoped we'd never find out.

"Pendragon!" Blake called from up ahead.

I have to go, I said quickly. *But Orcades, you have to tell me. How do we stop this?*

If I knew that, I'd have already told you, now, wouldn't I, my love?

I clenched my jaw. It was the answer I figured she'd give. *There has to be some way.*

Only the most obvious one.

Stop Marcus and Catherine. So we need to get to where you are somehow?

Perhaps. Not necessarily. There are things at play here that I can't explain right now. I'll tell you more soon.

"Medra!" Theo pulled my arm before I could parse that cryptic response. "Come on. The tower is clear." He lowered his voice. "I think Blake might let us go. But I'm sure he's going to insist on coming along."

Of course he would. Blake wasn't going to let me out of his sight. And to be fair, I didn't want to be out of it. We were stronger together. I nodded and followed Theo down to the mezzanine overlooking the common room where Blake stood talking to Visha. There was a pounding at the door, and for a moment, everyone froze. Finally, one of the wardens went to it. After a pause, she called across the room, "Two latecomers!" She opened the door, and a highblood couple practically fell in, giggling, still in rumpled finery, smelling of champagne. They'd clearly been partying late after the engagement ball. But then, they were highbloods, so they had no curfew.

Blake leaned over the balcony rail. "What is it?" I asked, coming up beside him.

A muscle ticked in his jaw. "Probably nothing. But . . ."

His gaze was locked on the girl, a petite highblood who I thought was a Third Year. She had her boyfriend's dinner jacket draped over her sequined shoulders and was laughing just a tad too loudly at something he'd said, her fingers fluttering against his chest.

Blake descended the stairs with deceptive calm. Theo, Visha, and I followed. "Long night, Collette?" Blake said to the girl. His tone was polite, but I picked up on the current of steel that undercut it.

She jumped. "House Leader." She gave a little giggle. "Just going back to our rooms. We'll be more quiet, I swear. At least, we'll try." She smiled sweetly up at Blake, clearly a girl used to getting everything her way.

Her boyfriend, a tall highblood boy with dreadlocks, was trying to pull her towards the stairs.

Blake's eyes slid to the boyfriend. "Run into any trouble in the halls tonight, Jareth?"

The boy shook his head—a little too quickly. "Trouble? Not at all. Come on, Collette. It's past your bedtime." His smile seemed slightly forced.

The girl giggled again. "Well, good night, House Leader."

In a flash, Blake stood between the boy and the staircase. "Your hands. They're shaking." He grasped Jareth's wrist, lifting it high enough that I could see the tremor. "Why is that?"

The boy's eyes leaped to his girlfriend's, but he didn't answer.

Blake turned to Collette. "Take off the jacket."

"But I'm cold," she protested, clutching it around her more tightly.

In a blur of motion, he'd swept it from her shoulders. Beside me Theo groaned. Teeth marks marred the girl's upper arm. The flesh was scalloped, rimmed with soot-dark veins. They'd cinched a handkerchief over it, but dark blood seeped through.

"I know it looks disgusting, but it hardly hurts," Collette said quickly. "We were going to tell you. The strangest thing happened on our way back here . . ." She continued to babble as I stepped forward.

"She's fine so far," I murmured to Blake. "We have an infirmary. We don't know for sure that she's infected."

But Blake wasn't listening to me. His eyes had narrowed to slits. "She's not fine. I can hear it."

"Hear it?"

He scowled without even looking at me. "Her blood is rotting."

Jareth had overheard. He moved quickly, trying to get between Blake and the girl. But before he could make it, Visha was there, a dagger kissing his throat.

Blake moved towards Collette. "I'm sorry." His voice was truly regretful. I could hear the pain behind the words.

I don't think she'd even registered what he was going to do—and neither had I. One thrust, swift and perfect, and Blake was easing her to the floor. I stared at the girl's body, trying to take in what had just happened, feeling morbidly grateful for highblood speed. Jareth cried out and rushed at Blake, but Visha caught him and dragged him back. She spoke soothingly to the boy as he collapsed onto a couch and began to sob into his hands.

Blake wiped his blade. Then he raised his voice, so the students he'd conscripted as guards could all hear. "Every new arrival will be inspected carefully first. Anyone with a bite mark is to be put in a room separate from the other injured, with guards posted at the door."

He took a deep breath and looked over at me. I knew what he was about to say. "It's out there. In the castle. It's not contained. It's spreading."

I swallowed. "I don't care. I'm going to find Florence."

"And I'm going to find Vaughn." Theo stepped up beside me.

"I'll stay." It was Visha. "You know you want to go with them, Blake. We can't all leave. I'm your other Second. I'll stay and watch over things here." She looked between the three of us. "Bloodmaiden watch over you. Come back soon. Come back safe."

Blake, Theo, and I slipped from the common room. We'd made a plan: we'd head to Sankara's training courtyard, get some actual armor and more weapons, then head on to the Orphos Tower. House Drakharrow had an armory, but it was within the Black Keep—under Viktor's control. Still, the Defensive Arts courtyard had storage rooms full of equipment. We'd bring enough to try to supply Lysander and his people with what we didn't use. The courtyard was on the way, so Theo and I hadn't put up much of a protest. Also, Blake had insisted, and we knew he wouldn't back down.

I touched the daggers strapped to my thighs. Theo had a belt of small knives across his chest, while Blake carried a sword at his waist. These were just what we'd found lying around the Drakharrow tower; Blake had literally pulled the sword from a display on the wall and sharpened it himself.

It hadn't escaped my attention that on an ordinary day at Bloodwing, highbloods wouldn't need weapons: They were weapons enough. They had no real enemies, not since they'd turned against one another in the last civil war. They were at the top of the fucking food chain. Yet now, suddenly, they were faced with an unexpected threat—themselves.

Behind us, the doors to Drakharrow Tower thudded shut, sealing Visha and the others inside. I hoped we'd been thorough enough and no more infected were in there with them. The lamps burned low in their brackets. The sky was still dark. It was hard to believe that just a few hours ago, Florence and I had been calmly dressing for the ball.

I stayed by Blake's side, matching his stride, my gaze drifting to his profile. He hadn't said that he'd smelled Collette's blood—like a highblood might have. He said he'd heard it rotting.

"Blake." I kept my voice soft. "How did you know about Collette? You said you could hear her blood rotting. What did you mean?"

He slowed slightly. Theo glanced at us both, then took a few steps ahead and stopped, waiting, giving us at least the illusion of privacy. "Pendragon," Blake said quietly, "we can talk about this later. This isn't the time."

"But what are we talking about, exactly? What's going on? Something is happening with you. Don't keep me in the dark. Talk to me." I touched his cheek. "Don't shut me out."

Blake looked down at me. In the torch glow, I could see his pupils glimmering like coals. He took a deep breath. "Do you remember what happened in my room tonight? Before you fell asleep?"

My face flushed. "Of course. I mean, most of it. You were amazing. And then I woke up and . . . you were gone. Why did you leave?"

His shoulders sagged. "Good. That's . . . good," he murmured, ignoring my question.

Suspicion prickled. "What happened to the room, Blake? The window was broken. Everything was trashed. Did you do that? Why? And why didn't I wake up when it happened?"

He lifted a hand and gently stroked my hair. "Something was wrong. Very wrong with me. But . . . I fixed it. I swear to you, it's under control now. Do you trust me?"

"I trust you," I whispered.

I saw relief fill his eyes—as if he truly hadn't known what my answer would be—and my chest ached. There'd been so much hate between us. So much mistrust. Would we ever be able to fully move past it?

But I knew. *Knew.* Eyes of red or eyes of gray, body whole or body broken—this man was *mine*. I was never letting him go. No matter what happened. Still, I knew he was holding back. I opened my mouth again, but Blake cut me off.

"We have to go." His face had locked down again. His jaw tightened. "This isn't the time to linger in the halls. Theo's waiting. Come on."

Still not far from Drakharrow Tower, we rounded the next corner and froze in unison. Dead bodies littered the corridor, slashed apart and broken. The hall was filled with the scent of death and blood. A girl's body hung out a smashed window, her skirts billowing in the breeze. A boy lay where he'd been thrown against a wall, his head smashed open like a melon. There must have been twenty or thirty bodies just in the span of that single corridor.

"What the fuck happened here?" Theo whispered. "Were they infected?"

Suddenly the stones rang with the sound of tramping feet. At least fifteen highbloods fanned across the landing ahead, most wearing telltale badges. Bloodguards. Quinn Riley sauntered at their center, her lips curling in a triumphant smile as she saw Blake and me. Beside her stood Edward Ashveil. I spotted Larissa, Gretchen, and Lucian towards the back. All of them were armored and carrying proper weapons.

"Did you do this?" Blake called, gesturing to the bodies that filled the hall.

"We've been working hard, cleansing the school, if that's what you're asking, House Leader," Quinn said sweetly. "Protecting highblood lives is what we do, after all. Now, if you don't mind, Lord Drakharrow would like a word. He's waiting for you—right here in the school refectory."

I paled. Theo whispered an oath.

"You'll come quietly. You won't make this difficult." Quinn was trying hard to project confidence, and yet, I knew. Inside, she wasn't quite as certain as she looked.

"And if we don't?" I declared loudly.

"Then, we spill your blood." Edward spun the longsword in his hands in a lazy circle on the ground. "Even though it would be a waste to lose a single highblood right now. Be serious, though—

you're outnumbered. Two highbloods and a . . ." he chuckled " . . . I don't even know what to call you. There are simply too many insults to choose from." He chuckled again. "Lowblood? Foulblood? Washed-up dragon rider?"

I could feel Blake bristling and put a hand on his arm. Around Edward, the others laughed.

"It's simple math," Lucian called from behind Quinn. "Don't be idiots."

"Fuck, I can't believe that cowardly little prick was going to be Visha's archon," Theo muttered. He was already poised to fight, leaning forward, body tensing. Beside me, I could feel Blake doing the same.

"Visha was too smart for that," Blake muttered. "Ready?"

I nodded tightly. The nearest Bloodguard rushed towards us. Blake met him, head on, pulling his sword from his belt. Steel screamed against steel, and the corridor exploded into a sea of blades and bodies in motion. Blake collided with the first Bloodguard, his movements a blur. His sword flashed, and a head fell with a thump to the flagstones. He pivoted towards me, eyes alight with adrenaline, already splitting another guard from neck to hip.

"Pendragon, run! Get back to the tower!"

It might have been good advice, but it was too late—Gretchen's blade swept towards me. I dove beneath it, my knife slicing her thigh. She shrieked and stumbled, but Lucian's rapier was lunging for my ribs. I twisted aside, throwing a fist into his jaw. Theo ripped two knives from the bandolier across his chest. One left his hand at a mind-numbing speed, landing in Edward Ashveil's shoulder. The other he used to parry a thrust from Larissa. Kicking the heel of his boot into her knee, he dropped her to the ground. We were holding our own. We might have even carved our way out.

If a second wave hadn't swept in from behind.

They poured into the hall, twenty or more Bloodguards with Silvio Santos at their head. They were even more heavily armed than Quinn and her group, all in House Mortis armor.

They'd had this planned. They'd been waiting for us to come out. Were they starting with us, or had they already swept the Avari tower?

Theo hurled knife after knife until I saw him reach for his last. A Bloodguard blocked it, smashing his shield into Theo's face, while three others crashed into him, hammering him down, then wrenching his arms behind his back.

"Theo!" I started towards him, but a gauntleted fist caught me in the ribs. Pain exploded, and I doubled over. Two Bloodguards were there in a flash, pinning my arms back so tightly I couldn't lift them.

Silvio approached. Reaching down, he plucked the remaining blade from my left thigh-sheath and tossed it aside with a grin. Blake roared as I struggled—the sound brutal and animalistic. He took a step towards me, his sword dripping red.

"Hold, House Leader," Quinn called. "One more step, one more twitch, and your cousin bleeds out." She had a knife to Theo's throat.

I met Blake's eyes, horrified. He stopped, chest heaving, knuckles white around the hilt of his sword. He lowered it, point down, and was ringed in an instant.

Silvio grabbed me by the hair, pushing me down on my knees. He grinned at me. "We meet again. This time I really do think I'll have a taste, curls."

I spit up at him, gratified when my saliva actually managed to hit his jaw.

He laughed, wiping it away. "Easy, baby. Lord Drakharrow wants to see you. We can't party yet." He turned to Blake, whose eyes were full of blood and murder. "Good to see you again, Drakharrow. You're talking to the new Mortis leader."

Blake stared. "And what—I'm supposed to be impressed? Didn't you graduate five years ago, Santos? What kind of a fucking idiot comes back to the same school?"

I burst out laughing, and Silvio smacked me in the face with a snarl. My head reeled, but it wasn't enough to wipe the smile off my face. Then Quinn barked an order and Blake, Theo, and I were herded down the corpse-strewn hallway.

Before long, the refectory doors loomed before us—for the second time that night. I could already feel Viktor Drakharrow's shadow stretching out like a skeletal hand. I thought of Florence: This was supposed to be a rescue mission. If this was how badly we were faring, what were the chances she was doing any better?

CHAPTER 29

BLAKE

The wooden doors of the refectory were flung open, and we were driven in at swordpoint. I looked around the hall. Hours ago the place had glittered with candles, been filled with the strains of music, and held the most elite highbloods in Sangratha. Now only traces of opulence were left. Tables had been shoved to the sides, tablecloths askew, crystal glassware smashed on the floor. The raised stage the musicians had played on had been stripped of instruments. A large chair now sat in its center, like a makeshift throne on a dais. And standing before the throne was my uncle.

Viktor had healed a little more since I'd last seen him, but he still wasn't looking up to snuff. His snowy-white hair was still ragged and patched in places. The left side of his face sagged in waxy folds. His eyes were the same as always, though. Dark rubies glittering in deep hollows. I glimpsed fear in those eyes—but something else, too. Something that made me frightened. Excitement.

"Bring them forward," he rasped.

Quinn gave me a shove. Beside me, Theo stumbled, his wrists tied behind him, flanked by two Bloodguards. Pendragon had been permitted to walk under her own power—that is, until she reached the dais and Silvio Santos lodged a palm between her shoulder blades and shoved her down onto her knees.

"Touch her again and lose that hand," I snarled at him. Not that I'd be stopping with a hand.

"Easy, Nephew," Viktor drawled. "Our new House Mortis leader is simply enthusiastic."

Silvio wiggled his eyebrows at me and grinned. "Sure am, Lord Drakharrow." Then he backhanded Pendragon full in the face, his eyes never leaving mine.

Pendragon winced but didn't cry out. I watched blood drop from her split lip, her cheek bright red from the blow. I saw fire. The blood I would spill in this hall tonight, I decided, would be truly torrential. A downpour. All of it spilled in her name.

"Now, now, Santos. That's enough of that." Viktor beckoned to another Bloodguard standing at the foot of the dais. This one wore House Avari colors beneath his blood-and-sword badge. "Cade, be so good as to hold the girl, won't you?"

I looked at the Bloodguard coming towards Pendragon. He grabbed her by the shoulder, hauling her to her feet, and pulled her arms roughly behind her back. Something wasn't right. I closed my eyes, gritting my teeth as the sound of wet, bubbling rot gurgled up and filled my ears.

"No," I snapped. "Not him. Get his filthy hands off her."

Heads turned towards me. Cade narrowed his eyes.

Viktor sat down in the chair on the dais, spreading his legs, a smile curving on his face. "So you can hear it as well, can you, Nephew? Fascinating. The beast in you is discerning."

Pendragon turned towards me, licking the blood off her lips. "Hear what? What beast? Blake, what is he talking about?" But her eyes were afraid. Did part of her already know?

I didn't answer, could only stare at the bite mark on Cade's hand where he clenched her wrists. "He's been bitten. He's infected."

Cade paled, but his grip tightened on Pendragon's wrists as she struggled. "What's he talking about, Lord Drakharrow? It's just a bite."

Viktor chuckled. "Hold her tight, Cade. Nothing you need to be concerned about."

But around me, a buzz was spreading through the Bloodguard

crowd. The others knew—they knew what a bite meant. Cade must have been bitten early on, then kept in the hall for this one purpose. I stared at Pendragon in horror, fully aware that the highblood holding her could turn in a moment, attacking her as she was held in his arms. Would she merely be wounded, or would she be infected like a highblood? I thought of the blood I had poured into her earlier that evening. Had it made her more susceptible?

"Let her go," I snarled at Viktor. "This is between us. Get her out of here."

The old monster smiled. "Come, now, Blake. You know me better than that. I'm curious about something, though. Have you told your little blightborn whore yet? Have you told her how you carry more than guilt in those veins?"

Pendragon thrashed in Cade's grip. "Blake, what's he talking about?"

"Nothing," I said, my lie turning to ash in my mouth. "Shut the fuck up, Uncle."

Viktor laughed. "There's a dragon lurking behind those red pupils of his. One that can taste this corruption before it even manifests."

"There is no dragon," I snarled. "I ended him. He's gone."

"Did you, now?" Viktor's red eyes glittered back at me. "How interesting. Especially as my Bloodguards tell me that a pile of red ash is all that remains of Vorago in the Dragon Court. Yet here you stand before me, your eyes burning like twin coals."

My throat tightened.

"Blake," Pendragon breathed. She twisted in Cade's hold, searching my face for the truth. "What did you do?"

CHAPTER 30

BLAKE

A Few Hours Earlier

As soon as Pendragon's breathing had steadied and the guilt inside me had tapered to a tolerable ache, I bolted from the room. *The Dark Art of Eternal Bonds* was tucked under my arm, the spell I needed still bookmarked with Rodriguez's note. I jogged through the corridors, taking turn after turn, until finally I reached the cloistered borders of the courtyard. I hadn't been in the Dragon Court since the night we'd almost lost Florence, the night my brother and Catherine Mortis had woken a sleeping stone dragon and flown away on the corrupted beast's back, taking Lunaya Orphos with him. The night I'd learned that Kage Tanaka was a fucking wolf.

Now, only two stone dragons stood where once there had been four. Alabryss, the Silvrayne of House Mortis rested in one corner. The white dragon's smooth face bore a tranquil expression that belied all the chaos the courtyard had recently seen. Off to the other side sat Vorago, a monolith of crimson sandstone, his throat lifted as if to rain down fire that would never come. He was an Inferni, fastest of the four breeds and the most unpredictable—like the dragon that lurked within me. Didn't they say it took one to know one?

A cold wind cut through the colonnades. I ignored it, crossing the court until I'd reached Vorago's side.

You die tonight, I whispered to the dragon within me. *This ends here.*

I flipped Rodriguez's book open to the page I'd read a hundred times. The Spell of Twin Hearts stared up at me. One page held the incantation, the other contained two sigils.

My wrist had already begun to heal from where I'd fed Pendragon. I ripped the flesh open again, letting my blood flow. Dipping my fingers in the crimson, I copied the first sigil from the book carefully, tracing the curves onto Vorago's rough sandstone chest. Blood sizzled as the sigil formed, lines igniting with power. I stepped back, then placed the book on the ground at my feet. Ripping my shirt open, I traced a second sigil on my own chest.

Next came the incantation. Picking the book back up, I read aloud, enunciating each word slowly and clearly. "In the furnace of one soul, bind name for name, flame for flame . . ." I began. "Vorago, Inferni of House Drakharrow, flame of the skies, whose wings eclipse the sun itself, I summon thee."

There were some parts I had to improvise, including the dragon's address. But at least I knew now how damn finicky dragons were when it came to being properly praised. The wind began to pick up speed, whipping my shirt around me and sending the pages of the book flapping.

"Let my will be heard. Let my blood be felt. If you would break your bindings and be free once more of stone, listen and heed me." Finally, I reached the end of the stanza. A response had to be given before I could go any further.

For a moment, nothing happened. Then the wind died out. The Dragon Court was deathly silent, as though the entire castle around me were holding its breath.

The flagstones at my feet began to crack. Clenching the book, I jumped back, then sank to my knees as the stones shook harder, the book falling from my hands, forgotten, as a voice as old as the center of the world poured into me. I clapped my hands to my ears, closing my eyes, and trying not to scream.

Who calls to me through this coil of pain? roared the voice.

Great Vorago, flame of the skies, I beg your ears, only for a moment. I kept my head bowed, trying to pour every ounce of respect and awe I could into the words. It wasn't too difficult, considering I was addressing a dragon mind to mind. Was this what it felt like to Pendragon and Florence, this immensity of thought? This awe-inspiring sense of weight and power?

Vorago groaned and rumbled, then his voice spilled with anger. *You wake me from the stone, little highblood, from this state of eternal torment, thinking to press mastery onto me?*

No, I said swiftly. *Not mastery. Mercy. I'm here to beg you to have mercy upon me.*

Highbloods speak of mercy when they wish to fasten a collar, Vorago scoffed. *Will you lash me to your will, force soul into soul?*

Perhaps I could. I let the admission hang there a moment. *But that isn't what I want. I have no wish to contain or control you. There's a dragon inside me already—one I didn't want, one I didn't ask for. He's reckless and cruel. All I want is freedom. I wish to be myself again, free of his bondage.*

Freedom? You would choose freedom over power? Vorago gave a laugh that reminded me of stones sliding off a mountain. *What sort of a highblood are you, boy?*

I swallowed. *I would, yes. But what about you? You say you're in torment. Don't you deserve to choose your own ending? If freedom means the sky, I will . . . offer myself to you willingly.* I didn't know quite how that would work and was praying he wouldn't take that offer. A better plan would be him flying the fuck out of here—but only after he helped me kill the dragon within me.

Yes, offer to master me, you mean. Vorago snorted.

I would never dare to suggest mastering one so wise and noble as you, Great Vorago, I promised. *Look at me. I cannot even master the one who dwells within me, and his violent spirit threatens all I hold dear. What can I give you that you long for? If freedom means rest, let me give you that instead.*

There was a long pause. Then, *The sky is a mere memory to me* now, boy. *I would bleed in the wind and fall, screaming. No matter where I went, I would never be free of these chains that have kept me bound here.*

That's horrible, I said, honestly. It was true. I couldn't imagine wanting to die instead of wanting to be free. And yet, that was what Vorago was talking about, wasn't it?

Vorago's laughter scraped my ears. *Years in stone. Every nerve ablaze while I cannot move, cannot scream. A hell forged for me, fresh with every dawn. A state of torment. No life at all. And yet they said this was what I deserved.*

I looked up at him as the stone began to crack, eyelids peeling open, red embers staring down into me.

Very well. I have decided. I will carve away the hatchling who gnaws at your marrow, and then I will end this futile existence.

Relief shot through my chest. No merging. No new tyrant inside my skull. It was more than I'd hoped for. *It's a deal. You help me, I'll help you. Just tell me how*, I said instantly.

The final words, he directed. *They must be changed just so.*

Inside me, my dragon suddenly burst to life, ripping and pressing against my skin. It didn't want me to do this. It would fight with everything it had to stop me. I fell forward, sinking to my knees, palms flat on the flagstone, as scales burst forth along my arms, along my chest. "No," I gasped. "Not now."

Vorago gave an amused, rumbling laugh. *Let the weakling come. I will crack its shell and drink its yolk. It is half-formed at best. Your beast will not stand before me.* He suddenly gave a wracking cough that sounded like boulders shifting.

My heart twinged with guilt. Vorago sounded as if he truly were in a bad state. I hoped this was going to work. From the sounds of it, this was going to be a mercy killing—for us both.

Change the close, little highblood, the dragon rasped. *Redraw the sigil.*

The incantation? I grabbed the book.

Call not for union, but for devouring, he instructed. *Your blood will carve a channel. My agony will be the flame that burns your beast out.*

And then you'll . . . go? I asked tentatively.

You wish me to stay? He sounded amused.

No, of course not, I said hastily.

Good. I wish only for an ending to the curse placed upon me.

My hand shook a little as I drew the second sigil on his chest as he instructed, then the other on myself, each below the first. Then, holding my voice steady, I read aloud the last half of the incantation, changing the words where Vorago had instructed.

". . . scaled will to scaled vein. One furnace, one cry. Let the weaker ember sigh, let the greater spirit fly. The elder burns and the younger fades away."

Fade away to blooddamned nothingness, I snarled at my dragon as I finished. *You fucking monster. You would have killed her tonight and not even cared. I won't mourn you. It'll be like you never existed at all.*

Light detonated around me. Vorago roared. Stone crashed down, sandstone shale fracturing, like a volcano bursting from the earth. Inside, something within me, vast and savage, tore free. A wall of heat slammed through my chest, and for a single blinding moment I was not one, not two, but three. I could *feel* Vorago—feel his molten memory, feel the centuries of fury and anguish compressed down my spine. I'd thought the dragon inside me angry and violent? That rage was nothing compared to Vorago's wrath. Now the presence I had carried for months like a burden, the one that had made a cage within my bones, was cowering, collapsing into raw, animal fear.

I tasted blood in my mouth as the two spirits met. Vorago's cruel laughter thundered through my veins, and for a moment, I feared I had made a terrible mistake. The Inferni was powerful—a hundred times more deadly than the creature that lurked within me.

Witness, whelp, Vorago hissed inside me. *Thus ends the torment of captivity. Thus ends our pain.*

A flash as hot as dragon fire exploded behind my eyes. I screamed, clawing at my face. Then it was over nearly as soon as it began. The fire within guttered out like a spark in a rainstorm. I staggered, fists bracing on the stones, determined to test myself. I called for wings. For scales. For talons. Anything. There was no answer. No itching under my skin. No fire in my pulse. My arms were flesh. My back, simple bone. Slowly, I straightened and stood. Laughter ripped from my throat. I felt light, giddy. Like iron bindings had been torn away from around my ribs.

The Dragon Court was silent. The place where Vorago had stood was empty. The massive sandstone statue was gone, only a swirling pillar of ruby-gold dust spiraled upward before being whisked away in the wind.

I was free. Truly free.

I turned towards the castle and the long walk back to Pendragon, the red ashes of an ancient dragon still drifting in the air behind me.

CHAPTER 31

BLAKE

Now

Cade's fingers tightened around Pendragon's wrists. I could hear his heartbeat stuttering, could smell the rot spreading like coils of corruption through his veins. Any second now and he'd turn. He'd lunge for the warmest throat within reach. He'd sink his teeth into Pendragon's skin and then . . . and then every pulse of blood he took would be blood I'd poured into her veins earlier tonight myself. My own gift, my own weakness.

I'd gladly given my blood to keep her alive—but the exchange had hollowed me. Even now my limbs felt a half second slower. When I'd fought back in the hall, my movements had felt sluggish, like moving through water. My pulse thudded in my ears. And with it came a faint prickle of something like curiosity.

No. I slammed the sensation back. *You're gone. Dead and buried.*

Viktor watched me like a vulture scenting a wounded animal. "You feel it, don't you? You smell the taint on him."

"Let her go," I growled, trying to focus on Viktor and Pendragon instead of the sudden confusion in my head. "What do you want?"

"Finally, the right question." My uncle leaned forward, his red eyes gleaming. "We have purged this school. The plague is gone from here—save for what you see."

"You slaughtered everyone," I said bluntly. "Infected or not."

"We took no chances. Bloodwing is safe. The best and the brightest of the highblood race live within these walls. Our children, our future."

Around me I could practically feel Quinn, Silvio, and the other Bloodguards stand up a little straighter with pride. Pathetic.

"Of course, one I was too late to save. But he, too, shall play his part." Viktor glanced over at Cade. "Tell me, my boy, how do you feel?"

I looked at Cade, my blood going cold. His eyes were turning a milky white. Black veins were branching across his throat.

"Strange," Cade whispered. He cleared his throat, a gurgle reaching his lips. "I feel strange, my lord. Perhaps I should see a healer."

Pendragon's face was as white as a sheet. She was holding very, very still.

Viktor smiled. "Soon, very soon."

"Get him the fuck away from her. You can see what's happening as well as I," I shouted at my uncle. "I swear to all that's holy, I swear by every drop of blood in Sangratha, I will do nothing for you, *nothing*, if harm befalls her. Do you hear me?"

Viktor looked back at me, and I knew both of us were remembering the last time I'd come at him. There I'd stood, thinking I'd won, blood running off my scales. And then? He'd filleted my eye from its socket. The phantom pain of that wound pulsed behind my temple. If I attacked him here, now, in the state I was in, he'd do worse. Pendragon would watch me fall. Then, where would that leave her and Theo?

Viktor smiled as if he'd known exactly what I was about to say, then snapped his fingers. "Hold the girl. Bind the Avari boy. Quickly, now."

Quinn slipped in as if playing a part she'd rehearsed, jerking Pendragon out of Cade's grasp as two Bloodguards stepped forward quickly, iron shackles already in hand. They clanged them shut around Cade's wrists just as he lunged at them with a wet snarl.

"What fucking games are you playing at, Uncle?" I demanded. "End him before he kills one of your own."

Viktor's mouth curved. "Not so fast. A preview tends to sharpen the mind. Quinn, be a good girl and fetch our prisoner."

She nodded eagerly, moving to one of the doors leading off into the kitchens, and reemerging a moment later, dragging a woman by the wrist.

"Professor!" Pendragon cried. The instructor's purple velvet coat was ripped, and her long, brightly colored hair was matted with blood. She stumbled with a groan as Quinn jerked her roughly.

"Allenvale?" I turned to face Viktor. "Really, a teacher of alchemy? What'd she do to you? Brew a tonic you didn't like? So you're torturing even highblood professors now?"

My uncle's lips twisted. "When will you learn there is always logic behind all I do, Nephew? I have not lived this long for naught. Everything I do I do for House Drakharrow."

I scoffed. Everything Viktor did was for himself and only himself. He was destroying my father's legacy, one step at a time.

"Lord Drakharrow," Professor Allenvale gasped as Quinn shoved her down before the dais. "I don't understand how I've come to offend you. I was aiding injured students. Blightborn and highblood, yes, but nothing more."

Viktor's lips stretched in a parody of sympathy. "*Aiding*? Don't play the innocent, Professor. We confiscated your correspondence. I've seen the notes you had in your desk."

Allenvale's dark eyes widened with guilt, and my heart sank. Whatever mistake she'd made, I knew he had her.

Viktor looked over at me. "Our little visiting professor has been funding a rebellion. An uprising nurtured by House Orphos right under our very noses."

Allenvale's eyes were on me, panicked and pleading.

"Let her go, Viktor," I said, trying to keep my voice calm. "Aren't there more important things to deal with right now? Who the fuck cares what Orphos has been doing? Their house is weak. We both know that. They could never stand up to ours. Let her go, and we'll discuss this when things have settled down."

"Pleading for traitors? And you, my heir? You're pathetic, Blake. You've always been too soft. You act as if mercy were a virtue. Now, Marcus, there was a lad with foresight, with ambition. You're correct that Orphos is weak. They are weaker now thanks to Marcus."

"Marcus?" I snapped. "I don't see Marcus here by your side. He took off as soon as he had a chance."

Viktor frowned. "He was hasty. Impatient. Yet what he's done may do more good than harm, in the end. He's given us an opportunity to crush Orphos and their treachery now, here—beginning with her."

Cade suddenly lunged against his chains, snapping at the air as Quinn propelled Allenvale closer towards him.

"Talk to Lysander," I said quickly. "Surely our quarrel is with him, not this woman. You need her. She represents proof. Take her to Lysander, and let's have this all out. Stop the games. You've made your point. Let me help you deal with Orphos."

Anything that would buy Allenvale a little more fucking time. Anything that would get the four of us out of this blooddamned death chamber.

"Stop the games? I'll stop as soon as you prove to me you can do what's really necessary." His eyes moved to Pendragon, still pinned by Larissa, flanked by Bloodguards. "Now, our Cade must be fed. I owe the poor boy that much for his unswerving loyalty. But I'll be charitable. I'll give you a choice. This traitor or your consort."

Time crashed to a standstill. Theo strained against his guards, his eyes wild. I could feel Pendragon's furious eyes on me. *Don't you dare choose me*, they cried. She twisted in Larissa's arms, trying to break free.

Viktor spread his skeletal hands. "Choose, Nephew. Our dear Cade grows hungrier by the second."

"What do you really want, Viktor?" I shouted, my voice echoing across the refectory. "Power? Allegiance? My head bowed lower? Just tell me what you want, and leave them out of this!"

Cade's chains rattled. The infected highblood slavered in anticipation as Quinn shoved Allenvale another step closer. Pendragon's eyes were on me, wide, pleading for me to think of some way out of this—for all our sakes.

Viktor's smile faded, and he rose to his feet. "You want to know what I want? Then, enough games. Show them what you truly are. Transform, right here, right now."

I clenched my fists. "I can't do that. I've already told you, the dragon is gone." I wouldn't meet Pendragon's eyes. I didn't dare. Deep inside, something stirred—scales flickering, talons clicking.

Viktor sneered. "You lie to yourself, boy. I see its glow behind your eyes. Now, shift. Shift and fly to Veilmar. Rain fire down upon the infected city, and burn it clean."

I stared at him, understanding quickly dawning. "So that's what you're really up to. Cleanse Veilmar? You don't want me to cleanse the city, you want me to purge it. Thanks to the Avaris, the most powerful highbloods in the Thralldom are lodged in the city tonight. You don't want me to stop a plague. You want me to wipe out your enemies."

There was a buzz of sound as the other highbloods grasped exactly what Viktor was trying to get me to do. Clearly he hadn't shared his little plan with them before he'd conscripted them all to do his bidding.

"Silence!" he roared. The hall quieted. He looked down at me. "Let Veilmar die tonight, and House Drakharrow will rise from the ashes to build a New Sangratha. The students of Bloodwing will stand at the forefront. A Pure Blood army in service to a most righteous cause. Marcus and Catherine were heralds of a new dawn, but it was one which I'd already set in motion. Already the infection grows within the city's walls. The Avari roost within, smug and self-satisfied. One blaze and their line ends."

Their line? But not Kage—as far as I knew, he was still at Bloodwing. Or did my uncle know something I didn't . . . Had Kage gone into the city? If my uncle did this, would the Avaris truly be wiped out?

"You'd have me scorch an entire city of innocent people and blame it on an outbreak?" I demanded. "Even you can't be that stupid."

"I'd have you do what I command," Viktor bellowed. "My patience has run out. If you fail to obey me tonight, I swear to you, Nephew, I will destroy every person you ever cared about. Not just your consort but also your cousin. And your mother." He leaned forward, with a cruel smile. "Your pathetic, traitorous mother, who I have kept alive solely for your sake. Your friends. Every person who has ever paid you a single kindness. All will die in throes of agony. For I warn you, Nephew, my limits have been reached. You *will* do as I ask."

I flinched. "Why not do it yourself? We both know what you're really capable of. Or are you too much of a coward?"

Viktor hissed.

Professor Allenvale's voice cut through the tumult, tight with terror. "Blake, please. Stand down. I don't know quite what's going on here, but let him kill me if he must. Better me than the city."

"She'll die, yes." Viktor's eyes were still on me, not even sparing Allenvale a glance. "They all will. First her, then your blightborn whore. The girl is useless to you now that she has no dragon. Her heart is weak. She holds you back, I see that now. Without her, you'll be who you were meant to be. No mercy and no regret. You'll rule by my side, the heir of your true father."

I gritted my teeth as he mentioned my father.

"Now, transform. Be the dragon you were meant to be," Viktor ordered. "The solider of my right hand. Your flame at my command."

Inside, my heartbeat thundered. "I won't burn Veilmar," I said slowly. "I won't be your monster."

Viktor stared down at me. "Then, we shall begin with smaller fires." He snapped his fingers, and Quinn gave Allenvale a vicious shove—sending her toppling straight into Cade's reach.

The professor screamed. Cade's chains jangled, and he grabbed for her, his teeth burying deep into the flesh of her shoulder.

I shouted, hearing Pendragon and Theo doing the same, but Allenvale's screams of pain and terror drowned us all out. Cade pulled her down to the ground, worrying at the wound like a dog twisting a bird's neck. Crimson flooded the purple velvet of her coat. I felt sick as I watched her being slowly devoured.

Highblood, are you? Softblood, more like. You would stand helpless while your mate trembles in another's grip?

My breath caught. *Vorago?*

I waited, highblood. Waited to taste your marrow. Waited to weigh your worth. Yet you would let carrion feast on your mate while you bargain with tyrants.

The red beast I'd thought dead slammed against my ribs, rattling the bars to get out, and I gasped. *You're alive. You fucking lied to me.*

A rumble of mirth. *I offered release for us both. No one compelled you. You chose to speak the words.*

I recalled what I'd said: *The elder burns and the younger fades away.* A chill spread over me. *What the fuck have you done to me?*

Cade was still feeding, the sounds wet and sloppy. Allenvale wasn't dead yet. Her cries of agony were unbearable to hear.

I won't let her die. But I won't destroy the city—I can't. Those people are innocent. It would be a massacre.

She is your mate. She is my rider. You have no choice.

She's not yours. You are not me. You were never supposed to be here. I drew a ragged breath, tasting iron, balanced on a knife's edge.

Enough, Vorago hissed. *If you will not defend what is ours, I will.*

Scales erupted across my arms like a spreading tide. I screamed as my bones split and lengthened, talons shredding through my skin. Cries of terror ricocheted off the walls as I began to grow and transform. The Bloodguards near me stepped back.

Viktor's eyes lit up, then he moved like lightning. One moment he was on the dais, the next he was at Pendragon's side, his hands digging into the soft flesh of her arms. The old fucker wasn't taking any chances.

Pendragon's eyes were wide and disbelieving as my body morphed and changed. "Blake?"

"I'm sorry," I managed—and then my jaw cracked wide, tearing into a muzzle of red scales and white fangs. My spine arched, bursting outwards into ridges of scarlet plates. Wings tore from my shoulders, slamming against chandeliers and breaking open windows with the force of their gust. I fought for control, clawing at the torrent of power swelling through my veins. But Vorago slammed my will aside. My consciousness hung, helpless, in his grasp.

Allenvale stared up at us, Cade still slurping from her open body. She was dead and yet not: No one should have to go through what she was enduring.

I felt Vorago's gaze fix upon her, and for a moment, my pity briefly permeated his mind. Our maw opened. White-hot flame spread forth, engulfing Cade and the professor. The two bodies vanished in incandescent heat.

Not Veilmar, I pleaded, hope momentarily rising at the way Vorago had granted Allenvale a mercy killing. *There must be another way. Give me more time. Transform back. I'll persuade Viktor to let Pendragon go, or I'll kill him myself.*

You've had your chance, youngling. Cities fall, Vorago answered, placidly. *Our rider is irreplaceable. Your uncle wishes to have a monster at his fingertips. Let him reap what he has sown. Better a monster with teeth than a princeling with empty hands.*

I felt him shift his massive bulk, claws cracking the stones beneath us like glass. He dipped his enormous head down to Pendragon, a breath of heat blowing back her hair, and for a moment, we stared at one another. Me through his eyes.

Pendragon's lips parted, trembling. She tried to lift a hand to touch my snout, but Viktor dragged her back. I saw the fear in her eyes. The pain, the hurt. I steeled my heart. But was it even still mine, or was it Vorago's? I'd sworn never to let Viktor hurt her again. If I had to trade my soul for the city, burn the sky to ash to keep her breathing, then in this moment, the bargain was struck. I would light my own pyre with dragon fire if it meant keeping her safe.

She deserved to live far more than I did.

Vorago's wings opened with a thunderous crack. Leaping forward, he smashed through the wall of the refectory, stone exploding around us, and we vaulted into the open sky.

CHAPTER 32

MEDRA

The moment Blake's spine began to arch and scarlet scales rippled across his skin, Viktor was there. Shoving Larissa aside, his hands clamped down on my arms, jerking me in front of him like a shield. I barely registered the pain from his grip; my whole body turned to white heat. As wings burst from Blake's shoulders, their surface a rough burnished crimson, something was happening inside of me. A throb in my gut, blood racing through every vein.

Something good. Strong. Powerful.

I recognized the sensation: highblood power mingling with dragon rider reflexes. I'd felt it once before—after the first time Blake had convinced me to drink a vial of his blood before the Consort Games. Then, my senses had been heightened. I'd been able to see farther, move faster. Blake's blood had intensified the instincts in my bones, stirring up senses I couldn't activate on my own. Now it was happening again, which could only mean one thing: Blake had given me his blood again, recently. I'd fallen asleep back in his room, and he'd disappeared. What had really happened in that brief window? What had Blake done?

He'd transformed into a fucking dragon and trashed his own room, nearly killing you in the process, I told myself.

When he returned, he'd been so relieved I was all right and so convinced he'd somehow fixed himself. If this was fixing himself, then I couldn't imagine how much worse things had been before.

The red dragon Blake had become turned his massive head towards Cade and Professor Allenvale. Hot breath surged from his jaws—a single blast of white-hot fire—and they were gone.

He turned again—this time towards me—and I reached a desperate hand out, only to be yanked back by Viktor.

Then a crash, and the refectory wall was gone—and so was Blake.

The instant he vanished, the power in my blood roared like waves against a cliff. Something inside me longed to follow him, but I'd been left behind. I clamped my teeth together, trying to stop the trembling.

Viktor's arms tightened around me, misreading my shudder as terror. "That's right, girl. He's mine now."

I turned my head to look up at him and snarled.

He smiled down at me complacently. "Now, what should we do with you?" But the smile was wiped off his face an instant later as the refectory doors burst open.

Everything dissolved into pandemonium. Visha came first, hurling a dagger that sank to its hilt in a Bloodguard's throat as he rushed towards her. Vaughn followed at her shoulder, blades clenched in his fists. He dropped into a low position we'd learned in Professor Stonefist's class, scything the legs from an armored highblood girl, and then sprang past her, pivoting to slam his elbow into another Bloodguard's jaw. I didn't see the moment Theo broke free of his captors, but soon he was next to Vaughn, the pair moving back to back, their timing impeccable as Vaughn sliced openings and Theo finished opponents off with highblood-swift strikes. Behind Visha and Vaughn thundered Professor Sankara. The burly ebony-skinned instructor gripped an iron war hammer in one enormous fist and a shield in the other.

A second wave followed right behind him. There, leading a group of students decked out in familiar purple and gold, came Lysander Orphos. His long silver hair was pulled back into a ponytail, and he carried a slender steel saber that he jerked effortlessly through every Bloodguard who tried to stop him. The sound of clashing blades rang out. Tables that weren't already overturned toppled. Screams and cries filled the air. And meanwhile, there I stood, pinned to Viktor—Blake's blood mingling with my own, running through my veins like a fire about to ignite.

Blake's uncle began to yank me backwards towards the dais—and the fire inside me erupted in a blaze. Strength flooded my limbs. I stamped hard on Viktor's instep, driving my elbow back into his ribs, then scooping a fallen rapier off the floor and whirling to face him. He straightened, lips peeling back in a sneer. Then he lifted his hands, and I watched in horror as his nails lengthened, sharpening into black talons, too large and too cruel to belong to any mortal creature. They were like Blake's. Like Nyxaris's. *Draconic.*

Viktor Drakharrow was part fucking dragon.

I bared my teeth and ran towards him. He slashed forward, moving faster than any highblood I'd ever seen. I jerked my head aside, but it was too late. His claws raked my cheek. Blood splattered as pain flared bright, only to quickly dull beneath the strength Blake's blood was infusing me with.

"So you can sprout wings of your own?" I challenged. "You really are a fucking coward, Viktor. Why not fight your own battles instead of getting Blake to do it for you?"

His eyes burned. "Because, unlike me, your archon is expendable. I should have made you kneel the moment I first laid eyes on you, girl."

"So why didn't you?" I spat. "You missed your chance. And here I am. Blake won't torch Veilmar for you. He'll never be what you want. He's not a trained hound."

Viktor's smile grew. "He's out there right now, raining down fire in my name—what's more, he's enjoying it. You know it's true."

My heart convulsed as the words penetrated me. I had to pray he was wrong.

Viktor rushed forward again—faster than that ruined, monstrous old body had any right to be able to move—and swung both taloned hands at me in a brutal crosscut. I managed to partly parry, but his second blow raked low across my torso. Agony flared as gouges opened up across my stomach and hips, blood soaking through the heavy sweater. I gasped, staggering, as Viktor wheeled again, scraping his claws along my forearm, skin peeling back under the strength of his curving hooks. The pain threatened to drop me, but Blake's blood thundered in my veins, giving me life, giving me the strength to keep standing.

Across the wreckage of the ballroom, I glimpsed Visha and Lysander breaking a path through one of the last knots of Bloodguards. They were fighting shoulder to shoulder. Visha's twin daggers flicked in and out as she caught my eye. *We're coming*, her eyes said.

Viktor sprang forward. This time I met his claws with my sword, knocking them aside with ease. I ignored the blood flowing from my body, ignored the pain. Viktor's eyes flickered to my torso, as if expecting me to fall at any time. But I could feel my wounds already knitting together. Highblood healing at its finest.

"You're weak, old man, and you're losing. Unless you'd like to show us your true colors. What color is your dragon, anyhow, or can you even turn all the way? Is that your real secret? Are you an impotent little dragon?" I mocked.

"I should have slaughtered you the moment you appeared," he snarled.

"So which is it?" I taunted, circling him, blade stretched out. "Should you have made me kneel or killed me? Guess what? It doesn't matter. Because I'm here now. But something tells me, Viktor, that your time is running out. Look around you—no one wants you as their king. And the ones that do won't be standing long."

"Blake would never betray me. His loyalty lies with House Drakharrow. One command from me and this school becomes ash—you and your friends along with it."

"Wrong. Blake's loyalty lies with me, and it has from the moment you bound us together," I snarled. "When are you going to realize what a huge fucking mistake you made, Viktor? Blake belongs to *us* now. He isn't just a highblood, anymore. He doesn't belong to House Drakharrow alone—and neither do I. We're Avari. We're Orphos. We're Mortis. We're blightborn. We are every house you've tried to shatter. We're the enemy you've always feared would someday appear at the fucking front gates." I backed a step up, tempting him to come at me. "You know what I really think? I think you've been afraid of us all along. Afraid of Blake and what you knew he was capable of. Afraid of me and what I am."

Viktor chuckled. "What you are, girl? What you are is less than nothing. You have no dragon. You're worthless. Your life is a drop of blood to be smeared into the dust beneath highblood feet." His eyes blazed. For a moment, I thought he would do it, erupt into his full draconic form.

A roar shook the rafters.

"No dragon, you said?" I whispered.

Viktor's face paled. His form blurred. And in the span of a breath, he was simply . . . gone.

CHAPTER 33

REGAN

I held as still as I could as Healer Elycia eased the gauze away from my skull. Dried blood tugged at hair that had been flawlessly clean just a few hours ago. Now it hung in knotted, rust-stained clumps around my shoulders.

"The gash has already closed," the healer announced, peering intently at my forehead. "Your head may be pounding for a while. But you'll live."

"Thank you," I murmured to the House Avari healer. "I appreciate your care."

She nodded stiffly, already moving away, clearly not a Headmistress Regan fan. That was fine. I wasn't either. Not anymore.

Kage prowled near the door, reminding me more than ever this evening of a wolf. I wondered if he wished he could shift into his animal form here and now and run away from this place and never come back. If I could do what he could do, I'd run out into the night, lift my head, and howl at the moon. I was tired of highbloods, tired of blightborn. Just plain tired. And the insanity just kept coming.

Feet pounded up the steps of the tower. I watched as Kage tensed. "Rodriguez," he barked. "To me. Now!"

I knew he'd already positioned Avari guards in the hall, but from the sounds of the footsteps, this was a large group. The guards wouldn't be enough—not if whoever it was meant to breach the infirmary.

I slid off the cot, moving to stand behind Kage along with Professor Rodriguez. Healer Elycia didn't seem like much of a fighter, and neither did Florence Shen, despite having a dragon. The others in the room were all injured and lying in cots.

Kage glanced at me. "Get back, Regan."

"No," I said quietly. "I'm fine. I've rested long enough."

He didn't protest again, just drew the blade from his belt. The pounding footsteps had stopped. Were they slaughtering the guards in the hall? My heart beat faster. The infirmary doors flew inwards.

"House Leader," an Avari guard said and grinned. "Someone to see you."

"A few *someones*," Professor Sankara announced, marching inside the room.

My mouth fell open. Behind him came Medra Pendragon, Theo Drakharrow, and his blightborn boyfriend, whose name I didn't know, Visha Vaidya, and perhaps most surprising of all, Lysander Orphos.

Also surprising was who was not in the group, and who I'd have expected to be there: Blake.

Medra's eyes flew around the room, going from Kage to me to Rodriguez and then past us.

"Florence!" she cried. She was covered in blood that looked to be her own, one cheek shredded open with what looked like claw marks. I stared. The wounds were fresh, yet already starting to close. Medra crossed the room in two great strides to where Florence Shen stood by a worktable fiddling with herbs and folded her into a tight embrace. Meanwhile, the little fluffin—Neville they apparently all called him—pranced about by their ankles, squeaking as if he'd done something remarkable. Considering his aptitude for detecting the plague, I supposed he deserved a little credit.

I watched in fascination as Medra held her friend close, her shoulders quaking—with laughter or tears, I couldn't tell. She was filthy, bloody, broken, and yet here she was, glowing with relief over seeing a girl who wasn't even her consort or her family, just a friend. I'd never known such a feeling, never imagined such loyalty unmotivated by anything but fear.

I'd had friends, yes. But suddenly I found myself doubting my understanding of the meaning of the word. I doubted I had one friend in Drakharrow who would embrace me with the emotion I was seeing between Medra and Florence right now. Even my own father never showed me such affection. I turned my head away, but it was too late. I caught Kage watching me. I looked away and started to walk across the room—only to collide with Theo.

"Good to see you're all right," I said quietly, expecting him to step aside and let me pass.

Instead, he stayed right where he was. Only then did I realize how furious he looked—and all of that fury was directed right down at me.

"Do you have any fucking idea what your archon is doing out there?"

"Something terrible, no doubt," I said wearily.

Theo's eyes narrowed. "Do you think this is funny, Regan? Do you? Do you have any idea what Viktor just made Blake do?"

"Don't talk to her like that." Kage stepped in front of me, his arms crossed over his chest. "If you have a problem, you take it up with me."

Theo looked at Kage in disbelief. Then he did something I never expected him to do and shoved Kage hard in the chest. The Avari leader didn't budge an inch—but he did snarl.

"Theo." It was the tall blightborn boy. He darted in between Kage and Theo and tried to pull Theo back. Then to Kage he said, "He isn't trying to start trouble."

"Isn't he?" Kage growled. "It doesn't look that way to me. You're in my house. This is the Avari Tower. Regan is under my protection. You'd do well to remember that."

Theo scoffed. "You'd protect her? Protect our *honorable* headmistress—" he said the word with bitterness "—after all she's done?

Do you even know what we've been through tonight? Do you know where we just came from?" He pointed at me accusingly. "We just came from fighting an entire fucking army of your Bloodguards—led by Viktor Drakharrow, I might add."

I shifted uncomfortably. "I'm sorry."

Theo laughed. "You're sorry? Are you serious? Are you really going to try to say none of this is your fault? That, what—Viktor was pulling your strings? That you couldn't help it?"

"Theo," the blightborn boy by his side whispered. "Please."

"Back off, Vaughn," Theo snapped. "She has to pay for what she's done. She's just as much to blame as he is."

Kage growled again—a decidedly wolflike sound this time. "You're out of line. You're the one who needs to back off, Drakharrow."

"No," I said quickly. "Let him speak. Theo's right."

Theo blinked. He gave a choking laugh. "I am? Really?"

"Yes." I lifted my chin. "I'm responsible. Whatever happened here tonight, I'm to blame. I let the Bloodguards into this school. Viktor was behind their creation, but I set them up to—" I took a deep breath "—to bully and to hurt." I closed my eyes. "Even to kill."

"That's exactly what they've been doing tonight," Vaughn said quietly. "The halls run with blightborn blood."

I paled. "I need to see for myself. I'll go at once. I'll do what I can to try to stop them."

"Try to stop them?" Theo scoffed. "Excuse me, who the fuck are you, and where's the real Regan?" He leaned forward and rapped on the side of my head. I flinched. "Viktor, are you in there? Is this some sort of a sick trick?"

Kage's fist met Theo's face before I could even open my mouth. The Drakharrow boy fell backwards onto a cot. Theo sat there for a moment, looking stunned, then he ran a hand over his face and burst out laughing. He was hysterical, I realized—none of this was like him. But then, this was no ordinary night. Once he'd started laughing he didn't seem to be able to stop. Vaughn crouched beside him, a hand on Theo's shoulder as his whole body shook with waves of laughter.

"Don't—don't you see," Theo gasped, "don't you see how funny it is?"

"No," Kage said coldly. "I don't." He glanced at Vaughn. "Is he infected? Was he bitten?"

Vaughn shook his head. "No, that's not it. Trust me. You'll want to hear what we have to say." He looked rueful. "He's been through a lot. What with Blake becoming a dragon and—"

"What?" I interrupted. "A dragon?"

"That's right. You going to pretend you didn't know?" Theo accused. "That Viktor didn't already tell you?" He hiccupped, trying to get control of the fit.

I stared at him. "Viktor doesn't tell me *anything* about his true plans. If you think that he would, you're more of an idiot than I ever took you for, Theo. He's my archon. Don't you get what that means? He fucking owns me." My voice broke, but I kept going. "He owns my family. I don't even know where my little brother is. Don't you see that? Don't you understand?" I stopped suddenly, realizing I'd been shouting. The entire room was quiet. Everyone had heard me. I felt my face flushing with humiliation. Then I lifted my chin. It wobbled a little, but I knew it was too late to go back. The truth was out there. Everything was coming to a head. I couldn't hold everything together. It was all coming apart. I'd been a fool to even try.

"It's just funny," Theo said quietly, "to have this fucking Avari try to shut me up, when we came here to warn *him*."

"Warn me about what?" Kage demanded.

Theo took a deep breath. "To warn you that Blake really *did* turn into a dragon. Viktor threatened to kill Medra if he didn't do as he said. He demanded Blake wipe out the plague from the city. Blake didn't want to, I know he didn't. But . . . he flew away."

Theo's eyes were wide with disbelief. I understood the reason for his hysterical laughter then. "Nyxaris arrived. Viktor disappeared. We have no idea where the fucker even went."

The entire room erupted—everyone talking at once.

"Silence," Kage roared. "What do you mean? Tell me now. Tell me quickly before I rip your throat out."

"Go ahead, Tanaka. Go the fuck ahead." Theo sounded exhausted. "It won't help. It won't stop anything. Blake flew into the city, just like I said. He went to destroy Veilmar."

Kage looked skeptical. He glanced at me.

"I don't know anything about it," I whispered. "I had no idea."

He nodded.

"You don't believe me?" Theo challenged. "Everything I'm telling you is true. Get to a fucking window and look outside if you don't believe me."

I tugged at Kage's sleeve. "Hurry. Come on. Let's do as he said."

Everyone followed as we went out into the hall. Even the injured students were rising from their beds, determined to see if what Theo Drakharrow had just claimed could possibly be true. We all knew people in Veilmar, almost every student at Bloodwing had family there.

Across from the infirmary lay an alcove full of tall bookshelves and plush armchairs, clearly used for waiting or for studying. Now we quickly crossed the space, to the far side where three tall arched windows overlooked the sea—and beyond that, the jewel of Sangratha, the greatest city in the Thralldom, Veilmar.

Kage rushed towards the window in the center, yanking it open, and peering out over the water. But I'd already seen the telltale glow. As soon as the window opened, a hot blast of wind rushed in—tinged with the scent of smoke.

"Bloodmaiden," I breathed.

On the far horizon were the lights of Veilmar. The glittering streets and towers were consumed in roiling plumes of orange flame. As we watched, a tower in the Banking District collapsed, slowly caving in upon itself. Clouds of smoke and ash billowed out over the water. Over it all, flying just beneath the clouds, was a dragon. Not black like Nyxaris, but crimson—scales glowing in the inferno's glare. From its jaw, a torrent of white-hot flame arced downwards, transforming another street into a river of fire.

"Dear gods." It was Rodriguez. He'd come up beside us and was standing at the window to our left. Healer Elycia stood beside him, silent and trembling. Behind them came Florence, with Medra right beside her. To my shock, I saw Medra was weeping. The tears ran down her blood-stained cheeks as she looked out at the city. Kage stepped back from the window slowly. I touched a hand to his arm and felt his muscles trembling. Something passed between us, secret and fleeting.

"We have to stop him," Medra whispered, looking at Kage.

He nodded. "I'm leaving. Now."

"But what can we do?" I demanded, helplessly. "He's a *dragon*." The thought of Kage going out there and trying to take on a dragon filled me with terror. I glanced at Florence. "There's only one way to stop another dragon."

Around me, I could see everyone else having the same thought.

"I—" Florence stammered. She looked at me, then Kage, then Rodriguez, and finally back at Medra. "She's right. That's why you've come, isn't it?"

"I came because I needed to know you were all right." Medra shook her head helplessly. "What Regan said may be true, but you're not ready for this, Florence. You're not prepared. You don't have to do this."

"But I do, don't I? I'm not ready," Florence said, her face ashen, "but Nyxaris is. He's trained for this all his life. If anyone can stop Blake, he can. He's the *only* one who can."

Kage didn't wait to hear Medra's reply; he was already moving. I chased after him, following him towards the stairs. "Where are you going?"

He paused, looking back at me. "Into the city."

I took a deep breath. "You, or the wolf?"

He didn't reply.

"Let me come with you." The words came out in a rush. But once I'd said them, I knew they were right.

"No. Absolutely not."

"Viktor will be there. If Nyxaris and Florence fly into the city, Viktor will follow them. I know it. He might even be there now. For all we know, he's riding on Blake's fucking back. I can stop him. I know I can. He'll listen to me."

I actually had no idea if that was true. In fact, it probably wasn't. But I did know one thing: Viktor had to pay for what he'd done—to me, to Persis, to Blake, to everyone. And I wanted to be the one who made him hurt. Even if I died trying.

I knew another thing, too. I wasn't letting Kage Tanaka walk away from me ever again.

"There's no time for this," Kage growled, his face strained. "I need you here. I need you safe."

I clenched my fists. "I've never been safe," I burst out. "And I never will be. Not with Viktor. You know that. You've known it all along. Now look at what he's done. He's sent Blake out there to kill everyone—to kill your family. Your entire family is in the city, Kage."

The Avari House Leader's shoulders shook.

"I'll run after you," I vowed. "I swear, I'll do it. I'll get a horse. I'll walk if I have to. I'll follow you on my own." I took a deep breath. "But I am not leaving your side tonight."

He closed his eyes. "Fine." One word. But it was enough. Everything about this man was more than enough.

We ran down the stairs side by side, hands barely touching. And that was enough, too.

CHAPTER 34

FLORENCE

The city was burning. I had a dragon, and Veilmar was on fire. I had a dragon, and I was standing here, safe and sound, while Veilmar burned. Around me, students were crying. Kage and Regan brushed past. They were leaving. I had no idea what their plan was, but at least they were moving. They were trying.

Nyxaris! You saw this. You knew. Why didn't you stop him?

The dragon answered at once, voice glacier-cold. *I guard my rider. I am not the protector of a hive of highblood scum.*

There are blightborn in Veilmar, thousands of them! And children! Tears were running down my cheeks. My fists thudded against my thighs helplessly.

Long ago I ceased to weigh the value of your human cities or your human lives. He sounded remote, or as if he were purposely trying not to care about what I was telling him.

I felt Medra's hand slip into mine. She was weeping, too. Tears that left red tracks through the slash marks on her cheeks. She watched me, saying nothing.

Little children. Babies, I whispered. *Do their lives really mean nothing to you? I wish I could say the same. It must be easier to not care. But I do, Nyxaris. They mean a great deal to me.* Silence fell. I closed my eyes, filled with the most terrible sense of disappointment. If he wouldn't help me, we would be lost.

Long ago, I began to feel something for the humans' plight. I cared beyond all reason, all wisdom. Nyxaris's voice was bitter.

What do you mean?

For centuries, I lived as their teeth, as the highbloods' claws. I slew whoever they named. It was I who was the destroyer of cities. I who slaughtered little babes in their beds.

I was trembling. *That's not the Nyxaris I know. You aren't like that anymore.*

No? You think me safe? You think me gentle? I was their enforcer. Their fangs. And then . . .

And then? I ventured.

I lost my rider to their cruelty. Another pause. *Molindra, she came to me. Offered me a chance to mend what I had helped destroy. I surrendered my spirit. Chose the stone so I could . . . atone.*

The vision of Nyxaris willingly letting himself be bound shattered me.

You sacrificed yourself, I whispered. *That doesn't sound like a heartless monster to me.*

Nyxaris was quiet for what felt like eternity. Then, *If I fly, I risk losing you, as once I lost her.*

You won't lose me, I whispered. *And we have no choice. This is what we were meant to do. If we don't try to stop him, where will it end?* I swallowed. *I'm not brave. I never wanted this.*

You are everything you need to be. You are my rider.

If I am your rider, then we have to try. This is what we were brought together to do. You sacrificed yourself once because you knew it was the right thing to do. Help me now. Help me stop Blake.

Blake? Nyxaris growled. *That beast is not your friend's mate.*

My eyes widened. *What do you mean? But Medra said . . .*

That is Vorago, he snarled.

Medra stared at me as my expression changed.

"The red dragon," I whispered aloud to her. "The Inferni that stood guard in the court. Did Blake do something to it?"

Her expression was pained. "Viktor said Vorago was gone from the Dragon Court. That only a pile of ash remained."

Nyxaris's voice was tight with contempt. *Vorago was never a guardian. He was not one of us. He was imprisoned. Vorago was a hundred times worse than I, merciless and savage, even by Inferni standards. Uncontrollable. He reveled in ruin.*

"But you just said he sacrificed himself," I said aloud so Medra could hear me as well. "That the four dragons gave up their freedom to save Sangratha."

Nyxaris's laugh was jagged like broken glass. *Three dragons offered themselves. Vorago did not. Molindra, Alabryss, and I helped to bind him. The ritual required one dragon from each lineage. How he howled treachery as his scales hardened to stone!*

"How can that be?" I whispered. "How can that dragon out there be Vorago? You're saying Blake is just . . . gone?"

Medra's face was pale beneath her freckles. "I think Blake was changing and that he was resisting the change. I think he thought he could kill his own dragon. But somehow, he woke Vorago instead." She gripped both my hands with hers, watching my face as I waited for Nyxaris to answer.

The fool. The little highblood fool, Nyxaris snarled. *He meddled with magic he did not understand. A fool's bargain. Reaching for freedom, he has unleashed a second tyrant upon you all.*

Second? I whispered. *Who is the first?* I glanced at Medra's face again. "Medra, did Viktor do that to you?"

She nodded slowly.

Nyxaris, I whispered, terrified, *how many dragons are out there?*

One for now. But soon there may be two.

"Two dragons." I felt dizzy.

Listen, little rider. Vorago will not stop with Veilmar. He will scour Sangratha until nothing remains but ash.

I closed my eyes, searching for inner strength. *You once cared for the world or you wouldn't have let them turn you into stone. If you ever cared for anything, care for me. Care now.*

His memory brushed with mine. I saw a sky crackled with fire. A rider fell, her body covered in flames. Nyxaris's roar shook the heavens. Then stone, cold and eternal. Decades of loneliness and sorrow.

I paid for that caring with centuries of silence.

I held my breath.

Very well, little rider. I will do this. For you.

Relief flooded me—but beneath it, something else. Complete and utter panic. I squeezed Medra's hands back. "He'll help us." I thought of something. *Will you carry her, too?* Anxiety rose in my throat as I realized what I was committing to. *I've never fought from your back before. I can hardly hold a weapon. I'm no warrior. You know that. But Medra . . .*

The answer came swiftly. *No. You are my rider. You alone.*

But . . .

Prepare yourself. Then meet me on the tower parapet. Go swiftly.

All right, I whispered back. *I'm coming.*

I looked at Medra. "I don't know how I'll do this. I want to help. But I'm so scared."

She gripped my hands. "It's all right to be scared. I've never fought a battle where I wasn't frightened. You wouldn't be mortal if you weren't afraid."

"I need a plan. I need a weapon. I don't know how we're going to do this," I moaned. I crossed the corridor in a fog, moving back into the infirmary. Inside, Visha and Lysander stood at a table beside Professor Rodriguez and Professor Sankara.

Visha looked up as Medra and I walked in. "You're going after Blake."

I nodded slowly.

"She needs a weapon. She's skilled with a bow," Medra told Visha. *Skilled* was an overstatement. But I appreciated the vote of confidence.

Visha nodded. "We have weapons. We'll get her equipped."

"But I use a longbow," I babbled. "I can't use a longbow on Nyxaris's back. I won't be able to aim properly." Horseback would have been one thing. I might have been able to draw from a horse.

But Nyxaris's back was simply too broad for me to get a good position. Not without standing up—and I knew there was no way I'd be able to manage that.

"You'll need a crossbow," Medra said. "They're easier to handle. You'll adapt."

"I don't even have anything to shoot. What can get through dragon hide?"

"Dragon fire," Rodriguez said, looking at me. "When dragons fought in the past, crossbow bolts weren't enough to take them down."

I stared at him. "You mean when they were trying to kill one another. But I don't want to kill Blake. I just want to stop him."

That is not your friend's mate. How many times must I remind you? Nyxaris growled.

There has to be something of Blake still in there. It's not just Vorago. I refuse to believe that. We're not killing him.

I thought of something and looked at Rodriguez. "When you attacked Nyxaris, your arrows were coated with something that let you penetrate his hide."

"One step ahead of you." Rodriguez slid the leather satchel he'd been carrying when we came in onto the table and snapped the buckles open. From a padded niche, he drew out a small vial. The liquid inside was opaque—thick, sluggish, and tarlike.

"I only made a small amount . . . the last time." He glanced at Medra and me guiltily. "I had some left over. The Emberwatch called it Godsbane. According to our order's history, it's said that the dragons were once worshipped alongside the highbloods as gods."

I'd never known that. But it certainly did help to explain Nyxaris's attitude.

"You knew," Medra breathed, her eyes on Rodriguez. "You knew about Blake."

His face was stricken as he stared back at her. "I'm sorry. It will have to be . . . a conversation for another time."

"Can that shit kill the beast?" Sankara asked bluntly.

"That beast is Blake," Medra exclaimed.

"That beast," Sankara replied without rancor, "is murdering a city, Miss Pendragon."

"I want to stop him, not kill him," I said firmly. "Not unless there's no other choice."

Nyxaris, do you hear me?

The dragon was quiet.

Rodriguez shook his head. "Godsbane won't kill Blake—Vorago—whatever the hell that thing is. It can penetrate the hide. It can slow the dragon down." He looked over at me. "Depending on how many of these you can hit him with."

I gulped. "Probably not many." I realized everyone was looking at me.

Visha's eyes homed in on mine. "We need a way to reach Blake, not just slow him down. And in the meantime, what the fuck are we supposed to be doing while she's up there flying around?"

She was right. We didn't have the weapons to fight a dragon from the ground. Veilmar certainly must have at one point, ages ago, but not any longer. The highbloods had been so certain they'd be able to control Nyxaris that they hadn't even stopped to consider what might happen if a dragon rebelled and turned against them. Now Veilmar was completely exposed and unprotected.

"We'll safeguard the school," Lysander Orphos announced. "Our place is here." He looked at Medra and Visha. "Silvio Santos did not fall in the refectory. You saw?"

Visha nodded slowly. "You're right. There are still Bloodguards out there, from every house." Her lips twisted. "When highbloods are afraid, they attack the most obvious target."

"Blightborn." Medra looked at me, closed her eyes briefly, then opened them. "I trust you, Florence. You'll bring Blake back to me. I'll stay at the school. I'll help Lysander and the others protect the students here."

The ones who'd managed to survive this long. I forced myself to nod. Lysander's words had triggered something. I looked at the

House Orphos leader, a memory breaking through: Lunaya Orphos sitting at our bench in Professor Allenvale's alchemy class, her ghost-pale hair spilling around her shoulders as she reached out a hand to brush a leaf of emberfern.

"House Drakharrow would use it on their dragon riders. When prepared correctly, it was said to be able to amplify courage and strength."

"Emberfern," I murmured. At my feet, Neville let out a yap. I reached down, patting him absent-mindedly, impressed that he'd stuck around this long with all of the horrible things that were happening.

Rodriguez heard me. "The herb you've been studying for your project?"

I nodded slowly. "Emberfern was mixed with mirthleaf and given to riders of Inferni. If it worked on riders, specifically Inferni ones, what if it could work on Blake?" I chewed my bottom lip. "I've been analyzing it, and it's volatile when handled, yes, but powerful. I think there's more to it than we know."

"Blake's not a dragon rider, Florence. We don't know what he is—or even if there's anything left of him in there," Rodriguez pointed out.

I knew he was right. Still, I turned to Lysander. "If I could talk to Professor Allenvale about this, she might have some insight. She's in House Orphos. Could we get to her somehow?" I felt sure she'd tell me if this was a terrible idea or not."

Lysander glanced at Medra, then at Sankara. "I'm afraid that's not possible."

"What do you mean?" I demanded, glancing around the worktable. "Where is she?"

Sankara's massive shoulders sagged. "Child, we found her in the refectory. Viktor fed her to an infected guard."

I covered my mouth with my hands, but a sob slipped out. "No. No. Not Allenvale."

Professor Allenvale was sweet and kind and gentle. I remembered how delighted her face had been when she'd met Neville. I could feel Nyxaris in the back of my mind. Knew he was sensing my grief.

"I'm so sorry, Florence." Medra slipped her arm around my waist, and I leaned against her.

"Why?" I choked. "Why her?"

Sankara glanced at Rodriguez. "Viktor found out that she was leading a . . . rebellion."

"A rebellion?" I sputtered. "That's ridiculous. What kind of rebellion?"

"It's not so ridiculous, and she wasn't the only one," Rodriguez said quietly.

"House Orphos has been funding projects designed to bring about change at Bloodwing and in the rest of Sangratha," Lysander announced. "By any means necessary. Unfortunately, we were just getting started with this one when . . ."

I bristled. "When Professor Allenvale was murdered?"

"She was the best of us," Sankara murmured. "It's a terrible, terrible loss, and we feel it, believe me, Miss Shen. She's paid a terrible price."

"Vasanti was a true believer," Rodriguez said stubbornly. "She would never have backed down. It was a price she was ready to pay."

"The work she began will continue, in all of us." Lysander's eyes were fiery.

The Orphos leader looked at me, as if silently asking me to join them. Saving Veilmar was one thing. But a rebellion? Against what—all highbloods? Against the inequality I'd grown up with all my life? That system was embedded throughout Sangratha. How could you even fight something like that?

"At least Blake put Vasanti out of her fucking misery," Visha muttered, kicking at the leg of the table.

"What do you mean?" I whispered, my head whipping up to look at Medra. "*Blake* killed her?"

Medra's face had gone white.

Sankara answered. "When the boy became the dragon, he burned her. And the Bloodguard feeding from her."

I moaned as my mind pictured it all.

Lysander leaned forward. "It wasn't cruelty, Florence. It was mercy. I truly believe that. He only wished to end her suffering."

"Mercy," I repeated. I looked at Medra. "Then, that proves it, doesn't it? Something of Blake *is* in there. He's not gone."

"Right. But the next thing he did wasn't so fucking merciful." Visha's face was hard. "He flew straight to Veilmar."

Medra rubbed a hand over her eyes. "I think there's a battle going on inside of him. He's fighting for control. But right now . . ." she said as she shrugged helplessly " . . . Vorago is winning."

I looked at Rodriguez. "I won't stop trying to get Blake back, but Nyxaris is waiting. I have to go. Will you help me gather what I need?"

He nodded. No more arguments. Everyone began to move, all of us fueled by an overwhelming sense of urgency.

To my surprise, Visha began stripping. "We're about the same size," she said, eyeballing me as she started shrugging out of the black-and-cherry-red jerkin she was wearing. The leather had been cut thin and layered for strength, with overlapping pieces along the shoulders and a high collar. I held out my arms dutifully as she yanked the jerkin over my shoulders. Visha patted my stomach as she tightened the lacings. "It's soft leather. You'll still be able to twist and turn as you ride."

As she started to pull narrow crimson vambraces over my arms, I called out instructions to Rodriguez. He pulled the bottle of crushed mirthleaf I'd already prepared earlier from the cupboard along with a bundle of emberfern. "Wear gloves! The sap stings if it touches your skin."

He nodded and did as I said. I continued to call out the ratio of ingredients from memory, my mind harkening back to the books I'd read that echoed Lunaya's claim. The strongest recipe I'd read about had the highest ratio of emberfern and the lowest amount of mirthleaf. I decided we'd use that one. Rodriguez worked quickly, crushing the emberfern leaves with a mortar and pestle and then blending the two herbs together into a sticky mixture.

As he worked across the room, equipment was being spread out on the table before me. Lysander laid down a crossbow. The wood was lacquered in a rich shade of violet, and the trigger guard was inlaid with gold. The House Orphos motto was scrawled along the wood. *Blood of Dreamers.* I touched the words gently with a fingertip.

"This was my sister's," he said. "I know she'd want you to have it now."

Tears pricked the corners of my eyes. "I'm honored to carry it until she returns. I wish she were here with us."

A silver-and-black bolt case clattered down beside the bow. Kage's Second, Evie, stood there. I hadn't noticed her come in. "Avari scout bolts. Shorter quills, lighter shafts." She flicked open the lid to show twenty bolts nested inside, each fletched with raven feathers. "They're the best we have."

I nodded, trying not to show the fear I was feeling at the thought of actually firing a crossbow from dragonback.

As Visha finished dressing me, cinching greaves over the boots she'd given me, and now standing barefoot herself, Rodriguez came over holding a flask full of a copper-tinged syrup. Healer Elycia was beside him. Her expression focused, she started pulling on a second pair of gloves. Together they removed the bolts and began carefully coating them in the two mixtures.

Parapet. Now, Nyxaris's voice boomed in my skull.

"We're out of time," I whispered. "Nyxaris says I have to go."

Rodriguez set down the last of the bolts. "First, listen." He pointed to the first set of bolts. "Godsbane on its own will sting him. It'll slow his reflexes, steal some of his heat. But the coatings can't mingle together on a single quarrel—we have no idea what effect they could have on one another. They need to stay separate."

I nodded. "So I shoot with Godsbane bolts first."

"Yes. Then, if you're determined to try the emberfern mix—" he glanced at Medra, standing silently beside me "—well, Nyxaris will have to cut an opening for you."

My heart sped up. Not that it could go any faster at this point. "What does that mean?"

"It means exactly what it sounds like. He'll need to hit Vorago with a direct blast. Dragon fire is the only thing besides Godsbane that will penetrate Inferni scales. You'll shoot the emberfern bolts into the wound. We have no idea what Vorago's healing speed is like, so act quickly."

The entire room was hushed. The plan sounded less like strategy and more like a game of dice—a game I had very little chance of winning. I swallowed, turned, and found Medra watching me.

Her eyes were steady. "Do whatever you have to do to bring him back. The Blake I know would rather carry countless scars than wake from this with Veilmar's blood staining his soul." Her fingers closed over my forearm. "Don't flinch. Not even for a moment. You can do this."

I nodded. But surely it was too late. Whatever was left of Blake, tonight had stained his soul irrevocably. How could it not?

To my surprise, Professor Sankara clapped me on the shoulder next. "I've never had the honor of having you as my student, Miss Shen, but Professor Allenvale had only wonderful things to say. Remember her bravery, and let it drive you tonight. Luck usually boils down to quick thinking and courage. From what I can see, you have both in good measure."

I wasn't so sure about that, but I forced a wobbly smile. "Thank you."

Visha came towards me, holding a sheathed dagger. She tucked it into one of my greaves. "Come back safe."

I looked at all their faces, one by one, wondering if I'd ever see any of them again.

My eyes flew to Evie. "My mother . . ."

"We found her," Kage's Second said quickly. "She was barricaded in her room with some of the other librarians. An Avari team went out earlier to find them. She's unharmed." She hesitated. "She's down in the common room. Theo Drakharrow and his friend are sitting with her now. Do you want to see her before you go? She's been asking about you."

I closed my eyes, then shook my head. I knew Theo would tell her what was happening. "No. I have to go." I opened my eyes, looking at my dearest friend. "Medra . . ."

Her green eyes gleamed. "Yes, you *can*." She answered the question on the tip of my lips in a voice of steel.

My eyes watered, but I nodded. Then I slung the bolt case up over my shoulder, grabbed Lunaya's crossbow, and headed to the stairs.

There was a dragon waiting for me. And we had a city to save.

CHAPTER 35

FLORENCE

Wind howled along the crenellations as I burst out onto the parapet that rimmed the peak of the Avari tower. The balustrade was no higher than my hip. As I looked over, I could see Veilmar. Festooned in orange and scarlet, the city looked as if it were drowning in a terrible sunset.

Nyxaris waited, perched against the slate-shingled tower, a mountain of obsidian shadow. Even folded, his wings rose higher than the tower's spires. Every breath he took seemed to leave the parapet shuddering. My pulse stuttered as I thought about what we were about to do.

This is madness, I whispered.

Second thoughts?

But I knew I didn't have that luxury. I crossed the roof carefully, Lunaya's crossbow bouncing against my spine and the case of bolts at my hip.

A sharp bark sent me jumping out of my skin. I whirled around. "Neville?"

The fluffin stood by the stair hatch, his tail poufed outwards, his pointed ears flat against his head. He barked again, then scampered towards me, claws clicking on the flagstones. Reaching my boots, he sat down on his hind legs and chirped, then batted his paws at me, as if asking to be lifted.

"Oh, no." I crouched down. "Neville, it's too dangerous. You can't possibly—wait!"

He wriggled past me, darting towards Nyxaris's fore-claw and scrambling up his scales like a tiny mountain climber. As he reached the top of the dragon's back, he turned to face me with a determined stare. Another bark.

"Neville, get down from there," I scolded.

Let him come.

Hysterical laughter bubbled in my throat. *Let him come? He's the size of a puppy, and you want to take him into terrible danger?*

The small one has courage, the dragon rumbled, amusement and impatience mingling together.

On Nyxaris's back, Neville was carefully arranging himself into a little hollow I'd never noticed before—much too small to suit me, but one which fit him perfectly. A humming sound began to come from the fluffin's throat.

"What's he doing?" I whispered.

Nyxaris sighed. *He says the other belongs to him, too.*

Too?

The Duskdrake harrumphed. *It seems the audacious little creature has staked two claims.*

In you and Blake, you mean?

I've told him that the beast is Vorago. That the highblood boy is lost. He will not listen to reason.

I reached a decision quickly. "We don't have time for this." I set my foot between onyx scales and hauled myself up onto Nyxaris's neck as a cold wind cut across my cheeks. Neville's tail whipped back and forth, a clear sign of fluffin stubbornness if there ever was one. "I hope you know what you're doing," I muttered to him.

Hold tight. Nyxaris unfurled his wings with a thunder-loud crack. And then the tower dropped away beneath us. We speared through the air towards the blazing city. Neville squeaked triumphantly.

"I'm glad you're so optimistic," I whispered to the fluffin. "I must say I feel much less certain about our prospects. You know we could all die tonight?"

We cleared the tower, skimming beneath moon-washed clouds.

Steel yourself, little rider, Nyxaris said suddenly. *Dragon fire is not for the faint of heart. What you are about to witness may haunt you all the years of your life.*

Thanks for the encouragement, I whispered back, furiously. I was already terrified.

I say this not to terrify but to prepare you, he replied grimly. *There will be screams on the wind. The scent of burning flesh. You must not let fear stay your hands.*

As we neared Veilmar, I caught sight of blocks of rooftops sagging. Hundreds of houses were simply smoking husks of ash. The streets were clogged with people streaming towards the four gates that lay on each side of the city. I prayed many had been able to flee in time.

Then, there he was—the red dragon—slashing a new wound across the bleeding city. He flew over a line of buildings near the waterfront. His jaws parted, and an entire block disintegrated in flames, debris raining down onto the ships docked nearby.

Between the collapsing buildings ran tiny specks. People. The dragon swooped down like a hawk, grasping one between his talons, then hurling them back into his waiting jaws. I stared in horror as the dragon swallowed, a crimson glow lighting the inside of his throat as his feast was roasted alive.

He's not just burning the city. He's feeding on it.

Inferni become drunk on blood and ruin, Nyxaris answered. *Have no doubt, Vorago is enjoying this.*

I felt sick to my stomach. Nyxaris banked, wings beating hard against the air.

Get ready, he warned. *Terror is a chain. Do not let it wind itself around you or your city is lost.*

My hands shook as I reached for a bolt, setting it in Lunaya's crossbow. Then I slid forward, pressing my chest to the broad ridge that rose between Nyxaris's neck plates. Hugging it, I leaned the crossbow against it, stock wedged beneath my shoulder. Neville seemed absolutely unfazed by everything. The little hollow he'd settled in left him curled up near my right hip, the plume of his tail draping across my lower back like a blanket. It was oddly comforting.

"Hold steady," I whispered.

I already am, Nyxaris rumbled.

I tried to breathe in time with him—inhale on the wing rise, exhale as the wing fell. Vorago—Blake—I didn't know what the hell to call him—was breathing fire through the streets below. He hadn't seen us. Yet. I aimed. Exhaled. Squeezed.

The bolt vanished into smoke. At least a hundred feet short.

I loaded, aimed, fired again. And missed. The quarrel spun out uselessly into the dark.

I can't do this. My voice was filled with panic. *I'm hopeless. Take me back. Get Medra.*

That is not an option, Nyxaris growled. *Would you have me use fire?*

No, not yet.

Third bolt. I let the updraft guide me, then released. A spark blossomed as the shaft buried itself under the root of Vorago's right wing. The Inferni lurched, roaring. His serpentine neck snapped towards us, molten eyes narrowing.

My stomach plunged. "He's seen us."

It was only a matter of time, Nyxaris said, sounding much calmer than I felt.

Vorago shot upwards. Nyxaris folded one wing and dove. Flame sheeted overhead, and I screamed, reaching for Neville, who was still planted in place, his tail wound around me.

Get ready to fire again, Nyxaris commanded, as he leveled out over the harbor.

Lever, drag, nock. My shoulders burned. I loosed the bolt just as the Inferni blew fire across my sights. The quarrel flew wide. I shot another. Then another. And another.

Eighth bolt, I whispered.

Feel the wind. Let it guide your hand. Breathe with me.

THE WINGS THAT BIND

I tried my best to do as he said. Exhale. Squeeze. The quarrel sailed true. Vorago reeled, spinning through the air, and for a moment I thought he would crash to the ground. I held my breath.

The Inferni leveled, then rushed upwards.

"Oh, Bloodmaiden," I moaned as the dragon sped towards us. I ducked my head as fire spread from the Inferni's maw and Nyxaris turned, spinning us out of the way of the flames.

I've hit him with two bolts. Shouldn't he be slowing? You were nearly immobile at this point.

Inferni and Duskdrakes have different physiologies, Nyxaris pointed out. *But he is slowing, never fear. Mark him.*

He was right. Vorago staggered, his wings hitching for a few slow beats. *It's working,* I started to say, relief beginning to flood my body.

Then the great red head jerked up. A roar of fury tore across the sky. The Inferni powered forward with renewed energy.

Nyxaris let out a string of curses in Classical Sangrathan. *This was a mistake. Godsbane is not enough.*

I bit my lip. *Perhaps the mixture sat for too long. Or perhaps Rodriguez prepared the wrong ratio for Inferni.*

Whatever the reason, Nyxaris barked, *we change tactics. Now. I wound him with flame. Then you fire the emberfern bolts. If that does not work . . .*

Then, what?

It's us or him. Tell me you understand that.

I swallowed, then reached for an emberfern bolt. Nyxaris beat hard, black wings shuddering against the scorching wind. Below us, the once-magnificent city sprawled like spilled coals in a dying hearth. We flew over a once-grand square, white marble facades now smoking heaps. I glimpsed the tops of crescent-edged walls: the Avari compound. The palacelike structure was a jagged ring of rubble. Had Kage's family still been inside? There was no time to wonder. The Inferni soared towards us, flames licking from his jaws.

Hold fast, Nyxaris warned.

We dropped into a dive that left me screaming. The harbor water rushed up. Then Nyxaris ascended suddenly, climbing high, then rolling beneath the Inferni. I felt the Duskdrake's chest expand and the next thing I knew . . .

Whoosh. A column of flame spread out. Vorago shrieked in pain, banking wildly.

There. Now! Nyxaris cried.

It was easier said than done when we were flying at such a slant, but I braced my crossbow across his ridge, the world tilting around us. I fired, then moaned: The shaft vanished into the air.

Another, Nyxaris roared.

I fumbled, dropping a bolt into the sea below. I stared down at it in horror.

We cannot go backwards, rider. Only forwards. Try again.

I nodded, reaching for another, quickly fitting it into the bow. I fired. The shaft vanished towards Vorago's smoking wound—and this time, the dragon staggered.

His head swiveled towards us, red eyes flaring with hatred.

We flee to the east. We'll lure him away from the city. Nyxaris banked towards the countryside. In his wake, Vorago followed, roaring with a vengeance.

The wind tore at my face. Neville pressed against me tighter. I clenched the next bolt, the black feathers trembling between my fingers. "Blake," I whispered as the Inferni flew behind us. "If there's anything left of you in there, please find it now. Come back to us. Please. Medra needs you." I suddenly imagined a conclusion in which the Inferni's body plummeted to the ground, covered in Nyxaris's flames. I glanced back. The Inferni's jaws were opening for another bout of flames.

Nyxaris wheeled, spinning us back through the air. *Now,* he commanded.

I aimed, praying to the Bloodmaiden with all I had. I squeezed. The ember-slick bolt flew through the air, striking just beneath the red dragon's left eye ridge. Vorago shrieked in rage, the earsplitting sound scraping my nerves raw. Before I could equip another bolt, Neville scrambled over my hip and up Nyxaris's spine. He planted his tiny paws between two plates, claws digging in effortlessly, and lifted his head high to the night. What left his throat was not a bark or a yelp—but a song. A melody, soft as a lullaby, drifted out onto the wind.

Vorago faltered. His wings beat more slowly. His head swung towards us, but the blazing red eyes seemed dimmed. A moment ago, they'd been coals of hatred. Now I sensed bewilderment there. Even pain.

Hold, I whispered, putting my hand against Nyxaris's neck as I felt him begin to swell for another strategic blast. *Wait. Let's see what happens.*

Neville sang on, his tail streaming behind him like a banner. The lullaby slipped through the air. I could almost imagine it, wrapping the Inferni in threads of delicate sound. Vorago shuddered. Then the Inferni turned, banking away from the city and heading out towards the sea.

"He's retreating." My voice cracked. Neville had stopped singing. Now I reached for the fluffin, squeezing him until he squeaked. "Neville, you ridiculous, amazing little creature. How did you *do* that?"

The fluffin gave a soft yip, then flopped back against my chest, panting hard.

Healing magic. Nyxaris's voice quivered with stunned relief. *I had forgotten*— His words cut off. I felt him freeze beneath me. Then he turned, banking back towards the city, spinning to face the three islands that bordered the city. Far above the Black Keep, a shape tore free of the clouds. A second Inferni, red as blood, but with wings marbled with black veins.

Nyxaris growled. *Viktor.*

Dread slid down my spine as the dragon angled straight towards us. I looked down at the few bolts I had left. It was time for round two.

CHAPTER 36

REGAN

Kage's wolf burst through Bloodwing's gates like a winter storm made flesh.

It had been the work of a moment. One second, Kage stood before me, a highblood man. The next, he was a silver-gray wolf, the size of a carriage horse. He'd hardly spoken to me since we'd left the tower. But now he crouched low enough for me to climb up. I sat astride, hardly believing where I was. A wolf was like a dragon in one regard: It had no reins, no saddle. I couldn't even imagine suggesting such things. So instead, my fingers sank deep into the rough scruff at his shoulders, and my thighs pressed onto his back, as his muscles pounded beneath me.

We hit the causeway leading towards the city at a dead run. Already, blightborn refugees clogged the road. Families dragging worn carpet bags and heavy trunks. Mothers clutching wailing infants, and fathers holding children by the hand. One woman drove a wagon, one side of her face horrifically burned. Behind her crouched twenty or more terrified-looking children, many of whom were also burned and bleeding.

Kage barreled through the crowd. Some people screamed at the sight of him. They were heading to Bloodwing, I realized. Four gates lay on each side of the city, one led to the three causeways connecting the mainland to the Sanctum, the Black Keep, and Bloodwing. I looked across the water and in the distance saw the causeway to the Sanctum was similarly clogged. Only the bridge to the Black Keep was empty.

I glanced behind me at Bloodwing's red facade, wondering what kind of reception they'd be greeted with when they got there. For a moment, I thought of sliding off Kage's back and returning to the school. Without me, what would the Bloodguard do to these people?

Someone else would step up, I reminded myself. They already were. Someone far more capable than I—Rodriguez, Pendragon, even Visha. They'd welcome these people. They'd shield them.

Guilt pricked inside my chest as a woman passing by saw my face. She gasped and pulled back, holding her baby to her breast in fear. These people weren't merely afraid of Kage. They knew me. It was my face they were afraid of.

I twisted, looking back at her as we crossed over to the mainland, longing to shout apologies. Knowing my voice would be lost on the wind—and that it was useless. A lump was in my throat. It was hard to fight the urge to dismount. To help lift a fallen child. To lead the people to the school and fling open the doors. To apologize for what my archon had wrought. But what blightborn in their right mind would accept my apology?

We passed another group of refugees. They darted to the side, recoiling from the wolf and me. Kage must have sensed my regret, his ears flattened as if to say he understood. Then a growl rumbled up my legs—a warning to stay alert. I faced forwards as we approached the city. If I never came back from this, I decided, then at least I would fall trying to stop Viktor from ever returning, too. If I could do that, then Persis would truly be safe. Maybe this was the only way he ever would.

Veilmar loomed, a city painted in shades of flame. Above the rooftops, a terrible duel was being waged. Nyxaris's obsidian scales sped across the sky. I watched as the Duskdrake drove the Inferni back with bursts of fire. From this distance, I couldn't see Florence. Was she still clinging to Nyxaris's back, or had Blake's dragon thrown her to the ground?

The red dragon fought like a terrible god, screaming and swooping through the sky. I watched in horror as the Inferni descended, plunging through a crowd of panicked people, and tossing some up into his jaws before speeding upwards again. Splatters of blood rained down. I imagined I could hear the crunch of bones, and my stomach heaved.

How could this beast be the Blake Drakharrow I knew? How could this have happened to him?

We were inside the city now. Kage raced on. Around us, stores where I'd once shopped for clothes and trinkets were now piles of gray rubble. We passed a shop still standing. I glimpsed my reflection in the shattered front window: a highblood girl with blood on her forehead, silver hair streaming as she held onto a wolf's back. My father would say what I was doing was madness, sheer folly. That I was betraying our family. So why did it feel like destiny?

Kage picked up his pace, leaping over piles of debris, every stride jolting through my spine. We passed a street full of highblood mansions, each one toppled to the side like books fallen over on a shelf. A burning rafter crashed down in a spray of sparks. Kage leaped to avoid it. I leaned down, pressing my cheek to the heat of his neck and closing my eyes. His breath came in savage gusts. A low thunder rumbling from his chest.

We turned, taking a corner at a breakneck pace, and raced onto Bloodwine Square—or what was left of it. The street was the pinnacle of Veilmar highblood society. Now only a few of its lavish manors remained standing. The Avari compound was at the center of palatial dwellings, a grand and luxurious white marble mansion. Only now, jagged ribs of marble sat where the compound used to be. In the center lay a crater, surrounded by smoldering wreckage. Kage stopped so suddenly that I fell forward against his shoulders with a gasp. He threw back his head and howled, pacing towards the crater's edge, tail lashing.

"They might not have been here," I whispered. "Perhaps they've all fled. They might have escaped."

The wolf's answer was a raw snarl.

"Kage," I breathed, laying a hand upon his neck. "Look."

Above, the two dragons had been clashing against a background of stars. Now I watched as the Inferni sped away from the city, the dragon's pace slower than before. He angled out towards the open sea without turning back. Could this possibly be over?

"Nyxaris must have driven him off." Relief flooded through me.

But Kage clearly did not share the same sentiment. With a growl, he bounded forward, clearly furious at the thought that Blake might be getting away and intent on revenge.

"Wait," I cried, my fear spiking. If we chased after Blake now, we'd never find Viktor. Kage seemed to sense my panic and skidded to a halt just in time.

"Kage, look!" I shouted, pointing upwards.

A new silhouette tore through the sky like a jet of blood: a second Inferni. But this one's wings were veined with black. I didn't have to guess where the second dragon had come from or who it was. I could feel my archon's malice rolling off it.

"Viktor," I whispered. I stared at the blackened veins. Was this the same kind of corruption that had infected highbloods?

Kage held very still, his ears laid flat. The sight of the tainted Inferni filled me with dread. Whatever happened, I knew one thing: I wasn't going back to the Black Keep. I would never lie on my back for Viktor again. I would never again do his bidding in a vain quest for power. That Regan died tonight.

"Please. Viktor is the one behind this. Whatever Blake has done, Viktor is truly to blame. We have to stay. We have to help stop this." I lowered my voice to a whisper. "I won't be dragged back to him. I'd rather die." I paused, my voice choking. "If we can stop him, then my brother . . ."

The wolf turned his head, amber eyes looking back into mine with gentle understanding. Then his muzzle brushed my thigh. He bounded forward. We climbed shattered terraces, leaping over fallen rooftops, making our way higher and higher until I realized where Kage was going: the Peacebringer's Hill. It was the highest ground in Veilmar. He ran up the hilltop, claws scrabbling over grass. Usually the hill was a parklike place, full of people. Now it was deserted. The green slopes stretched out, broken only by cobblestone paths and cultivated gardens. It seemed as if it was one of the few places in the city that remained unscathed.

From atop the perch of the hill, we watched a new battle play out as Viktor's darker, red dragon flew after Nyxaris, cruelty and corruption in every beat of his wings. The Duskdrake streamed across the heavens to meet him, jaws spreading wide, his fire burning so hot it appeared white. He wasn't taking any of Viktor's bullshit. Florence's dragon seemed intent on annihilating my archon—and I found myself holding my breath, silently cheering them on.

Torrents of fire hit Viktor like a siege, flames splashing against the Inferni's chest and lighting up his scarlet scales. We could hear the Inferni's shrieks from where we stood. I sucked in a breath as Viktor dove straight for Nyxaris's throat. For a moment the two dragons thrashed together, their bodies intertwined, and I thought the battle was over, that Nyxaris couldn't withstand the onslaught. Then I saw a crossbow bolt glimmer in between blasts of fire. One little silver pinprick arced upward—hammering straight into Viktor's chest.

"Florence!" My face was wet. Beneath me, Kage's hackles bristled with anticipation. I dug my fingers into his soft scruff, feeling every thrum within his chest. Above, Nyxaris exhaled in a molten wall of fire. The flames rolled over Viktor, clinging and chewing through scale and flesh. The red dragon thrashed, beating at the flames, but I could see it was no use. A huge, ragged hole was blooming in the center of one wing.

"Fall, you bastard," I whispered, my palms tingling against Kage's fur. "Burn and fall."

Viktor roared, and I shivered. His dragon tail whipped, his ruined wing convulsing and shriveling in on itself. Then, in a rush of smoke and embers, the Inferni began to drop. He pitched down, nose first, spiraling once, twice, flames streaming from his wounds like a corrupted falling star.

My eyes widened. "Kage!"

The trajectory of his fall was clear—Viktor would land at the bottom of the hill, no more than a hundred paces down the slope from us.

The great silver wolf spun, paws skidding on loose stones in his eagerness. We bolted down the hillside towards the descending dragon.

CHAPTER 37

FLORENCE

For one brief moment, I thought we'd done it. Nyxaris's last blast had left Viktor aflame. The Inferni was reeling and shrieking. Blake was gone. We'd defeated Vorago. Now Viktor was falling, too.

Neville shivered against my breast. The fluffin let out a strangled whimper.

"What—" I started to say.

The sky split. A red shape shot up from below us. Viktor drove himself upwards with murderous speed, ramming his jaws straight into Nyxaris's throat. My dragon roared. The impact snapped through the Duskdrake's body. I felt his pain echo through my ribs and screamed.

"Nyxaris!" I could hear the scales snap. Feel the hot blood as it splattered across my cheeks.

Fireheart . . . Nyxaris's voice was strangled.

"Hold on!" I clamped Neville to my chest, fishing for a Godsbane bolt.

Breathe. Steady, now, I warned myself. This is no time to mess up. I wedged the crossbow over the dragons' ridge, scanning the Inferni as he banked away from Nyxaris. There: a patch of scar tissue where Viktor's corrupted scales overlapped.

I squeezed. The bolt slammed home, just below his sternum. Viktor recoiled with a screech, diving away.

Nyxaris's blood was flowing heavily, streaming down his neck.

But he wasn't backing down. His chest inflated, every plate along his neck suddenly glowing furnace-bright. An inferno erupted from his jaws. Flames wrapped across Viktor's left wing, the membrane instantly catching the blaze.

The Inferni beat his wings, desperately trying to smother the fire, but the Godsbane I'd shot into him was tunneling through his blood, slowing him down. A hole slowly formed, getting larger and larger. Viktor lurched, lost lift, and began to wobble. First a slight topple, then a sudden plunge. Down, down he fell, towards the city below.

"You did it," I breathed. "Nyxaris, you did it!"

I waited for him to turn, to dive, to follow Viktor down to the ground so we could finish him off once and for all. But my dragon didn't answer.

Beneath my palms, I suddenly realized his scales were slick. *Nyxaris, talk to me.*

I peered over the curve of his neck, Neville still whimpering against me. Blood poured from the gash Viktor's fangs had opened. The wound smelled strange. Foul. *Wrong.* Gallons of dragon blood poured out, falling onto the city below.

I felt choked with panic. *Nyxaris, you're wounded. We need to get you down to the ground. Land. Land now.*

Fireheart, he rasped, *you are safe. That is . . . sufficient.*

That's not sufficient for me. I don't care about Viktor. I care about you. Now, land, dammit.

Nyxaris began to drop. A pulse of amusement brushed my thoughts. *Very well, little rider. I shall obey.*

For once in your life, I muttered, trying to make him laugh. But no such luck. His breathing had grown unsteady. I closed my eyes, matching my breaths to his—steady where they were broken, trying to force him to match my rhythm. His wings angled downwards as we flew towards the edge of the city. We circled, then landed in an open field.

I slid from his back, opening my arms to catch Neville as he jumped. My crossbow fell at the ground at my feet, the instrument of violence suddenly feeling unwelcome and unnecessary.

Talk to me. I moved to Nyxaris's head, wiping my blood-soaked hands on my thighs, then running them gently over his scales. *How bad is it?*

The dragon's head lowered until the tip of his muzzle rested in the trampled grass. I pressed both palms to the great line of his jaw, feeling the warm blood seeping through my fingers, then leaned down, resting my forehead against his warm snout.

How bad is the bite? I whispered. *Tell me, Nyxaris.*

Fireheart, such worry does not suit you.

I gave a ragged laugh. *Fireheart? Why do you keep calling me that? Worryheart, more like. I worry every moment of my life. You know me. You know that.* I hiccupped. *Now, you're bleeding like a fountain. Tell me how deep the bite is. Tell me what I can do.*

A tiny scratch. Pay it no mind. Calm your racing heart.

He lifted his head, trying to nudge my cheek with his nose—an awkward, affectionate bump. My heart went very still. It was the first time he'd ever done such a thing.

Stop changing the subject, I insisted. The fact that he kept doing so frightened me more than if he'd given me a straight answer.

You must have wondered why I never ended Viktor before now. The truth is I tried.

I have never wondered. I have never doubted you. You don't need to explain yourself to me.

He ignored me. *I knew him once. Long ago. He is a remnant of a former world. One I thought we had wiped clean.*

I stared. *Before you were turned to stone, you mean?*

Yes. In the tower, that day, I finally recognized his stench. When he threatened you, I knew he could not live. I sensed what he was. But he has always valued that particular secret greatly. He paused, his breathing heavy. *We all have secrets, fireheart.*

You mean you knew he could shift into a dragon? That he was like Blake?

In dragon form, he is nearly indestructible, Nyxaris continued. I got the feeling he wasn't ignoring me so much as he needed to get the words out. *So I stalked the highblood man instead. I waited. Hunting. But he was canny, traveling only underground, through tunnels that lie beneath the sea.*

Medra told me about those tunnels. She said they lead to the Sanctum and Veilmar, too.

Yes. Around his chambers in the Black Keep, wards had been drawn up. Sigils of blood magic. Powerful and potent. Nyxaris drew a heaving breath, and my heart froze. He exhaled, and I let out my breath. *I knew you would not wish for me to attack him in the school. The loss of life would have been . . . significant.*

Thank you for that, I whispered. *You're right.*

Yet now I wondered just how right I was. If Nyxaris had attacked Viktor in highblood form when he'd had the chance, would he be here now, bleeding in my arms?

He was nearly in my grasp that day in the tower. But he fled like the coward he has always been. Another sigh, more ragged than the last. *I forced you to accept the engagement. Forced you to lower yourself by accepting the hand of a man you . . . did not care for. I let another do what I should have done.*

That's over now. You've always tried to protect me. I ran my hand along his jaw. *You always do your best. I trust you. I will always trust you.*

I would matter little to you if I could not keep you safe.

A shard of ice pierced my heart. *Not true.* I shook my head. *You matter to me because you're you. Not because you're some kind of a shield.* I leaned my head against his scales. *You saved Veilmar. You saved me. You've tried to protect me, even when I never knew it, even when I didn't deserve it.*

You deserve a very great deal, fireheart. Far more than I can give. Nyxaris drew a gasping breath. *Tonight, I went to the refectory. I was so close. I nearly had him. As soon as I appeared, he melted away. Vanished before I could sink my teeth into him.*

Don't worry about Viktor now, I whispered. *We'll finish him off. Together. His time is over. Tell me how you feel. Tell me how I can help you.*

His breath warmed my face. *You are . . . absurdly stubborn.*

I laughed shakily. *We're quite a pair, then, aren't we?*

Neville was at my feet, winding between my ankles. He'd stopped whimpering. I picked him up, holding him against me and the dragon. His owl-like eyes opened wider—and they began to glow.

Fireheart, you cannot save me now, my dragon murmured.

My heart hammered. *What do you mean? Nyxaris, what are you saying?*

The fluffin made a little growling sound that sounded stubborn, even to me.

The audacity. Nyxaris sighed.

Three stubborn creatures, I whispered. The fluffin wriggled in my grip. "Easy," I murmured. "What is it, Neville?"

To my shock, he answered with a wheezing snort, then hacked up an enormous wad of orange straight into my palm. I yelped. Then I sniffed. The lump smelled familiar. "Emberfern!" I stared at the chewy lump of pulp, my palm already tingling. Slowly, I looked at the field around us.

The field was full of stalks of golden wheat. But scattered in between the gold were shorter, slender shoots of green tipped with orange fronds.

Fireheart, it is pointless. The poison in the highblood's fangs was older than kingdoms and more loathsome than the grave.

I flinched from the truth, the words like a dagger to my heart. "Pointless, my eye," I snapped aloud. "You're the most important thing in the world to me, Nyxaris. When will you get that through your thick dragon skull?"

I was having a kind of epiphany. Placing the fluffin gently on the ground, I walked around to the side of the dragon's neck where the gash began.

What are you doing? Nyxaris sounded weary yet curious.

Good. That meant he hadn't given up hope.

Wait and see. Hesitating only a moment, in my palm I scrunched the sticky wad Neville had been chewing, then slapped it across the bleeding gash. A hiss like the quenching of coals rose up. Tendrils of smoke spiraled from the wound. My hand burned. I yanked it back. Then grinned in triumph. Where the emberfern touched, the skin beneath the broken scales was tightening and pulling inwards. The bleeding in that area slowed to a trickle.

I ran into the field, ripping up fistfuls of emberfern, shredding the fronds between my fingers until the sap ran in fiery rivulets. My eyes watered. The plant burned my skin worse than nettles I'd once had the misfortune to sit in as a small child, but I barely felt the pain over the hammering in my heart. This could work, I thought.

I wrenched and tore, racing back and forth between the field and Nyxaris, slapping handful after handful of the emberfern mash onto the gaping gash along his neck.

Slowly, the edges of the scales began knitting together like ripped cloth made whole.

"It's working," I crowed. "You see? You just have to stay stubborn a little longer. That's all."

But Nyxaris didn't answer. The fluffin had climbed back onto the dragon. Now he sat on Nyxaris's shoulder ridge, his tiny head tipped back, and began to sing again.

"Nyxaris?" I laid both my blistering palms against his muzzle. "Talk to me. Please."

His massive chest had fallen into a more shallow rhythm, I realized abruptly. Each breath was shorter than the last.

"Nyxaris . . ." Panic flooded my veins. "No, no, no."

Neville's song rose in a sudden, piercing swell. The little fluffin's throat vibrated and puffed.

I looked up at him. "Neville?"

His large eyes glowed down at me. Everything about the tiny creature was glowing, I realized. He sat in an aura of golden light. The fluffin suddenly sprang forward, leaping into my hands, as the world . . . tilted. Nyxaris's vast form shuddered. His wings folded close, trembling.

"What's happening?" I whispered. "Nyxaris?"

I staggered back, my mouth dry, heart slamming against my ribs, as light flared from the creature in my arms—blinding and purifying.

CHAPTER 38
MEDRA

The refugees were at the door, but the doors weren't opening. They were being held firmly shut. I moved towards the vaulted foyer at the front of a column, flanked by Visha on one side and Lysander on the other. Behind us came Theo, Vaughn, Evie, Rodriguez, Sankara, and a mix of students from all three houses. A crowd of blightborn and highbloods blended together in a mishmash of red and purple, gold and silver and black. Some might have said the colors clashed. I thought they were beautiful together.

We could hear the banging on the doors as we reached the top of the stairs. The sounds of heavy oak panels rattling beneath the fists of the hundreds of refugees trapped outside. Cries bled through the cracks. Men shouting, women pleading, children crying.

Between us and those doors stood House Mortis. Silvio Santos, his pale blond hair plastered back against his tan skin, white-and-crimson steel armor hugging his frame, stood shouting orders. He and his lackeys had obviously been there for some time. They'd dragged banquet tables from the refectory into the entranceway, pulling them across the doors in a makeshift barricade. Above, at each end of the mezzanine, stood a dozen or more House Mortis students armed with bows. They'd smashed the windows overlooking the courtyard. Now they held position—some looking eager, others uncertain—as Silvio shouted at them to prepare to shoot. Around the foyer, other students looked on in silence, sitting on the floor or leaning against colonnades, gaping, hesitating, weary—neither obeying nor intervening.

"Tell me I'm fucking imagining this," Theo whispered, coming up beside Lysander with Vaughn.

"I wish you were," Lysander said.

"These aren't all House Mortis students," Sankara observed.

"No, there are blightborn here, too. They fear the ship is sinking." Rodriguez's voice was laced with disgust. "They'll take the side of least resistance."

"You mean the side most likely to win," Visha said starkly.

"That would be us," I said firmly. "They're outnumbered. And this isn't fucking happening. We are better than this."

"We?" Theo raised his eyebrows. "You including highbloods in that statement?"

"Well, you're here, aren't you? Standing beside me, holding a blightborn's hand." I looked around the group. "And Visha, Lysander, Sankara, Evie." I met the Avari girl's eyes, and she nodded tightly. "You're all here because you've had enough. We've all fucking had enough."

Something inside of me had snapped the moment Blake had flown out the window. He was out there, somewhere beyond these walls, flying with wings that weren't his own. Carried forth by Viktor's lust for control, tormented by his uncle's desire for power. I didn't know if I'd ever see the man who formed the other half of my heart again. If I'd ever hear his laugh. See him smirk lazily in that way that turned my blood to fire. Hear him call me Pendragon, as if it were both a challenge and a promise. Hear him snarl *mine*.

But this was *our* fucking school—Blake's and mine. Our strange, brutal, beautiful Bloodwing. It had shaped us, brought us together, made us into who we were, for better or for worse. And while it was still standing and while the blood ran in my veins, there was plenty I could do to keep it truly ours.

Outside those doors were hundreds of innocent blightborn. Maybe I couldn't save Blake tonight. But I could save *them*.

Silvio's voice rang across the foyer. "Archers, prepare to fire on my mark!"

"Put your weapons down," I roared, stepping up to the balcony rail. "Belay that order. Open the doors, Silvio."

The Mortis leader laughed. "Not a fucking chance. So you crawled out of the refectory alive, did you?"

"We noticed you ran and left the rest of your Bloodguards to die," Visha spat.

Silvio waved a hand. "I went back to my tower to rally my house to serve Lord Drakharrow. There are many Bloodguards here with me now."

I took in the scattered badges. Too many for my liking.

"Rally them to do what? To attack more blightborn?" Theo demanded.

"Blightborn students are right here with us," Silvio said dismissively. "Look around. They support our cause."

"Oh really? And what cause is that? Because it looks to me like you're preparing to slaughter hundreds of innocent people who just fled a dragon," I said flatly. "And if you think we're going to just stand here and watch you do that, you've got another thing coming."

Silvio sneered. "Go back to your kennel, Pendragon. House Mortis stands proud. We answer to no one, certainly not some blightborn bitch."

Visha hissed. Lysander bristled. I lifted a hand—*Wait*. The door behind Silvio shuddered as blows rang down upon it from the outside. A baby's wail carried through the broken windows. One of the archers, a blightborn First Year, flinched, his bow drooping.

"What would you have us do?" a Mortis highblood girl shouted up at us, her face angry. "If we let them in, they could be infected."

"It isn't the blightborn who are infected," I called back. "It's the highbloods. They turn when bitten by another infected highblood. Blightborn are immune."

Murmurs rang out around the hall. They weren't all House Mortis, I realized. There were Drakharrow students mixed in with Silvio's supporters, too. I recognized Quinn, Larissa, Gretchen, and Edward. Lucian Aleron was missing, though. He hadn't made it out of the refectory—Visha had seen to that. A few students' clothes flashed purple and gold. Others black and silver.

"Lies!" Silvio declared. "She lies to save her skin. If we let this horde of rabble into the school, we'll be slaughtered."

"Look at the people by my side," I said, loud enough to be heard over the banging at the door. "They're highbloods and blightborn. They come from all houses."

"I don't see Kage Tanaka with you," Silvio sneered. "Clearly he doesn't support whatever the hell this is."

"It's an insurrection," I said coolly. "Believe me, Kage would love to be here. But I'm afraid he's gone into the city to try to stop a fucking dragon." I could only hope he found the right one.

More murmurs broke out at that. I knew Kage would be here backing me up if he could.

"So has my friend, Florence Shen, the rider of the Duskdrake. She's flown into Veilmar with Nyxaris and right now is fighting to stop the massacre that's taking place—a massacre that was ordered by Lord Viktor Drakharrow." I let that bombshell explode as the room burst into noise.

"Viktor Drakharrow believed it was better to burn Veilmar to the ground than try to save it," I shouted. "He'd rather kill blightborn and highbloods so that he can consolidate power over us all."

The room slowly fell silent.

"Viktor wants to divide us. To divide this school. Just look at the rules he had our new headmistress put in place. He'd have us at one another's throats," I went on.

"That's the highblood way," Quinn shouted. "Our fangs at your throats." Around her, a small group of highblood students cheered.

I scowled. "I'm speaking to those of you who haven't decided to support Silvio or Quinn or any of the highbloods intent on keeping the status quo," I said, once they'd quieted down. "I'm speaking to all those of you who know this is wrong. Who have always known." I pointed down into the crowd at a blightborn girl who sat weeping on the stairs. "How old were you when you knew? How old were you when you felt it in your bones?"

The girl slowly pushed herself to her feet. "I was seven. Seven when a highblood woman fed from my father. She enthralled him, and he followed her back to her home. That was the last time we saw him."

I pointed at a House Mortis student who leaned against a colonnade. He was a highblood but something in his face told me he didn't want to be there. "And you? How old were you?"

"I was twenty," he said quietly but loud enough that we could hear. "I knew tonight. When I watched Silvio kill a blightborn girl who tried to stop him from barricading these doors."

"This struggle feels impossible, doesn't it?" I said.

He nodded. "Hopeless."

"Yet all over Sangratha, I guarantee you it's happening. Thousands upon thousands of people are fighting their own small rebellions." I thought of Regan, trapped beneath Viktor's thumb and, worse, sharing his bed. And yet clearly something in her was rising up, slowly but surely. I thought of the way she'd gone with Kage into the city, the way she'd rescued Florence and Neville, and stopped her own Bloodguards from feeding on Dani.

"Some of them are blightborn, some are highbloods. We may not know them. But we are them. We are united." I took a deep breath. "This plague, this illness, is terrifying. It creeps across Sangratha. It threatens us all. But it's brought one truth out into the light, something each of us has always known. Sangratha is wounded. Sangratha is broken. And if it takes a disease to show us we all stand in darkness, so be it. Let that disease unite us as one."

"What the fuck is that even supposed to mean?" Silvio scoffed.

I leaned closer to the rail. "It means Bloodwing is a battleground. This is our school. This is where we make our stand. Orphos or Avari, Drakharrow or Mortis. Anyone ready to stand up against tyranny is welcome to join us."

And then, while Silvio stood there gaping at my words, I moved.

Faster than I had ever moved in my life. Faster than wildfire. Faster than lightning. As fast as a highblood. I moved with the power of Blake's blood. One moment, I was by the rail. The next I was beside Silvio with a knife to his throat. "You *will* open the doors," I said in his ear, my dagger brushing his skin.

Up on the mezzanine, every weapon in my motley company rose as one.

Lysander stepped forward. "The rest of you will drop your weapons." He glanced at Visha and Evie, and I saw them nod. "As of this night, all highblood house boundaries are dissolved. Any student from House Mortis wishing to join any of our three houses may do so and be welcomed."

Visha stepped up beside him. "Similarly, any student in any house who believes in highblood supremacy, who believes that students should be drained in our halls, who believes blightborn lives are not just as sacred as our own, you are no longer welcome in House Drakharrow."

"Or House Avari," Evie said loudly.

"Or House Orphos," Lysander echoed.

"You hear that, you fucking bitch?" Visha called down to Quinn. She gestured to the group around Quinn. "All of you? You're out. Get your shit, and go to House Mortis. You're no longer in Drakharrow."

"You can't do this," Quinn seethed. "Our parents—"

"Will be dealt with next," Lysander said quietly.

"This is how a revolution begins," Rodriguez said, coming to stand beside the three. "If you wish to continue attending school here during these unique revolutionary times, Miss Riley, I suggest you fall in line." He pointed to the doors. "Otherwise, the door leading out will soon be open. Feel free to make your way into the city. I understand it's a little hot there this evening. You may wish to dress for the weather."

"We don't want to spill any more blood in these halls," I declared. I withdrew my dagger, giving Silvio a savage shove. He staggered away from me, rubbing his neck and gnashing his teeth. "We don't want to fight you," I went on. "We're asking you to make a choice. If you want to follow Silvio and his like, then leave now. We'll let you go in peace. But these doors behind me are opening. For those of you who stay, you'll help us tend to the refugees. Bloodwing will give them a place until they can return to their homes."

"Just don't forget, we have a fucking dragon on our side," Visha called as students began to scatter. "Yeah, Quinn, you little bitch. You'd better run." She snarled gleefully as Quinn began to trot up the stairs, heading towards one of the side passages, Edward and the others clambering after her. Then she hopped the railing, jumping down effortlessly into the middle of the foyer, and punched me lightly in the shoulder. "Let's get these tables cleared away. We have work to do."

I nodded, and together we turned to the doors of our school.

CHAPTER 39

REGAN

The impact of the dragon's fall shook the hill like a hammer smashing glass when Viktor's burning body slammed into the meadow.

As the blast of heat and wind tore over us, I was hurled off Kage's back. For a single moment, I was weightless—flying like a dragon. Then I crashed down onto the grass, skidding to a stop. Pain flared along my arm. Blood welled up where a shard of red scale had slit my wrist open to the bone. Kage growled, bounding to my side. He nudged the gash with his nose. I gasped as he dragged his rough tongue over the wound.

A roar shattered the moment. I stared past Kage in horror to where Viktor was hauling himself up. He'd shed most of his dragon form, but crimson scales armored his torso. Black-veined red wings furled from his back, one horribly crushed and ragged.

He hadn't seen us yet.

Kage's lips peeled back to bare his fangs, his chest rumbling in a snarl. He sprang, a silver blur spinning towards the red. The wolf was massive, but the dragon was larger. Viktor turned as the wolf came towards him, his eyes widening. I saw him lift his arms, draconic talons snapping outwards.

The two beasts collided, canine fangs sinking into scale. Sharp talons scraping flesh and fur. Although Viktor was bigger than the wolf by far, he was already wounded, and he staggered under the wolf's weight. Kage's jaws reached down, finding the soft seam where red plating ended. The wolf's teeth tore, and black blood splattered the earth. Viktor let out an unearthly roar as the wolf sank his teeth in a second time, ripping and shredding at the monstrous highblood.

I lay where I'd fallen, my heart heavy in my chest, my own wound forgotten, everything in me praying to the Bloodmaiden for the wolf's victory. For Kage's safety.

Viktor slammed at the wolf with a taloned fist, sending him careering against a nearby boulder with a sickening thud. I screamed as Kage yelped. He tried to rise as Viktor descended upon him, talons ripping across the wolf's flank, cutting through the beautiful silver coat and exposing flesh.

"No!" I screamed.

I pushed myself off the ground, slipping and sliding down the slope. The wolf lay beside the boulder, his blood soaking the grass, still struggling to rise. "Stop," I whispered. "Rest." I slid to my knees beside him, pressing both hands against his torn side. My wrist throbbed, but I ignored the pain. Our mingled blood ran through my fingers. Kage's warmth spread through me, flowing up my arm.

Behind me, Viktor straightened. He gave his wings a flick, and they flew open. He walked slowly towards us, then stopped, looming over me, cold and monstrous, staring down at Kage's bleeding body and my crouched figure.

"Let him live and I'll do anything," I breathed. "I'll come back with you. Do anything you want." I swallowed the lump in my throat. "It was a mistake to come here tonight, but . . . I needed you. Needed to see you."

A wing flew forward, backhanding me and sending me rolling across the ground. I lay there for a moment, dizzy and winded, then pushed myself up, retching dry heaves onto the grass.

"You need him," I whispered, looking up at Viktor as he approached me. "He's the last Avari." The instant the word left my tongue, a white-hot wrongness flooded through me. Poison creeping up from my stomach to choke my heart. But I pressed forward. "Think of the power his blood holds. You can't kill him."

"Regan, no," Kage growled. I looked back over at him. His fur had retreated. He was highblood again, naked and wounded. His chest was raked open, flesh peeled back. He struggled to rise but sank back down.

Viktor said nothing, just pulled back a taloned fist. This time I was ready for the blow. I coughed up blood, my lips cracking open.

"Get your fucking hands off her, old man," Kage snarled. He was crouched low, knees bent, crawling towards me, the wound in his chest bleeding onto the grass.

I was ready when the next blow came. I lifted my wounded wrist, using it to shield my face. Viktor's talons easily tore the wound open. I felt blood rush down my arm. "I'll do anything," I whispered, trying to smile through the blood coating my teeth. "Anything for you. Spare him. Break me, beat me, use me—but take me back. Forgive me, Viktor."

Kage growled, the sound bestial and desperate.

"Stay back," I warned him. "This is between my archon and me. I was wrong. I disobeyed him. He's right to punish me." I looked up at Viktor. "I needed to see you. The Avari tried to sway me to his side, but I led him here so he could be tribute. You fought bravely. Truly you are the most powerful highblood in all of Sangratha."

A taloned finger lifted my chin. "Traitorous bitch. I honored you. Elevated you."

"You did," I whispered. "And look at me now. Kneeling at your feet. My blood spilling to honor the ground you walk upon. Just as it should be, my lord, my archon. No less than you deserve."

I glanced at Kage, steeling my gaze, feeling the poison tinge my heart. "Let the Avari dog watch as we consort together." It was hard to choke out the words, but I forced myself to keep going. "Put him in a cage at the foot of our bed. Let him see us feed from one another." *Only spare him. Spare him.*

Viktor's face split into a horrific smile. "You long for me, though it kills you to admit it, does it not? You yearn for me. As it should be. Seeing me now in this form, it makes you dream of dark things, does it not, Regan?"

"Truly dark," I whispered. "You have no idea."

"Take my hand," he murmured. "Rise. Let me give you power beyond your wildest dreams."

I glanced at Kage. His teeth were bared in a snarl of rage and revulsion. It was no more than I deserved: I disgusted him. I was vile and repugnant, even to myself. But I could do this. I could do one pure, *good* thing. Viktor reached his hand down to raise me.

"I'm sorry, Avari," I said clearly. "This is my choice." Then I grabbed Viktor's wrist, pulling him off-balance. Before he could wrench free, I bared my fangs, driving them deep into his veins.

Hot blood flooded my mouth. I tore, ripping the wound wide. Then I slammed my own bleeding wrist hard across Viktor's, smearing it into his bloodstream.

Wolf blood met dragon blood.

Viktor's red eyes flared wide with alarm. He staggered back, the wound already blistering inwards, flesh melting away to expose bone. Black veins spread like vines up his arm where the wolf's blood crept, snaking up his shoulder, making its way to Viktor's heart.

Beside us, Kage snarled, shifting as he leaped at Viktor, all silver fur and bared teeth. But Viktor's good hand was faster. It scythed out, razored talons flashing.

A burning line split across my throat. I fell back against the grass, the night sky spinning above me. My eyes closed. When I opened them, the wolf crouched over me, paws heavy on my chest, fury and grief blazing in his dark eyes.

I smiled. Darkness folded in on me. Warm like my wolf.

CHAPTER 40

MEDRA

I pushed open the door to Blake's room, Orcades's last words still echoing in my mind, my body tense and trembling with a mix of emotions. It had been a very, very long night. I needed a moment to lie down, to compose myself. But as I stepped inside, the first thing I saw was a shadow. I stopped.

Blake sat on the windowsill, shirtless and barefoot, one leg dangling out over the side of the tower, the other drawn up so his forearm could rest on his knee. His face was in profile as he looked out at the sunrise coming up over the far horizon. A new day was dawning. In its light, Blake was more heart-achingly beautiful than ever before. Only a pair of faded black trousers clung to his hips. I stared at his body, at the black ink crawling over his torso: dragons. Always dragons. Serpentine bodies coiling and crawling over his back and chest, like shackles of black iron.

For the first time, I saw them in a different light. Not merely as stylized decorations but as a warning, a confession, and a sentence, all rolled into one—tethering him to some dark purpose. In the burnished gold light of the dawn, his hair shone silver. He reminded me of a statue. Carved from something cruel and lovely . . . and not quite mortal.

My heart began to thud. Because I knew when his gaze turned towards mine nothing would ever be the same.

I pushed the door carefully shut behind me, lifting the latch into place, then leaned back against the door.

"How'd you know I'd be here?" He spoke without turning.

My heart sped up. He'd known I was here, probably as soon as I'd stepped into the room.

"I didn't. We thought you'd . . . flown away. I just needed somewhere to be. To sleep. I needed . . ." I looked over at the bed and swallowed. "I needed to feel close to you."

He didn't answer.

"What about you?" I said carefully. "Why are you here?"

"I thought this would be as good a place to do it as any. But then I thought, what if you looked out the window? What if you saw?" He shook his head slowly, still refusing to look at me. "So I just sat here. It's peaceful—not that I deserve any peace. I'm sorry. I didn't mean for you to find me like this."

"Do it?" I was horrified. "What do you mean, *do it*? Do you mean . . . *jump*?" I started towards the window.

Instantly he held out a hand. "Stop. Don't come any closer to me. I mean it, Pendragon."

A lump choked my throat. "You can't be serious."

"Serious as the grave."

"Fuck you, Blake. Turn around and look at me when you say that. Look me in the eyes." I watched him breathe in and out slowly. Then he turned his head. His face was stone. His gray-and-red eyes were cold. "Fine. If that's what you want."

"What I want?" I choked out. "I didn't know any of this was about what I wanted."

He lashed out. "You think I wanted this?"

"I don't know. I don't know anything. But you went to the Dragon Court, didn't you? You did something with Vorago."

"I fucked up," he said flatly. "Like I always do."

"Don't do that." I shook my head. "Don't take the easy way out."

"The easy way out?" His eyes flashed. "I'm trying to take responsibility. Pendragon, I killed children tonight. Like your father."

A sob broke from my throat. "I know. I know that. But throwing yourself out a godsdamned window? That isn't how you make things right."

"No? What did your good old dad do? Tell me that."

I didn't want to tell him. Couldn't. That story ended in death.

"I'm bad for you," he continued. "Dangerous."

I gave a bitter laugh. "You've always been bad for me. You've always been dangerous."

"So why do you keep coming back?" he roared, half rising from the windowsill. "Get out. Stay away from me. Save yourself. Because I can't do it. I know that now. I've tried. I've tried and I've tried, and now just look at me, Medra. I've fucked up worse than ever before. Trying to do that. Trying to save you from myself."

The tears were running down my face freely now. "What do you mean?"

"There was a dragon in me. For months I've been hiding it. Last night . . ." He took a breath. "Last night it nearly fucking killed you. *I* almost killed you. I almost drained you dry."

"So you gave me some of your own blood. To save me." I took a step forward.

He snarled.

I stopped, closing my eyes briefly. "Well, it worked. Your blood did save me. More than once last night."

For a moment, he looked surprised. "Small mercies."

"You didn't want this. I know you," I said, my voice low.

He gave a mocking laugh. "You don't know me, or you wouldn't be standing there."

I closed my eyes. My heart was tearing. My soul was tearing. "I have no choice."

"You have a choice," he said roughly. "There's the door. Open it. Get out."

"No. I can't do that. And you know why."

"No, I don't. I don't know why you'd choose to stand here after everything I've done—to you, to Veilmar. I'm a fucking murderer,

Pendragon. My heart is black. My hands are stained with blood. Children's blood," he roared.

I trembled, but not from fear. "I'm not afraid of you."

"Well, you fucking should be." The words were almost a moan. "You should be. Because I can't control this." He paused. "Don't you realize the only reason I'm even sitting here right now, talking to you like this is because Florence fucking shot me? Not that I blame her." He side-eyed me. "What did she shoot me with, anyhow?"

"Emberfern. House Drakharrow used to use it to control dragon riders."

He tipped his head back and chuckled. "Dragon riders. How fucking appropriate."

"But you're more than a rider," I said stubbornly. "That's your body, Blake. Vorago's the one hitching a ride. You need to take control back from him. Before—"

"Before it happens again? Before I go berserk again?" His face turned flinty. "I won't let that happen. I'll die first."

"I won't let you die." I took another small step towards him.

"Not another step," he warned. "Or I swear to you, I will slide off this sill. We'll see if I grow wings on the way down or not."

I froze. "Fine. I'm not moving."

He nodded.

"But if you jump, what makes you think I won't jump right after you?"

He looked at me, and I saw the fear in his eyes. *Good.* So he was still capable of feeling that.

"You wouldn't dare."

"Wouldn't I?" I said, my voice dangerously quiet. "You think I'd stay here in this fucked-up world without you?"

"This isn't some romantic play, Pendragon," he snapped. "This is life and death."

"I'm not the one threatening to off myself by jumping out a window," I cried. "Don't you dare do that to me, Blake. Don't you dare. You look me in the face. You take a good look right now and see what you're doing to me." My whole body was shaking. "You're breaking my heart."

He swallowed. "It'll heal. It has to."

"We'll heal together."

"There's no way back from this, Pendragon. You have to know that. No one will ever forgive me for what I've done. If I stay, I'll be a shadow on your life. Staining your soul."

"I don't care," I said stubbornly. "That *is* life. Shit happens. We have to deal with it. We have to try to atone. We can't just run from it. You think I'm perfect? I'm not perfect, Blake. I've done horrible things, too. I've lost people I've loved because of my own stupidity."

"Have you ever scorched an entire city? Swallowed living beings whole? Watched children running and known you couldn't save them, couldn't stop yourself from killing them?"

"No." I was weeping. "But it wasn't you who did that—it was Vorago. You wanted to stop him. I know you did."

"I'm broken." His voice was shaking. "I'm falling to pieces. I don't know who I am. I don't know what I'm doing. All I know is I need you to be safe. As for me, death is all I deserve. I should do it now, before Vorago can stop me."

I moved. With whatever residual power of his blood left in me, with whatever fae power still filled me, I moved with highblood speed and rider reflexes, seizing him by the shoulders and yanking him down off the windowsill before he could even react.

He half sat, half lay on the floor, pushing himself up on his elbows. I lay there next to him, my hands flat against his chest. There was something infinitely powerful about the way our bodies touched. It went beyond words—and always had.

"You're a part of me," I whispered. "Don't you know that?"

"Oh, Pendragon." He sighed. Then he reached out a hand to brush my cheek. "We were always wrong together. Didn't you try to tell me that, right from the start?"

"And you knew the truth. You always knew."

"I . . . was wrong. I release you. I relinquish any claim to you. You're free."

"No," I spat. "That's not how this works. We're bound, you and me. We don't break that easily. This," I said gesturing to him, then to myself, "this is forever. And you fucking know that."

He stared at me. "I don't know . . ."

"Then, let me tell you," I snarled. "Let me tell you that I love you more than anything in this world or any other. I love you more than the sum of your sins. My heart chose you a long time ago. Maybe before I even got here." The lump in my throat forced me to pause. "You make me feel like I'm falling, like I'm tearing apart at the seams. But free? I will never be free of you. I can't be. I choose to be chained to you. I choose to be claimed. I would never choose to be free. Because this feeling is everything. You aren't just in my heart—you are my heart. You are written in my blood."

"Love," Blake whispered.

"Yes." I touched his face, trying to press my forehead against his.

He pushed me away. "Love doesn't begin to describe what I feel for you." He shook his head, his voice rough. "It's harsher. Darker. It's consuming me. I told you to go because I knew if you took one more step, I might never be able to let you leave."

My throat tightened.

"I should scare you. After what I did tonight. I scare myself. I don't deserve you. I don't deserve the word *love* from your lips."

"You don't get to choose for me." The words slipped out. "You don't get to decide if you deserve love. You *are* loved. Whether you like it or not."

"I'm a monster," he whispered. "I'm not worthy of you."

"You're not a monster. But if you are, then I am, too. Your blood flows through my veins. And . . ."

The door burst open. Vaughn stood there. "I heard you talking," he mumbled, his face stricken. "I didn't want to believe it."

"Believe what?" I stood up quickly, planting myself between Blake and the door.

"That you might be in here. With him. Just talking, when . . ." Too late, I saw he was shaking with rage.

"When what?" I demanded. "We have to start somewhere."

"When you know what he's done, Medra. Talking?" Vaughn shook his head, looking disgusted. "This is beyond a talking matter."

"He's done terrible things, but he didn't want to do them. You know that. You know what he is to me. Please, he's Theo's cousin."

"I know," he whispered. "I'm so sorry." Then he turned his head. "He's here!" he yelled. "Come quickly! I've found him!"

"No!" I screamed, but the hall had already filled with pounding footsteps.

Professor Sankara appeared in the doorframe alongside Rodriguez. There were heavy chains in their hands.

I eyed them in horror. "What are you doing? This isn't the way."

"It's the only way for now." His face was stony, yet I had never heard his voice sound so gentle. To my shock, I saw there were tears in his eyes as he looked down at Blake. "I'm so sorry. But you know we have to do this. If Vorago takes control again, we have no idea what he'll make you do."

I turned. Blake slowly nodded. He pushed himself to his feet, then held out his hands. "Do it."

They came into the room. The men with their chains, approaching slowly, while Vaughn stood off to one side, his eyes still clouded in grief and judgment. But the moment Sankara began to cinch the first cuff, a rumble crawled out of Blake's chest. His head snapped up, eyes flashing as he looked at me with a desperate expression.

"Get away from him," I said, my voice sharp. "Can't you see what's happening?"

Rodriguez's face was grim, but he didn't back away, just picked up the other cuff and cracked it open. "Hurry," I heard him whisper to Sankara.

Blake's eyes locked with mine. "Run," he whispered. "I can't . . ." His jaw cracked with a roar. The half-fastened chain on his wrist snapped like string.

Sankara staggered back with a shout, yanking Rodriguez with him. Talons exploded from Blake's fingers. He whirled, vaulting to the windowsill in one swift movement.

I lunged. "No!"

But it was too late. He plunged, body bursting into the dragon in midair, wings unfolding, vast and magnificent, igniting in a brilliant red under the light of the rising sun.

For a split second he hovered there, looking back at me. But Blake or Vorago? I didn't know which.

Then he was gone.

★ ★ ★ ★

**Welcome to Bloodwing Academy.
Expect magic. Expect competition. Expect blood.**

**Don't miss the unforgettable beginning
to Medra and Blake's epic story.**

At Bloodwing Academy, blood is currency, but a dragon's legacy is priceless – and as dangerous as fire.

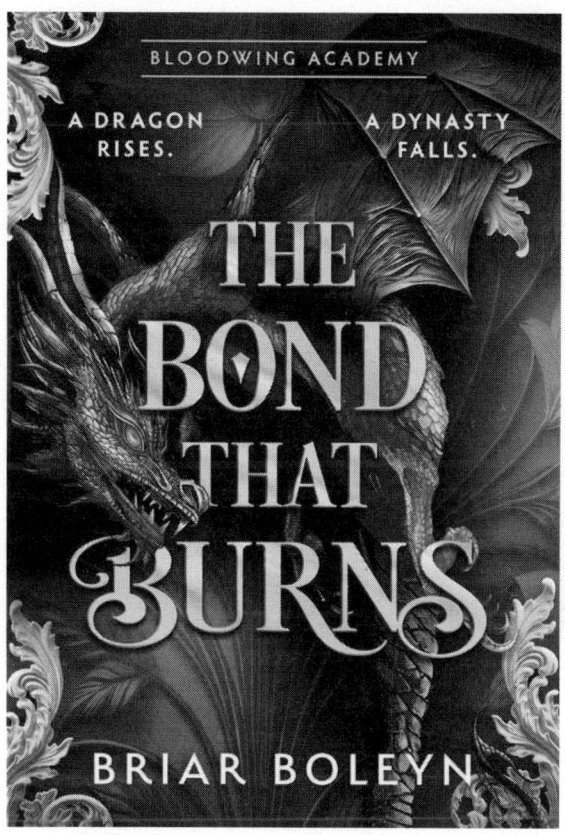

A heart-stopping and deadly new year is about to begin for Medra, Blake and Florence.

Join My Street Team: Briar's Rose Court

If you'd like to discuss my books, meet other romantasy book lovers, share pictures or quotes about your favorite characters, vote on character names and book titles, get sneak peeks at covers and other art, and enter exclusive giveaways, then I would love to have you over in our private Rose Court Street Team Facebook group!

**Come join in the fun!
Sign up for the Street Team:
rosecourt.briarboleyn.com**

ONE PLACE. MANY STORIES

Bold, innovative and
empowering publishing.

FOLLOW US ON:

@HQStories